PRAISE FOR AM

.9

"Part traditional police pr... redemption and the possib... cleverly and apparently effortlessly builds a future world that is both engaging and utterly terrifying."

Kaaron Warren, award-winning author of The Grief Hole *and* Tide of Stone

"*The Wire* meets *Blade Runner* in this enthralling near-future crime thriller."

Nathan M Farrugia, USA Today *bestseller*

"An intelligent, believable future wrapped around an intriguing mystery."

Kylie Chan, bestselling author of the Dark Heavens trilogy

"Bridgeman does not just build up her characters, but punishes them, and the thrills are all the more visceral for that."

Aurealis Magazine

"Incredibly vivid and bursting with tension."

Just A Guy That Likes To Read

"Nail-biting edge of the seat action and suspense that I expect from much more seasoned writers. The tension that Bridgeman maintained here was brilliant."

Adventures of a Bookonaut

"As I've come to love from her books, Bridgeman builds tensio... and points all the pie... finish. This is the kir...)ok hangover. Get re...

West...

By the same author

THE AURORA SERIES
    Aurora: Darwin
    Aurora: Pegasus
    Aurora: Meridian
    Aurora: Centralis
    Aurora: Eden
    Aurora: Decimus
    Aurora: Aurizun

The Time of the Stripes

AMANDA BRIDGEMAN

THE SUBJUGATE

ANGRY ROBOT

ANGRY ROBOT
An imprint of Watkins Media Ltd

20 Fletcher Gate,
Nottingham,
NG1 2FZ
UK

angryrobotbooks.com
twitter.com/angryrobotbooks
Code blue

An Angry Robot paperback original 2018

Cover by Argh! Nottingham/Lee Gibbons/Mauritius Images
Set in Meridien and Taurus Mono by Argh! Nottingham

Distributed in the United States by Penguin Random House, Inc., New York.

ISBN 978 0 85766 771 7
Ebook ISBN 978 0 85766 772 4

Printed in the United States of America

9 8 7 6 5 4 3 2 1

To the many victims of crime who've never received the justice they deserved, and to the law enforcement officers who did everything they could within the constraints of the law.

1 : THE VIC

Detective Salvi Brentt stared at the dead body. She wondered what had been going through the killer's mind at the time of the attack. It was meant to be a quick, easy mugging. But a hard shove, the victim fell back, and his skull met horribly with the pavement. The mugging had turned into murder. And for what? An expensive smartwatch and a gift card to Kiki's virtual shopping service.

The perp had run. They always ran. But in the dead heart of the city that was a useless thing to do. With the constant rotation of police drones, watching everything from on high, there was little one could get away with out in the open. And if you shove a man, he dies, and you run? The police have you. And if you manage to get away, they have your face and they will track you down. They'll get you for the murder, and the city will lay a compensation claim for the cleaning of the bloodied pavement.

That's why many thought the security companies ruled the cities. In a world where no one trusted anyone, everyone wanted evidence – not just the cops. Cities watched residents, businesses watched employees, people watched their property, their spouses, their kids. Of course, some people made good money hacking these systems and erasing all traces of certain goings-on. But not this perp. No, he was a fool who lived just one block away. One block… At first Salvi couldn't decide whether he'd been desperate or just plain stupid.

When they found him, he ignorantly answered the door.

He took one look at her, Mitch, and the holo-badges glowing at their chests, then slammed the door in their faces. When her partner barged into the apartment, hot on his heels, the perp was already at the window climbing onto the fire escape. Salvi ran back down to the street to meet him head on. Well, it was more like side on. She kept herself hidden behind a wall and heard him running toward her. As he raced by, she kicked out her leg and sent him slamming down to the ground, his chin and hands raking along the sidewalk. He barely had time to give her a panicked look before Mitch was on top of him. Despite the circumstances, the perp still tried to struggle free, but her senior partner soon put an end to that. With an arm around his throat, Mitch hauled him to his feet, then slammed him hard against the wall, where Salvi swiftly snapped a pair of digital cuffs around the man's wrists.

Turns out the guy had lost his job and had four kids to feed. So, he was both desperate *and* stupid. Regardless, he took an innocent life. The man had to pay.

Salvi tapped the glass display of her console, closing the image down. She finished reading over the report, ensuring all the detail was there. Riverton, the department's dedicated AI, always prefilled the data for them; transcriptions from interviews and the like. But it always took a human to add the finishing touches and ensure the thing was readable and would stand up in court.

When she was done, she pressed her left thumb against the authorization panel beside her console. It flashed blue as it read her print, then green, indicating the department's system had accepted it. She then scrawled her signature onto the scratch pad. It registered on the display, then she tapped "File Report". And off it went. Another case closed.

She heard the soft whirring sound of Sadie approaching, the homicide department's assigned robo-cleaner. Salvi looked up as it moved past her desk, sweeping the floor.

Rounded and white, it looked much like a rubbish bin with a ball-shaped head atop. It swiveled its face toward her, lights flashing where eyes, nose and mouth would normally appear.

"Good morning, Detective Brentt," its electronically generated voice sounded.

"Morning, Sadie," she replied as it swished on by.

Chimes sounded across the six screens on the wall to her left. The mugshows were being updated. Salvi watched as the screens went black, then one by one, the new images appeared featuring the latest persons of interest. Five were male, one was female, all mixed races.

The mugshows still gave her the creeps. Staring at a single photo was one thing but watching moving footage was something else. As if on cue, one by one the persons of interest turned, offering a side profile. Creepy, yes, but valuable. Seeing footage of a criminal, of how they moved, their mannerisms, twitches and tics, even the way they smiled or frowned, made it that much easier to identify them in real life. They turned again, offering the view of them from behind. She waited until they came full circle and faced the front again. When they did, she scanned the row of faces, trying to etch each one of them into her memory. If the drones in the sky didn't pick them up, maybe she could.

Hernandez approached and stopped by her desk. His dark eyes shone with curiosity, but no smile met his mouth. She studied the thick gold chain he wore around his neck and the wide collar of his shirt. He was always one for keeping up with the latest trends, but this outfit was reminding her of some weird fashion from almost a century earlier that probably should've stayed there.

"Morning," she said.

"Guess who we ran into last night at the Chinese takeout?" he said, running a hand over his dark gelled hair.

"Who?" she asked.

"Old man Stan."

"Old man Stan!" Bronte's deep voice thundered as he came to stand beside his partner. A good head taller and muscular in build, Bronte's dark skin made Hernandez look white.

"Yeah?" she gave them both a slight smile. "And how's Stan doing?"

"Good." Hernandez nodded, dark eyes studying her. "He asked how you were doing."

"Yeah?" Her smile broadened. "He asked about me, or was he asking about the job? He misses it, doesn't he? I knew he would."

Bronte beamed a big smile. "He'd never admit that, but yeah, he misses it. But he *did* ask about you, Salv."

"*How's Mia doing?*" Hernandez grinned, imitating Stan's New Yorker accent.

"Don't call me that," Salvi said. Stan had given her the moniker because she reminded him of some character from an old film. "I don't look a goddamn thing like her," she said, crossing her arms.

Hernandez chuckled. "Spitting image, Salv. You got the dark brown bob, the red lips, and you're always wearing the white shirts and black pants. You're Mia!"

Bronte laughed and walked off toward his desk on the other side of the bullpen.

"So," she said, pulling Hernandez's attention back. "Stan. How's he doing?"

"He's doing good. You should go see him sometime. I think the old guy would appreciate that." He glanced over to the empty desk opposite hers. "Where's your new partner at?"

Salvi checked the time on her police-issued iPort, a thick data-enabled wrist cuff. "He can't be too far."

"How's he been doing?" Hernandez's eyes sharpened on hers. "It's been nearly four months. You must have a good feel for him by now."

"He's doing fine."

"Really? Seems to me he's been drinking a bit."

Salvi went to respond but Ford called out from her office. "Brentt and Grenville! You're up!"

"The boss calls," she said to Hernandez, then stood and glanced at Mitch's empty desk, wondering where the hell her partner was. Hernandez checked his iPort and pursed his lips, just as Mitch finally walked in.

She caught her partner's eye. "Ford's office."

Mitch nodded as he made his way toward her with two takeout cups of coffee in hand. He held one out for her and she took it. For whatever reason, every morning he brought her a coffee. At first she thought it was just a gesture from one new partner to another, but three and a half months had now passed and he was still bringing her one every day. She wasn't complaining.

"What's up?" he asked, pulling his dark wraparound shades onto his head.

"You're late," Hernandez said, studying him. "Big night?"

Mitch's hair was still wet from a shower, his face unshaven, his eyes a little bloodshot, but he smelled of aftershave and mints. He smiled and pointed at Hernandez. "You'd make a good detective, you know that?"

Salvi grabbed him by the arm and ushered him toward Ford's office before Hernandez could respond.

They found Ford sitting at her pristine desk, which was empty aside from her console display, a hologram of her wife and kids, and a cup of what smelled like Strawberry Cofftea. Back in the day she'd been attractive, athletic and known to hold her own in the field and in a fight, but now she carried a little extra weight and the stress of being detective lieutenant.

Salvi eyed the large glass screen affixed to the wall behind Ford, displaying a map of the city with various lights glowing and flashing, indicating the current location of all callouts.

She wondered which one would be theirs.

"Don't get too comfortable," Ford said as they took a seat in the guest chairs, her light blue eyes fixed on her console's display. "You got a drive ahead of you."

"Where're we going?" Salvi asked.

"The body of a young female has been found inside her home in the unincorporated community of Bountiful, just outside the city. Looks pretty nasty and the sheriff's office is small, so they don't have the manpower to work it. Weston and Swaggert will be handling the forensics. They're already on their way. This is a first for the community so it's big news. You heard about Bountiful, right? It's one of the tech-pullaways."

"Survivalist or religious?" Salvi asked.

"Religious," Ford said. "But Bountiful was founded before the Crash."

"How religious?" Salvi asked. "Cult religious?"

"Cult's a pretty strong word," Ford said. "Let's go with extremely devout."

"I think I heard about that place," Mitch said. "Bountiful is the one next door to the Solme Complex, right?"

"Yeah," Ford said, resting her elbows on the table. "I need you to get out there and get a handle on it. Let's be discreet on this one. We want to keep the media out of things if we can. The first place people will be looking to throw blame is the Solme Complex given what it houses. We need to manage that. From everything I hear, the place is doing good work and the people of Bountiful have accepted them. But I guess you never know. So, get out there, see what you can find out." She turned back to her console and tapped at the screen. "I just uploaded the case file to your accounts. The contact out there is Sheriff Holt. He's expecting you."

Mitch stood and tapped his iPort, checking the information had come through. "We'll get on it," he said.

"Maybe use the autodrive today, huh?" Ford said, studying him carefully.

Mitch looked back at her.

"I can see the red in your eyes from here, Grenville," Ford said, "and I know it's not your comms lenses."

"I'm fine to drive," he said.

"Next time use some drops, for Christ's sake. At least try and hide it."

Mitch didn't say anything, but gave a nod, then turned and left the room, his long black coat swishing behind him.

Salvi watched him leave as she stood, then glanced back at Ford.

"He doing OK?" Ford asked.

"Seems to be," she said with a shrug.

"Keep an eye on him, huh?"

Salvi eyed Ford curiously. "Something I should know?"

Ford shook her head and looked back at her display. "Just making sure the new guy is settling in."

The drive to Bountiful from their police hub took an hour in Mitch's sleek black Raider. It was the latest model in unmarked police-issue vehicles, with plenty of grunt under the hood and an array of features set into the dash that essentially provided them with a functioning office on the road. Every team was assigned one, but the senior officer was the one who got to claim it as theirs and take it home at night. The windows were unbreakable, the locks unpickable, and inbuilt cameras transmitting data back to the station's AI meant that thieves knew to keep walking.

Between the Raider and the fact that they were outside peak traffic, heading north away from the Bay Area, they made good time. Despite Ford's request, Mitch refused to engage the autodrive, taking the wheel himself. Salvi didn't bother arguing the point. He hadn't once used the autodrive since she'd known him. She often used the autodrive in the Zenith, her own personal vehicle, but with just about everything in life now automated, she admitted that it felt nice to occasionally take the wheel herself and be in control.

Staring out the window, she noted how quickly the concrete, glass, and bright flashing LED lights of San Francisco slowly gave way to fields and hills and swathes of trees bursting with golden autumn leaves. The hustle and bustle of traffic and stereos fading into the sounds of silence. It was both refreshing yet strange at the same time. All that open space. All that fresh air.

"The quiet life," they called it. And it was growing in popularity by the day. Different communities of like-minded people were springing up, establishing their own way of life off the grid, away from the cities – yet still within easy reach of them. The movement started with religious and survivalist groups, each decrying the Crash as the start of the end of the world. They thought the only way to secure any future for the human race was to pull away from technology and go back to the simple way of life of their ancestors.

For some people, though, it was simply more cost effective. They worked in the cities for their cash and just wanted to get away from them as soon as they were done. With the high speed "SlingShot" trainline running the coast from LA to San Jose, San Francisco and Seattle, and servicing smaller communities along the way, it was easy for people to dwell away from the dark, neon shadows of their local metropolis. Away from the technology. Away from the stress. Away from each other.

Salvi actually liked living in the city. It had its faults, sure, but she liked the anonymity of it all. Walking the streets, she was just another face. Invisible to people when she wanted to be; hiding within its claustrophobic confines. After spending the day soaked in murderers, she was happy to be alone and away from everyone, trapped up high in her Sky Tower apartment overlooking the Golden Gate Bridge.

"It's quite picturesque out here," Mitch thought aloud, breaking her reverie.

"Yeah," Salvi said, eyeing the trees and hills as they flew by. "I've never been out this way before."

"No? You haven't lived in the Bay Area your whole life?" Mitch asked.

Salvi looked at him. Despite having been her partner for a few months now, they hadn't really talked much outside of case work before. Polite talk, sure, but nothing that ever ran deeper than the weather or good restaurants. He'd been one to keep his personal distance, and so had she.

"No," she said. "I grew up east of here."

Mitch eyed her, then looked back at the road. The dark sunglasses he wore to hide his bloodshot eyes matched nicely with his dark shirt, black jeans and black coat. And his black car. *The mysterious man in black,* she thought, mulling over both Hernandez's and Ford's comments that morning, wondering if there was something she didn't know that maybe she should.

"What about you?" she asked, taking the line of conversation and giving it a little tug. "Were you a Chicago native before you moved here?"

Mitch nodded. "Born and bred."

"So, are you adapting to our city?" she studied him. "Or maybe not. That what those bloodshot eyes are about? You homesick?"

Mitch glanced at her again, then back at the road ahead. "I thought I transferred to a unit of homicide detectives. Not hall monitors."

A smile curled Salvi's mouth and she shrugged. "People tend to notice when you turn up hungover during the working week."

A loud whoosh sounded and they both looked to their

right to see a SlingShot train race past them. Running parallel to the road it looked like a hurtling gray snake with mirrored windows and curved cabins.

"We're almost there," Mitch said, ignoring her comment.

Salvi looked through the Raider's windscreen and saw a large handpainted wooden sign approaching them on the left-hand side of the road.

WELCOME TO BOUNTIFUL
POPULATION 3,271
God's Country

"Extremely devout," Salvi said aloud, noticing the goosebumps that rippled up her arms despite the jacket she wore.

The autumn trees began to thin, making way for tidy timber houses with lush gardens and old-fashioned storefronts that led into the small town center – a single main street. It felt like Salvi was driving through a museum town, like it was a postcard from a wholesome America that existed well over a century ago. She glanced in the rearview mirror. The gray shadow of the city was nowhere to be seen. The hills had closed in behind them, blocking the view, as though denying its very existence.

They approached the center of Bountiful. Dominating the landscape around it, as though the very heart of it, was a grand white church. Made of stone, it had small statues of various saints and deities built into its walls, and atop was a tall bell tower with a pale green cross sprouting out of it. She stared at it as they neared, the church looming large above like a tidal wave about to crash. She felt her heart kick up a notch and couldn't help but turn her eyes away.

"A town built on religion, huh?" Mitch said, studying it as they drove past.

Wanting distraction, Salvi busied herself tapping at the Raider's console, contacting their department's AI.

Riverton appeared on the screen as it always did, in its bald, androgynous form, pictured from the shoulders up, a shimmering gold in color. Human enough to feel comfortable talking to, but not quite human enough to avoid the uncanny valley.

"Yes, Detective Brentt," it answered.

"Request background on the unincorporated community of Bountiful."

"Yes, Detective," it answered. "According to my records it was founded in 2034 by Preacher Graeme Vowker, his wife Elizabeth, and fifty members of their religious group, the Children of Christ. Population steadily increased over the years, however after the events of the Crash in 2040, numbers spiked due to the backlash against technology. The community is considered one of the lead examples of the pullaways and one of the most religious towns in the state of California. There's no internet, no mobile phones, no computers. However, devoted to its religion as it may be, the town does engage in a symbiotic relationship with the Solme Complex located nearby. This may be of interest, Detective, as the Solme Complex embraces both religion *and* technology in the treatment of its residents."

"Religion *and* technology?" Mitch said with an air of sarcasm.

"Well," Salvi said, as the church shrank in her rearview mirror, the threatening tidal wave receding from view, "someone around here's been acting unholy of late."

Mitch threw her a glance and she looked back to the Raider's console screen. "Thank you, Riverton. End request."

Riverton disappeared from the screen as the Raider's inbuilt geolocater system sounded, directing them to turn into the vic's street. They pulled up on the side of the road behind a county police vehicle, parked in front of a suburban house.

Salvi noticed the crime scene was cordoned off with the old-style yellow police tape, which she hadn't seen in years. In the city nowadays, the beat cops would set out small discs that would project laser walls of light declaring the "Police Line Do Not Cross" message. It certainly stopped the prying eyes of nosy neighbors, and the discs came with sensors that would alarm loudly if anyone tried to cross without authorization. It seemed odd now to look at the thin piece of tape and think about how little protection it gave such an important investigation site.

She glanced around the street. A small cluster of neighbors stood back staring at the house, whispering. She accessed her iPort and scrolled through the minimal information Ford had sent them. All they knew was that the victim, Sharon Gleamer, was eighteen years old, lived at home with her parents, and they had been the ones to find her.

Salvi studied the house as she got out of the Raider. It was large and white, two stories, and immaculately presented. Surrounded by lush green lawn, it had a wide wooden porch decorated with pots of colorful flowers. It looked nice. Perfect, in fact. Just like every other house in this pretty, cookie-cutter street.

It was a good neighborhood, in a good, clean, old-fashioned town. At least, that's what it appeared from the outside. Now it was time to look inside.

Salvi and Mitch ducked below the tape and made their way up onto the victim's porch. They tapped the holo-badges pinned to their left upper chest, activating them, which projected the hologram of their ID and signaled they had commenced recording. The county cop at the front door began noting their details on a clipboard with a paper and pen. Salvi and Mitch exchanged a curious glance, as her partner tucked his sunglasses into a pocket. They knew Bountiful was a pullaway, but they hasn't expected the local sheriff's department to be tech-free also. Then again, looking at the officer's badge, it was a simple old-fashioned one; literally just a badge. Salvi and Mitch's badges, however, once activated, would record everything, which would then be uploaded and transcribed by their AI, Riverton. It was department protocol, and public knowledge, that the badge must be activated when interviewing witnesses.

"Were you first on scene?" Mitch asked the county cop.

He shook his head. "No, Sheriff Holt was. He's across the road at the Fizzraeli house with the parents. Your forensics team is inside."

Mitch nodded, and the officer eventually waved them through into the victim's house, handing them a pair of basic crime scene coveralls. Again, a little old-fashioned compared to the suits and sole plates they had in the city, in which the materials themselves could pick up and detect all sorts of things, but they shrugged and put them on, then snapped on their gloves and double checked their badge-cams were recording. As they stepped inside the Gleamer residence, they could see straight down the polished wooden hallway into a brightly lit kitchen, and that was where the vic lay. She was on her stomach, her head, shoulders and arms visible through the doorway, dead eyes staring out at them.

They began making their way carefully down the hallway toward the body, eyeing their surrounds. A staircase sat flush against the left wall, most likely leading up to the bedrooms. They passed a doorway on the right-hand side that led into the living room. Salvi paused and glanced inside. It was simply furnished with two couches, soft cushions, and a fireplace. On the walls she saw pictures of Jesus and Mary, a wooden crucifix, and framed hand-stitched quotes that looked to be taken from the Bible.

They continued toward the kitchen, past a closed doorway nestled under the staircase. In the kitchen they found Doctor Kim Weston, the medical examiner, and Chuck Swaggert, the forensics modeler, already at work, dressed in the synthetic city suits. They noticed their colleagues' arrival and exchanged a nod of greeting.

Salvi stared down at the young, naked, dead woman. She'd seen enough dead bodies now to be able to handle them, although some were more gruesome than others. The truth was, she always found dealing with the vic's relatives harder. She pictured the parents finding their baby girl like this. Eighteen years old, soft supple skin, toned body, innocent face; her body sprawled across the pristine white kitchen tiles; bloodied, battered and probably raped. What a thing to come home to.

Salvi's eyes flicked to study Mitch. Her partner's stubbled jaw was rigid, and his eyes focused sharply as Weston ran a scan over the body, committing the vic to data memory. Swaggert moved around carefully, recording the scene from different angles on his camera. Its red laser light scanned the room forming 3D images in its internal software with a bright flash of color accompanied by a three-beat chime that rose in tenor.

Salvi noticed Swaggert shooting Mitch curious glances in between the imaging. Too many curious glances. She wondered briefly whether the rumors about her partner had made it down to forensics as yet. The evidence seemed to indicate they had.

She turned back to the body and centered her focus. Sharon Gleamer's sky-blue eyes stared across the floor at nothing; her cheek lay pressed against the tiles, arms laid out before her, long blond hair scattered messily around her. Salvi scanned the room. There were no signs of a struggle. Her attacker must have killed her elsewhere, then left her here to be found. The question was, by leaving her here like this, was he staging the vic to throw them off the trail, or was he posing the vic to satisfy some fantasy?

"I estimate the time of death as somewhere between 2pm and 6pm yesterday," Weston told them.

Salvi motioned to a blue bath towel already bagged and tagged in the corner of the room. "What's that?"

"Her parents covered her with that after they found her," Weston said.

Swaggert's state-of-the-art camera hissed and clicked, its red laser-imaging flashes reflecting off the vic's dead eyes. Salvi crouched down beside the body. She could see no sign of major wounds on her back. Just some bruising. The same with her wrists, bruising where the killer had held her down. She could see patches of blood under the body, however, and wondered what he'd done to the front of her. If it was a "he", that is. History indicated that it most likely was, but as her old partner Stanlevski would always say: *Never rule anything out, Salvi. Not until you have undeniable proof.*

Mitch moved, and she looked up at him. His green eyes were troubled, and they met hers briefly, the whites still pink, but they didn't linger long. She watched as he turned his attention to a printed photo on the fridge, while Weston and Swaggert moved in to turn the body over.

Salvi stepped back while they did, then paused when she saw the front of the vic. Across her bare stomach the word "PURE" had been engraved with a sharp object, and her neck was badly bruised. Strangled? The left side of her face, which had been pressed against the floor, was battered. That meant her attacker was most likely right-handed.

Salvi turned to see Mitch standing behind her with his hands by his sides, eyes fixed on the body again. He raised a gloved hand to show the photo from the fridge. Salvi took it in her gloved hands and saw the dead woman with a small group of people standing in front of a large banner that read *God Saves, God Aids*.

"Pure," she mused aloud, then glanced back at Mitch.

His eyes showed agreement before he turned to stare at the body again. He then glanced around the room before his attention fell to the floor. Salvi's eyes followed and saw the occasional starburst patterns of blood drops. Eyes fixed to the floor, Mitch began to move back down the hallway, following the drops of blood, until he paused outside the door under the staircase. He glanced back at her, then placed a gloved hand on the door handle and opened it. She moved toward him, careful to avoid the blood drops, angling her badge down to record the evidence.

She reached the doorway as Mitch stepped inside. His hand found a light switch and turned it on, then he peered down the dimly lit stairway. It seemed to lead to a basement, out of sight to the left of the stairway wall.

Bathed in a dull yellowy glow, Mitch's eyes flicked to hers again, and he began to descend. She followed, her flat-heeled boots tapping on the wooden steps as she did, avoiding any blood spatter that Mitch pointed out to her.

He stepped onto the basement floor, ducking his head below a low-hanging beam. Salvi, a good head shorter than him, only tilted slightly to miss it.

Mitch came to a sudden stop, staring at something. Salvi stepped around him and saw a fold-out couch in the middle of the floor with blood stains on the mattress. The room, otherwise used as a laundry and storage space, looked neat and tidy. The killer either cleaned up after himself or had subdued her quickly so there was little struggle. He probably did what he did to her down here so people wouldn't hear her screams for help.

Salvi noticed the room held a musty aroma that smelled uncomfortably like a mixture of blood, sweat, sex and a strong cleaning agent. She eyed the blood stains on the mattress again and moved to take a closer look, but Mitch caught her arm, stopping her.

"Chuck!" Mitch called over his shoulder.

"Yeah?" Swaggert replied from the top of the stairs.

"Kill the lights and give us a bio-scan down here," Mitch ordered. "Watch the drops on the staircase."

The basement lights went out and they stood momentarily in pitch blackness before a dull blue light emanated from atop the stairs. They heard the squeaking of the wood as the chubby Swaggert carefully descended to join them. Salvi watched intently to see what biological evidence his light picked up.

"There's no sign of forced entry," Swaggert said, as he scanned the light carefully over the steps and walls of the stairwell, the occasional splash of blood showing up in a startling white. "It's a relatively clean scene."

"No, it's not," Mitch said, eyeing the concrete floor in front of them, which lay in darkness outside Swaggert's blue light.

Salvi looked down through the darkness and saw light patches of fluorescent green. She peered closer and made out what looked like smudged footprints. Now Swaggert's blue light was off the stairway, she noticed the occasional faint green smudge leading up to the hallway too. Both Mitch and Salvi crouched down to examine the smears in front of them.

"What is that?" she asked.

Mitch dabbed a gloved finger in one of the florescent green smudges and brought it closer to study it, his face now lit in the dull blue light of Swaggert's scan.

"Looks like BioLume," Mitch offered.

"That natural lighting stuff?" Salvi asked. "The bacteria?"

Mitch nodded.

"The vic doesn't have BioLume lights," she said, glancing around. "This house is still on electricity."

"Yeah, she doesn't have it." Mitch stood back up. "But maybe our perp does."

Salvi studied the smeared prints again and compared them to Mitch's feet. "They look about your size."

Mitch nodded, placing his foot closer beside the smear. "Yeah. Near enough." He activated his iPort and engaged his lenses. A silver sheen swam over his eyes as he made a call.

"Riverton?" he said. Mitch looked down at the BioLume smears, angled his iPort and took an image. "I need you to identify who in Bountiful is off the electrical grid, using BioLume lighting. Upload the information to the case file." He pressed his ear, adjusting his ear bud. "Yes... Thank you. End request." He tapped his iPort, ending the call, and the silver sheen vanished from his eyes.

Salvi looked around the room again. Swaggert's bio-scan picked up very little. Just those patches on the mattress and some drops on the stairwell.

The stark white patches, the blood, they had expected to see. But the green patches, alight of their own natural accord, they did not.

"You better switch your gloves," Salvi told Mitch, standing back up herself. "You don't want that bacteria getting on you or in you."

A slight smile briefly turned the corner of his mouth. "No. I don't."

Mitch carefully made his way up the stairs again, turning the lights back on as he left the room.

Salvi glanced at Swaggert, then motioned to the room. "Over to you, Chuck. Start modeling."

He nodded, double chin wobbling. "Will do," he said, killing the blue light of his bio-scan, then raising his 3D camera to her face and snapping a shot.

"Jesus!" Salvi said, holding her hand up to protect her eyes from the red laser flash as it danced over her.

He laughed. "You're wearing your lenses," he said. "Relax."

She looked back at him with a plain expression. "You never dated, did you?"

His grin fell away and an unhappy look took its place.

"Asshole," she muttered, heading back up the stairs.

She stepped into the hallway again, blinking away the after-effects of the red light from her vision. When it was near enough gone, she looked back toward the kitchen to see the top of Sharon's body through the doorway, those pretty dead eyes staring out at her. Had she been killed in the kitchen, Salvi would've said those eyes had been staring at the front door in the hope that someone would save her. But they hadn't.

Mitch emerged from the kitchen, his hands covered by fresh gloves, and they spent the next while examining each room inside the house; the bedrooms, bathroom, the yard, the entries and exits. But everything looked neat and tidy and innocent, and very Christian. Aside from the body in the kitchen and the bloodied mattress in the basement, that is.

When Salvi was done examining the scene, she deactivated her badge recording and found Mitch studying Sharon's pretty pink and white bedroom.

"Let's go talk to the parents now, huh?" she suggested.

Mitch nodded and they descended the stairway.

Free of their coveralls and gloves, they crossed the street to the porch of the neighbor's house and knocked on the door. Salvi glanced around to see the other neighbors still standing in the street. Some were praying, heads down, hands clasped together. And some were staring at her and Mitch as though they'd been the ones to kill Sharon.

"Yes?" a child's voice demanded. They turned back to the screen door to see a girl of maybe eight years old with long red plaits, wearing a frilly yellow polka-dot dress and socks to her knees.

Salvi and Mitch projected their badges. The girl gasped, taking a step backward.

"We'd like to talk to Mr and Mrs Gleamer," Mitch said. "I believe they're inside."

The girl stared at Mitch for a moment, looking him up and down, then at Salvi.

"Only the devil uses technology," the girl said, unmoving.

Mitch glanced down at his badge, then at Salvi's. He looked back at the girl. "Are they here?" he asked again. "The Gleamers."

A plump woman in a gray dress with flushed cheeks moved anxiously toward the door. "Sophia, let them in."

"They're strangers with devil devices," the girl said firmly, as the woman elbowed her out of the way and unlatched the door.

"They're police, from the city," the woman scolded quietly. "You saw their badges."

"Mrs Fizzraeli?" Mitch asked.

"Yes, come in." Although she was more welcoming than the child, Salvi noticed she kept her eyes on the ground, refusing to look at either of them.

"We don't allow technology here," the young girl said to Mitch, her narrowed eyes darting to his badge. "It's sinful."

"Well, these are special circumstances," Mitch answered patiently, stepping inside as the woman motioned the girl away.

"This way," Mrs Fizzraeli said. She led them through to a living room not dissimilar to the Gleamers' house across the road. Pictures of Jesus and of saints adorned walls, and Salvi paused as she noticed a home-made wooden pulpit standing in one corner where a Bible lay upon its ledge. The redheaded child moved toward it, standing up on a box, and laid her hands on the pages. She glared back at Salvi as though she were the devil himself and the girl was guarding the book with her life.

Salvi looked away to the vic's parents, huddled together on a couch, their faces and eyes flushed with despair. Beside them sat the sheriff. Noticing the visitors, he stood and approached. Blond haired, early forties, standing around 5'11 and weighing maybe 190 pounds, he had a soft belly and sharp eyes.

"Ben Holt. County sheriff."

Mitch shook his hand. "Detectives Grenville and Brentt." He motioned to Salvi as he glanced back at the grieving parents. "You didn't separate them for questioning?"

Holt glanced at the Gleamers then back to Mitch, lowering his voice. "No. I did not. I know these folks, they're good people. And they just found their daughter like that." He pointed across the street and gave Mitch a look that said it wasn't up for discussion. "Besides, they were with the Fizzraelis, so they have an alibi."

"We need to talk to them," Mitch said.

"I know." His voice lightened and body softened. "The investigation is yours. I'm just here to assist." He motioned for Mitch to approach the Gleamers, then gave a nod to the homeowner. "Mrs Fizzraeli?"

"Come on, Sophia," the woman called to the child still standing at the pulpit. "Let's leave them in peace."

"I'm praying," the girl said, closing her eyes, hands still laid out flat upon the Bible's pages as though she were reading via osmosis, "for their souls."

Salvi stared at the girl, knowing it wasn't the Gleamers she was praying for. The girl was praying for her and Mitch.

"Sophia," the woman said firmly. "You can pray with me in the next room. Come!"

The girl huffed and threw Salvi and Mitch another glare, then stomped out of the room.

Salvi glanced at Holt. "Did you get a statement from the Fizzraelis already?"

"Yes, of course I did."

"May we see them?" Salvi asked.

Holt gave a small nod and pulled a paper notepad out of his pocket, licked his fingers then flicked through to the relevant page, before holding it out to her. Salvi took a photograph of the pages on her iPort, then uploaded them to Riverton with the message "Riverton, transcribe. End request."

"Thank you," she said to Holt, then pulled up the case file to check the parents' names: Paul and Christine. She looked back at the Gleamers as they finally noticed the two strangers standing in front of them.

Christine bowed her head and squeezed her eyes shut, pressing a tissue over her nose and mouth, while one hand clutched a silver chain around her neck. Paul stared at them, a vacant yet shocked look glazed in his red eyes.

"Mr and Mrs Gleamer," Mitch said, as they lit up their badges again and activated the record mode. "We need to ask you some questions?"

Salvi motioned to Mitch. "This is Detective Grenville and I'm Detective Brentt."

The grieving parents nodded silently, eyeing their holo-badges cautiously. Aged in their late forties or early fifties, just like the house around them, they were middle class and well maintained.

"We're very sorry for your loss," Mitch said. "We won't take too much of your time."

"You were the ones to find your daughter?" Salvi asked gently.

Paul nodded, while Christine buried her face in her tissue again, the other hand's knuckles turning white as she clutched firmly at whatever hung off her necklace.

"What time was this?" Salvi asked.

"A-about nine this morning," Paul replied softly.

"Had you been out, or had you just awoken?"

"We…" Paul's voice came out rough and croaky. He cleared his throat and tried again. "We'd just gotten home from a week away."

"Where had you been?" Salvi asked.

"Out at Green Pines, a few miles outside town. We help the church with their retreats. Volunteer."

Salvi nodded. "How regularly do you go on these retreats?"

"Once every quarter."

"And your daughter didn't attend these with you?"

"Sometimes. If she could get holidays. But she had to work this time."

"Where did she work?" Mitch asked.

"At Joan's Veterinary Clinic, on the main road in town."

"So, you arrived back today. Who knew you were out of town?" she asked.

"Who knew?" Paul asked, confused.

"How widely advertised was the retreat and your involvement in it? Who knew that your daughter was home alone?"

"The… the whole town knew," he said. "The Children of Christ are the backbone of Bountiful. Everyone here knows about the retreats. Everyone attends the church. I work at the local library and Christine works reception at the doctor's office. Everyone in town knows us."

"Who goes to these retreats?" Mitch asked.

"People from town."

"No outsiders?"

"No."

Salvi nodded. "Is there anyone you know that may have wanted to harm your daughter?"

"No." Paul shook his head, his eyes lost and confused. "Sh-she was a good girl. She was a Child of Christ. Everyone in Bountiful is. No one here could do this."

Christine nodded in agreement. "Everyone liked her.

Everyone. I-I don't understand how this could happen. It doesn't make sense. This... awful *sin*. *Here!* My beautiful baby..." Her mouth began to shake and she squeezed her eyes closed. "This *cannot* be God's will," she whispered, before breaking down in tears again. Paul wrapped his arm around her shoulders and pulled her closer.

"Did Sharon have a boyfriend?" Mitch asked.

Paul shook his head again. "No. No, we don't encourage that behavior here."

"That behavior?" Salvi's brow furrowed.

"Maybe Tobias or Ellie..." Christine looked up at Paul, then back at Salvi and Mitch. "Tobias and Ellie might know something. They're Sharon's friends."

"Tobias?" Mitch asked.

"He volunteers down at the church with Sharon," Paul said. "They spent time together, but he is a good boy. He's a Child of Christ."

"Surname?" Mitch asked.

"Brook," Paul said. "Tobias Brook."

"Was Tobias at the retreat with you?" Salvi asked.

Paul shook his head. "No. No, he was here. Same with Ellie. Ellie Felling. She works at Vonn's café."

"And where might we find Tobias?" Mitch asked.

"He works at the hardware store."

"Is there anything else you can tell us?" Salvi asked. "Anyone else your daughter had contact with that might know something?"

Paul shook his head, then shrugged helplessly. "Everyone in town knew her. Just like they knew us. There's no one in the town that would... *do* this. I-I don't understand..." Paul seemed to choke on his words as they tangled with his emotion. He touched his forehead, his chest, then each shoulder, marking a sign of the cross upon himself.

Christine watched him, shaking her head as tears spilled

from her eyes again. She turned back to Salvi with a vacant look, raised the hand that had been clasping her necklace. A smear of fresh blood sat across her open palm, as it did the crucifix she'd been clutching. "This is the work of the devil..." She marked a sign of the cross over herself as well. "No one here would do this. *No one.*" She started crying heavily and Paul wrapped his arms around her again.

Sheriff Holt stepped forward. "I think maybe they've had enough for a while."

Salvi turned and met eyes with Mitch. He looked back to the mourning Gleamers.

"Thank you for your time," he said. "Again, we're very sorry for your loss. We'll be in touch if we have any more questions."

They moved into the hallway and the sheriff motioned for them to head outside. Holt and Mitch stepped out onto the porch, but Salvi hesitated upon seeing the young girl standing down the hallway staring at her.

"The devil was here," she told Salvi, her face emotionless.

"Do you know who hurt Sharon?" Salvi asked her.

The girl shook her head. "But he was here. The devil. And now he's brought you."

Salvi gave the child a soft smile. "We don't work for the devil. We're police."

"You live in the sinful city. It's full of filth. It corrupts you."

Salvi felt a pang of pity for the girl, spouting words she didn't really understand the meaning of. Spouting words fed to her since birth. She turned for the door, but the girl's voice stopped her.

"Are you going to catch him?"

Salvi looked back at her. "The devil?"

The girl nodded, her face tilted as she eyed Salvi's white shirt and the rest of her black attire.

"I'm sure going to try," Salvi told her.

The girl glanced at Salvi's badge, at her iPort, then looked back at Salvi's face, eyes fixed to her red lipstick. "Technology is the devil," she whispered, making a sign of the cross upon herself. "It's going to eat your soul."

Salvi gave her a nod. "I'll keep that in mind."

As she stepped onto the porch, she glanced around the quaint suburban street again; at the pretty flowers, green lawns, and the clear drone-less sky. She felt a slight chill in the air, heard chirping birds, then faint sobs. Just down the street, the group of neighbors still stood huddled together and staring at the Gleamer house, at the ambulance and police cars, at the sleek black Raider from the city. Their idyllic surrounds broken by something apparently unimaginable in this religious pullaway town.

"So, you got any leads?" Holt, now wearing mirrored sunglasses, asked Mitch as the three of them stood on the Fizzraelis' porch.

"Not yet, but we'll work on it," Mitch said.

Holt glanced around the streets, shaking his head. "Such an awful business."

"First time something like this has happened around here?" Salvi asked.

Holt nodded, and she watched herself in the mirrored reflection. "You bet. I've worked this area some ten years now. Worst we get around here is the occasional car or farming accident. We've never had anything like this." He glanced around the streets and shrugged. "But that's why you're here, I guess. This has never happened here before, and they can't afford to have this happen again."

"They?" Mitch asked.

Holt seemed to analyze him for a moment. "The Solme Complex. I take it you've heard of it?"

Mitch nodded. "Just outside of here, right?"

Holt nodded back and eyed the surrounding streets. "You'll see the Serenes walking around the town. They're pretty quiet folk. Handy to have around. They keep the town clean and help people out." Holt looked back at Mitch. "But you also see some of the Subjugates walking around here too. They're the ones they've haven't finished converting yet. They're close, but not finished." He stepped closer to Mitch and lowered his voice. "If one of them did this?" He shook his head again and pressed his lips together in concern. "A world of trouble will go down."

"A world of trouble?" Salvi asked.

Holt nodded. "The Solme Complex relies on this community for support. And the town relies on the Solme Complex in return. But at the end of the day, they need us more than we need them. No one else will have them on their doorstep. The only reason we do is because the Children of Christ are all about forgiveness. If it weren't for them, the Solme Complex would be stuck out in the desert somewhere. But boy, I tell you if one of those Subjugates did this to that little girl in there," he motioned back into the Gleamer house, "Attis will have to close his doors."

"Who's Attis?" Salvi asked.

"Attis Solme. He's the founder of the Complex. It's his baby. He lives here now but he grew up in the city, has a lot of connections. That's why the Complex is located here."

"Thanks," Mitch said. "We'll look into it."

"You can't just drive out there, you know," Holt told him. "Their facility is effectively a prison. Just a special one. You'll need approval to get in there and interview people. My advice would be to get on that asap. It might take a while to get clearance."

"Will do," Mitch said.

Holt gave him a nod. "You get any leads you need me to look into, just say the word. It's my job to watch all the pullaway communities in the area. And I live right here in Bountiful, so I know the people around here, and they know me."

"You live here in Bountiful?" Salvi asked.

"Yes, I do."

"Is that why your officers don't use technology?" Salvi asked.

Holt nodded. "We respect the wishes of all the communities. They're pullaways, so we are too. You get used it after a while. You don't need technology to police."

"So knowing the townsfolk, I take it you have no suspects in mind?" Mitch asked.

Holt stared at him. "I know this. No one in Bountiful did this. They're good, kind people. That's why I live here. So if I were you, I'd be talking to the Solme Complex. I've already canvassed the other neighbors for you. I'll send you through my notes."

"Please do," Salvi said. "Send them to our AI, Riverton, care of SFPD Hub 9."

Holt's eyes narrowed at the mention of the word 'AI' but he gave a nod, then moved past them to re-enter the Fizzraeli house. She watched him go, then looked back at Mitch.

"Let's go talk to Tobias," he said, then made his way down to the sleek black Raider, parked on the street.

2 : VOWS

Salvi stepped out of the Raider and looked around the center of Bountiful. It really did feel as though she'd stepped back in time to an early 1950s country town. There was hardly any traffic on the wide-open street, no horns, no yelling. There were no bright LED lights flashing in her face telling her to buy something. No tech addicts, booze or drug addicts pestering passersby. The buildings were mostly one story, sometimes two, but she could clearly see an expanse of sky overhead as the autumn sun shone down. Used to the dense intensity of the city, it was so strange to have so much space and peace and quiet.

And no drones watching you.

She looked across the broad street to where the large white stone church stood with its green cross atop. Looming big and mighty, it felt like a deity silently watching over its worshippers. She eyed the cross again, thinking it odd for it to be green in color, but then she suddenly realized why.

"Is that BioLume in the cross?" she asked Mitch.

He studied it then nodded. "Looks like it." He glanced back to the hardware store. "Come on."

Hudson's hardware store sat opposite the church wedged between the café and the vet, in a line of stores that threaded through the main street of the town. The people of Bountiful were going about their day, dressed neatly and tidily and in muted colors. She saw no piercings or tattoos, no colored or spiky hair. And everyone seemed happy, walking around

35

with a smile pasted upon their face. One woman even sang a hymn aloud to herself as she walked along pushing a pram. It seemed that word of Sharon Gleamer's murder hadn't quite spread to everyone just yet. It surprised her, but then she remembered they didn't use mobile phones. News here had to spread by word of mouth or old-fashioned telephones. That was a good thing. Being able to question suspects before they had the heads-up to get their stories straight was helpful.

News may not have spread yet, but their presence was certainly drawing some curious stares... Mitch and Salvi, dressed mostly in black and pulling up in their sleek black Raider, certainly did stand out.

They entered the store and saw a few people milling about. Salvi approached a young woman, about 5'4" in height, 120 pounds, with blond curls, standing at a counter with an old-fashioned cash register – the kind where you press buttons, manually punching in the price of each item. Salvi stared at it a moment. She'd never seen one before.

"Good... morning, ma'am" the young woman said tentatively, as her eyes drifted over Salvi's red lipstick, dark suit and technology.

"Good morning," Salvi said. "We're looking for Tobias Brook. He in today?"

The woman's eyes drifted over her again, then she nodded. "Yes, ma'am, he's in today. May I ask what this is in relation to?"

"We'd just like a chat. Where can we find him?"

The young woman suddenly looked past Salvi to Mitch, as though just noticing him. She eyed him over then straightened a little and smiled nervously. "Last I saw he was in the back corner stocking shelves." She pointed in the direction helpfully, her eyes remaining on Mitch.

"Thank you," Salvi said, throwing her partner a look and suppressing a smile. He was oblivious to young woman's attention as he scanned the store before him. She guessed in a small town, new faces would always strike interest among the locals, even in a religious town like this and with a mysterious man in black like Mitch. He was certainly very different to the guys around here. Salvi figured he was handsome in his own disheveled, hungover kind of way.

They headed in the direction the young woman pointed and finally came across an employee folding lengths of rope. Salvi analyzed him quickly like she did any potential suspect. He stood around 5'10", about 160 pounds, and was dressed in a plain sweater, jeans and apron, with neatly combed short brown hair.

"Tobias Brook?" Mitch asked.

The young man turned to face them. "Yes?" He smiled. "How may I help you?"

Mitch lit up his badge. "Detective Grenville, this is Detective Brentt." He motioned to Salvi. "We'd like to ask you some questions."

"W-what about?" Tobias asked, the smile falling into surprise.

"Sharon Gleamer," Salvi said.

Tobias' smile fell further. "What about her?"

"You haven't heard what happened?" Mitch asked.

The color slowly drained from Tobias' face as his eyes darted between them. "No. What? What happened?"

"I'm afraid she's dead," Salvi said. "Her parents found her body this morning."

Tobias stared blankly at her. "Sh… She's dead?"

Mitch nodded. "She was murdered."

For a moment Salvi thought she was going to have to catch the kid.

"Can you take a break, so we can talk?" she asked.

Tobias stared blankly for another second, then seemed to shake his head as his face grew paler. "Y-yeah. Just… just give me a minute, ma'am." He put down the rope and walked away, removing his apron as he did.

Mitch moved to the rope Tobias had been winding. He activated his lenses and took a few pictures.

"There was no rope at the scene," Salvi commented quietly.

Mitch threw her a glance as he deactivated his lenses. "No, but fibers like this cling to jumpers like the one Tobias is wearing."

Tobias came back with flushed red cheeks. "Um, w-where would you like to talk?"

"Let's head out front," Mitch said, and led the way.

"So how did you know Sharon?" Mitch asked.

"We went to school together," he said, eyes wide like a child, the shock still enveloping him. "We're both members of the Children of Christ Junior Corps." He motioned vaguely to the large white monolith standing on the opposite side of the street. "I saw her at church all the time. We helped make clothes for poor communities in Africa. Sh-she worked at the vet next door." As he pointed to the vet, Salvi noticed how much his hands were shaking.

"So you spent a lot of time with her?" Mitch asked.

Tobias nodded, his blue eyes welling with tears, troubled against his pale and freckled skin.

"How much time?" Mitch asked.

Tobias shrugged. "A-a lot, I guess."

"Was she your girlfriend?" Mitch asked.

Tobias looked away. Salvi couldn't tell if it was through shame or embarrassment. "No."

"Pretty girl like that?" Mitch said. "You didn't think to ask her out?"

Tobias glanced back at him, a look of hurt or maybe anger flashing in his eyes before he looked away again. "That's not what we do here."

"What, you can't have a girlfriend?" Mitch asked. "What's wrong with that? What's wrong with being in love?"

Tobias didn't answer, kept his eyes on the ground.

"Did Sharon have another boyfriend?" Mitch asked. "Was that it?"

"No," Tobias said quickly. "She wasn't like that!" His face looked tortured, like a sharp pain was running right through him.

"Do you know of anyone who would wish her harm?" Salvi asked.

Tobias shook his head, trying hard to contain his emotion. Salvi felt for him. He'd just found out his friend was dead, and it was clear he didn't know how to release his pain. Or whether he was *allowed* to release it.

"We need a list of all the friends you knew she had," Mitch said bluntly, taking a Noteb00k from his pocket and handing it to Tobias. The young man eyed the small, rectangular pane of glass as though it might burn his skin at the touch, then he glanced around nervously to see who might be witnessing him holding such a device. Mitch reached out and activated it, and the screen came to life as its keyboard display lit up. "Type the names into that, and while you're at it, you can note down where you've been these past few days."

Tobias held the Noteb00k in his shaking hands. "Where I've been? You think I...?"

Mitch stared at him. "We'd just like to know where you've been these past few days."

"I-I've been working here all week," Tobias said, motioning back to the hardware store.

"When did you last see Sharon?" Salvi asked.

Tobias thought for a moment. "A couple of days ago."

"Where?" Mitch asked.

"At the Children of Christ. Then we had pizza afterwards." He looked away again. Salvi was sure this time it was in shame.

"So you work next door to Sharon," Mitch said, "you both attend the Children of Christ, and you hang out in your spare time and eat pizza. It's fair to say you were very good friends, then?"

She saw a haunted look on Tobias' face as he nodded, still avoiding eye contact with either of them.

"You're good friends and yet you didn't see or speak to her for a couple of days? Is that normal?"

"I-I was busy," he said quietly.

"It's a small town. You didn't run into her? You didn't call her at all during that time?" Mitch asked.

Tobias glanced around nervously. "I called her, but she didn't answer. I thought… I thought…" His voice trailed off.

"You thought what?"

"I thought she must've been busy." His face screwed up as he fought to contain the tears that wanted to pour from him. "I should've checked on her," he whispered, as his eyes fell to the ground again, flooding with tears. "If I'd kn-known…" He raised his arm up and wiped the sleeve of his jumper across his eyes.

"If you'd known what?" Mitch asked.

Tobias sniffed and continued to wipe his eyes. He swallowed hard to clear his throat. "If I'd known she was in trouble."

"You have absolutely no idea who might've done this to her?" Mitch pressed.

Tobias shook his head. "No. I… I can't believe she's gone…"

"We're sorry for your loss, Tobias," Salvi said gently, "but we need your help to find who did this to her."

"Start typing those names," Mitch pushed. "And be aware that your fingerprints will be recorded as you do it."

Tobias looked up at Mitch with wet, red eyes.

Salvi threw Mitch a look, then glanced back at Tobias. "I'll go check your hours with your boss."

• • •

Salvi and Mitch stood beside the Raider watching a shaky Tobias leave. Mitch put the Noteb00k back into his pocket.

"His alibi checks out," Salvi told him. "He's been working full time at the store."

"Well that covers the day. What about the night?" Mitch said looking at her.

"Weston estimated the time of death as between 2pm and 6pm." Salvi shrugged. "He looked genuinely shocked to hear of her death. But I did get the feeling he was hiding something."

"Me too. Let's let him squirm for a bit, then we'll question him again."

"Alright. Let's go find her other friend, Ellie Felling," Salvi said.

They moved toward the café next door. The pristine window displays showed plastic cakes and cups of coffee and synthetic flowers, laid neatly on clean white embroidered cloths with rosary beads placed either side like an offering. As they opened the door, a song began to play in what sounded to Salvi like chipmunk voices.

"We welcome you! We welcome you! Have a wonderful day!"

Mitch winced a little and Salvi smiled thinking the song must grate with his hangover. They moved into the café and saw pastel blue booths along the sides and round wooden tables in the middle. Several people sat strewn about the tables as the tinkling of crockery sounded, and a religious hymn played softly in the background.

"Good morning," a tall woman, around 5'11", said cautiously from behind the counter at the far end. She was stick thin and plain faced, with her graying brown hair pulled back tightly in a bun. "Take a seat and someone will be with you shortly."

The other café patrons looked at them warily, eyeing them up and down.

"We'd like to see Ellie Felling," Mitch said as he approached the woman. "Is she working today?"

"Yes, she is. She's out back on a break. Is everything alright?" The woman's brow creased in concern as she wiped her hands on her pastel pink apron.

"We'd just like a chat. Is she out this way?" Mitch pointed toward a door behind the woman.

The woman stared at them, her hollow cheeks and beady eyes darting between the two like a bird nervously eyeing a potential predator. "May I ask who you are?"

Mitch did the introductions as they tapped their badges. The café fell so silent, Salvi could hear herself breathe. Even over the soft hymn playing in the background. She glanced around at the faces, all eyes fixed to the holograms projecting from their chests.

"We'd just like a chat," Salvi reiterated Mitch's words with a calm tone to her voice.

"Yes. OK. She's this way." The woman waved them forward past the kitchen to a doorway that led out the back of the café.

Sitting on an upturned milk crate with her nose in a paperback was a young girl of Asian descent. She wore a pink blouse and skirt beneath her waitress apron, comfortable shoes, and her socks were pulled up to her knees.

"Ellie?" the woman said. "These people would like to speak with you."

Ellie looked up from her book. She folded the corner of the page she was on and stood, curious about the visitors in black.

"Yes?" she smiled at them, displaying a fine set of braces. Barely 5'1" and very childlike, she seemed much younger than Sharon Gleamer. "How can I help you?"

Salvi and Mitch showed their badges again.

"Oh." Ellie's face took on a look of concern. "You're from the city."

"Yes," Salvi said. She introduced themselves then proceeded to break the news about Sharon's murder. The woman from the café gasped in horror at the news, quickly marking a sign of the cross over herself.

"Murdered?" Ellie's voice wavered, eyes and mouth gaping wide as she looked up at them. "Here in Bountiful?"

"I'm afraid so." Salvi nodded.

Ellie's face fell much like Tobias' and she slumped back down to the crate, the book falling from her hands to ground.

"When did you last see her?" she asked gently.

"Yesterday," Ellie said, hand to her mouth as tears fell. "At the Children of Christ. We had our youth group meeting."

"What time was this?" Mitch asked.

"Three o'clock. We finished at four."

"What did you do after that?"

"I went home to do my chores."

"When you last saw Sharon how did she seem to you?" Salvi asked.

"She was fine," Ellie said, then paused and tilted her head slightly. "Well… maybe she was maybe a little quiet."

"What do you mean by quiet?" Salvi asked.

"She was always… so bubbly," she said. "She was always smiling. But she was a little flat yesterday."

"Did you ask her why?"

Ellie shook her head as tears fell. "But Preacher Vowker did. I heard Sharon say she wasn't feeling well. I'd noticed she'd been a little off for a few days."

"Off?"

Ellie nodded. "She hadn't been herself."

"You don't know why?"

Ellie shook her head, then dropped her eyes to the ground.

"Ellie, if you know something you should tell us," Salvi said, placing her hand on the girl's shoulder. "No matter how small. It could help."

The girl looked up at Salvi, mouth scrunching into sobs. "I don't know... We weren't speaking to each other."

"Why?"

"We had a fight. It was a silly fight..."

"What did you fight about?" Salvi asked.

"It was silly..." She shook her head, tears raining down now.

Salvi squeezed the girl's shoulder. "You can tell us, Ellie. We won't judge you."

"No," the girl said softly, shaking her head. "Only the Lord can."

Salvi felt her stomach tighten at the girl's words. "So, what were you fighting about?" she gently pushed.

Ellie looked at her with wet eyes. "I was upset because she hadn't been spending much time with me. It was so silly." Ellie curled over, placing her head into her hands.

Salvi crouched and wrapped her arm around the girl's shoulder. "It's OK, Ellie. That must've been tough on you. Who was she spending her time with?"

The girl glanced at the café owner.

"Ellie?" Salvi verbally nudged. "Who?"

The girl looked nervously at Salvi. "Tobias Brook," she said quietly.

Salvi nodded. "How much time were they spending together?"

"A lot," she cried. "She didn't seem to have time for me at all any more. It was so silly."

As the girl began to rain more tears, Salvi looked to the café owner and motioned her to step forward and care for the girl. As the woman stepped forward, Salvi reached down to pick up Ellie's paperback. It was a Christian adventure series. On the cover stood a saint surrounded by teenage girls and boys smiling with excitement at the mission that lay ahead of them. She passed the book to Ellie, who took it, sniffing and wiping her face.

"She's really gone?" Ellie whispered looking up at her. "She's really dead?"

Salvi nodded. "I'm afraid so."

The woman moved to comfort Ellie, wrapping her arms around her.

"If you think of anything, Ellie," Salvi said, "anything at all, you call me, OK?" She reached in her pocket and handed over a contact card. It was old and slightly crinkled at the edges. In the city, it was rare to have to hand over paper cards like this, but every now and then they'd come across someone on a tech diet and it was the only way of exchange.

Ellie took the card and nodded. As Salvi and Mitch left, the woman took the girl's hand and said: "Come, child. We must pray for Sharon's soul."

"What do you think?" Mitch said. "A teenage love triangle? Or maybe Sharon pissed them both off and Tobias and Ellie ganged up on her to exact their revenge."

Salvi shrugged. "Even if it was true, I don't think Ellie could've done that to Sharon. She didn't look like she could even hurt a fly. But I guess it could've just been for show."

"She was definitely crying with guilt."

"Yeah," Salvi said. "Religion tends to be good at making people feel guilty for things."

Mitch glanced at her, then looked across the street at the church. "I think it's time we pay the Children of Christ a visit and talk to Preacher Vowker," he said.

Salvi glanced at the looming white church facing her, then back to Mitch, and plucked the Noteb00k from his coat pocket. "Why don't you do that, and I'll go chat to some of the other names Tobias gave us," she suggested, and began scrolling through the list.

"Salvi, this is a religious town and Sharon, Tobias and Ellie spent a lot of time there. That's where we start."

"So, you start there, and I'll start on this list Tobias gave us."

Mitch plucked the Noteb00k back from her hands. "There'll be too many at the church for me to question alone. Come on." And with that he turned and departed. She watched him for a moment, then hesitantly followed.

Salvi approached the church with a heavy reluctance. It was stupid, she knew it. She was working a case, this was different. Still, once upon a time she'd sworn that she would never, *ever*, step inside another church, and now here she was. How many years had it been? Too many. Her heart kicked up a notch and an anxiety rose within as she stared at it – rearing up in front of her like a cobra about to strike. It was like she and the building were two magnets and hers was the one fighting violently not to connect. She was about to break her vow. She didn't want to, but she didn't want to make a big deal about it in front of Mitch either. She took a subtle breath in, wiped her sweaty palms, and bit the feelings back. Like it or not, she was here to find Sharon Gleamer's killer. It was a necessary measure.

They found the doors to the church were locked and she felt an instant sense of relief wash over her. Mitch motioned to the adjoining building, however, where broad double doors were open and welcoming. The sign on the building read "Bountiful Town Hall", but Salvi noted they were not exclusive buildings. The Town Hall was very much an extension of the church as though they were one and the same. It wasn't exactly surprising. This was a community founded on religion. In this town, the church and the state were very much united.

They made their way to the doors, and Mitch entered. Salvi hesitated a moment, glancing down at the building's threshold. She felt that invisible force trying to stop her, trying to push her back again. But she ignored it, took a deep breath, and stepped over.

Before them she saw a large open space with fine polished wooden floors and rafters, cream walls, and a large statue of Jesus at one end that seemed to watch over the room. His arms were extended, palms and eyes up, addressing the man upstairs. A group of people, mixed in age, were sitting together in a circle before Jesus, holding hands and praying. Their heads were lowered, their eyes closed. Along one side of the hall trestle tables were lined up with various bits of clothing and sewing machines. On the other side a coffee and tea station with baked goods.

One of the men in the circle seemed to sense them there and opened his eyes. If she was to pick a leader among them, it would be him. She guessed this was the preacher, Vowker. He studied them a moment, then stood, as the rest of the group eventually broke their prayers and looked over at them too.

"Keep praying," the man urged gently, joining the two hands he'd been holding, before leaving the circle and moving toward them.

"Can I help you?" he asked, coming to a stop in front of them. Salvi picked him to be in his late fifties, around 6' and close to 200 pounds. His face was soft, his eyes intelligent, and short curly hair sat snug around the sides of his skull as though nestling the bald patch above.

"Graham Vowker?" Mitch asked.

"Yes," he said. "Is this about Sharon?"

Mitch nodded. "You've heard?"

"Yes," he said solemnly, signing the cross. "Sheriff Holt called me immediately to comfort the parents. I stayed with them for a while then I came back here and called our volunteers to pray for her."

Mitch nodded and went to light up his badge, but Vowker stopped him.

"Please," he said, "we do not permit that in here."

"We need to record all conversations," Mitch said.

"We may speak, but not in here in front of my parishioners," Vowker said, glancing back at the circle of praying townsfolk. "Do you mind if we take this elsewhere?"

"Not at all," Mitch said.

"Please come through to my office." Vowker turned and began to lead them over to a door on the right-hand side of Jesus.

They stepped through the doorway into a medium-sized room that seemed to be wedged between the hall and the church, essentially joining them. This was Vowker's office. Or perhaps chamber was a better word. It had an expensive looking desk of dark wood on one side, and an area lined with his robes for mass on the other. Another closed door stood opposite the one they'd entered, which Salvi figured led directly to the church's sanctuary. Again, she felt the internal struggle of that magnet pushing herself away. The preacher closed the door behind her, sealing the room, and she couldn't help the feeling of suffocation that swept over her. Of claustrophobia. Of being trapped. The uneasiness of being so close to the church, to know it was just on the other side of that wall, and to want to run as far away from it as she could.

Or burn it down.

She subconsciously clenched her fists but released them when Mitch glanced at her curiously. She swallowed hard and brushed it off.

Vowker motioned to the two guest chairs opposite his desk as he took a seat.

"I just don't know what to say about this." He shook his head. "Such atrocity in our peaceful town. Can you tell me what happened exactly? I mean I... can imagine, but... talk is already beginning to spread around. I want to clarify the rumors if they're not true."

"What have you heard?" Salvi asked.

Vowker looked at her hesitantly for a moment. "That she was defiled."

"Defiled?" Salvi asked. "What do you class as defiled?"

Again, Vowker hesitated. "Things were done to her that a Child of Christ would not take part in."

"From what we can tell Sharon didn't take part in anything," Mitch told him. "What happened in that house was forced upon her."

Vowker nodded and lowered his eyes, quickly performing another sign of the cross. He shook his head again. "Dreadful business. I will continue to pray for her and her family."

"What kind of girl was Sharon?" Mitch asked.

"She was a good Christian. Caring. Loving to those less fortunate. She was well liked. A solid contributor to our parish."

"You don't know of anyone who would want to hurt her?" Mitch asked.

Vowker shook his head. "No," he said adamantly. "Absolutely not."

"Who did she hang around with?" Mitch asked.

"Her fellow Children of Christ. They are all good kids, well behaved, like any Child of Christ should be."

Salvi felt an involuntary twitch of the muscles in her neck. A flinch of anger maybe. "Did she have a boyfriend?"

He seemed to ponder something for a moment. "I suspected she had become curious about boys, but that's to be expected at her age. We counsel our young and provide them with the support they need to avoid such temptations. I had the utmost faith that her vows to Christ were intact. She was a model citizen at the Children of Christ... For someone to do that to her… to corrupt such a pure heart…"

"Pure?" Salvi said. "An interesting choice of word."

Vowker looked at her. "Purity and chastity are two important vows the Children of Christ live by."

"And do you live by these vows?" Salvi asked, then motioned to his wedding ring. "I see you're married."

Vowker looked down at his wedding ring. "Yes," he smiled. "Twenty-three years last month."

"And did you practice chastity before marriage?" Salvi asked, unable to help the sharpness of her words. "Or do you just expect everyone else to?"

Mitch threw her a glance, while Vowker stared at her with surprise.

"Elizabeth and I were then married in the eyes of God and that is how we live. And anyone else who chooses to marry in the eyes of God can do so too."

"How long was Sharon a part of your group?" Mitch took the conversation in another direction.

Vowker turned his eyes to Mitch. "Ever since she was born. Her parents are devoutly religious, were one of the founding residents of this town alongside myself, and they have raised her as such."

"You never directly answered my question about Sharon having a boyfriend?" Salvi pressed.

Vowker stared at her for a moment as though in analysis. "No. As I said, she was a Child of Christ."

"They can't have boyfriends and girlfriends and just abstain from sex?"

He analyzed her again. "I don't expect non-believers to understand, Detective. Especially those from the city," he said with an air of condescension. "But *we* believe. This is our faith. This is our way of life. This is why we established this community, so we could live good, clean lives, live the way *we* want to. Away from the city. Free of temptation."

"I understand how it works," Salvi said with a smile. "You cut them off from the outside world so the only life they know to exist is the one you tell them that does."

Mitch glanced at her again, and Preacher Vowker stared.

"You didn't answer my question," Salvi persisted, her eyes piercing the preacher's. "Can't they have boyfriends and girlfriends and just abstain?"

Vowker gave her a patient smile. "If one does not want to be tempted, then one should avoid temptation in the first place. We encourage our flock to have friends. If their friendships deepen, that is when they know the time is right to marry. That is when they know their friendship is special."

"How young do they marry here?" she asked.

"As young as their parents will consent to, within the boundary of Californian state law."

"Did Sharon ever have any special friends?" Mitch asked, taking the reins of the conversation.

Vowker hesitated a moment, considering his answer. "She was friends with one boy. They seemed to be getting close, so I counseled them. Reminded them of their vows."

"Which boy?" Mitch asked.

Vowker looked back to Mitch. "Oh, he would never–"

"Which boy?" Mitch asked again, more firmly.

The preacher hesitated, then answered. "Tobias Brook. But he is dedicated to his faith. He would never do anything like that."

Salvi and Mitch exchanged a look.

"Is there anyone else in town you think we should talk to?" Mitch asked.

"Anyone that may have strayed from your restrictive values?" Salvi added, unable to hide the acidic tone to her voice. "Anyone you think might be living an unclean life?"

Vowker stared at Salvi again. Mitch did too.

"No," Vowker said calmly. "This is a good town full of good

people, Detective. We live good lives and we work to help others. That is what Bountiful is all about. That's what this town was founded on. Love, peace, and goodwill to others." He smiled again as though explaining something to a child. "The people around here do not believe our values are restrictive. Our values protect us from the devil that lurks in the outside world."

"When was the last time you saw Sharon?" Salvi asked, eyes still fixed firmly upon him, her face unrelenting.

"She was here for the weekly Youth Corps meeting. She left around 4pm."

"And what did you do after that?"

"I closed up the hall and went home for supper."

"Your wife, Elizabeth, can verify this?"

Vowker paused, eyes narrowing in analysis of Salvi. "Yes. She can."

Mitch pulled a card out of his pocket and offered it to Vowker. "If you think of anything, please give us a call."

Vowker took the card and read it, then opened a drawer at his desk and pulled out one of his own. But instead of offering it to Mitch, he offered it to Salvi. She looked at his proffered arm and the card it held.

"We have certified counselors here, including myself, who can talk about anything you want," he said. "Your job must be a tough one, Detective. You shouldn't bear the burden of that alone. If you ever want to talk, please call my number."

Salvi looked from the card back to Vowker's face, a slap of anger burning up her cheeks. She stood, ignoring the card and Vowker, and walked out of the office.

"What the hell was that about?" Mitch asked as he climbed back into the Raider, where Salvi was waiting.

"What was what?" Salvi asked, nonchalant.

"You giving the preacher a hard time. Asking him those

questions about his sex life."

Salvi shrugged. "I just think it's hypocritical. While he screws his wife every night, he expects those teenagers to abstain."

Mitch stared at her.

"What?" she asked.

"Since when did you become an advocate for people's sex lives."

Salvi stared back.

He shrugged. "You're suddenly the spokesperson for free sex?" he said. "From what I hear you've been single a long time. What do you care if people choose to abstain? Doesn't that make *you* hypocritical?"

"You've been asking people about my sex life?" she questioned, the muscles in her back tightening.

"No. But I've heard the guys at the hub joking about it."

"You really think I'm going to report in on my sex life to them?"

He shrugged again as he looked out the window, but he didn't answer.

"Alright, what about you, then?" she shot. "How long have you been single, Mitch?"

"Ever since my girlfriend was murdered," he shot back. "Almost four years ago."

They stared at each other for a moment, Salvi caught a little by surprise. It was the first time he'd mentioned her.

"But is that what you're asking me?" Mitch said. "Or are you asking how long it's been since I had sex? Because the answer is a lot different."

Salvi turned to look out the front windscreen. "Just drive."

"Ah," a smile broke his face, "there's the partner I've come to know. Forever sailing on an even keel."

She threw him a confused look. "What's that supposed to mean?"

"You," he said, eyes twinkling with curiosity. "You've been a constant flatline these past few months, but five minutes with the preacher and suddenly we have a pulse."

"I told you, I think he's a hypocrite."

Mitch studied her curiously. "So?"

"What?" she demanded.

He shrugged. "I'm just curious is all. You keep this façade, pretending to be this emotionless vessel, so in control, when clearly you're not."

"I'm not emotionless, Mitch. I just don't wear my heart on my sleeve like you seem to. You're the one turning up to work hungover."

"I don't wear my heart on my sleeve, Salvi. It's called being normal. I'm human. It's normal to have emotions."

"I keep my emotion out of my job. Something you should do."

"You didn't just then." He pointed back to the hall. "You, Miss Controlled, just let a little emotion escape. Something about that preacher got you wound up. I'm curious."

She turned back to stare out the window. "Your desire to see me be an emotional mess like you, is clouding your judgment, Detective."

"Emotional mess?" he said. "Ouch. That was cold, Salvi. Even for you."

Mitch went to start the Raider up, but his eyes caught on something and he paused.

Salvi followed his line of sight and saw two men moving along the sidewalk, heading toward the church. They were dressed in beige uniforms: long cotton pants covered by a long-sleeved cotton robe, tied with a beige cotton belt. They wore brown sandals and they carried baskets of fruit. Their heads were shaved, and a strange strip of silver sat wrapped around backs of their skulls, somewhat reminiscent of an ancient Roman laurel wreath.

"Well, would you look at that," Mitch said, not taking his eyes off them. "They must be the Serenes. Just walking around the streets of Bountiful, free to do whatever they want. No guards present."

Salvi studied the men. They looked like their names suggested. Serene. Placid. Content. She watched as they approached members of the Children of Christ and handed over the baskets of fruit. One of the women smiled, and Salvi lip-read a "thank you". The Serenes both bowed and smiled, then turned and began to walk away again.

"The Serenes are the ones they've fixed, though, right?" she said. "How do we know that's a Serene and not a Subjugate?"

Mitch tapped at the Raider's controls and Riverton appeared on the screen.

"Riverton, can you tell us how the Solme Complex distinguishes between the Serenes and the Subjugates?"

"One moment," Riverton said. A few seconds passed before the AI spoke again. "There is little information publicly available on the Solme Complex," it said. "But according to what information is available, the ones they have converted, the Serenes, wear the belts. The ones they call the Subjugates, that haven't yet graduated, don't."

"A belt?" Salvi asked, looking at Mitch. "A belt is all that differentiates between the converted and the unconverted?"

Mitch nodded, then started the Raider and set it in motion.

It was late by the time Salvi and Mitch had finished canvassing the known associates of Sharon Gleamer, in conjunction with Sheriff Holt, then driven back into the city to finalize their reports. All their interviewees had said the same thing; Sharon was a devout Child of Christ, and she was well liked. No one seemed to have any idea who could've murdered her. The last time Sharon had been seen was at the Youth Corps meeting. No one saw anything else. And without a circulation of drones in the sky, Salvi and Mitch couldn't verify her movements. Or that of her killer.

Mitch had been quiet and focused on the drive back to the station. She glanced at him from time to time in study, curious. He'd never spoken to her about his girlfriend before. Salvi had heard the rumors, of course, but she'd never asked him about it. She didn't like people prying into her life, so she never did it to others. Besides, she figured if he wanted to tell her, he would. And until now he hadn't.

Until now, the few cases they'd worked together had been relatively simple; victims of muggings gone wrong, or those on the losing end of a street fight or drug deal, or cases of domestic homicide. This was the first case they'd worked together that apparently resembled the death of his girlfriend.

"Stop it, Salvi," Mitch said, back at their hub. He looked up from his console opposite hers, the glow of his display splashing him with strands of color.

"Stop what?" she asked.

"Analyzing me."

She didn't respond, just stared at him some more; his angular stubbled jaw, his green eyes, his dark brown hair that was maybe a little longer than it should be, hanging low on his forehead near his eyes.

"I'm fine," he told her.

"Never said you weren't." She made sure her tone sounded even; just one cop talking to another.

"You didn't have to," he said. "You think I haven't heard the whispers around here? One mention of my dead girlfriend and suddenly you're on alert."

Salvi stared at him. "I'm on alert for Sharon Gleamer's killer. Not you."

"Well, good. But just so we're clear, I'm fine. And you can tell Ford that too," he said. "I know it's your job to watch me."

"Watch you?"

"Yeah. Apparently you're stable and in control. And a woman too. That's supposed to soften a male cop, right?" he said, then smirked. "Don't worry, Salvi, I won't tell them about the way you handled that preacher. Your secret's safe with me."

She ignored him, deciding it best to move on. "You find anything?"

He exhaled heavily and leaned back in his chair, then pointed back at his console screen. "Riverton's identified seventy-two homes and thirty-nine businesses on the electrical grid, which means everyone else is off the grid using BioLume lighting or some other form. We're talking near eight-hundred homes."

"Great. We've narrowed it down, then," she said dryly.

Mitch stared at her but didn't smile back. "Of course, there's also the Solme Complex that actually produces the stuff." His eyes narrowed.

Salvi dropped her smile. "Yes. But could someone from there have actually done this?"

Mitch shrugged. "A group of sexual predators and murderers supposedly reformed into priestlike community servants. Yeah, I'd say there's a good chance."

"From what Riverton's managed to find out, they've had an excellent success rate out there," she countered. "The Subjugates are tightly controlled, otherwise they'd never be allowed outside the Complex. The ones that are, are no longer deemed a threat to society."

"No," Mitch sat forward again, "*the Serenes* are no longer deemed a threat to society. The Subjugates have not yet graduated."

"But they're always escorted by guards."

"No system is infallible."

"What about their curfew?"

"Weston estimated the time of death as yesterday afternoon.

A Subjugate could've easily done it, then gone back to the Solme Complex last night as normal."

"And what about traces of blood?" she asked.

Mitch shrugged. "Maybe he knocked her out, removed his clothes, then did what he did, before washing up and putting his clean clothes back on."

"Possibly. We'll need the full forensic report to confirm that though. And what about the guards?" Salvi said. "A guard would've had to have lost sight of one of them for at least an hour or so."

Mitch shrugged. "We need to talk to them, find out which ones were in town at the time the murder took place."

Salvi contemplated him for a moment. "Yeah, we do. But we can't just turn up there. We need to get that approval happening."

"Already have."

"You have?"

Ford came out of her office then, pulling on her jacket, her heels tapping on the floor as she headed over to them.

"You've got your approval to head out to the Solme Complex," she told Mitch. "I just got off a call with Attis Solme, the guy in charge out there. He'll arrange a time for you to meet with the key members of his staff. I'll let you know when, but it'll be in the next day or two."

"We can't get out there any sooner?" Mitch asked.

"Hey, it's the best I can do," she said. "I take it we've had no hits in the VICAP system? No other murders with the 'pure' carvings?"

"No, not yet, but Riverton's searching as we speak."

"Alright. I've put in a request to rush through the rape kit as well. You should have the results tomorrow morning. Let's hope we confirm some DNA and get a hit on CODIS."

"Let's hope," Mitch said.

"Remember it's a delicate situation and it needs to be

handled carefully. You got it? Let's make sure our evidence is tight. The Solme Complex seem to be doing good work out there, so we gotta be sure where we point the finger."

They both nodded and watched Ford leave for the night. Salvi looked back at Mitch.

"Thanks for the heads-up, partner," she said sarcastically.

A smile curled the corner of his mouth, but before he could retort, Beggs and Caine walked in.

"Hey!" Beggs greeted them, his craggy face indicating he probably wasn't too far behind Stan in retiring. "Pulling an all-nighter?"

"Gotta work that golden forty-eight hours, right?" Salvi said.

"Ain't that the truth," Beggs said, as he and his partner Caine came to stand near their desks. "We just came from McClusky's. Hernandez and Bronte are still there, if you want a drink to clear your head."

"Thanks, but no thanks," Salvi said.

"We would've stayed longer," Beggs said, motioning to Caine, "but pretty boy here needs his beauty sleep."

Caine smiled his Hollywood smile. The guys always teased him about his good looks, Hernandez and Bronte often referring to Beggs and Caine as "the mobster and the movie star".

"Hey, it's OK to be jealous, Beggs," Caine said. "I understand. I got this beautiful face and you look like you've been hit with a shovel. I get it."

"Yeah, you'll keep, junior," Beggs said, walking off.

"Sure thing, old man." Caine smiled again, following him.

Salvi shook her head and looked back at Mitch.

A chime sounded and they both looked at their console displays as their AI, Riverton, appeared in its golden androgynous form on the display.

"Detectives," it greeted them. "All the interviews

undertaken today have been translated and can now be found in your case file, along with the notes submitted from Sheriff Holt. The timeline has also been established and the relevant witness testimonies linked where applicable. I've also submitted the warrant to access phone records of the victim."

"Thanks, Riverton," Mitch replied. "Can you also cross check all clients of the vet store where Sharon worked against any of the homes off the electrical grid and most likely using BioLume lighting?"

"Yes, Detective. Please note the information I provide will be of 89 percent accuracy, as those living off the grid may not be using BioLume lighting and instead may use candlelight or other methods. My records indicate Bountiful as a high consumer of candles for its population size."

"Understood, Riverton," Mitch said. "It'll be hard to get immediate accuracy with the pullaways being offline as they are. Sometimes we gotta do things the hard way."

"Do you require anything else from me at this time?"

"No," he said. "That's it for now. End request."

"Good evening, Detectives."

Riverton disappeared from their screens and Mitch checked his watch. "Let's call it a night."

"Yeah," she said, then looked about. "Sadie!" She heard the whirring as the robo-cleaner emerged from its holding cupboard and approached her. Salvi placed their take-out boxes in its receptacle and Sadie whirred off again.

They both stood, grabbed their coats and headed for the door.

"I want to head off early," Mitch said. "Maybe if I pick you up from your place–"

"No," she said. Maybe a little too quickly because he gave a curious glance. "Here at the hub works better for me."

"Alright," he said. "See you in the morning."

Mitch headed to the Raider and she moved to her compact, pearl-colored Zenith. It was the perfect kind of car for zipping around the city, although perhaps a little extravagant for a cop's salary.

She noticed that Mitch waited for her to leave first. She threw him a wave, then checked her rearview cameras to make sure he hadn't followed.

Salvi walked into the grand foyer of her apartment complex. As she did, the auto-concierge came to life, projected from the sensor console on the wall.

"Good evening, Miss Brentt!" It smiled, the image reflecting in the white polished tiles on the floor. She eyed the hologram. It was so lifelike, it kind of freaked her out a little. She didn't respond to it, but instead headed straight for the elevator.

As she entered her apartment and the door closed behind her, she listened for the musical chime of her digital lock indicating the apartment was secure. The lights came on automatically as she made her way into the open-plan living space. A single door stood to the left leading to her bedroom and bathroom. The white walls were aglow with soft lighting and it instantly made her relax. This was her personal space, the place where she locked herself away from the world outside. The world of murderers, rapists and thieves. This was her comfy cloud; her cushioning from reality.

She walked into her bedroom, unholstered her gun and placed it on her bedside table, then removed the iPort from her wrist, the lenses from her eyes, and the ear bud from her ear. Shedding the tools of her job was the first step to releasing the day and relaxing.

Her apartment was in the Sky Tower complex, of which there were four separate buildings. Standing tall and slim like shiny silver-white needles, they formed an integral part of the city skyline. Her Sky Tower, number 4, offered a view over the city and the Golden Gate Bridge beyond. When it wasn't covered in fog, that is. She often found herself staring out the floor-to-ceiling glass panes into the night. The lights twinkling all around her were inviting and peaceful, but only at first. Soon she would spot the rotation of police drones flying around the city. And soon enough she would start wondering what was happening out there behind those lights, in the buildings, in the depraved minds of the people living within them. And inevitably, she would walk away from the view then, not wanting to think about it any more.

Salvi hid the location of her home from her co-workers. An inheritance had enabled her to buy this apartment and her Zenith, and it was something that not many people in her line of work would understand; to live in this luxury by night and slum it with murderers by day. Being a cop was deemed the kind of job that girls with money shouldn't want to dirty themselves in. But Salvi didn't buy into that. She wanted to make a difference. She wanted justice to be dealt for those who could no longer claim it for themselves. So why should money stop her from doing that. Not all criminals were poor and uneducated. Some were rich and smart. Some were people just like her, so why shouldn't she use her skills to catch them?

She'd been working in homicide for three years now. Her old partner, Stan Stanlevski had finally retired in June, and that's when Mitch had transferred out from Chicago to fill his spot. Well, official word was that Mitch had transferred, but the story going around was that the transfer wasn't Mitch's doing. Word was that Mitch was sent away for a fresh start after his girlfriend's murder, because he was on the verge of burning out. Or lashing out. But Salvi wasn't sure moving locations would help much with that. She knew from personal experience that no matter how far someone traveled, it was hard to escape the memories of the past.

At first Mitch had kept to himself, but as the weeks had rolled on, little by little, she saw the emotion inside that would occasionally bubble over. On the last case with the killer mugger, after Salvi had tripped the guy and Mitch stepped in to subdue him, he'd done so a lot more roughly than was required. But Salvi knew that sometimes you had to do what you had to do. So it was hard to judge him on that. When your life was spent dealing with dead bodies, crying family members, and lying perps, emotions were bound to bubble over at some point. She had always managed to keep her emotions in check, despite how difficult it could be sometimes. In some ways she actually envied him for being so in touch with his feelings. For not being afraid to let go.

But still, she also knew that feelings could get messy. Feelings could make you miss important evidence. Feelings could make you overstep the mark. And he had. With that comment about her sex life today and his curiosity over her animosity toward the preacher. It was the first time he'd shown any interest in her life outside of work. It made her uncomfortable. Stanlevski rarely talked personal stuff with her, and if he did it would be an offhand comment about his wife Conchetta or his adult children. And she liked that. He never pried into her life. He'd learned from the start that she was a guarded person and he never tried to fight it. Maybe because Stan was a little like herself.

But Mitch, she was starting to realize, wasn't.

She turned on her entertainment portal, to get her mind thinking about other things. While she ate a pre-prepared, nutritional micro-dinner, she watched a current affairs show spouting the latest figures of tech addiction and the spiraling resultant crime wave. Afterward she moved to the corner of her living room where she had a small workout space set up. She ran for a while on a treadmill, then lifted some weights, then moved into her bathroom and took a long hot shower under the hydro-spray, as the streams of water massaged her tired muscles. When she was done, she donned a robe and made her way to the windows once more where she wondered briefly what Sharon Gleamer's killer was doing right now.

She moved into her bedroom, to her soft white bed, and snuggled down into it. She longed for sleep, but images of the day kept circling her thoughts. Sharon's pretty blue eyes, her crying parents, little Sophia with her hands upon the opened Bible, Tobias Brook's pale face and his shaking hands, Ellie's tears for a lost childhood friend, and Preacher Vowker's proffered card.

Especially Vowker and his proffered card.

She saw his face analyzing hers and recalled the words he'd said to her before they'd parted. The gall of him to offer counseling when he knew nothing about her.

She fought hard to clear her mind but found herself tossing and turning. She reached up to the console embedded in the wall above her bed and engaged the SleepHarmony program. It came to life and suddenly there were numerous 3D jellyfish swimming about her, their long tendrils flowing gently as they moved to soft, soothing music. She focused her breathing and eyed the muted colors of pink and purple and blue.

But still she couldn't sleep.

She realized there was something else clawing at her psyche, that would not leave her alone. And she knew what it was. Giving in to it, she threw back her sheets, pulled herself out of her bed and turned the lights on. She eyed the set of drawers opposite her bed, beneath her inbuilt entertainment screen. She moved toward the top drawer, pausing a moment, before pulling it open.

Before her were three rows of neatly folded blouses in shades of white and gray. She reached in and slid her hand beneath the left-most pile, right to the very back corner. When her fingers touched the soft silken material of the pouch, she paused again, then pulled it forward.

The golds of the silken material shone in the lights. She traced her fingers over the front of the pouch, then slid them beneath the press-stud button and flicked it open. She inhaled and exhaled for a single breath, then reached her fingers inside and curled them around the contents. Slowly, as though pulling out a rattlesnake, she raised her hand in line with her face. She stared at the dangling rosary beads as they hung limply before her; the cross hanging off the end like a tear drop that failed the shed. She turned the beads and the cross around in her hands for a moment, thinking of Vowker, and thinking of… *them*.

A sensation of tightness in her throat and the sting of a tear in her eye took her by surprise.

She quickly stuffed the beads back into the pouch and slid them underneath the shirts, into the far corner again. Shutting the drawer and moving to her bed, she cursed herself for letting Vowker get to her. She lay back down in her bed and pumped up the intensity of the jellyfish swimming around her, then drowned herself within.

3 : CONFESSIONS

Salvi approached Mitch, waiting in the Raider outside the station hub. The engine was purring softly like a kitten, such a contrast to the hard, sleek, black body of the vehicle. He popped the door open with a hydraulic hiss and she sat down in the passenger seat, the aroma of strong coffee filling her senses. Mitch handed her a tall takeout cup, her usual order. She gave a nod in thanks and he set the Raider in motion.

"Weston confirmed cause of death was strangulation," Mitch told her, motioning to the Raider's high-tech console and the screen displaying the relevant report. "The vic was raped, possibly more than once. They're still waiting on the results of the kit to figure out if there was more than one perp, but we should have them soon going by what Ford said last night."

Salvi nodded. She'd just finished reading the report at her desk inside the hub.

"Swaggert got minute traces of the BioLume from the front door to the basement," Mitch continued. "It's evenly spread until the basement door, then the traces appear more erratically placed. Looks like the initial attack happened there, then he's dragged her down into the basement."

"So, she knew the killer," Salvi said. "She let him inside the house, walked down the hallway as far as the basement door before he attacked her."

Mitch nodded. "Unless she left her door unlocked and he walked in and surprised her."

"If she knew him, the question is, did they argue over something first?" Salvi mused aloud. "Or was the attack a surprise to her?"

"I think the attack was premeditated," Mitch said. "He knew her parents were away. He knew she'd be alone. The scene is otherwise pretty clean. If he didn't plan it and it was spur of the moment, then he's smart. No one saw anything, and he's covered his tracks pretty well."

Salvi stared out the window in thought, watching as the SlingShot train whizzed by, a blur of curved mirrored windows. "It might not have been planned. He might have seen an opportunity and seized the moment," she said. "He came onto her and she rejected him, making him angry. Or he outright attacked her, knowing she was alone. Then cleaned up after himself, but he didn't notice the minute traces of the BioLume on the floor. There were no windows in the basement. He had the house lights on and didn't notice." She looked back at Mitch. "Forensics bagged up the cleaning products and they found no fingerprints. Looks like he wore gloves. This guy did everything he could to remove all traces and stop himself being caught."

Mitch nodded again. "Like I said, he's smart. I think he's been through this before and knows what got him caught last time."

Salvi glanced at him, knew what Mitch was thinking: that it was one of the Subjugates from the Solme Complex.

"Maybe," she said. "Let's just wait for the kit, huh? Perps always leave DNA at the scene, no matter how careful they are."

"Which is only good to us if he's already on the system somewhere. I doubt there's many folks in Bountiful with a prior record. The Subjugates however ..."

She threw him a glance. "I think the key here is the BioLume."

"Speaking of which," Mitch said, "I asked Riverton to look into the hardware store where Tobias Brook works. Turns out they're the biggest seller in town for BioLume products."

Salvi eyed Mitch again, staring ahead at the road as he drove. He'd obviously worked on the case from home last night. "The Children of Christ seem quite devout," she said. "Sharon and Tobias were apparently strong in their faith."

Mitch shrugged. "Maybe he got sick and tired of being devout?"

"She was tortured, Mitch. Raped, possibly more than once, then he carved the word 'pure' into her. This wasn't about sex, this was about control. About punishment."

"I know," he said, looking over at her. "This was about someone who lost control and wanted to punish *her* for it."

Salvi stared at him, then turned her eyes back to the road again, sipping her coffee. "Her family knew everyone in the town. A lot of those homes have BioLume lighting. That's a long list for us to get through to narrow it down." She looked out the window again. "And let's not forget the SlingShot. How long does that take from the City? Twenty minutes? And how many communities does it service on the way to Seattle and back to LA? That provides access for a whole lot of people."

"Yeah," he said. "But you saw the way people looked at us in Bountiful. We were strangers. A stranger walking around Bountiful on the afternoon that Sharon was killed would be noticed."

Salvi smiled in amusement. "We were the only ones in town wearing black."

"I think people would notice if a stranger drove in or walked in off the SlingShot, wearing black or not," he said not sharing her humor. "It would have to be someone people wouldn't think twice about. Someone invisible."

Salvi nodded. "Until the evidence proves otherwise we

assume it was a local."

"Until we can speak with the Solme Complex, then Tobias stays on our suspect list."

"It's odd that he hadn't seen her for a few days," Salvi said. "One minute they're spending all this time together, enough to make her fight with Ellie, then suddenly their contact stops."

"Maybe the fight with Ellie triggered Sharon to stop seeing him."

"But even after she hadn't seen him for a few days, she still wasn't talking to Ellie. No, something else happened."

"Between Tobias and Sharon?" Mitch shrugged. "Maybe the Children of Christ weren't so chaste after all."

"Maybe," Salvi said. "Or maybe they'd agreed to spend time apart so as not to risk their vows."

Mitch chuckled. "Innocent until proven guilty, huh?"

"Yeah, that's how it's supposed to go," she said.

"Except with the preacher." He smiled, eyes twinkling.

Salvi gave him a blank stare.

Mitch looked back at the road. "Well, you know, you just be might be in luck, Salvi. Both the Children of Christ church and hall have BioLume products, as does the house of the good preacher." He glanced back at her. "What do you say, would you like to poke around the preacher's bedroom?"

Salvi didn't respond but opened another file on the display and began looking through the imaging that had come in from Swaggert. She studied the vic's house again. It was neat and tidy, her bedroom girly, innocent, colored in whites and soft pinks. Fluffy teddy bears rested on her bed. There were statues and figurines dotted around her room; of doves, and Jesus, and Mary, and...

"Hello..." she said, leaning in closer as she looked at the image of Sharon's bedroom displayed.

"What?" Mitch asked.

Salvi zoomed in on the photo, right up to the white-silled window.

"Put it on autodrive. You better look at this," she said. Mitch kept driving but studied the screen in between glances at the road ahead.

"Is that...?"

"A friendly neighbor?" She smiled, studying the image. The window of Sharon's bedroom was aligned perfectly with a window in the house next door. And there, standing at the other window looking through, was Sharon's male neighbor, casually sipping from a mug.

"The neighbor's house on that list of BioLume properties?" Mitch asked.

Salvi pulled up the relevant report and scanned through it. "Well, I'll be," she said. "We might just have a peeping-tom BioLume killer next door."

"Sheriff Holt canvassed him, though, right?" Mitch asked.

Salvi scrolled through the data to find the Holt's notes that Riverton had transcribed. "Yeah. Claims he'd been at work, in the city. He's an accountant. James Stackwell. Thirty-two and single."

"Alright, we'll start there, then pay another visit to Tobias."

They pulled up at James Stackwell's house at 7.45am, hoping to catch him before he left for work. He was partially dressed and halfway through a shave when he answered the door. Salvi picked him to be just shy of 6 foot and about 180, maybe 190 pounds. From his shirtless torso it was clear he worked out.

"Yes?" he said.

Mitch lit up his badge and introduced them.

"I've already spoken with the local police," Stackwell said.

"We'd like to ask a few more questions," Mitch told him. "It won't take long."

Stackwell sighed, but let them in. "I have to leave for work soon."

They moved into the lounge and took a seat. There were hand weights on the carpeted floor and a health bar wrapper on the coffee table. Salvi looked up to the ceiling and saw a BioLume globe, a faint green tinge mixing with the early-morning sunlight that filled the room.

"What's this about?" Stackwell asked. "I already told Sheriff Holt that I was at work and didn't see anyone coming or going around the time she was murdered."

"You never heard any screams or sounds of struggle at any time?" Salvi asked.

Stackwell looked at her. "No. Do you think if I had, I'd just leave it? I assure you if I heard something I would've called the cops."

Mitch stood and moved to the window, looking out onto the vic's house. Stackwell watched him.

"Had you seen any regular visitors?" he asked. "Or anyone unusual visit recently?"

"No." He shook his head. "She hung out with the Children of Christ. I saw them visit from time to time. But they were all, you know, like that." He shrugged.

"Like what?" Salvi asked him.

"Like *that*," he said. "Religious."

"And you're not?" Salvi asked. "I thought the whole town was?"

Stackwell gave her a nervous look as though he'd said something he shouldn't have. "Hey look, I've got nothing against religion, but I'm normal. This was my uncle's house. He was religious but didn't have any kids of his own. When he died, he left the place to my dad, hoping that he would see the religious light and move here, but he didn't. My parents were going to donate it to the church and I said 'hell no. I'll take it.' It's free rent! It's nice and quiet and a hell of a lot more spacious than anything I'd get in the city. And the SlingShot gets me there in no time."

"You don't mind the technology ban?" Salvi asked.

Stackwell looked at her. "Honestly, I'm trying to cut down." Again he looked nervous. "I'm kind of here to... get away from it."

"Why?"

"Health reasons," he said shortly, then looked back at Mitch.

"Anyone visit the Gleamer house more than any others?" Mitch asked, still staring out the window.

"Look, I got better things to do than watch who comes and goes from her house."

Mitch looked around at him, his face suggesting that Stackwell think harder.

Stackwell understood the request. "There was one guy. But he was part of that religious group. They used to, like, pray and stuff."

"How do you know that?" Mitch asked.

"Er," Stackwell stammered, "sometimes they'd do it on her porch. Sometimes... I'd see them through the kitchen window."

"She wasn't one for drawing her curtains much, was she?" Mitch said, looking out the window. "Too trusting."

"Excuse me?" Stackwell said.

Salvi held out her iPort, engaging the hologram function. The image of Stackwell staring through his window into Sharon's bedroom appeared.

He paused upon seeing it and looked back at Salvi.

"You had a nice view into her bedroom," Salvi said. "What room are you standing in here?"

"Oh, hey," Stackwell said straightening, "I was just seeing what all the commotion was about."

"What room were you standing in?" Salvi asked again.

Stackwell hesitated, "My... bedroom."

Mitch looked around at him again.

"Mind if we take a look?" Salvi asked him.

"Do I need a lawyer?" Stackwell asked.

"I don't know," Mitch said. "Do you?"

"We just want to take a look," Salvi said. "May we?"

Stackwell considered them both, then nodded cautiously. He led them upstairs to his bedroom. His bed was unmade and there were clothes on the floor. Salvi and Mitch moved to the window and looked across at Sharon's bedroom.

"You had a good view," Mitch said.

"What are you getting at?" Stackwell asked. "Look, I have a girlfriend, alright? She lives in the city at the moment, but we've been together a long time."

"You told Sheriff Holt that you're single," Salvi said.

"Well, we're not married," he said.

"Your neighbor was pretty cute, though," Mitch said. "You're telling me you didn't peep just once?"

Stackwell stared at him. "I think I'm going to call a lawyer."

"There's no need to panic," Salvi said soothingly. "Did you ever... *accidentally*, look over and see her in there with anyone?"

"Look, what she did was her business, alright? I don't want to get involved."

"Mr Stackwell, she was brutally raped and murdered right next door to you," Salvi said bluntly. "I'm sorry if we're putting you out here, but she went through hell and we'd like to find the person responsible. So, if you saw something, you should tell us."

Stackwell looked between them. "Look, I didn't see anything."

"You did," Mitch said. "You're a bad liar, James. You need to work on your body language."

"Excuse me?"

Mitch looked down at a strewn shoe and placed his beside it. "What size are you?"

Stackwell looked agitated now. "Look, you want to talk to someone, go talk to her boyfriend. Or whatever he was. He was the only one I ever saw step foot in her bedroom."

"She didn't have a boyfriend," Mitch said.

"Well, he sure looked like it to me," Stackwell said, putting his hands on his hips.

"What makes you say that?" Salvi asked.

"I…" he hesitated. "I saw them kissing."

"In her bedroom?" Mitch asked.

Stackwell hesitated but then nodded. "Yeah, but that's all I saw. I swear," he said, averting his eyes.

"Body language," Mitch warned again and Stackwell huffed.

"Who was the boyfriend?" Salvi asked.

"I don't know. One of those religious guys." Then he scoffed a laugh. "Guess he wasn't that religious."

Salvi moved over to Stackwell and projected an image of Tobias from her iPort. "That him?"

Stackwell eyed the hologram and nodded. "Yeah. That's him."

Salvi nodded and glanced at Mitch. "Thank you for your time."

They moved back downstairs toward Stackwell's front door. "If you think of anything else, please get in touch. Hub 9, SFPD."

Stackwell nodded, and Salvi and Mitch stepped out the front door again. As they did, they noticed a Serene standing at the front door of the Gleamers' house. They paused and watched as the Serene knocked on the door and waited. Upon hearing no response, he bent down and placed the flowers he carried onto the doormat.

Mitch looked back at Salvi, then turned to Stackwell. "How

often do they come around?"

Stackwell looked at the Serene then back at Mitch. "At least once a week. They knock on your door and ask if you need help with anything."

"They help the Gleamers with anything?" Mitch asked.

Stackwell nodded. "Yeah, I've seen them in their yard from time to time."

"You didn't think to mention that?" Mitch said.

Stackwell shrugged. "This is Bountiful. They help everyone with stuff. I gotta admit I was hesitant at first, but they're harmless. They're pretty handy too. They train them to garden and fix stuff at the Complex. Who's gonna turn down a free worker if it saves you time and a buck or two, right?" Stackwell looked between the Serene and Mitch's fixed stare upon it. "What, you think one of them did it? I thought they were like eunuchs or something?"

Mitch stared at the Serene as it made its way back to the sidewalk, heading toward Stackwell's house.

"I think it's good," Stackwell said. "Making them pay for what they did. Putting them to good use. Better than sucking up our taxes while they sit on their asses in prison, right?"

"Thank you for your time," Salvi said to Stackwell, then tapped Mitch on the arm. "Come on."

They moved down the steps of Stackwell's porch and onto the sidewalk, just as the Serene reached them.

The Serene smiled and bowed to them. As he did, Salvi studied the strange silver device wrapped around the back of his skull, from one temple to the other. The Serene stood straight again and went to enter the Stackwell property, but Mitch stepped in front, blocking his path.

The Serene stepped back and looked at him. "I'm sorry," he said calmly. Pleasantly. "May I pass you?"

Mitch stared at the Serene for a moment, his eyes cold and hard, before he stepped around him and continued on to the

Raider. Salvi watched his brooding figure, then glanced back at the Serene now talking with Stackwell on his porch. The Serene was still just that. Serene. Mitch's disposition hadn't affected him, hadn't upset him. She turned back to the Raider, saw Mitch sitting in the driver's seat, revving the engine, and she moved toward it.

Before Salvi could deconstruct the Stackwell conversation or the Serene incident with Mitch, her iPort signaled an incoming call. She didn't recognize the number, and the call was audio only. She switched her iPort to private and pressed the receiver in her ear.

"This is Detective Brentt."

"Detective Brentt? This is Martha Felling, Ellie's mother."

"Mrs Felling," Salvi said, glancing at Mitch and switching the call to speaker so he could hear. "How can I help you?"

"Ellie has something she needs to tell you." There was a muffled sound as Mrs Felling passed the phone over to her daughter. "Tell them."

"Miss Brentt?" Ellie's childlike voice said tentatively.

"Ellie, Hi. It's Detective Brentt. You had something you wanted to tell me?"

"I-I don't want to get anyone in trouble but–"

"Tell them!" Ellie's mother could be heard in the background. "God is your witness!"

Salvi could hear Ellie gulp deeply with nerves. "Sharon would sometimes go down to the SlingShot station. I saw her."

"Tell them why!" Mrs Felling pestered her daughter.

"I don't know what they were doing! Honest!"

"They?" Salvi asked. "Who was she with?"

"I saw her walking there with Tobias." Ellie hesitated. "We're not supposed to go there. Preacher Vowker warned us not to. He said bad people were there. He said the SlingShot station was a doorway to sinners and temptation."

Salvi exchanged a look with Mitch. "And you really don't know what Sharon and Tobias were doing down there?"

"No. I stopped following because we're not supposed to go there. I... I knew she was straying from the Lord. I knew it. I should've pulled her back... I should've done more. May the Lord forgive me."

"I'm sure you did what you could, Ellie," Salvi said. "Thank you for the information. I'll be in touch if I have any more questions. If you think of anything else, you let me know."

"OK," she said, the misery evident in her childlike voice.

Salvi ended the call and looked back at Mitch.

He gave a single nod. "It's time we have another chat with Tobias."

They went to the hardware store but found that Tobias hadn't shown up for work, so they headed to his house, a couple of blocks away from Sharon's. As they drove, the Raider's console signaled an incoming message. Mitch tapped the screen, read the message, then looked at Salvi.

"Rape kit's in," he said. "Check it out."

"Ford's pulled some strings to get it this fast," she said, tilting the screen toward her and reading through the results. "Rape kit positive... Weston found a single DNA source external to the vic and on the mattress. So, we've got a single perp."

"I take it there's no hits on the DNA?"

Her eyes scanned the report, then she engaged her lenses and contacted Riverton.

"Yes, Detective Brentt," it answered.

"Riverton, confirming you've registered the forensics report on Sharon Gleamer and will run the DNA through CODIS?"

"Yes, Detective. The DNA has been submitted."

"Great. Can you also provide a background check on James Stackwell, Sharon's neighbor?"

"Of course. One moment." Silence sat in the Raider while Riverton processed the request. "It would seem Mr Stackwell is in financial difficulty," the AI said. "He has defaulted on several loans and appears to owe a substantial amount of money to a company called Winchester. According to my records they are a sports betting company."

"So that's why he's hiding out in Bountiful," Mitch said. "The guy's got gambling debts."

Salvi nodded. "The free rent and abstinence from technology would be very appealing in that case."

"Yeah, but does he really want to live here, or did his parents push him into it?"

"Thank you, Riverton. End request."

"Stackwell's admitted to peeping through the window," Mitch said. "I think we can work up enough of a case to get DNA warrants for him and Tobias. Once we get the names of the Serenes and Subjugates that have been servicing her street these past few weeks, we'll check them out too."

Salvi glanced at him, and Mitch returned the look.

"It fits their previous MO, Salvi. They're convicted murderers and sex fiends."

"Who have supposedly been cured of their murderous ways and passed all examination."

"They're more likely to have done that to Sharon than one of these religious guys."

"Maybe," Salvi said with a shrug. "But people snap all the time, Mitch. It could easily have been one of these religious guys. From what information Riverton has gathered, these Serenes and Subjugates make these Bountiful folks look bad. Those things wrapped around their heads somehow stop them from reoffending. These guys are apparently numb to all the feelings that once excited them. They can't feel those things any more. The guys of Bountiful can."

"Check in with Ford, would you?" Mitch said. "We're still

waiting for our time to visit the Complex."

Salvi sighed and engaged her lenses. She called Ford, watching the connection screen in her vision. The call went unanswered. White text began to scroll upward, asking her to leave a message. Salvi hung up.

"She's not answering."

"Why's it taking so damn long?"

"It's like Sheriff Holt said, it's effectively a prison. There's hoops we have to jump through."

"Screw protocol."

"Easy tiger," Salvi said. "Let's go chat with Tobias first and see where that leads us."

Mitch looked at her. "Is Tobias smart enough to cover his tracks and leave the scene pretty clean like that?"

Salvi stared back but couldn't answer.

They found Tobias at his home. His roommate answered the door. Salvi recognized him from the group photo Mitch had taken from Sharon's fridge.

"He's... not well," the roommate, Kevin Craydon, said when they'd asked if Tobias was home. About 5'11 and maybe 140 pounds, he had longish auburn hair and brown eyes.

"We need to see him," Salvi said.

Kevin nodded and let them in. They waited in the living room while he tried to rouse Tobias. Salvi looked around the house and saw candles, an empty pizza box, Christian comics, and a framed picture of Jesus on one wall.

"Electricity," Mitch said, looking up at the ceiling. Salvi did too, then scanned the lights in the other rooms that she could see.

"No BioLume here," she agreed.

"But there *is* down at his work," Mitch said quietly.

Kevin came out again, pulling on a jacket. "He'll be out soon. I must leave now."

"One question." Mitch stopped him. "Where were you the day Sharon was murdered?"

Kevin looked a little stunned by the question. "At the city library," he said. "I study by correspondence, but I head into the city to attend some lectures and study in the library."

"I thought the people of Bountiful were encouraged to stay away from the city?"

"We are, but I have been allowed to attend due to my studies."

"What are you studying?" Salvi asked.

"Teaching," he replied with a smile. "I'm hoping to teach at the Children of Christ one day. After I gain my teaching degree, I plan to join the Children of Christ seminary and become a priest. I hope to one day travel the world and spread the word of God."

Mitch and Salvi exchanged a look.

"When did you last see Sharon Gleamer?" Mitch asked him.

"Last Sunday at church."

"Were you good friends?"

"Yes. Not as close as her and Tobias, but I would call her a friend. Yes, of course."

Mitch nodded and Salvi gave him her card. "If there's anything you think we should know, please give us a call."

Kevin nodded, then grabbed a lunchbox off the table and left.

Within a few moments Tobias emerged wearing a thick blue robe. He looked terrible, his skin pasty, his eyes puffy and red.

"Tobias," Salvi greeted him. "You don't look so well."

"No," he said quietly rubbing his throat. "I think I've got the flu."

"We need to ask you some more questions about Sharon," Mitch said. "You weren't entirely honest with us the other day, were you?"

Tobias looked at Mitch and his face seemed to pale even further. Salvi swore she saw his eyes pop a little in fear. Mitch could be intimidating when he wanted to be, and to someone like Tobias he could probably be terrifying.

"She was your girlfriend, wasn't she?" Salvi said.

Tobias took a few steps away from them, averting his eyes. "It wasn't like that. She wasn't like that."

"A witness saw you kissing her," Mitch said. "That sounds like a girlfriend to me."

Tobias quickly marked the sign of the cross as he looked at the floor.

"Did you want more than she was willing to give you, Tobias?" Mitch pushed. "Did you lose control and take it too far?"

"No!" Tobias raised his face. "No. It wasn't like that."

"What was it like?" Salvi asked him.

"What was *she* like?" Mitch asked. "She tease you?"

"No!" Tobias said, a glimmer of anger flashing across his face as he looked at Mitch. "*Don't* talk about her like that."

"You were seen kissing her, Tobias," Salvi said. "Isn't that against the Children of Christ teachings?"

"We… didn't mean to–"

"Didn't mean to what?" Mitch asked.

"We're not like th-that," Tobias fumbled. "We just…"

"Just what?" Mitch pushed again.

"We just…"

"Just what?" Mitch snapped. "Spit it out, Tobias!"

"It just happened!" Tobias blurted, tears bursting out and running down his face. He dropped suddenly to his knees and clasped his hands in prayer, eyes squeezed tightly shut.

Mitch stepped forward, but Salvi held up her hand to keep him at bay. She crouched down and placed her hand gently on Tobias' shoulder.

"What happened, Tobias?" she asked softly. "Tell me what happened?"

Tobias sobbed, hands still clenched together. "I-I loved her... I w-would never hurt her."

"And she loved you?"

Tobias nodded, more tears spilling down his cheeks, as he rocked back and forth upon his knees. "We knew it was wrong... We tried so hard not to. It just happened... but we loved each other..."

"Tell me what happened," Salvi said, her voice soft.

Tobias sniffed and wiped his face. "We're going to hell," he whispered. "I know it."

"What happened, Tobias?" Salvi asked again. "You loved her, she loved you. Why do you think you're going to hell?"

"We were weak... we gave into temptation... and n-now she's dead."

"You think she's dead because you kissed her?" Mitch asked doubtfully.

Salvi shot him a look to keep quiet, then looked back at Tobias.

"You did more than kiss, didn't you, Tobias?" she said, keeping her voice soft.

Tobias began sobbing again, the eighteen year-old looking very much like a small boy. "We'd been so good. We were strong in our faith... We would just hold hands, nothing more, but... I couldn't stop thinking about her. I just wanted to spend all day with her. And she said she couldn't stop thinking about me either. We tried not to. We tried... other things, to keep our bodies pure. But one night... We didn't mean to... It just happened. We know it was wrong but..."

"What happened?" she asked again. When Tobias didn't respond, she answered for him. "You had sex with Sharon, didn't you?"

Tobias began to sob again, his face so red and distraught.

Salvi squeezed his shoulder, trying to offer him support and ease the words out of him. Eventually he nodded. "Yes…" His voice was barely a whisper.

"Why do you think it was wrong?" Salvi asked.

"B-because God said–"

"Did Sharon sleep with you willingly?" she cut him off. "Did she give her consent?"

"Yes!" Tobias looked at her with his wet cheeks. "I would *never* hurt her! We were going to get married."

"So why do you think what you did was wrong?" she asked.

"Because God said–"

"God created Adam and Eve," she interrupted him. "He created them for a purpose. He wanted them to fall in love and bring children into this world. How could that be wrong?"

"But we made a vow," Tobias said. "We were weak and we broke that vow. We let the devil possess us!"

"Above all, love each other deeply," she said, "because love covers over a multitude of sins. 1 Peter 4:8."

Tobias' wet face looked at her, surprised. Mitch did too.

"Hatred stirs up conflict," she continued, "but love covers over all wrongs. Proverbs 10:12."

Tobias wiped his face as though trying to get a clearer look at her.

"Whoever does not love does not know God, because God is love. John 4:8." She smiled at Tobias. "You've done nothing wrong, Tobias. You fell in love. There's nothing wrong with that."

"But we broke our vows…" he said quietly. "We let the devil take hold. We–"

"You did nothing wrong," she said firmly, feeling her jaw tighten as she did. "The person who killed Sharon did."

Tobias stared at her a moment, before he broke down crying again. "Who would do that to her?"

"I don't know, Tobias," she said, feeling her heart racing in her chest and echoing in her ears as she watched the distraught boy. She saw the guilt that plagued him, saw the torment. She took his chin and brought his face up to look him in the eyes. "But I promise you, I'm going to find him."

Tobias stared back at her for a moment before he curled over in a sob again.

"Get off your knees," she said, as she pulled him to his feet then sat him down on the couch. She glanced back at Mitch and saw his eyes burning with curiosity at hers. She looked back at Tobias as Mitch stepped forward.

"Tobias," he said, "we heard you and Sharon used to go to the SlingShot station. Did you go into the city at all?"

Tobias looked up at him and wiped his face. "Why?"

"Because it was forbidden, wasn't it?"

Tobias shrugged and averted his eyes again. "We went in there with Kevin."

"Why?"

"He wanted me to join him in the priesthood, wanted Sharon to as well. He wanted to show us the sinners in the city, how they needed our help. Our guidance."

"How many times did you go in?"

"A few times. We didn't like it there."

"But you were seen going to the SlingShot more than a few times," Salvi said.

"Sharon and I would go to the café at the station." He dropped his eyes to the ground in shame. "We didn't want anyone in town to see us holding hands."

"That's all?" Salvi asked, noticing his eyes wouldn't lift from the ground.

He shrugged. "We sometimes played arcade games too." He looked up at her. "Not the online games. They're banned from the Bountiful station. They're sinful ..." He began to sob again. "They're so very sinful." Salvi and Mitch exchanged a glance.

Salvi sighed. "Someone will be around soon with a warrant to take a DNA sample from you."

Tobias looked up at her frightened. "Why?"

"Don't worry. This can rule you out as a suspect in her murder."

"B-But we fornicated?"

"How long ago?" Salvi asked.

Tobias thought for a moment. "F-five days ago."

Salvi smiled. "You'll be fine, Tobias." She stood from the couch, walked into the kitchen, poured a glass of water and brought it back to him. "Is there anyone I can call for you? Your parents? Your roommate, Kevin?"

Tobias took the glass and shook his head adamantly. "No one can know about this. *Please!*"

"It's alright. They don't have to," Salvi told him.

"You won't tell anyone?" His eyes were wide and childlike.

"No one in town needs to know," she reassured him.

"Except my preacher," he said, looking down at his glass. "I'll have to confess it to hi–"

"It's none of the preacher's goddamn business!" Salvi snapped, the hardness of her voice making Tobias look up at her. "What happened between you and Sharon can stay between you and Sharon. It's nobody's business but yours. Don't let anyone tell you differently." And with that Salvi walked out the door.

4 : WRETCHED SOULS

Salvi sat in the Raider and waited for Mitch to join her. He did so, staring at her curiously, but before he could speak, his iPort beeped. He read the message and sighed.

"Shit," he said.

"What?"

"It's Ford. We can't get out to the Solme Complex until tomorrow morning. Attis Solme had to leave on business. He'll be back later tonight."

Salvi sighed heavily and turned to view the road ahead again. "So much for the golden forty-eight hours, huh?"

"Sounds like he's trying to stall us."

"Or he just had business to attend to."

Mitch shrugged. "It doesn't matter. Forty-eight hours or forty-eight days, we'll get him."

"Let's go pay the preacher another visit," she suggested.

"Why?"

"Why do you think?"

Mitch sat silent and still, those dark green eyes analyzing her.

"The attack on Sharon was about control and punishment," Salvi said. "She was obviously a virgin who gave into temptation. Someone found out and they punished her for that. Who else would punish her? Maybe she'd already confessed it to Vowker."

Mitch shrugged, still staring at her.

"Someone carved the word 'pure' into her belly," Salvi said. "The preacher used that *exact* same word describing her."

"Tobias said it too. He said they were trying to keep their bodies pure."

"Vowker knew Sharon and Tobias were growing close, that's why he counseled them. The preacher, the man whose job it is to guide the flock, to keep these Children of Christ true to their vows, true to this very town, found out his two star members of the youth corps had disobeyed him. Disobeyed Christ. So maybe he punished them for that. He punished Sharon by doing what he did, and he punished Tobias by leaving him behind with his good old-fashioned Christian guilt."

Mitch continued to study her for a moment in silence. "Don't look now, Salvi," he said, "but you're showing emotion. And it might just be clouding your vision."

"I'm stating the facts," she said. "How can that be clouding my vision?"

"He's a preacher. It's his job to counsel the flock. Preachers also generally tend to be non-violent types. Occasionally child molesters and perverts, but not killers."

"You're defending him?"

"They abstain outside of marriage. That's what they do."

"So?"

"So, it's their choice, Salvi. They chose that religion, they choose to live by those rules. Who are we to tell them they're wrong?"

"They *are* wrong. They punish people for having normal human tendencies. They try to control bodies that aren't theirs to control."

"It's their belief system. What do you care? Why does it bother you so much?"

She turned back to look out the windscreen. "A young woman with her whole life ahead of her was brutally murdered. I want to find her killer and fuck up the rest of his life too."

"Yeah. So do I," he said, studying her again.

"Then, what?!" she snapped.

"Why is this case getting you so wound up?"

"Why does *every* case get you wound up?"

"Because I wear my heart on my sleeve apparently," he told her.

"Well, *oops*, mine just slipped out a little."

Mitch stared at her again for a moment, then, deciding not to argue, turned back and set the Raider in motion.

"Why aren't you taking me to the preacher?" she asked, as they passed the church and Mitch kept driving.

"We're going somewhere else first."

"Where?"

He didn't answer. They appeared to be heading out of town, before eventually he pulled up at the Bountiful SlingShot station.

"Why aren't we going to the preacher?" she asked again.

"I'm not taking you to the preacher like that. We've got enough reports to sign off."

"I can handle myself," she said. "Remember? I'm the emotionless one."

"Not today, you're not," he said, getting out and closing the door.

Salvi followed. "Are you telling me you don't want to get this guy? *You* of all people?"

"Yeah, I want to get this guy," he said moving up to her and lowering his voice, "but I want to get the *right* guy, Salvi! Not go on some witch hunt for the preacher."

"No, you just want to pin this on one of those Serenes or Subjugates! How are you any different to me?"

Mitch threw her a dark look, then grabbed her arm and ushered her up the platform to a row of stores. She snatched her arm back, but followed him, if for nothing else but curiosity about the SlingShot station. They passed the arcade Tobias had referred to, then the café. Mitch entered and led her to an empty booth at the back.

She glared at him as she sat down. "You grab my arm like that again, I'll break yours."

"Yeah, yeah," he said. "What are you drinking?"

Salvi folded her arms and looked away. The café was brightly lit and smelled of incense. A mellow Christian tune sounded from a speaker somewhere, the singer preaching about "giving yourself to Him". Mitch walked to the counter and after a discussion with the server, he came back with two shots of whiskey.

"They serve alcohol here?"

"Don't Christians love their wine? The blood of Christ and all that," Mitch said with a smirk. He downed one of the shots and slid the other in front of her.

"You trying to turn me into a drunk like you?" she said.

"You need to relax, Salvi. Take the shot and calm down."

"I am calm."

"Yeah? That's what bothers me. If this is you calm, I'd hate to see you fired up."

Salvi glared at him and he glanced around the café, then looked back at her.

"You going to drink that?" he asked.

She stared at him. He stared back, then reached out and downed her shot too.

"Are you calm now?" he asked her.

"Are you?"

"How did you know those Bible verses?" he asked.

Salvi stared back but didn't answer.

"Were you raised in a Christian religion?" he asked.

"You're going to interrogate me now?"

Mitch shrugged. "If you've got some beef with these religious folks, then maybe you shouldn't come with me to talk to the preacher."

"If I have some *beef*? What, like the beef you have with the former criminals dwelling out there in the Solme Complex? You're the last person who should be accusing me of prejudice."

"Salvi, I haven't seen you like this before. In nearly four whole months of working together you've been one long flatline. Now, just like that," he clicked his fingers, "we suddenly have a pulse and it's *racing*."

"So you said before." Salvi took a deep breath and centered herself. "Look, I felt sorry for the kid, that's all it was."

"How do you know those Bible passages?"

"What business is it of yours?"

Mitch stared back at her.

"Have I ever asked you about your girlfriend?" she said.

"No."

"No, I haven't, because I don't pry. You should follow my lead on that."

"No, you haven't asked me about my dead girlfriend because you don't know what to say or how to deal with it."

"What?" She furrowed her brow.

"I don't know much about you, Salvi, but I know this. You wear this mask. You don't deal with emotion, so you don't go near the death of my girlfriend because you don't know how to handle it. Or me. *Or* my emotions. Just like you don't know how to handle whatever emotions that preacher has stirred up in you now."

"Remember last night at the hub when you demanded I stop analyzing you? Well, ditto. Stop analyzing me now."

He shrugged. "Can't help it. Comes with the job. It's my job to know how people tick. And I'd like to know how my partner ticks."

"I tick like any other cop, Mitch."

"Do you?"

"Look, we have a job to do," she said, changing the subject. "There is a sick bastard out there and we need to catch him."

"Yes, we do. *That*, we can agree on."

"So, what are we doing here then?"

"I'm keeping you out of trouble."

Salvi gave a short sharp laugh. "Give me a break. I think you should focus on keeping yourself out of trouble." She stood, walked out of the café back to the Raider, and waited for him to follow. Eventually he did, and without a word or a look in her direction, set them in motion for the Children of Christ church.

"I do the talking," Mitch said as they arrived. "You so much as open your mouth, I'm hauling you out of there."

He hadn't pulled rank on her before. This was new.

Salvi studied him but said nothing. She was calm now. Mitch's questions earlier had made her bristle, but he was right. She was supposed to be the stable one and there was Mitch lecturing her about control. She didn't know what had come over her to behave like that. She took a deep breath and looked up at the grand white stone church with its BioLume cross atop. She centered her focus and beat back the resistance that didn't want her going inside.

They entered the Children of Christ hall and saw a small hive of activity before them. People were gathered around the tables filled with rolls of material and sewing machines. Preacher Vowker stood by one of the tables examining some of the material and talking with Ellie, his hand resting on her shoulder. Although there were a few older people in attendance, most of those present were under the age of twenty-five.

And there among them, moving around freely, were three Serenes; shaved heads, silver devices snug around their skulls, beige belted uniforms and brown sandals.

Then she noticed one of them did not wear the belt. This one was a Subjugate.

Salvi glanced at Mitch and saw his eyes were fixed on the Serenes and Subjugate. Vowker noticed their arrival and swiftly ushered them through into his office again, wanting to remove the strangers in black with their technology from the eyes of his delicate flock.

"More questions?" he asked, closing the door and moving to his seat at the desk.

"Yes," Mitch said. "Were you aware of the strong friendship between Tobias Brook and Sharon Gleamer?"

Vowker considered the question carefully before answering. "As I said the last time, I suspected they had grown close."

"What do you do when you suspect members have grown too close?"

"We counsel them. Remind them of their vows, of their promises to Christ."

"And what would happen to members of the Children of Christ if they were found to have broken their vows?"

Again, Vowker considered the question before answering. "They would need to confess their sins, repent, and ask the Lord for forgiveness."

"That's it?" Mitch asked.

"We would provide them with support to ensure that it doesn't happen again."

"What kind of support?"

"They would be assigned guides. Someone to pray with, who would accompany them around and stay close should they fear temptation rising."

"That sounds like what happens with the Subjugates from the Solme Complex," Salvi said.

Mitch flashed her a warning stare to keep quiet, then turned back to the preacher.

Vowker smiled. "Part of the treatment the Subjugates

receive at the Solme Complex is very closely aligned with how we run things in the Children of Christ. I have worked closely with Attis Solme on that part of the program."

"How so?" Mitch asked.

"The very core of their rehabilitation is the continual religious guidance we provide. We teach the Serenes and the borderline Subjugates allowed into town, the way of Christ. We let them know the Lord has forgiven them their sins, and they have been born again, free from that sin. Like with all of our flock, we counsel them, we support them, we provide them work. You know what they say about idle hands. We are the first ones to welcome them back into society. Without our support, the Solme Complex could not survive, and these men would be rotting in prison, unreformed."

"Are you aware of anyone else here who grew close to Sharon?"

"Like I said last time, she was well liked. She had a lot of friends."

"Did any of them require a guide to help them fight temptation?"

Vowker stared at Mitch. "I know you want to find her killer, but I assure you, you won't find them here. We are a peaceful, gentle people. If I were you I'd be focusing your attention on the SlingShot and the sinners it carries from the city."

"What about the Serenes?" Mitch ignored him. "How often do they come here?"

"Every day," Vowker said. "They are repentant sinners, who must give back to the Lord."

"What hours do they come here?"

"It varies. They are generally in town every day between 8am and 6pm. It depends what other tasks they are assigned to do at the Complex, of course. But generally you will find at least two of them here at the Children of Christ every day."

"So, every day, you welcome murderers and rapists to come and mix with your innocent congregation?"

Vowker paused. "That's not who they are any more. The Complex has made sure of that. We believe in forgiveness, Detective. Everyone on this Earth, should he repent, can be forgiven. We all make mistakes, and everyone deserves the chance to be forgiven for them."

"And if that sinner attacked Sharon Gleamer? Raped and mutilated her, then strangled her to death? Would *he* deserve forgiveness for taking an innocent life?"

"That is not for me to decide," Vowker said, his pale blue eyes fixed on Mitch's. "Only God can."

"You don't care for the girl or her family?" Mitch asked furrowing his brow. "For their justice?"

"Or is that just God's will?" Salvi spoke up. "That an innocent girl should die like that?"

Mitch threw her another sharp look but turned back to hear the preacher's answer.

"No one deserves to die like that," Vowker said, making a sign of the cross. "But we are all born with souls stained of sin. Most of us move on from that. But for some, society or some*one* has not let them forget that sin. Some are raised in sin, abused, taken for granted, mistreated. They have been taught to do the same to others. Do these poor souls not deserve a chance at forgiveness and freedom from their sin? At redemption? At resetting their lives and getting a second chance?"

"No," Mitch said bluntly. "If they take an innocent life, they deserve nothing."

Vowker smiled sadly at Mitch. "So black and white, Detective. It's as easy as that, is it? I know you must've seen some things that have tainted your point of view. And for that you have a troubled soul. I can see that. But you harbor a hatred that can be freed by forgiveness if you let it." He leaned over the desk toward him. "Let your hatred go, forgive, and you will be happier than you've ever been." He looked over at Salvi then. "Both of you."

Mitch and Salvi exchanged a glance. Despite the tension between them, right now they felt an alliance. An alliance of law enforcement over religion.

"I'm going to need a list of the Serenes and Subjugates who come here," Mitch said, indifferently.

"Are you prepared to provide your DNA to help us solve this case, preacher?" Salvi asked.

"Excuse me?" Vowker looked at her.

"DNA was found at the site of the murder. Semen. Should you provide your DNA it would be most helpful to our investigation. We could rule you out–"

"Wait," he said, absolutely aghast. He sat back in his seat. "What do you take me for?"

"We take you for someone who had contact with the victim," Mitch said bluntly, taking the reins back. "Someone displeased with her recent behavior. If you have nothing to hide, you'll be happy to volunteer the sample."

Vowker stared at him, face falling into an unhappy mask. "You do not have any evidence for a warrant, Detectives. Do not take me for a fool."

"That's why we asked you to volunteer it," Salvi said.

He stared at her, his face now full of hard lines. "If it is required, I shall do so," he said, "but I *thoroughly* object to your *foul* insinuation."

Mitch gave him a smile. "Thank you for your cooperation."

With that he motioned for Salvi to stand. She did, and they made their way toward the door, but upon reaching it, Mitch stopped and turned back to the preacher.

"By the way, thanks for the advice on the whole forgiveness thing." He pretended to be considering it for a moment. "But I like my hatred. I think I'm going to keep it."

They left the preacher's office and crossed the hall. As they did, Mitch's eyes were fixed on the Serenes and Subjugate again. He slowed his pace and Salvi could tell what he was thinking.

"You know we can't question them without an official from the Solme Complex present."

Mitch threw her a look and shrugged. "Surely we can just have a conversation with them?" He went to move in their direction, but Salvi caught his arm. Mitch looked down at her grip.

She smiled at him. "Looks like order has been restored. I'm the one holding you back." She let his arm go. "Come on. Let's go."

Salvi and Mitch walked back into the hub around five. They dumped their jackets at their desks as Beggs and Caine approached.

"You guys nailed that suspect yet?" Caine said cockily. "It's been two days already!"

Mitch flipped him the bird and Caine laughed, flashing his straight white teeth. He really was far too pretty to be working homicide.

"I don't know what's worse for you," Beggs said, brushing his fingers over his graying moustache, "dealing with the religious freaks or those Serenes. Give me a regular perp any day of the week."

"I don't know," Caine said. "There's something kinda cute about those religious cult girls. They're either virgins or they like to share their love around. I could handle that." Beggs gave a raucous laugh and Mitch humored them with a smile. Salvi just stared.

"Does all this laughter mean we've cracked a case?" Ford asked, walking up to their desks. With her sharp blue eyes and athletic stature, she didn't need her detective lieutenant's rank to be obeyed. Beggs and Caine ceased their laughter.

"Still working on it," Mitch said, as Caine and Beggs went back to their desks. "Did you see the request for DNA warrants?"

"Yeah, they should be approved by morning. Where are you at?"

"We think we ruled out the boyfriend, but the DNA will confirm that officially," Mitch said. "And as much as Salvi hates the preacher," he shot her a look, "I don't think he's the one either. He'll provide us a sample if we officially ask for one. There's still the neighbor too. James Stackwell. He's a city guy who's hiding out in Bountiful."

"Hiding out from what?"

"Loan sharks, probably."

"So you still think she knew her attacker?" Ford asked.

"Yeah," Salvi answered for Mitch. "They may not have been well acquainted, but we think the vic and the perp knew each other. She let him inside the house, then it turned nasty. And he punished her for something. Something that she did to affront him in some way. That much is clear."

Mitch shrugged. "It might not be anything specific. She might've just been an example of the kind of woman who always turned him down."

Ford nodded.

"We really need to talk to the Serenes and the Subjugates," Mitch said. "They're all over Bountiful, many without guards watching them."

Ford nodded. "Solme has confirmed your appointment for 8am tomorrow. Do you have any other suspects at this stage?"

Mitch shook his head. "None that stand out. Riverton's given us a list of homes and businesses we think have BioLume lighting and it's cross-checked them with clients of the vet clinic where Sharon worked. There's a handful of names. Some were at the retreat with the parents, so they've already been erased. The rest Sheriff Holt is canvassing for us.

If there's any of interest, we'll follow them up. But I think it's important we rule out the Serenes and Subjugates sooner rather than later."

Ford nodded again. "Alright. Update me once you've spoken to the folks out at the Solme Complex."

Ford walked back to her office, just as Hernandez and Bronte entered the hub.

"Hey," Salvi said.

"You guys having any luck?" Hernandez asked.

Salvi shook her head. "Not yet."

"Hey, who's up for a drink?" Beggs asked walking over to them. "Niiko from Narcotics said there's a bunch heading to McClusky's for a few rounds. They just nailed the perp they've been chasing the past several months."

"Yeah, we're up," Hernandez said, as Bronte nodded in agreement. Beggs looked at both Salvi and Mitch and raised his eyebrows.

"We'll pass," Salvi said.

"What are you, his mother?" Beggs asked and Caine laughed.

Mitch shot her a glance, then looked at Beggs and shrugged. "What the boss said."

The four cops laughed among themselves as they left. Salvi looked at Mitch.

"Showing some restraint tonight?"

Mitch stared at her. "If we're going to the Solme Complex tomorrow, I want a clear head."

"You should want that every day."

He studied her a moment. "You're such a good little girl, Salvi."

She turned back to her console screen, scratching the side of her face with her middle finger. A smile curled the corner of Mitch's mouth as he turned back to his screen too.

• • •

Back at her apartment, Salvi hung up her coat and placed her gun and comms gear on the bedside table. She kicked off her shoes, placing them in the cupboard, then moved to her exercise station and worked up a sweat. Afterward, she moved to the bathroom and began to disrobe for a shower. She stared at herself in the mirror. Her dark brown hair, cut into a blunt bob with square fringe, looked perfect. Not a hair out of place despite the day just done. Her red lipstick had mostly worn off, but her lips were still stained a color deeper than their natural shade. Her body was smooth and toned, only two marks disrupting her skin. Two tattoos. The large black scorpion that ran up her side from hip to waist, and the single word FAITH tattooed over her heart. Remnants of her former lives that she hadn't yet erased.

She turned away from the mirror and stepped into the shower. As she stood clouded in steam, she ran through the day's events. She thought of Sharon and Tobias' secret, wondered just how much control the preacher had over the Children of Christ, wondered just what he would do if he found out they'd broken their vows. She thought of Sharon's neighbor, wondered how often James Stackwell looked through into her bedroom. Wondered who else might've watched her too, through that bedroom window. She wondered how much contact the Serenes and Subjugates had with Sharon, wondered whether they really had been converted from their former selves or whether the monsters they once were still lay within. Most of all, though, she wondered about the things Mitch had said to her these past couple of days. The comments about her sex life, his curiosity over her attitude toward the preacher, his fixation with the Solme Complex. And both Ford and Hernandez asking her how Mitch was coping.

She stepped out of the shower, pulled on a robe, and heated her dinner. As she sipped her miso soup, she stared out of her Sky Tower windows at the city lights below. The drones buzzed here and there, golden lights twinkling like fireflies. She turned her eyes downtown, wondered whether Mitch had really gone back to his apartment or whether maybe he'd gone out drinking with the guys instead.

There were three types of cop in this world. The ones who only hung out with other cops. Most of them fit into that category. The ones who preferred to hang out with regular people. And those that liked to be alone. Salvi was definitely the latter.

She cleaned her teeth and slipped between her sheets, staring at the drawer that held the rosary beads. She thought of the deep dark secret she had buried there underneath the clothes in the far back corner. She smiled sadly as she thought of her sister, couldn't remember how long it had been since she'd thought of her. Since she'd allowed herself to think of her. Since she'd locked her away in the deep, dark recesses of her mind.

She touched her bedside lamp and extinguished the light. Then, as she lay there in the silence, she whispered to the darkness. "Faith."

5 : COMPLEXITY

Salvi stood outside the hub and checked her iPort. Mitch was late. She moved to activate her lenses but suddenly saw the Raider in the distance. He pulled up in front of her and the door sprang open with its hydraulic hiss.

"You're late," she said getting in.

He glanced at her briefly, then turned his eyes front again. She studied him. His hair was wet, he hadn't shaved, but he was awash in aftershave and mints.

"Early night, huh?" she said.

He looked at her again but didn't answer. Instead he held out her coffee. His eyes were clear, he must've taken Ford's advice, but she could still detect a tired, pained expression within them.

"Thank you," she said, taking the coffee. "Need some aspirin?"

"You know me so well, partner," he said, voice sounding a little rough.

"I'm a detective. It's my job to know people," she said, harking back to their conversation the day before.

"No, you just like to make people feel guilty," he said setting the Raider in motion.

Salvi looked at him. "I'm not making you feel guilty."

"Yes, you are."

"For what?"

"For getting drunk and releasing the day. You're good at it. You don't say anything, but it's there in your eyes. The judgment. Remember not all of us can bottle it up like you, Salvi. Some of us need to purge."

"So we've reached this point in our partnership, huh?" she said. "The critique phase. I guess that means you're comfortable around me now."

He threw her another glance. "It's not a critique. It's called clear and open communication. Can't have a partnership without it. I know it must bother you, having to talk about your feelings."

She looked out the windscreen; she wasn't getting drawn into another argument. She had to admit she was beginning to feel a little melancholy for past days, of working with Stanlevski. He never antagonized her like Mitch had been doing lately. Poking, prodding. Stan kept to himself and focused on the job. It made her work easier. Mitch was beginning to be equal parts focused on the job and focused on her. She didn't like being the topic of his curiosity, his hobby, his own personal investigation. And she didn't like the amount of time her mind was getting caught up thinking about his behavior. This wasn't her. She was focused and driven and hardworking, not the distracted kind.

The rest of the trip to Bountiful was done in silence. Mitch focused on the road ahead, while Salvi looked out the passenger window at the landscape as it turned from the dark gray hues and neon lights of the city, to the muted colors of an autumn country town. And while they drove, the SlingShot raced past them as though trying to beat them there.

Salvi studied the tall silver gates of the Solme Complex. Cylindrical posts topped with spear-like ends, it was the most prison-like aspect of it. But that wasn't the overall look the Solme Complex was going for. In order to be accepted by the people of Bountiful, and the outside world, this facility had to look different. It had to look secure, yes, but not frightening to outsiders. And it generally succeeded in that. The gate looked secure, as did the boundary fencing, but inside it looked like any other state-of-the-art industrial facility. A business that, according to the information Riverton had stored in their case file, supplied fresh goods, BioLume products, and a friendly, trustworthy, community of workers willing to help others, for free.

She glanced at Mitch. He sat clenching his jaw, eyes narrowed as he studied the perimeter, while the checkpoint guard scanned the Raider for contraband.

"If it was someone from the Complex," Salvi said, eyeing the fences, "they'd have to be rostered on for service in the town. No one could just walk out of here without authorization."

Mitch didn't answer, instead he watched the guard carefully on the rearview camera footage screening on the Raider's console. Salvi looked into her rearview mirror to watch the guard as he moved around to her side of the Raider. As she did, she caught sight of the bright red lipstick she wore. Pressing her lips together in thought, she wondered whether maybe she should've gone without today.

Something moving in the distance caught her eye and she looked through the windscreen to see a guard drone flying toward them. Mitch shifted his eyes to the drone then looked back at the guard again, who was now approaching his window. As the guard appeared, they exchanged a nod.

"Follow the drone to the parking area," the guard said through the data-enabled silver helmet visor that covered his entire face. "Do not deviate." The guard looked at Salvi then and back to Mitch. "And keep her with you," he said. "Don't go anywhere you're not supposed to."

Mitch glanced at Salvi, as she lit up her badge and flashed it at the guard.

"I can take care of myself," she said. "Thank you."

The guard seemed to find her comment amusing. "You

haven't met some of our residents, miss." He looked back at Mitch. "Follow the drone."

Mitch threw her another glance, then put the Raider in motion.

As they followed the drone she was impressed by how expansive the Solme Complex actually was. She'd known it was part prison, part BioLume manufacturing plant, and part rehabilitation center for the Serenes, but hadn't quite appreciated the sheer scale of it. It was almost an entirely self-sufficient community. They made their own furniture and clothes, fixed their own vehicles and machinery. They grew their own fruit and vegetables. The only food sources they relied upon from the outside world were fresh meat and dairy products, as it was deemed inappropriate for their rehabilitation to have the Subjugates butchering animals or milking cows.

To the left of the main building, in the outer grounds, Salvi saw six huge silver teardrop-shaped silos connected to each other and then to a processing plant by a long silver pipe. Beside that were the farms that supplied the Serenes and some of Bountiful with all their food. In the middle was the main facility, a large hexagonal-shaped prison where the processing took place. Curved white panels layered the outside giving it a strange appearance like some kind of alien cocoon.

Behind the main building she could see the tops of the housing units for the processed Serenes, oval-shaped habitats that looked like white wicker baskets stacked on one another. To the right of the housing units were the vineyards. Beyond that were workshops for carpentry and the like.

"It's a lot bigger than I realized," she mused aloud.

"Yeah," Mitch said. "Might take us a while to check everyone out."

"Well let's just start with the ones who had contact with

the victim, huh?"

The drone started flashing its lights, indicating they were arriving at their destination. A Serene stood waiting for them, beige uniform and belt flapping gently in the breeze, almost the same color as the man's skin. He smiled pleasantly and gracefully waved them forward. Salvi recognized him as the one Mitch had blocked on the sidewalk outside Stackwell's house the day before.

Mitch pulled the Raider up and turned off the engine, staring at the Serene, who moved toward him as Mitch popped the doors.

"Welcome to the Solme Complex," the Serene said, then walked around to Salvi's open door. "I am Serene-41, at your service." He bowed.

"Hello," she said, getting out of the Raider. "I'm Detective Brentt and this is Detective Grenville." They flashed their badges. The Serene, who looked to be in his late forties, about 5'8 and 150 pounds, smiled and bowed again.

"Mayor Solme is expecting you," Serene-41 said. "This way, please." He turned and began to make his way to the main building's entrance. Salvi threw Mitch another look as he moved up beside her.

"Goddamn freaks," he muttered.

As they reached the building, Serene-41 stood by the door waiting for them.

"This way," he said, leading them into a hollow reception, bare except for a plain curved desk. No artwork, no seats, just curved walls and soft green BioLume lighting. A doorway sat along the back wall by the desk, but it was a second door to the left that the Serene led them to.

The Serene knocked lightly upon it.

"Enter," a voice on the other side answered.

Serene-41 smiled, opened the door and bowed once more as Mitch and Salvi passed.

Attis Solme stood from his desk and walked around to greet them both. Like the rest of this building, his office was neat and tidy, all soft curves and gentle tones. The only thing distracting from the smooth lines and calmness was a small wooden cross that hung on the wall behind Solme's desk, adorned with a silver, crucified, Jesus Christ.

"Detectives Grenville and Brentt," Mitch announced.

"Yes," Attis Solme said. "Detective Lieutenant Ford told me to expect you." Standing at 6' and about 260 pounds, Solme shook the detective's hand, then turned to Salvi, softening his face as he shook her hand also. She gave a nod back, eyeing his pale blue suit and bolo tie, making him look somewhat like an old Texan rancher. "Heila and I go back a ways. She's been a big supporter of what I've accomplished out here."

Salvi and Mitch exchanged a glance. This was news to both of them.

"Will that be all, Mayor?" Serene-41 asked politely.

"Yes, thank you, Serene-41," Solme said. "You are excused."

The Serene left, closing the door as Attis Solme motioned for them to sit in two white rounded chairs positioned for guests.

"They call you Mayor?" Mitch asked as he took the proffered seat.

Attis Solme smiled. "Well, the Solme Complex is a community, after all. And it sounds a lot nicer than warden. Especially after they've been processed. It's important they feel a sense of accomplishment. It's all a part of their treatment, you see. We reward them for good behavior."

Mitch nodded, while Salvi's eyes caught on a stone statuette of Mary on Solme's desk. The statue captured Mary from the waist up, looking gracious, gentle, chaste, her eyes turned toward the ground in servitude. At least, that was what Mary was supposed to look like. Salvi always took her for looking sad. But sad for what, she wasn't sure. Sad at how her life turned out? How her son's life had turned out? That she was known simply as the mother and nothing more? That she'd had to take a back seat to everyone else's glory? That her job was simply to look gentle and patient and give the Christian girls an icon to follow? Who the hell was Mary, really?

"I believe you wish to interview some of my Serenes," Solme said.

"And your Subjugates," Mitch said.

"I understand." Solme's face fell serious. "I've been praying for the Gleamer family. Word is, Sharon's death was quite heinous."

"Yeah," Mitch said. "Something along the lines of what some of the people in here did once."

Solme gave a small smile. "I understand the natural reaction is to look here given the history of our residents, but I assure you only those sufficiently processed are allowed out of the Solme Complex and into the town. Our Serenes go through years of stringent treatment. This facility has been running for nine years and of that only the last three have seen Serenes released into the town's service. Do you know what that means?" he asked.

"Tell me," Mitch said.

"It means, generally speaking, and of course each case is different, that the standard treatment is seven years. The first two years here they are kept in solitary confinement. During that time, they deal only with their medical personnel, their psychiatric team and the guards. They are implanted with our special neural technology and undergo intense daily therapy. *Extreme* therapy. The following two years see them put to work in the farm and vineyard, all the while continuing the intense treatment. They only have contact with their medical teams, the guards, and now other residents. The next two years see them progress to work in the BioLume factory. There they come into contact with the people from the outside. Mostly it's those delivering supplies and salesmen with orders. Again, all the while they undergo the treatment. It is only after that that they are allowed into town with an escort. For twelve months they must keep this escort." Attis smiled. "So you see, Detective, that is seven years of supervised treatment."

Mitch nodded, scratching his jaw. "So that means for the past two years some of your Serenes have been walking around free of escorts."

Solme stared at him a moment, his face passive. "Yes. That is correct. And there have been no incidents."

"Until now," Mitch said.

"This was not one of my Subjugates or Serenes."

"Do you know how many pedophiles and rapists manage to stay away from temptation for years, only to reoffend in a weak moment?" Mitch countered.

"Have they been implanted with our neural technology? Have they undergone years of the intense treatment that we offer?" Solme asked.

Mitch stared back at him but didn't respond.

"Have they been chemically castrated to control such... weak moments?" Solme continued, analyzing Mitch carefully. "The Solme Complex has been running for nine years and we've never had an incident. Not even inside these walls. Trust me, our treatment is thorough. Our program is the best in the world."

"How many inmates do you have here?" Salvi asked.

"We currently have a total of one hundred and sixteen, with more due next month. But only twenty-three of them are Serenes – *Serene* being the name we give to those who have been successfully converted. The ones unconverted, as you know, are referred to as Subjugates. They arrive here as inmates, but the Solme Complex *subjugates* them and turns them into Serenes."

"So, you have twenty-three Serenes and ninety-three Subjugates?" Mitch asked.

"Yes."

"The Serene that showed us in," Salvi said. "He was Serene-41. How can that work if you only have twenty-three of them?"

"When they arrive, they are assigned a number. They keep that number through the process. Serene-41 was the forty-first inmate we had. However, his treatment went very well, and he was allowed to progress to a Serene more quickly than others. He's one of our longest serving Serenes, in fact. We've given him the position of Serene Supreme. He helps to watch the others."

"I thought you just said they all generally undergo six years of treatment and one year of supervision. They don't all undergo the same level of treatment, then?" Mitch asked. "How can you be sure the treatment worked?"

"The Subjugates we receive come from different backgrounds and have committed varying degrees of crimes. Each must be assessed on a case by case basis and the intensity and length of treatment provided tailored to their individual needs. Serene-41 came to us as John Holden, a man convicted of many accounts of indecent exposure. He never physically harmed anyone, but he was obsessed with showing his private parts to women. He had a particular fetish for mothers out walking with their young daughters." Solme smiled. "Perverse, yes, but he was never violent. He was easier to treat than some of the others here for more serious crimes, so he progressed through each stage more quickly."

"Why *was* Serene-41 sent here?" Salvi asked. "His crimes are minor."

"How does someone come here?" Mitch added. "Do you select them?"

"No, but we do assess each candidate before accepting

them," Solme said. "This facility, despite how successful it has been, is still fairly new. We are being watched by a lot of agencies, our reports reviewed with interest, but we are not yet accepted as standard practice by the federal authorities. Our treatment is considered a specialist program. Niche. And to some… controversial. Given what happened in the crash of 2040, there is a strong mistrust for neural implants, and the technology we use here is a step back in that direction. However, our success is slowly winning back the confidence of the federal agencies. But that's why, right now, each prisoner must volunteer to undergo the program. Normally, the families hear about our services and apply to send the Subjugates here for treatment, part of their plea deal. The families are the ones who believe, and perhaps hope, that these men can change. That they can be saved. On rare occasions, such as with Serene-41, he volunteered for the treatment himself. He wanted desperately to be cured."

"Can you tell us a little about the neural technology you use on the Subjugates?" Salvi asked. "I'm intrigued by the silver… *crowns* they wear."

"Halos." Attis smiled. "That's what we call them."

"Halos?" Mitch asked.

"Yes," Attis said. "The halos turn them from sinners into saints." He smiled again, a man impressed with his own cleverness. "Our society has been using similar neural applications for years to treat physical diseases such as Parkinson's and dementia. However, we are the first ones to treat psychological conditions. Each Subjugate first undergoes neural imaging to map their brains. Once this has been done, a minor surgical procedure to implant the tech is undertaken with exact positioning according to their neural imaging. The implants are small but powerful and they sit inside the skull wall, on each side of the brain. The implant, thanks to the precise neural imaging, records electrical activity in the centers of the brain that control emotion, sexual arousal and the like. When the implants detect increased electrical activity in these areas, a signal is sent externally along the silver panels you can see on the outside of their skull. Heightened emotion, such as anger, or sexual arousal, will trigger a visual alarm warning us that action needs to be taken before the Subjugate can act out."

"What exactly is the alarm?" Salvi asked.

"Their halos will turn ice blue."

"And how often do you find them turning blue?" Mitch asked.

"While the Subjugates are still in early treatment, often. But as time marches on, the more we hone our treatment to the individual, they trigger less and less. We've never had a code blue in a Serene. Ever."

"Is that how you determine their graduation from Subjugate to Serene? The lack of code blue?"

"That's the primary indicator, yes. We submit them to all sorts of stimuli and when they no longer react to it, we know we've won our battle and have exorcised the demon within them."

"So, the neural tech you use is effectively just a warning system," Mitch said. "It doesn't stop them."

"It can if required," Attis said, sitting back in his chair.

"How so?" Mitch pushed.

"If required, if a Subjugate were to be considered a threat, considered dangerous, we could use the implants to shock them into submission."

"Shock their brains?" Salvi asked. "Wouldn't that be dangerous?"

"Yes it would, at high levels. The levels we would submit them to would be minor, equating to something similar to a brain freeze or brief fainting spell, but enough to halt their actions."

"And have you ever had to use this measure on any?" Mitch asked.

"Rarely."

"But you *have* had to use this method?" Mitch said.

Attis stared at Mitch a moment. "Once or twice a Subjugate has needed this method, but it is extremely rare. Normally our guards would handle such outbursts or misbehavior. But again, even that is rare in the later stages. Between the chemical castration we give them and our stringent therapy, they are well controlled. Their desire for evil has been fully suppressed."

"Suppressed but not eradicated," Mitch said, eyes fixed on Attis.

"Fully suppressed, meaning eradicated," the mayor replied firmly.

"So, you honestly believe the Subjugates and Serenes you put on the streets of Bountiful are no longer a threat to society?" Salvi asked.

"Absolutely," he said, sitting forward, placing his forearms on the desk and clasping his hands as though in prayer. "We're fixing the ultimate problem that others have not been able to fix. The problem of reintegrating these people into society. Do you know how hard it is to send convicted sex offenders back into the public? Even after they've done their time in prison? No one wants them living in their neighborhood. *No one.* Their options are limited. They either end up sitting in prisons or other special facilities because they have nowhere else to go. Some are lucky and get sent to special living quarters on the outside. But it's very difficult for them to reintegrate with ankle bracelets, constant check-ups from parole officers, the restrictions on where they can go, what they can do. Those convicted of pedophilia must never go anywhere children may be. The beach, a shopping mall, parks. They're listed online for all to see, for the rest of their lives. That's no way to live."

"Wait a minute," Mitch raised his hand, "you're talking about convicted sex offenders here. The public has a right to know if a potential threat is living next door to them and their children."

"Exactly." Attis pointed at him. "And I agree. But what is the system to do with all these unwanted offenders? The only way the public will ever accept them back into society is if they are cured of their demons once and for all. When the public has one hundred percent assurance the individual has lost all desire and will not reoffend. A one hundred percent assurance that the individual has in fact been taught to never harm another human being, and instead, to always help those in need. And that is what we do here. We take them, we fix them, we turn them around, and we send them back out into society as non-violent, non-threatening, non-offending individuals that give back to the society they once stole from."

"But how do you fix them, exactly?" Salvi asked. "The neural tech you describe is effectively an alarm system and a possible weapon against them, but how do you train them against their natural thoughts? These men often have personality disorders, brain dysfunctions, that are beyond their control."

"Again, it depends on their individual needs. We can apply a variety of treatments. All undergo the chemical castration as I have said. They receive twice-daily injections to control their testosterone levels and keep them on a subdued plateau. As any patient with a medical disorder, they must take their meds for life. If this proves unachievable there are more permanent measures we can take. As I also said, they undergo intensive daily therapy with psychiatrists, sitting regular testing. If we fail to see any progression, then we apply special brain tweaks that see an end to their attraction to murder and sexual violence."

"Brain tweaks?" Mitch asked.

Attis smiled. "We... numb... the relevant parts of their brains, but I'll let my lead psychologist explain that in more depth when you meet him."

The silence sat for a moment before Salvi broke it. "Are there any female Subjugates?"

"Not as yet, no. In time I would like to incorporate them, but the truth is, most murderers and sexual predators are indeed male."

"So, the families can petition to send inmates here?" Mitch asked.

"Yes. Requests are made and considered by the federal prison board." Attis sighed heavily. "It's been a long road, but word is spreading about the work we do here." He smiled again. "It's hard to think that I started this program with just five Subjugates. By next month we will exceed a hundred and twenty. We're already drawing up plans to expand the compound."

"And you've never had any problems with the treatment?" Salvi asked. "No setbacks? Faults?"

"No. Neither our Subjugates nor our Serenes have inflicted harm on anyone."

"And after the Crash you're not worried about using neural implants?" Mitch asked. "Do they have any connectivity with a wider program that can be hacked?"

"Not yet, but we are working on a second phase that would include such connectivity."

"How so?" Salvi asked.

Attis smiled again. "Our numbers are growing. Soon we will need to set up other facilities to house them, and soon we will need to release the Serenes back into the wild permanently. Connectivity to a wider program will enable us to keep an eye on all of our Serenes once released back into society. They will effectively still be prisoners but live in the outside world."

"Why do you need to keep an eye on them if you believe they're cured?" Mitch asked.

"To appease the federal prison board and disbelievers like yourself, Detective."

"Have you received federal permission to roll out connectivity with the Serenes' implants already?" Salvi asked, unable to hide her surprise. "They banned connectivity after the Crash. They're really going to open it up again?"

"Neural implant connectivity has never left the table," Attis said. "It was just put on hold to allay fears after the Crash. I have no doubt it will be a strong part of our future."

"And if another terrorist organization comes along, hacks the system and fries the brains of your precious Serenes?" Mitch said. "Or worse, somehow sends them on a killing rampage? There will always be hackers. Connected neural implants will never be safe."

"Well, I plan to show them otherwise." Attis smiled.

"How?" Salvi asked. "How exactly will connected neural implants help them?"

"We've studied and recorded the neurological patterns which precede the errors in their behavior. We know what each of their brains do when they're aroused to things they shouldn't be. We've mapped the signals, the triggers. And if they register on our systems, we can intercept their mistakes before they make them." He smiled again with a twinkle in his eye. "Just think, one day we may be able to apply this to the wider population. Imagine a world where we can shut down threats and stop murders and rapes before they occur. We may not need the police any more."

"Unlikely," Mitch said.

"Well, for now we'll settle for stopping criminals from reoffending. We will ensure our Serenes are trained to never harm another human being again."

Salvi nodded. "So, the government is effectively letting you use these prisoners as lab rats. Lab rats that no one will miss if the tech fails and they die."

Attis looked at Salvi and took a moment to collect his thoughts. "Let's get one thing clear, Detective. I am here to save these men. It is the path the Lord has asked me to walk and walk it I shall. I am saving these sinners. I am turning their eyes to the Lord. And neural tech is the tool that allows me to do this, along with religion and therapy of course. It's the only way to rescue their minds from the devil. We exorcise that devil and we banish it for good. And should that devil ever think of returning, their halo will stop it."

"No," Mitch said, "their halo will just warn you. And how will that warning system work once you 'release them into the wild' and they're a hundred miles away?"

"That's what the connectivity is for." Salvi nodded to herself. "Someone sits in a control room and watches. If a halo codes blue, they shut it down. Freeze their brains."

"That's a lot of halos to watch," Mitch commented.

"Not with a fully automated system overseen by a superior AI," Attis said. "Within mere nanoseconds of a code blue, the Serene would be on the floor."

"Has the treatment you apply affected any of the Serenes or Subjugates unduly?" Salvi asked. "Have there been any physical or psychological issues reported?"

"We've, er, only ever had one issue with treatment."

"And what was that?" Mitch asked.

"A Subjugate by the name of Fontan Pragge. He reacted poorly to the treatment provided."

"In what way?" Salvi asked.

Attis hesitated a moment. "He acquired brain damage," he said, but quickly held up his hand in a motion to let him finish. "That was in the early days of the program. A setback which we've now overcome."

"How much brain damage?" Mitch asked.

Attis considered his words. "For the most part he has normal function. He's... just a little slow."

"Who was he?" Salvi asked. "Before coming here?"

"Fontan Pragge was a serial rapist," Attis told her. "Anything went. His youngest victim was four years old, the oldest was eighty-two. He showed no restraint nor any repentance for his crimes. He resisted us at every turn, so he was issued the most rigorous of treatments. The kind that involved our highest level of brain tweaks to numb the pleasure zones. Unfortunately, he received one tweak too many. It caused brain damage."

"Where is he now?" Salvi asked.

"Oh, he's around," Attis said. "He's another of our longest serving residents. Subjugate-12. You can usually find him in the vineyard or the farms, lending a hand."

"He allowed in town?" Mitch asked.

"Yes," Attis said. "He goes with the other Serenes, but I assure you he's as harmless as a fly. He doesn't have the, er, *physical* capacity let alone the intellect to launch an attack such as the one on Miss Gleamer."

"How many of your residents are cleared to go into town?" Salvi asked.

"There are twenty-three Serenes, and we have another fifteen in progress to become Serenes," he said. "Although not all of those are allowed into town just yet."

"So, several of those fifteen Subjugates are allowed into town?" Salvi asked.

"Yes, but they are nearing the end of their treatment, soon to become Serenes," Attis said.

"But they're not one hundred percent processed?" Mitch said.

"No, but at some point, they need to be reintroduced into society. They are taken on excursions to town. At first, it's one day a week and slowly it builds until it is every day. They help the other Serenes in service of the town, they spend time at the Children of Christ. All the while they are accompanied by guards and other Serenes," Attis said. "I assure you the guards keep an eye on the Subjugates."

"And if a guard gets distracted?" Mitch asked.

Attis gave him a look that hinted his patience was ebbing, and leaned back into his chair again. "They are watched very carefully. And I remind you, they have had years of intense treatment prior to these trips into town."

"But they could still code blue?" Salvi said.

Silence sat for the briefest of moments before Attis replied. "My borderline Serenes do not code blue."

"We'll need a list of all those who were in town the day of Sharon's murder," Mitch said. "We'll need to speak with each one of them. And I think a good place to start would be with these borderline Subjugates, Mr Solme."

The Complex's mayor stared at Mitch as his mind ticked over.

"First, I think, you should tour my facility and see our results for yourself. Then, you talk to my lead psychiatrist," Attis replied, sitting forward in his chair and clasping his hands in prayer again. "Then you may talk with my Subjugates. But I'd like you to promise me something, Detectives?"

"What's that?" Mitch asked.

"Promise me you'll investigate this thoroughly and *fairly*."

Mitch glanced at Salvi then back to Attis. "We plan to," he told him.

"I know this crime has rocked Bountiful," Attis said. "But I will not help you launch a lynch mob on my doorstep. I know with crimes like this, emotion takes over and people start looking for someone to hang. I have worked long and hard to get the Solme Complex to where it is. I have been successfully treating these people and releasing them back into society and making them useful again. If you try to pin this on one of my Serenes or Subjugates without sufficient evidence, you could destroy everything I have worked hard for all these years." Attis stared at them both firmly. "And I cannot let that happen. I will not stand by and let you pin Sharon Gleamer's murder on one of them because you need to appease tensions in the town. I will protect my residents with the full force of the law."

"And if one of your Serenes or Subjugates did do this?" Mitch asked him.

Attis stared at him a moment, considering the question. "If one of my Serenes or Subjugates did this... then I will take full responsibility for that girl's death. I will accept whatever punishment may come as deemed by the Lord. But I am *confident* that you have come to the wrong place."

A moment of silence sat in the smooth, hollowed-out room.

"I'll grant you the interviews," Attis said, "but you keep this quiet and out of the press. I told Ford, that's the deal. You will not destroy all my hard work."

Salvi watched as Mitch stood from his chair.

"Let's get started with the tour, shall we?"

6: BIOLUME

Salvi and Mitch followed Serene-41 down a tubular corridor awash in that green BioLume glow. The neutral walls were covered in a soft felt-like material and the scent of some kind of soothing essential oil wafted throughout. Everything about the place was geared toward pleasantness and harmony. No sharp corners, no bright colors. Salvi almost felt like taking a nap. As they passed other Serenes in the corridor, she noticed they all stopped, smiled and bowed to them, lowering their eyes to the floor as they passed, their halos tarnished under the green lighting. And with each step she saw Mitch's disgust and unease grow.

Attis Solme had stayed behind in his office to make a call, promising to find them soon, but he'd requested the Serene take them to the caretaker's office. The caretaker, they'd been told, was the term for the head guard, the man in charge of the day-to-day security of the inmates and the Complex as a whole.

When they arrived, she noticed the caretaker's office was a third of the size of Solme's. He sat at a small desk near the back wall, facing the door, while a large glass panel was affixed to the wall beside him, alight with data, prisoner numbers and maps. A gum wrapper and coffee mug sat on his desk, while the sound of a baseball game sounded through speakers somewhere. At the touch of a button, the sound ceased, however.

"Caretaker," Serene-41 said, lowering his eyes as he bowed. "I bring you Detectives Grenville and Brentt."

The caretaker stood from his desk. Appearing to be in his early forties, his face held the hard features of a man who'd seen some tough times. Or at least the look of a man who faced hardened criminals every day. He was fit and toned, stood around 6'1, and weighed maybe 210 pounds.

"Levan Bander." He gave a nod, tucking his thumbs behind his belt. Although he was called caretaker, he dressed like a regular prison guard. His uniform was dark brown in color and made from a fitting, synthetic, impenetrable material, while he was equipped with a baton, some kind of taser, and wireless comms gear that sat wrapped around one ear.

"You know why we're here?" Mitch asked.

"Yeah." Bander rubbed his jaw. "The mayor says you want a look around and to interview some of the Subjugates. This to do with that girl's death in town, huh?"

"Yeah." Mitch rested his hands on his hips.

"You think one of them did this?"

"We don't think anything yet," Salvi answered quickly with a smile. "We just want to look around and talk to some of them."

"Shall we start the tour?" Mitch said eagerly.

Bander stared at him a moment, then moved around the desk toward them.

"She coming too?" Bander asked Mitch.

"Yes, I am," Salvi said, not letting Mitch answer for her.

"The mayor approved that?" Bander threw a look to the Serene.

"Only the green zones," Serene-41 said, bowing slightly. "No access has been granted to Section A or B."

"A or B?" Mitch asked, looking back at Bander. "What's in A and B?"

Bander turned his eyes back to Mitch. "Section A is the new guys. They're not broken yet. Section B, they're only half broken. Still a risk."

"So where do you keep the Serenes?" Salvi asked.

Bander turned to her. With his dark blue eyes and square jaw, he was almost attractive. Except for the fact that it looked like his nose had been broken more than once.

"Serenes are housed in Section D," he said. "Section C have been broken but we don't like to take our eyes off them just yet. That's the Subjugates we allow into town."

"Let's do it, then," Mitch said.

Bander nodded. "This way."

"Caretaker, do you require my services any longer?" the Serene asked, keeping his eyes on the ground. Something about him reminded Salvi of a geisha. The softness. The servitude.

Bander waved him off, uninterested, and Serene-41 bowed and walked away.

Salvi and Mitch followed the caretaker back down the tubular corridor toward reception, then took another corridor to the opposite side of the Complex. All curved, smooth corridors and soft BioLume lighting, it felt like walking through some kind of human ant colony.

She noted that every Serene they passed quickly stopped and moved back against the walls, lowering their eyes or bowing until they passed. Some almost looked terrified. Fearful. Almost. Perhaps they would be if they were allowed to feel anything any more, if the extreme therapy and chemical castration hadn't taken it away.

Or had it?

Were they simply bowing out of courtesy and respect? Or were they bowing in pure servitude. Bowing out of necessity?

They ascended in a glass elevator to the second floor and soon emerged onto a walkway bridge. Enclosed like a glass cocoon, with white concrete pillars and circular support beams, it seemed to be leading them away from the main building toward what she suspected was the BioLume plant.

"Through there is the farm." Bander pointed to the right-hand side.

Salvi saw a tractor in the distance and crops. And, of course, both Serenes and Subjugates, who seemed to pause and watch upon seeing them. Dressed in their beige uniforms and brown sandals, she realized now how wrong she'd been in thinking the silver devices wrapped around their skulls were like laurel wreaths. As she looked at them now, the silver headwear glinting in the sunlight really did appear eerily like halos. Solme's sinners very much appearing as saints to make the residents feel safe.

"How long have you worked here?" Mitch asked Bander.

"Since the beginning," he said.

"Yeah?" Mitch asked. "You ever seen any of the Serenes break their serenity?"

Bander walked on and shook his head confidently. "Nope. We've had a one hundred percent success rate." He glanced back at Mitch. "I make sure of that."

"Have you always worked in the corrections industry?" Salvi asked.

"Not in the prison system, no. I've worked in security most of my life, ran my own business, but a few years back I was looking for a change and got a job at a local prison, found I was good at it, then the mayor offered me a job here. He was looking for someone who knew how to secure both people and property. I had skills in both, it was paying well, so," he shrugged, "here I am."

They came to the other side of the walkway bridge and approached a circular, white metal door sealed with a series of mechanical locks. It looked like something from a submarine. Bander swiped his pass on a console beside the door and submitted to a retinal scan before the door unlocked.

"This is the BioLume plant," he said, tugging hard on the heavy circular handle to open the door.

Before them, Salvi saw a large circular facility with wide circular windows cut out of the walls. On the ground floor, sat a broad expanse of concrete topped with several bulky silver metal vats, which she guessed were responsible for the strong odor of wet moss that filled her nose. About twenty workers were spread across the floor at various posts; some working consoles, some checking samples, some undertaking mechanical work. All wore biohazard suits to stop contact with the bacteria that made up the BioLume product. She stepped onto the elevated grid platform that ran the perimeter of the plant. From her birdseye view she could see into each vat and noticed they were different shades of green; each vat at a different stage of the process to become the final BioLume product which would eventually be packed into globes and shipped to stores. All for the purpose of natural light and environmentally sustainable homes.

Within seconds of them coming to stand on the observation platform, all the workers below noticed their arrival, paused, and stared up at them. Although it felt like they were only staring at her. Dressed head to toe in their white protective-wear and face masks, their bodies tinged by the green glow emanating from the vats, they looked alien in appearance. She wondered how many of them were Serenes and how many were Subjugates.

Levan Bander pulled the baton off his belt and smacked it hard three times on the edge of the railing. The workers below immediately went back to work.

Mitch shot Salvi a look before he began with more questions.

"All of these workers are almost transformed?"

Bander nodded, eyeing the residents below. "Most of 'em are Serenes. Some are Subjugates about to get their wings back." Bander looked at Salvi. "A few of them probably haven't seen a woman in the flesh for several years. Let's hope you haven't set their treatment back."

Salvi eyed him. "I'm covered head to toe in a suit. I'm sure seeing one woman from afar won't set them on a killing rampage."

Bander grunted a laugh. "You'd be surprised."

"How many work in this factory at any one time?" Mitch asked.

"Depends. Normally about what we got here now. We undergo daily testing on the vats to check the culture level. It's a fine art. If the conditions are too acidic, they die. Too alkaline? They die. Every twelve weeks we clear out a vat and start a new batch."

"Where does it go when it's ready?" Salvi asked.

Bander motioned for them to follow him, as he began to walk along the platform to the left. They came to one of the circular windows and he pointed out. "The storage cells."

Salvi looked out to see the six teardrop-shaped silos, shining a brilliant silver in the mid-morning sun.

"After the vat is done, we let it ferment a while in the storage silos. Then when it's fully cooked, every month we load the readied BioLume into the special globes with the sheath cover that slides up and down to enable the light to be turned out, then we send them out to stores."

"And the Serenes load the globes too?" Mitch asked.

"Yeah," Bander motioned in the distance, "over in the next building."

"Looks like it keeps the residents pretty busy," Salvi said.

"Sure does," Bander said. "We're almost at a point where we're struggling to keep up with demand." He looked at them and smirked. "Business is booming."

"We got orders from Japan just the other day!" Attis Solme's voice sounded behind them.

They turned to see him smiling as he approached along the grid walkway.

"Word is spreading and it's growing by the day," he said. "This here," he waved his hands like a game show hostess over the plant, "is benefiting the Solme Complex at large in more ways than one. Not only are we are starting to ease the pressure on prison populations by taking in criminals, healing that terrible element of society and putting them to good use, but we're using a natural product and making this world more sustainable for everyone." Attis turned and smiled at Salvi. "And we are self-funded. We're not taking a dime from the government or other funding bodies. Self-funded, self-sufficient, self-governing. We're helping society, not burdening it. How could anyone not want this?"

"I guess so," Salvi said.

"Unless they reoffend," Mitch said. "Then there's a chink in the chain."

"There's no chink in my chain, Detective. This here is utopia."

Salvi moved over to the railing and looked down again. She watched as one worker took a sample from a vat then moved to pour it into another container for study. As he turned back around, Salvi noted bright green splotches on his white biohazard uniform.

"Do they need any kind of specialized training to handle the BioLume?" she asked.

Attis moved to stand beside her. "They're given detailed training when they first start and are watched carefully onwards by the more experienced ones."

"What happens if they get any BioLume on their skin?"

"It's incredibly difficult to do in their suits, but should a worker get even the slightest drop on their skin, they take a special cleansing shower afterward to kill the bacteria. We are audited regularly. I assure you, Detective, we have the highest quality standards here and health and safety are paramount to us. I used to run a fertilizer plant in my former life, so I know what I'm doing."

"Yeah?" she asked. "From fertilizer to the rehabilitation of criminals. That's quite a change in career."

He smiled again, looking out upon the factory with pride. "I am a religious man now, but I never used to be. I was a successful man, had wealth, but somehow in my foolishness, my greed, I lost it all. But then I met my wife and I realized I was being given a second chance. She changed my world, helped me build up my fortune again. She taught me about kindness and care, and forgiveness. She showed me the light of God. The Solme Complex, in a way, is for her. In her honor." He smiled again sadly. "I think she would be so proud of what I've done here."

"Your wife passed?" Salvi asked gently.

Attis nodded. "Cancer. She taught me so much about strength. She could've been so bitter and angry about her life being cut short, but she wasn't. This was her path, she told me. This was God's plan. And it was," he said. "She inspired all of this." He waved his hand again across the plant floor. "She always believed that criminals were misunderstood and needed a second chance and a guiding hand, that if only they had religion in their lives they could be saved. Her strength, her courage, her death... it led me to this. This, *here*, is God's will."

Salvi saw the look on the mayor's face as he eyed the workers below, saw a slight shine to his eyes. Pride in his creations. She glanced back at Levan Bander, who stared stony-faced and unaffected by his boss's passion. Further along was Mitch, not really listening, too focused on studying the residents below, eager to interrogate them.

"Shall we commence the interviews?" Salvi asked Attis.

He looked back at her. "First you must meet Doctor Remmell. He's in charge of the medical and psychiatric care of our residents. Nothing can be done without him present."

They made their way back to the exit and stepped onto the sealed glass walkway again. As they crossed over to the other side, Salvi noticed one of the residents standing close by on the ground, staring up at them. He showed no facial expression, just stood, mouth slightly open, one hand reaching into a hessian bag he held, groping the seeds within. She saw no beige belt, so this was a Subjugate.

"Ah," Attis Solme said seeing the man. He glanced at Salvi. "Subjugate-12, also known as Fontan Pragge."

Salvi studied the man; old and stooped and gray, his mouth glistening. His brain damage was apparent just by looking at him; the glaze in his eyes, the drool along his mouth. A small part of her felt sorry for him. But then she thought of his victims, of the four year-old girl, the eighty-two year-old grandmother, and it quickly ebbed. She shared a glance with Mitch, and the look on his face told her that he felt no pity at all.

Upon entering the main facility again, they parted ways with Attis Solme once more and followed Bander to the ward where the Subjugates were processed. They walked down more tubular corridors of soft BioLume light and felt walls, eventually entering the treatment wing, passing the doors of the individual processing rooms. Curious, Salvi slowed and moved to peer through the window of one. The room was small with a laid-back chair in the center. She noticed the chair had head, arm and leg restraints. A small table with a semi-circular edge cut out was attached to the chair, positioned over it. Another table sat beside the chair that held a pair of VR glasses and various implements that looked like they belonged in a surgical theater. Or perhaps a torture chamber.

Mitch stood beside her and peered in also.

"Hey!" Bander called. "Keep up. Don't deviate."

Salvi exchanged a look with Mitch then turned to follow Bander. They moved toward him as a Subjugate approached from the opposite direction, escorted by another guard. The Subjugate's face was sweating, his nose bleeding, and more blood was splattered down the front of his beige tunic. A bewildered look was plastered on his face that soon turned to terror upon seeing them. Upon seeing *her*. The Subjugate averted his eyes, scrunching them closed, and turned his body toward the wall in a cowering pose as though afraid he was about to be beaten. As they passed she heard him whispering to himself, pleading, "No, no, no, no, no."

Salvi glanced back at him after they passed and saw his escorting guard tugging him by the arm and hissing something into his ear that made the Subjugate curl into himself even more.

"I'm sure Doctor Remmell will go over this," Bander said, bringing her attention back to him, "but you need to watch your language with the Subjugates. You are not to mention any words that may incite or remind them of their prior criminal activity. Death is one of them. So is murder. So is rape. Get the picture? You can only speak of the present. You must never bring up their past. Do you understand?"

"Why's that?" Mitch asked.

"Because we've erased it," Bander said plainly. "They don't know that person any more. That was a different person and that person is now dead and buried. We do not resurrect that person. We do not speak of the dead. You don't mention their old names. You refer to them by their Subjugate or Serene number only. No names, no past. Understand?"

Salvi and Mitch exchanged another look then nodded at Bander.

They eventually came to a wide silver door. Bander submitted to the security clearances and the door slid open silently. The caretaker waved them through and Salvi saw another hollowed-out, curved room, with the BioLume lights glowing along white walls. A single white table sat in the middle of the room, with chairs set back a little either side.

Bander motioned for them to sit, as another man entered the room. Dressed in a white uniform, similar to that of a dentist, he stood around 5'11 and weighed maybe 170 pounds.

"Doctor Dunstan Remmell," he said in a British accent, shaking their hands. He looked back at Bander. "Would you bring in Serene-23?" The caretaker gave a nod and left the room.

Remmell's hair was short and blond, the face beneath his brown rectangular glasses looked young, but Salvi guessed that was more to do with lack of sun than his actual age. His small brown eyes stared back at hers with a look of intellect as he took a seat on the other side of the table. "I'm in charge of overseeing the medical and psychiatric treatment of the Subjugates. Mayor Solme asked me to speak with you and provide a list of the Subjugates soon to graduate to Serenes."

"Yes," Mitch said. "There are approximately fifteen, is that right?"

"Yes," he answered. "Fifteen in that phase of the treatment, but only seven of those are close to graduation and hence allowed into the town."

"And were they in town the day of the murder?" Mitch asked.

"Yes," Remmell answered in a calm, measured voice. "They were."

"Do you normally have that many Subjugates in town on any one day?" Salvi asked.

"No. On that particular day extra hands were called for to help clear a vacant block, readying it for building on. Every month new families are moving to Bountiful to lead the tech-free religious lifestyle."

"Where was the block of land?" Salvi asked.

"Not far from the center of town."

"How far from the Gleamer residence?" she asked.

Dr Remmell hesitated a moment. "I believe it was a couple of streets away."

"So who were the seven Subjugates in town that day?" Mitch asked.

Remmell pressed his hands against the table and a keyboard embedded within lit up beneath his fingers. He tapped the keys and soon a thin glass pane emerged from the wall to their right. Upon it, a list of names appeared. Salvi looked back at Remmell.

"How long have you been working with the Subjugates?"

"I've been here from the start, but this will be my seventh year in charge of their care," he said.

"Who did you take over from?"

"Doctor Roman Broucharde. He retired. But I assisted him for the first two years of my employ here."

"So, you would know these seven Subjugates quite well, then?" Salvi asked.

"Yes," he said confidently. "Better than anyone."

"Are any of these Subjugates the type to relapse?" Mitch asked, pointing to the seven names on the screen. "Have any given you signs that their treatment isn't working?"

"No," he said, again confidently. "If they did, they wouldn't be allowed into town. I personally authorize the transition and will not authorize it unless I'm entirely sure there is no chance of re-offense."

"Can you give us a rundown on these seven men?" Salvi asked. "Show us their criminal files?"

"I can," Doctor Remmell said. "However, it's important you understand, these men you wish to interview are not the same men as those in their criminal files. We've seen to that."

"We'll be the judge of that," Mitch said.

"Our processes here are impeccable," Remmell said. "We take every precaution."

"Mr Solme outlined the treatment, but can you walk us through it?" Salvi asked.

"Of course," he said, as Bander came back into the room, along with another Serene. Remmell saw them and turned back to Salvi and Mitch. "Would you care for tea?"

"Thank you." Salvi nodded, but Mitch shook his head. The Serene bowed and left again.

"So how do you transform a hardened criminal into that?" Salvi asked, watching the Serene leave.

"With years of treatment," Remmell said. "What type of treatment and the amount of which depends on the patient. We hold daily psychological sessions. We work to keep them calm and we work to extricate the hate and violence from their systems. Many of these criminals were abused themselves as children or young adults. Many come from broken and violent homes. Many are battling addictions when they arrive here."

"Many other people come from these places too," Mitch said, "and yet they don't inflict harm on anyone else."

"This is true," Remmell conceded. "And some were born with neurological and psychological deficiencies that couldn't be controlled. There are many murderers who came from loving families," he said with a smile. "But there was something wrong with their brains to make them this way... This is why it is crucial to treat each one individually. Just like our fingerprints we are each individually wired in our own unique way. Each of us a result of our genetic makeup, our upbringings and the societal effect. Some residents just require a chemical or hormonal re-balance. This of course, we do to all our Subjugates. They receive twice-daily injections, a chemical castration. In time these injections will decrease, once we're certain their treatment has worked and any adjustments made to their brain and behaviors have become permanent. Once this is the case, they will be weaned off their medication. Some may stay on the injections for life. Again, this is decided on a case by case basis."

"So that's the chemical castration," Salvi said. "What about the other treatments?"

"We use various methods. For those deemed sexually violent, the ultimate way is to submit our Subjugates to regular PPGs–"

"PPGs?" Salvi asked.

"Penile plethysmography." Remmell pressed a button on his console and a section of the desk opened to reveal a drawer. He pulled out what looked like a rubbery sock. He held it out to Salvi and she took it and examined it. "This is a haptic sheath. It's one of the ways we test our Subjugates. It measures blood flow to the penis. We subject them to certain stimuli and see if it results in arousal. If it does, we work to remove that arousal from them."

Salvi held the rubber device out to Mitch, who glanced at it, furrowing his brow, and shook his head. She passed it back to back to Dr Remmell, suppressing a smile.

"So how do you do that?" she asked. "Remove the arousal?"

Remmell paused a moment. "By any means necessary."

"Which means?" Mitch asked.

"I can't go into specifics, exactly," Remmell said, "but trust me when I say that they come to associate violence and sexual debauchery with *intense*, unwanted pain. They are taught to never want to experience that pain again, and in so doing, they never desire violence or sexual debauchery again. As I said, each case is different. We have many murderers here, who although extremely violent, never engaged in sexual violence. Their treatment will therefore be different from the pedophiles and rapists."

"Is it legal? What you do to them to associate this *intense* pain with their previous pleasures?" Salvi asked.

Remmell stared at her for a moment. "In our facility, yes. We are essentially reprogramming their brains. Granted we are trialing this treatment and some may question our methods, but we have found that what we do works."

"And this works on all of them?" Mitch asked. "Every single one?"

"This particular treatment? Yes. For some, years of this reprogramming treatment, psychiatric consultation and chemical castration is enough. But for approximately thirty-five percent of cases we will resort to brain augmentation."

"Brain augmentation?" Salvi asked. "The brain tweaks?"

Remmell nodded. "We insert electric currents into the parts of their brains responsible for sexual arousal and violence, and we... numb those parts. They become deadened to those feelings. After that, nothing excites them. Nothing."

Salvi stared at Remmell, unsure what to think or say.

The Serene walked back in with the tea. Salvi smelled it from across the room, the scent of strawberries and elderflower.

"Ah! Tea. I do hope you like it," Dr Remmell said. "We make it here on the premises. Unfortunately coffee is banned onsite, but I think you'll find this acceptable."

The Serene placed the cup down, averting his eyes, and stepped back. She thanked him, then took a sip and placed the cup down.

"It's good," she said, tasting the strawberry flavor on her tongue.

The Serene stepped forward again and wiped the rim of her white cup. She looked at him quizzically.

"The lipstick," Remmell explained. "It is considered... *unsavory*. The print of your lips on the cup." He motioned to it.

"Your Serenes can't handle a little lipstick on a cup?" Mitch asked.

"They can. But they've been taught to remove such sights from themselves. Anything that once may have turned them on. You'd be surprised what can, Detective. We've found lipstick to be one of them. For the heterosexual ones anyway. The imprint of a woman's open mouth on something…"

The room fell into a heavy silence for a moment, as both Salvi and Mitch stared at him.

"I'm sorry." Remmell bowed an apology. "I am used to speaking with the Subjugates, and they respond best to direct speech." He smiled, a little embarrassed perhaps. "This is why Attis Solme usually handles any discussion with outsiders. He often tells me that I have spent too much time with these men."

"We're police," Salvi told him firmly. "We appreciate direct speech also. And we'd like to witness the treatment you apply to your Subjugates, if possible."

"As part of your investigation or out of your own curiosity?" Remmell smiled.

Salvi smiled back. "Both."

"It's… not for the faint of heart, Detective."

"I'm sure I've seen worse on the streets."

"I would need to clear this with Mayor Solme first. We've never allowed outsiders to witness our treatments before."

"Understood," she said, "but if you could fast-track it, that would be great."

"Tell us about the seven Subjugates," Mitch said, moving the conversation on.

Remmell gave a nod and motioned to the screen again. He worked the keypad alight beneath his fingers and the list of names disappeared. Salvi watched as a mugshow appeared, of a lean but toned Caucasian man, covered heavily in tattoos and piercings, with short spiky brown hair and a gnarly scowl. She watched him turn to provide his side profile.

"This was Lucius Dolles, now known as Subjugate-46. He

was a serial rapist who targeted college students. He was a high school dropout who, at the heart of it, had class issues. In his mind these college girls thought they were better than him and he didn't like it. He wanted to put them in their place. He raped and beat three, attempted a fourth, but she managed to get away and later identified him. He's been a resident of the Solme Complex for just over six years now and he has made wonderful progress." Remmell brought up a still image of the now-subjugated Lucius Dolles. He was barely recognizable to his former self; his head shaved and crowned with his silver halo, the tattoos bleached from his skin, the piercings removed, the look of anger gone from his eyes; the scowl erased from his face.

Salvi nodded to herself as a realization washed over her. "We saw this Subjugate at the Children of Christ yesterday."

"Yes. He is one of the seven allowed into Bountiful," Remmell said, then looked back at his fingers as he patted the keys. "Next we have Felix Gomes. Now known as Subjugate-65." Remmell brought up the mugshow of a Hispanic man with a long goatee. "Gomes was involved in gangs, had several weapons and drugs charges against him, but it was for the single count of date rape that he was sent here. His family petitioned to have him reformed. Personally, I think it was simply to get him off the streets and away from the gangs, but regardless, he has progressed to graduation swiftly." Salvi eyed the photo of the subjugated Gomes. Again, a placid look rested on the face where hardness had once reigned.

Remmell brought up the third mugshow. It showed an African-American man with cold, uncaring eyes. "This was Junior Malcolm. Now known as Subjugate-51. He had several charges of rape and battery against him. It didn't seem to matter how many restraining orders they put on him, he kept finding where his ex-girlfriend was hiding and assaulted her. There are at least four separate hospital reports for her injuries. The assaults were bad." Remmell showed the subjugated photo of Junior Malcolm. The eyes were no longer cold. A smile of contentment rested upon his lips. With the silver halo against his dark skull, he looked very much like a saint.

The doctor moved on. "This is Kenton Poole, now known as Subjugate-39." The mugshow on the screen was of a pale-skinned man with curly blond hair and big round eyes. "Poole had a fetish for young boys. He'd been arrested three separate times but kept reoffending, so they sent him here. He's been doing very well in our care." The photo of Poole as a Subjugate displayed. His face held a blank look, a little similar to that of the brain-damaged Fontan Pragge, Salvi thought. She wondered if he'd been one of those to receive the tweaks.

"Then we have Vincent Margola," Remmell said. "Now known as Subjugate-27." The man in the mugshow had olive skin, longish black hair and a bored look upon his face. "Margola worked for an organized crime outfit based in New York. He was convicted of three gruesome murders, but we suspect that is only a fraction of those he actually committed. The authorities just haven't been able to tie him to any others. A sadistic and violent man, it has been a slow process in converting him, but we have finally made headway with this Subjugate and he is doing very well." Remmell showed a picture of Margola now. The mobster hitman looked more like an aging choirboy.

"Next we have Alexander Neuben. Now known as Subjugate-48." The mugshow was of a slightly chubby Caucasian man with a strawberry-blond bowl cut. "Neuben emigrated from Russia as a teen. He liked to frequent dance clubs, spike women's drinks, then dump them in alleyways once he was done with them. He was a drug user himself, and a repeat offender. This is him now." The subjugated Neuben filled the screen, showing a content, less chubby face where a look of bitterness had once been.

"Lastly we have Edward Moses. Now known as Subjugate-52." A mugshow displayed of a broad, well-built Caucasian man with a handsome face and a dark, soulless look in his blue eyes. Salvi watched as he turned to provide his side profile to the camera. Remmell seemed to stare at the mugshow in consideration before speaking. "Edward Moses was once a narcissistic lawyer with an incredibly high intellect. He is a special case... He was supposed to die, you see. A brutal serial rapist and murderer, he was handed a death sentence for his crimes. But of all people, one of his victims' families opposed the death penalty brought against him. They were devoutly religious and did not believe in an eye for an eye. They believed in forgiveness and reformation and believed his name, *Moses*, was a sign from God that they must try to save him. Somehow they'd heard about the Solme Complex and petitioned rigorously for him to be sent here instead. They had friends in the right places."

Remmell smiled softly. "Edward Moses has been one of the hardest men to break... He was very smart, you see. Despite telling police that he wanted to be caught, that he wanted someone to finally best him, at the start he fought us at every turn... but we prevailed. We broke that man down and we rebuilt him. Of all the Subjugates I have treated, of all the work we have done, he is the one I am most proud of." Remmell brought up the photo of the subjugated Moses. Still broad, although he seemed to have less muscular definition than at the time of his arrest, his head was shaved and crowned with his halo, and the look of evil was gone from his eyes.

Mitch leaned forward. "This man, once on death row for his brutality, for rape and murder, has been allowed into the town," he said, unable to hide the disbelief in his voice.

"Yes. All seven have. But as I said, I do not authorize them to do so unless I am satisfied they are more Serene than Subjugate."

"Have all seven had the brain tweaks?" Salvi asked.

"No. All seven obviously have the neural implants for monitoring, but only four needed the brain augmentation. To varying degrees, of course, depending on their condition."

"Which four?" Mitch asked.

"Subjugate-46, Subjugate-39, Subjugate-27 and Subjugate-52."

"Which one was who again?" Salvi asked.

"Subjugate-46, Lucius Dolles. Subjugate-39, Kenton Poole. Subjugate-27, Vincent Margola, and Subjugate-52, Edward Moses."

"The college rapist, the one into young boys, the mobster guy and our narcissistic lawyer," Mitch said.

"Yes," Remmell said.

"You said to varying degrees they had the brain augmentation?" Salvi asked.

Remmell looked at her. "Yes. For example, Lucius Dolles required less than the others. We focused on the class issues in his therapy and he learned not to hate women who were more privileged than he."

"So why did the others require more augmentation?" Mitch asked. "By the way, I like that you call it that. Why don't you call it what it really is: partial brain death?"

Remmell turned his eyes back to Mitch. "Because, first of all, we do not kill parts of their brains, just effectively numb them. Secondly, there is such a thing as a process called neurogenesis. Certain areas of the brain will regenerate, however slowly."

Mitch stared at him. "So, your treatment isn't foolproof, then."

"I said 'however slowly'. The brain will continue to create new cells in certain areas, but that is what the Serenes' halos are for. Should the augmented brain of a Serene begin to increase in activity again, we will be warned immediately and then take the appropriate action to recalibrate them."

"Tell me about the other three?" Salvi said. "The others who needed the augmentation."

Remmell exhaled as though trying to rein in patience. "Margola was so immune to violence, and so good at it, it took some work to make him abhor it. Poole was much less violent but his lust for young boys took work to erase. The thought of young boys now repulses him so much, he physically vomits at the sight of them."

"He vomits at the sight of young boys in the street?" Mitch asked.

"No, he vomits at the sight of young boys naked and in situations that would once excite him."

The silence sat for a moment. Salvi wondered what treatment they'd given him to result in such a strong response.

"And Edward Moses?" Salvi asked.

"With Margola it was the violence. With Poole it was the sexual deviancy. With Moses, it was both. We needed to bleach both aspects from him. The traditional treatments only did so much, so brain augmentation was called for. In truth, I've never met a human being who more perfectly fit in the psychopath spectrum. He felt no remorse for what he'd done." Remmell removed his glasses, rubbed his eyes and placed them back on. "We do not enter into the brain augmentation lightly, Detectives. It's a fine art to numb certain areas of the brain and not destroy them so they can no longer function at all. We start small and we continue until we see results. Thankfully, most have responded with minimal tweaks and we haven't had to take things further. We just need to numb them enough for the rest of our treatment to work. And as you can see, we have succeeded; they can still function in society without being a threat to it."

"Alright. When can we talk with them?" Mitch asked, tapping at his iPort.

Remmell looked from Mitch to Salvi, his mind ticking over. "I am not sure that is wise."

"We need to question them," she said.

"The detective can," Remmell motioned to Mitch, "but I would like you to stay out of it, in the observation room. I am not quite ready for a woman in your position to push them too hard with questions."

"And yet you allow them into town," Mitch said.

"Yes, to sweep streets, fix buildings, pick up rubbish and pray with the Children of Christ. Not to be interrogated by a woman in a position of power who wants to accuse them of something they haven't done. If you wish to interrogate them, she must stay out of it."

"Wouldn't this be good practice for them out in the real world?" Salvi countered.

"No."

"What about Poole. He liked young boys. Surely I can interview him?" Salvi said.

"I said no."

"Alright," Mitch said with finality. "We'll do it your way."

Salvi shot Mitch a look, but he shot her one back that told her it wasn't up for discussion. Pulling rank on her again...

He looked back at Remmell. "Let's get started," he said. "Oh, and we'll need a copy of their files for our records. I notice we no longer have access to them on our systems." He motioned to his iPort.

"No," Remmell said, "because we've erased their pasts. They belong to the Solme Complex now, as do their criminal files. But I will see to it that you're given copies."

"Good." Mitch stood. "Let's go."

7 : SUBJUGATES AND SUSPECTS

Salvi stood in a small darkened control room studying Doctor Remmell as he sat before a glass-topped console of dancing lights. In front of the console was a large window of one-way glass, granting them an unhindered view of the interview room beyond. Like a small cave, it was curved and colored in a calming neutral hue. Inside, Mitch sat alone at a small table, awaiting the first of the seven Subjugates.

The door to the room eventually opened and she watched as Bander escorted Lucius Dolles inside.

"Subjugate-46," Remmell announced to her. He reached out and pulled the thin stem of a microphone toward his lips. "You may begin when ready," he said, then paused and tapped a spot on the glass console. Whatever he hoped would happen with the tap of his finger, didn't. He frowned in response and stubbed his finger into the screen again.

Salvi looked back through the window and saw Mitch eyeing the Subjugate that Bander had placed in the chair opposite him.

"You're Subjugate-46?" Mitch asked.

"Wait!" Bander scolded him. "You don't start until we're recording! All conversations must be recorded."

Mitch stared back at Bander unaffected. "You're right." He activated the camera on his badge.

Bander looked into the mirrored window for a moment then raised his hands in question.

"You may start when ready," Remmell spoke again.

Bander continued to stare into the mirror. Impatient, he turned back to the table, pointed a warning finger at the Subjugate, then left the room. Within seconds, the door to their observation room swung open.

"Are we ready or not?" Bander asked.

"Yes, but," Remmell said a little flustered, still stabbing his finger into the glass, "I think the audio system is on the fritz. Sound is coming in, but not going out."

Bander exhaled annoyance. "Excuse me," he said to Salvi, then barged between them. His fingers danced over the console, tapping and typing here and there, accessing various screens. When he finished, he gave Remmell a condescending look.

"Camera working?" he asked the doctor.

Remmell reached out and tapped at the console, darting his eyes to a small screen beside the console, but nothing came on. Bander exhaled again and bent down, reaching underneath the console. She saw him grab a cable that appeared loose and reconnect it, before he stood again. "Try it now."

Remmell worked the console and the screen came alive showing Mitch and Subjugate-46. Remmell smiled. "That is why you're the caretaker, Mr Bander."

"Yeah, yeah," he said walking out the room. Within moments Bander was back in the interrogation room, motioning for Remmell to speak.

"You may begin when ready," Remmell said into the microphone. "We are now recording this conversation."

Salvi eyed the psychiatrist. "Is it normal for the AV feeds to be disconnected like that, given you're supposed to record every conversation?"

Remmell glanced at her briefly, before turning his eyes back to the room. "Probably one of the Serenes when they were cleaning in here," he said. "They must've knocked the wires."

She stared at Remmell for a moment, before folding her arms and settling in to watch Mitch's interrogation of Subjugate-46.

Salvi watched as Mitch stared at the Subjugate sitting before him. The young man's face was even, placid. The memory of the Subjugate's mugshow, complete with tattoos and piercings, compared to the image of the man before her now was, she had to admit, intriguing. Could the treatment here really, *permanently*, change them? Or did the monster still linger beneath their neutral façade? Were they just going through the motions, pretending to be healed to escape the Complex's treatments? Would these criminals simply do what they had to, to get on the outside again? The chemical castrations were obviously not permanent if they required twice daily shots. So how stable were they really? And what would happen if they missed one of those injections? Would their overall treatment collapse?

"Do you know who I am?" Mitch asked the Subjugate.

"No. I do not," he replied in a voice sounding like that of a boy's. The only thing hinting that it wasn't was the depth of sound. Something changed by puberty that not even the treatments of the Solme Complex could erase.

"I'm Detective Grenville," he said. "I'm investigating the death of–"

"He's here to ask you questions about Sharon Gleamer," Bander cut him off.

The Subjugate marked a sign of the cross over himself as Bander stepped toward Mitch. He leaned down and whispered into her partner's ear, but Salvi heard it just fine through her connected iPort's earpiece.

"I told you before, you are not to mention any words that may incite or remind them of their prior criminal activity. Death is one of them." Bander pulled back and gave Mitch a warning stare.

"We've taught them to protect themselves from evil words," Remmell told Salvi. "When they hear an evil word, they mark a sign of the cross upon themselves to protect them from the evil."

"Death isn't always evil," Salvi said. "Death is a part of life."

"According to our Subjugates, people don't die. They simply pass into heaven."

Inside the interview room, Mitch stared at the caretaker for a moment before turning his eyes back to the Subjugate. Dolles sat there as calm and serene as before. Salvi could sense an unease in Mitch as he eyed the silver device that crowned the man's skull. She wondered what it looked like when a Subjugate flashed a code blue.

"Did you know Sharon Gleamer?" Mitch asked.

The Subjugate stared at him but did not answer. Salvi darted her eyes to Remmell's monitor, which captured the Subjugate's face in close-up. His eyes moved, his mind thinking, recalling. Mitch held his arm out and projected a hologram of her from his iPort. "This is Sharon Gleamer. You seen her before?"

Dolles looked at the hologram of the pretty blonde Sharon, beaming a broad smile. He turned his pear-green eyes back to Mitch. "Yes. I saw her at the Children of Christ."

"How often?"

"Every Sunday for mass. Sometimes during the week also."

"You ever speak to her?"

The Subjugate paused a moment, thinking again. Recalling. Salvi wondered if the delay in his response had anything to do with the brain tweaks. She noticed a dark spot flecked the white of his left eye. "Yes," he finally said. "I helped her once in the hall. We were preparing the material to be sewn into clothes."

"Preparing the material. You mean cutting it?"

Bander threw Mitch a glance of warning. Obviously "cutting" was another banned word. The Subjugate marked another sign of the cross over himself. Mitch looked back at the Subjugate. "Who did that? You or her?"

"She did. I held the roll for her. It was heavy."

"Did you ever see her outside of the church and hall? Ever see her around town?"

Again, the Subjugate thought this over. "I have seen her walking along the road. Sometimes riding her bicycle."

"Did you ever speak to her then? When you saw her outside the Children of Christ facilities?"

"No. She would wave. I would wave back."

"Did you ever go to her house?"

"No."

"Did you know where she lived?"

"Yes."

Mitch paused, studying him carefully. "So, she was friendly to you, but you never went to visit her at home?"

"No."

"Why not?"

"We have work to do. When we are in town we must work."

Salvi analyzed the Subjugate for a moment. The guy was of decent height, a little on the lean side, but even in his subjugated state he probably could still have overpowered Sharon Gleamer.

If there were cracks in his treatment, that is.

"When did you last see her?" Mitch asked.

Again the Subjugate thought. "At Church. Last Sunday."

Mitch pulled his iPort back toward him and looked at the hologram again.

"Sharon was pretty, huh?" he said.

Bander cleared his throat loudly, gave Mitch another glare. The Subjugate paused, tilted his head to the side like a curious child. "Why do you ask about her?" he asked.

Mitch eyed him. Dolles stared back with flatline eyes and a flatline face.

Even. Steady. Serene.

Neutral. Just like the walls around him.

"Because something bad happened to her," Mitch said, flicking his eyes to Bander's. "Someone sent her to heaven earlier than she was meant to go."

"She's in heaven now?"

Mitch nodded. "We're trying to find that person. They need to pay." He flicked his eyes to Bander again. "They need to repent for what they've done."

"Yes," Dolles said, signing the cross over his body again. "They must. We all must."

"Do you know who might've hurt Sharon?"

Bander cleared his throat again. 'Hurt' was obviously another word.

The Subjugate made another sign of the cross. "No. I do not," he said.

"It wasn't you?"

Dolles body stilled, just slightly, as he stared back at Mitch. "Did I send Sharon to heaven?"

"Yes."

"No." Dolles glanced at Bander, then back to Mitch. "I held the roll while she scissored it. I did what my Serene Supreme told me to do."

"You didn't feel strange, standing that close to her? That pretty college-aged girl?"

Bander stepped forward, right up to the table between them, and stared down at Mitch.

"Last warning," he said.

Mitch glanced down to see the caretaker's hand resting on the baton attached to his belt.

"Understand?" Bander said.

"I'm not one of your Subjugates," Mitch said. He turned his eyes back to Dolles. The Subjugate sat there with his eyes fixed on the table in front of him, the close proximity of Bander's dark cloud forcing him into submission. Mitch looked back at Bander and gave him a serene smile.

"I think I'm ready for the next Subjugate, please."

Salvi eyed the motel they pulled up in front of. The strip of five units with pale blue walls and white window frames looked like something from an old movie but she couldn't think which one. The sign out front read: "Bountiful Beds" and was framed with a border of yellow globes. The air was cool, Salvi could smell freshly cut lawn, and she thought she heard the SlingShot whizzing by in the distance.

Mitch had only made it through interviewing four of the Subjugates that afternoon, and they decided it was more time efficient to put a call into Ford for approval to stay put overnight, as there were three more interviews to get through tomorrow.

"This'll do," Mitch said, eyeing the motel as he turned the Raider off, then popped their doors with a hydraulic hiss.

"It's probably the only one in town anyway," she said, getting out. She followed him to the reception window. Behind it sat a wrinkled old man about forty pounds overweight, who glanced up at them, then darted his eyes to the Raider.

"I'm sorry, I don't charge by the hour," he said in an uppity voice, as he looked down his capillary-flecked nose. "You need to find another town."

"Excuse me?" Mitch said.

"I don't charge by the hour if that's what you're looking for," he said, moving his eyes to Salvi, then back to Mitch.

Mitch glanced around at Salvi, a slight look of humor on his face. "Well that's good because we want all night," he said, turning back to the man. "*Two* rooms, all night."

The man eyed Salvi again. "Your sister then? Colleague?"

"Irrelevant," Mitch said with a firm look.

Salvi stepped forward. "Do you often have people wanting to rent your rooms out by the hour in a town like this?"

The man looked up at her briefly. "Not on my watch. Bountiful Beds is a reputable establishment. The sinners can stay on the SlingShot. And I'll send you there too if I catch any funny business." He looked back at Mitch. "That'll be eighty, please. Each room."

Mitch muttered something under his breath and pulled out his wallet.

"Cash only," the man said.

Mitch stared at him. "I don't carry cash. No one does any more."

"In this town, we do," the man said firmly.

Mitch sighed and tapped his badge. "We'd like two rooms, please, and we'd like them charged to Hub 9 in the city."

The man leaned back from the holo projection, eyeing it like a snake about to strike. "How do I know you're who you say you are?"

Salvi stepped forward and tapped hers too. "You can't forge these. That's the point of them." She showed him her iPort, and sent her lenses silver briefly, before turning them off again. "We're SFPD. Trust me."

"Stop that now! We don't like that technology here," he said.

They both stared at him as Salvi turned the holo off.

"Aren't you worried that stuff will rot your brains?" the man asked, then shrugged upon receiving no response. "You can never be too sure of people. We've got reason to be wary of strangers. Some bad things have been happening here of late, and I don't plan to enable any more of it."

"What's been happening of late?" Mitch asked.

"Sin," he said leaning forward. "Evil has been trying to invade our town. It started with the Solme Complex, then Attis went and got the SlingShot station built, now the doors have opened and non-believers are being allowed to live here. It's the start of the end, I tell you. You let the sinners and non-believers live here, they'll corrupt the whole town. Just look at what happened to that young Gleamer girl."

"Well, that's why we're here," Mitch said. "We're investigating her murder. So, if you would just give us a place to stay, we can help you fight the sinners."

The man studied them both again, then reluctantly took some old-fashioned brass keys and handed them over. "I'll be watching you."

Mitch gave a nod. "And we'll be watching you." He turned to Salvi and they moved to find their rooms. She suppressed a smile upon learning the gentleman had placed them at opposite ends of the small strip of units. Just in case temptation overtook them during the night. Mitch gave Salvi the key to the room closest to reception, while he took the farthest.

"You hungry?" Mitch asked. "Wanna grab a bite to eat?"

"Yeah." Salvi nodded. "I'm starving."

"Meet back at the Raider in fifteen."

After freshening up, they looked for a place to eat and eventually settled on a rustic-looking Italian joint opposite their motel. The restaurant, like much of Bountiful, appeared to have been left in another decade with its exposed brick walls and red and white chequered tablecloths. Salvi didn't care though. She needed food, and fast, and pasta would do just fine.

As they entered she heard what she thought was the music of some crooner from the 1950s, but she soon realized that the crooner was singing an ode to God. They took a booth by the window and ordered a drink from the waitress who scribbled it down on a small pad of paper, then left.

"Drinking on the job, Salvi?" Mitch teased. "That's not like you."

She shrugged. "Just following my senior officer's lead."

A slight smile curled the corner of Mitch's mouth as the candle on the table reflected in his dark green eyes.

"Besides," Salvi said, leaning back against the booth seat, "it's been a long day."

"Yeah," Mitch agreed, face falling serious. "So, what's your take on the Subjugates I interviewed today?"

Salvi thought for a moment, looking out the window to the quiet street beyond. "Subjugate-46 is a possibility."

"Lucius Dolles?"

"Yeah." She turned her eyes back to him, flashbacks of the interview playing in her mind. Dolles had appeared very serene, but prior to his transformation he was a serial rapist of college-aged girls. Girls similar in age to Sharon. "I'm not liking any of the others you spoke to though."

"Why?" he questioned. Salvi sensed it was more of a test than a question – to see what she'd picked up.

"Subjugate-57, Felix Gomes, he ran with gangs, and only had one count of date rape against him. The crime doesn't fit his MO."

"And Subjugate-48?"

"Alexander Neuben," she said, pausing to turn her thoughts around in her mind. "He did commit multiple rapes, but he drugged them. This wasn't a man who liked the sight of blood and gore. He was lazy. He was a coward. He didn't want to have to fight them for it, that's why he drugged them. I don't see him putting in the effort to do what Sharon Gleamer's killer did, do you?"

Mitch shook his head in agreement, accepting his scotch from the waitress and taking a sip.

"And Kenton Poole?" he asked.

"Poole liked little boys. Women weren't his thing." She took a sip of her drink, a gin and soda, eyeing the slice of lime that danced around in the glass. "Your thoughts?"

"I agree. But I don't really like Dolles for it either. Of all four Subjugates, he was the one who seemed most like a choir boy. Whatever they did to him, they did it good. And he was younger than the others, so he got his treatment earlier in life than the others did." He shrugged. "Maybe that counts for something."

"Does that mean you're a believer in the program now?" She smiled.

"No." Mitch stared back at her. "I just don't think it was him. *Yet.*"

"Well, we still have the other three to interview," Salvi said.

"Yeah. The mob murderer, what's his name, Margola? Junior Malcolm and Edward Moses."

"While you were interviewing, I read through the criminal files that Remmell submitted," Salvi told him. "Margola was charged with three counts of murder, and they liked him for killing a lot of people and very violently, a little sickeningly actually, but he didn't have one charge of rape against him. Nothing sexual at all."

"So?" Mitch asked.

"So, I think he's capable of carving 'pure' into our vic, but rape wasn't his thing. According to witness statements on his character, he was actually a ladies' man. He was a little old-fashioned and believed in treating a lady like a lady."

"Maybe he got carried away in the moment. It would've been a while since he had some and she was an attractive woman."

"Not one of his victims was female. Not even the ones he was suspected of but never convicted for."

Mitch shrugged. "Junior Malcolm only ever assaulted his girlfriend. He never touched another woman outside of her.

Why would he do so now?"

Salvi shrugged back. "His girlfriend's not around. It would've been a while since he had some," she repeated Mitch's words. "Maybe he got caught up in the moment."

His eyes shone a little at her challenge. "But he never killed anyone before. Just roughed them up."

Salvi shrugged indifferently.

Mitch stared at her. "You and I both know of all the Subjugates, the one that fits this most is Edward Moses."

"Yeah." Salvi exhaled heavily, tiredly. "The Subjugate they're most proud of."

Mitch nodded. "The one they saved from death row. The one they turned around for the greater good." He sipped his drink. "The one that would make a hell of a story and garner them all kinds of golden PR if his treatment was successful. Imagine the kudos Attis Solme would receive."

Salvi nodded. "And imagine what would happen if Moses reoffended after all that treatment."

"Imagine what would happen if he reoffended after all that treatment," Mitch repeated her words. "And did *that* to such a good, holy, innocent, *pure* girl… The monster they thought they'd turned back into a man, was actually still a monster all along. They'd be ruined."

Salvi considered things for a moment. "Did you pick up Solme saying that he and Ford went way back?"

Mitch nodded. "Yeah. I want to ask Ford about that. You think that's why she wanted us to deal with this quickly and quietly? Why she was pulling strings to get the forensics processed so fast? Is Solme an acquaintance or a buddy?"

"Don't know."

Mitch paused a moment, his eyes narrowing in thought. "You don't think Ford would help Solme cover things up, do you?"

"Cover what up?" Salvi asked. "We don't know who the

perp is yet. It could be someone from the Solme Complex, but I'm not prepared to rule out any of our friends from the town or the Children of Christ just yet."

"Still stuck on the preacher, huh?" Mitch said.

"Looks can be deceiving, Mitch," she said, taking another sip of her drink. "All that glitters is not gold. You forget that most religions are built on punishment and control of human freedoms."

He sat staring back at her, like he was trying to figure something out.

"We need to keep going back to the crime scene," Salvi said, echoing the words Stanlevski would always say to her. "Someone cut the word 'pure' into her. Someone was angry at her for breaking her vows and having sex with Tobias. Someone found out and they wanted to punish her."

"Or someone just got a thrill out of doing those things to someone they thought was pure," Mitch countered. "You're only seeing it the way you want to see it, Salvi."

She stared back at him, as he continued to eye her curiously.

"You wanna pin something on the preacher or one of those religious folk," he said. "You're making the crime fit the suspect. That's bad police work, Salvi."

She looked away from him, glancing around the restaurant as she took another drink to put out the steam that had risen at his words. A new song began to play. This time a choir sang in a language she couldn't understand. Within moments a family sitting two tables over began to sing along, loudly, while others watched on smiling and nodding. Mitch eyed them strangely, then turned back to her.

"How did you know those bible verses?" he asked.

She moved her eyes back to his; dark in this lighting yet shining with intrigue.

"Were you one of those girls once?" he continued to prod. "Good. Holy. *Pure*."

"What's it to you?"

He shrugged. "Just curious. You're perpetually quiet. Reserved. Restrained. Yesterday when you comforted Tobias Brook and quoted those Bible passages, that's the first insight I've had into my partner in nearly four months. Well, that, and when you were snapping at the preacher."

"I spout some useless Bible passages and you think that's me showing a part of myself?" she said.

"Prove me wrong, then," he said. "I'll lay my cards down if you do."

She shook her head, looking away again. As she did, her eyes caught on a man and woman walking through the front door of the restaurant. It was Preacher Vowker and what she assumed was his wife.

"Well, well," Mitch said, eyeing them. "It's the preacher." He looked back at Salvi. "You're not gonna start a fight, are you?"

"That's your job, isn't it?"

He stared at her. "Only if people ask for it, Salvi. And the preacher's not there yet."

Other than a nod of acknowledgment, the preacher did not speak to them, choosing to sit on the other side of the restaurant. Many of the other diners got up from their seats to talk to him, shake his hand. One woman even bowed and kissed his hand. The Preacher was a rock star in this religious town.

"It's odd, don't you think?" Salvi said. "This being a pullaway town and yet they let the Solme Complex get built close by, then the SlingShot station. Attis Solme doesn't appear to be as against technology as the good preacher. That must cause some friction."

Mitch shrugged. "Well, it depends if Attis is lining the preacher's pockets."

They exchanged a look but said nothing. In fact they ate

their dinners in relative silence, noticing other tables stopping to pray before each course of their meal. Mitch had a few more drinks and Salvi noticed people in the restaurant giving them furtive glances; curious to the strangers in town. The city folk dressed in black with their high-tech gadgets and their black devil car. The detectives here to solve the heinous murder of good little Sharon Gleamer. But so far, they hadn't solved anything.

Salvi threw her napkin on the table. "I'm done. I'm going to bed," she said, standing up. Mitch watched her but didn't move.

"You're staying?" she asked.

He nodded. "Yeah, I'm going to peoplewatch for a bit. Maybe have a nightcap."

Salvi shook her head and left. She stepped outside into the cool night air and glanced around the streets of Bountiful. It felt like a ghost town, the quiet, the open space. It made her feel uneasy. Her eyes caught on the large green BioLume cross adorning the Children of Christ church a couple of blocks down and she felt a shiver run down her spine. As she crossed the street she turned her eyes back to the motel and suddenly noticed a hooded figure loitering near the Raider.

"Hey," she called out, lighting up her badge. "Keep walking."

The hooded figure quickly walked away, disappearing behind a building further down. She moved up to the Raider and peered in, but everything looked fine. She knew it was virtually impossible to break into anyway. It was a nice-looking car and high-spec for a place like this, so she guessed it was bound to draw attention. It was probably just a curious kid.

She shrugged it off, throwing a final glance back to the restaurant. As she did, she saw Mitch still sitting in the booth, sipping a fresh drink and watching her.

8 : THE SECOND COMING

Salvi knocked on the door to Mitch's room. She waited a few seconds, then knocked again. He finally opened the door, holding one hand up to shade his eyes from the morning light; the room behind him was dark. He'd thrown on his jeans but hadn't quite gotten around to doing them up, and he was shirtless, his hair all messy like he just got out of bed.

"So, you had a few nightcaps, then?" she asked plainly.

He lowered his hand, shot her a hungover glance then turned and walked to his bed. She eyed his lean, toned back and saw a long red scratch running down the right side.

"What the hell did you do, Detective?" she asked.

He looked back at her as he grabbed his shirt from the floor beside the bed.

She held her hand up. "No, forget it. I don't want to know." She threw him a can of deodorant and he caught it. "We gotta go, so it's shower in a can for you."

He used it, then pulled on his shirt. "We got time for breakfast?" he asked as he moved into the bathroom and washed his face and rinsed his mouth.

"There's coffee and mints waiting on top of the Raider." She smiled. "Let's go."

As they drove along the road heading back to the Solme Complex, Salvi studied him. He'd insisted on driving again.

"You gonna be up for the interviews today?" she asked.

He glanced at her, sipping his coffee. "Of course."

"You don't look like you had much sleep."

"I didn't."

"Maybe I should do them today."

"You heard Dr Remmell, they don't want you to do them."

"So? It's our investigation."

Mitch threw her another glance then turned his eyes to the road ahead again. "The Subjugates are property of the Solme Complex. We want to talk to them, we gotta follow their rules."

"You don't strike me as someone who listens to rules."

Mitch looked at her. "And you strike me as someone who does."

"Look, if we want to see if any of these Subjugates have cracks, we should put me in front of them," Salvi shrugged.

"No," he said. "I can handle it."

"Can you?"

"Yes. I can."

She stared at him as he drove, and he flashed her glances back.

"Salvi," he said. "I didn't get much sleep, but it's not what you're thinking. I had a few drinks, sure, but I got back to my room early enough. I just couldn't sleep."

"Why?"

Mitch averted his eyes, sipped his coffee again and shrugged. "I don't know. Going over the case, I guess."

Salvi continued to stare at him.

Mitch looked back at her. "I can handle it … *Brentt*."

Salvi stared at him. He hadn't used her surname before. She waved her hand with an indifferent air. "Fine."

He analyzed her for a moment. "Open the glove compartment. Pull out the black container."

She did. It was rectangular in shape but with curved edges. He reached out and placed his fingertips on the top of it, a screen lit up as it read his prints, and the box opened up.

Inside, wedged in foam surrounds, was a needle and three vials.

"What the hell is this?" she asked.

"It's called ReVitalize," he said. "It's basically a vitamin and mineral solution with some other good stuff added, designed to give you a kick. Wanna load one up and stick it in my arm?"

She looked at him. "Excuse me?"

He stared back. "It's legal, Salvi. And a genuine cure for hangovers and lack of sleep."

"I know what it is, Mitch. I'm assuming, given the fingerprint access, you have a prescription for it?"

"Yes," he said dryly, "hence the fingerprint access. Prescription is legal and in my name. So, load it and shoot me in the top of my arm, would you."

"Put the car on autodrive and do it yourself."

"You know I don't like autodrive."

"It's what the Raider is designed to do."

"I like to stay in control."

"If that were true, you wouldn't need one of these shots."

"Fine," he said. "Hand it here."

"You're going to do it while you drive?"

"Well, you won't help me."

Salvi glanced between the road and Mitch. "Do you have a death wish or something? Is this a cry for help, Mitch?"

"Maybe I like to live on the edge," he said, a smile curling the corner of his mouth. "Does that bother you? I know you like to play safe."

Salvi gave him a plain stare. "You want me to stick you? I'll stick you." She studied the label on the vial, then pulled out the needle and began to prepare it. "You take this every day?" she asked, studying the loaded needle in her hands as she shot a little fluid out.

Mitch shook his head. "Only when I've had a rough night."

"Why didn't you have this yesterday morning then? You looked a little rough."

"Because I didn't need it then. Besides, I was still trying to figure out how you'd take it. Me shooting ReVitalize. There's still a little stigma over it."

"That's because people run themselves near death, then shoot up to revive. It's a lazy way of taking care of yourself. It also enables the partiers to party harder. Of course there's stigma. They're saying the vita-heads are almost as bad as the tech-heads."

"Oh, come on. That's bullshit. Shooting vitamins and minerals and whoring yourself for tech are two different things."

"Some people whore themselves for the vitamins too. They're not cheap and it's hard to get a prescription."

Mitch gave her an unaffected look.

"Anyway," Salvi said, "what makes you think I'm cool with it now?"

He shrugged. "I guess you showed me a little of yourself with the Bible verses, so I'm showing you a little of myself." He angled his shoulder toward her. "Shoot me."

"Shoot yourself," Salvi said, holding out the needle.

"I'm driving."

"Autodrive, pull over, or wait a few minutes until we get there."

"And have people see me shooting up in the Solme Complex's parking lot?"

"You know, if we weren't running late because of *you*, you could've done this in the privacy of your hotel room. What did you get up to last night?"

"Come on, Salvi," he said ignoring the question. "Live a little. Stop being such a good girl. Take a risk once in a while."

"I'm a cop, Mitch. I don't take risks unless I have to."

"We take risks every single day." He looked back at the

road. "Look, if you're not game–"

She stabbed the needle into his arm.

He grunted in pain. "Don't have much of a bedside manner, do you?"

"No," she said, injecting the fluid into his arm, then yanking it out. "And if I find out that I just shot you with something other than ReVitalize, I will take you down."

His eyes glinted. "I don't doubt that for a second."

By the time they arrived at the Solme Complex, Mitch was a new man. Whatever was in that needle worked fast and brought him to life. He looked fresher than she did.

Serene-41 was there to greet them again. He escorted them through to the same interrogation room they had been in yesterday. Salvi stood in the control room with Doctor Remmell, while Mitch sat waiting for the caretaker to present Subjugate-27, aka Vincent Margola, the gruesome hitman.

When they finally arrived, it was another guard escorting the Subjugate, not Bander. According to Remmell this was guard Jones, Bander's second. The man stood about 5'11 and weighed maybe 200 pounds, with a closely cropped blond haircut and moustache.

Salvi turned her eyes to Margola as he took his chair. The man appeared rather unassuming. Yes, he was a Subjugate soon to graduate to Serene, but even then, he didn't look like the monster she expected to see. Over the years, she'd learned how to pick violent men. The way they carried themselves, the look in their eyes, even those with overt politeness and friendliness – she could often sense something dangerous, something not-quite-right underneath the facade. She'd read Margola's file and the man who did those things, who'd butchered those people so gruesomely, didn't seem like the same man sitting in that room.

"Subjugate-27," Mitch said. "I'm Detective Grenville

and I'd like to ask you some questions about a resident of Bountiful."

"Yes," Margola said, in a calm, even voice.

"A woman by the name of Sharon Gleamer attended the same church you did. The one run by the Children of Christ. Do you know her?"

Margola stared blankly back and Mitch slid his arm across the table, displaying the same hologram he'd shown the others the day before. Sharon Gleamer beamed a smile at them in traces of white light.

"Oh," Margola said in recognition, although the emotion was hollow. "Yes. I saw her at church."

"How often did you see her at church?"

"Once a week for mass," Margola said. "I also saw her in the hall on other days."

"And what would you do at the hall?"

"Clean the yard. Arrange the donations for distribution to the city. Such things as that."

"Why do you go to mass?"

"It is good for us," he said. "It shows us the enlightened path."

"The enlightened path?" Mitch asked.

Margola gave a small, pleasant smile. "It keeps us true to God."

Mitch stared at him.

"We Subjugates once walked a less honest path," Margola said, slowly, calmly. "We have turned from that. We wish to be Serene and lead others on the enlightened path."

"Just like that?" Mitch asked. "You go from brutally murdering people to suddenly on the enlightened path?"

Dr Remmell immediately leaned forward and spoke into the microphone. "Detective! Caution."

Margola marked a sign of the cross upon him, as Mitch glanced over to the mirrored window.

"I don't understand the cautions?" Salvi asked Remmell in the control room. "Surely they need to be tested, prepared for the real world."

"The Subjugates in their later days of treatment are not reminded of their past. It is all we talk to them about in the first few years. During the latter stages of their treatment, once we've wrenched out every ounce of pleasure for their previous crimes, we focus on erasing their former selves. Part of their treatment once they reach a certain point is to never mention what they once did ever again. Certain words, or triggers, must be avoided to bleach their meaning out of their systems."

"But how can you erase their memories?"

Dr Remmell looked at her in such a way, that for a moment she thought he was Serene too. "Through years of finely tuned treatment and through the Subjugate's sheer willpower. Through their trained, selective remembrance. When the memories no longer excite them, when the memories of their previous crimes only cause them fear or repulsion, it is easy to forget. To avoid what causes them harm. The human body will do what it must to survive. We erase their pleasure and in turn they erase their own memories. They disassociate from their old selves in order for their present self to survive." He studied her. "Have you ever been so drunk that you've done something you regretted the next day?"

"Who hasn't?" Salvi said.

"I'm not talking little things, I'm talking big things. Have you ever done something that you were ashamed of the next day? That you regretted horribly?"

Salvi stared back but didn't answer.

"Regrets, embarrassments, lies, cheating, they're all swept under the rug out of sight. People work hard to forget the things they'd rather not remember. This is similar, but of course much more extreme. We make them abhor their previous actions and offer the ability to be able to forget them. They all accept Christ into their lives in order to forget that which causes them pain."

"So, you torture them until they break, make them come to detest their previous actions, then you offer them absolution if they turn to religion and pray away the memory of their past selves. You make them sell their soul to God in order to stop the pain."

Remmell eyed her through his dark-framed glasses. "They don't sell their soul. They *offer* their souls. Voluntarily. That's the power of it."

"And if they don't offer you their soul, you torture them until they do," Salvi said. "You realize that could possibly be a motive right there. If one of them attacked Sharon Gleamer, that would call into question your treatment and cause a lot of problems for the Solme Complex. And this place, and your torture, could be shut down."

"You say torture like we do it for fun. It's not torture. It's treatment."

"Well, I wouldn't know. You haven't shown me the treatment yet. Prove it."

Remmell turned back to the console. "I'm afraid Mayor Solme has not approved that."

"Why not?"

"Because, as I told you the other day, it is not for the faint of heart."

"And as I told you, Doctor Remmell, I'm a cop. I can handle it."

He looked at her. "I don't think you can, Detective. I watch it every day and still I struggle."

"Well, until I see it with my own eyes, if the treatment is *that* physical it makes them vomit at a mere thought, I'm going to call it torture."

He looked back at her. "Are you telling me you've never overstepped the mark in your job as a police officer? Hmm?

You've never been excessively rough with someone you've apprehended? Sometimes the result justifies the action, Detective. You of all people, in your line of work, should know this."

Salvi looked back through the window at Margola, then pictured the mugshow footage she'd seen upon his arrest. Based on what she'd read in his file, Margola was once a man who didn't think twice about cutting out another man's intestines, wrapping them around a Christmas tree as decoration and spiking the man's heart on top as though it were a star. All because some mob boss's eight year-old daughter was not given the lead role in a school play.

"Twisting someone's arm a little tighter than necessary is quite different," she said to Remmell. "You torture them. You chemically castrate them. You brainwash them. And for those that need it, you tweak their brains. Numb the parts you don't like. What you do, is it really that much different to what these men did on the outside?" She wasn't sure she necessarily agreed with what she was saying, but Remmell was opening up to her, so she was going to milk it for what it was worth.

He turned to look at her. "You make us sound like monsters, Detective." He motioned back to Margola. "They're the monsters. And we're their saviors. We systematically raze their former selves and we build new people from their ashes. *Good* people, through religion. Religion has the power to control behavior. Make them believe in something enough, they will obey its commands. It's the only way."

"Obey its commands..." Salvi said, thinking aloud as she stared at Remmell. "But are you building new people from their ashes, or are you building a religious army of slaves who will never question your commands?"

Remmell stared at her. "We build people who give back to their community. Something lacking in society these days. If that's called making them slaves." He shrugged.

She nodded. "People who clean your streets, grow your crops, work in your BioLume factory. They make you a nice profit with their free labor. That's slavery, you know."

Remmell's face became less serene. "Would you rather we put them back on the streets as they were so they can hurt more people?" He paused a moment, before finding his own serenity again. "This topic is out of my area of concern, Detective. If you wish to continue that line of discussion, perhaps you should speak with Mayor Solme." Remmell turned back to his console.

Salvi looked through the window at Margola, again unsure of how she felt. Somewhere deep inside, an unease filled her at thoughts of what treatments the Complex might be doling out to its inmates. They were, effectively lab rats. Manipulated, put through extremely violent therapies, and controlled through drugs and neural tech for years on end. She hadn't witnessed the treatment herself, but after seeing the room with restraints and surgical tools, she could just imagine what they were doing to them. She pictured the terrified Subjugate she'd passed in the corridor on the first day; his bloodied face and tunic, the way he turned into the wall away from her. This would not be allowed on a member of the public, and hauntingly harked back to the very early days of the treatment of mental health patients, so was it right to do this to a criminal? They were still humans, after all.

Or were they?

Were these monsters, with their horrendous crimes, no longer able to be considered men?

It was a hard question to answer. It was Salvi's job to pursue justice for up the bodies these monsters left behind. She'd seen the victims and their families, knew their suffering. These monsters had tortured and killed many, so was the treatment they received now simply karma slapping them back hard? Many of the residents' victims were now dead so they never had to live with the memories of their torture, but the Subjugates were left alive and faced with the torture every single day if they stepped out of line.

But what if the treatment really was curing them? Turning them around? If it stopped them from being a menace to society, wasn't that a good thing? If they now served the community at large instead of taking from it, did the good outweigh the bad? Did their victims' suffering justify the Subjugates' suffering now?

Salvi still didn't have an answer. But there was only one question she really cared about. Was the monster still alive inside one of these men? Could one of these Subjugates be faking their cure? Could one of these Subjugates have killed Sharon Gleamer? Was one of these Subjugates playing a game that would close the Complex down and end their suffering, end their torture? Or had the treatment simply failed? Had one of these Subjugates broken their serenity?

Toward the end of Margola's interview, Attis Solme entered the control room.

"How is it going?" he asked, his large stature making the room seem that much smaller.

"Good," Remmell answered. "The detectives only have Subjugate-52 to go."

"Ah! Edward Moses," he said with a smile.

"Yes," Salvi said. "The best of your worst. Or is that, the worst of your best?"

Solme eyed her curiously. "You must have a good stomach to handle such cases, Detective Brentt."

She eyed him back. "It's a prerequisite of the job."

"You stayed in town last night?"

"Yes," she said, then paused. "How did you know?"

"I ran into Preacher Vowker. He said he saw you in Bianchi's restaurant."

She nodded. "Are you close to the preacher?"

"Quite," Solme said. "My wife was his sister. We founded the community together. I attend church every Sunday."

Salvi recalled seeing the crucifix on the wall of Solme's office, the stone statuette of Mary on his desk, remembered him talking in the BioLume factory about being a religious, born-again, man.

He smiled at her. "Our Father has led me on the righteous path and now He is leading our Subjugates."

Salvi stared at him, thinking of Margola, of the preacher, of the Children of Christ. "Did you know Sharon Gleamer personally?"

"Everyone knew Sharon," he said.

Salvi waited for him to elaborate.

"She was the heart of the youth corps of the Children of Christ," he said. "She spent a lot of time at the church, volunteering across town. She even tutored some of our residents with their reading and writing."

"Wait," Salvi said straightening. "She had direct, one-on-one contact with the Serenes? You didn't think to mention this?"

"Everyone in Bountiful has contact with the Serenes in one way or another. She taught them in the Children of Christ hall. There were always others present in the room. They were never left alone."

"But she taught them one-on-one? Just her, dealing directly with a Serene?"

"Yes, I guess you could say that. But like I said, it would be in the hall and others would be present elsewhere in the room. They would not be alone together."

"And what about the Subjugates?"

Solme looked back at her but didn't answer.

"Did she have similar contact with the Subjugates?" she pressed. "One-on-one?"

"No," Solme said firmly. "The Subjugates, with their escorts, would help the church in group activities only. They did not have one-on-one contact with her."

"And your guards can confirm this?"

Attis glanced at Dr Remmell, who was watching them both carefully.

"Yes," he said. "Now have you found any evidence from your interviews so far that indicates one of my Subjugates did this?"

"Not as yet, no."

Solme nodded. "And you won't, Detective. The men who emerge from the Solme Complex as Serenes are nothing like the men who first came here. We have seen to that. These men will not reoffend. Ever."

"You believe in your program," Salvi said. "I understand."

"Do you?" He stared at her, face serious. "You're not the first to doubt what we do here, Detective. And you won't be the last. But I tell you, we have fought tooth and nail to get where we are today. When I first planned to open this place, you can *imagine* the opposition I got, housing criminals of this caliber so close to the human population, with plans to eventually let them out and reintegrate them into society. But you see, this was the best place for the Solme Complex. Right here alongside Bountiful. Right in the heart of those who believe in love and forgiveness. Those who believe in shunning the devil and avoiding temptation. We are turning these sinners into children of Christ. And it is *working*!"

Solme paused, taking a moment to control his demeanor. He unfurled his clenched fist, which had been raised beating the air with passion, and wiped at the saliva gathering in the corner of his mouth.

"As I said before, Detective, do not try to sling mud at this community without sufficient evidence. Because it won't stick. You're not the first and you won't be the last. The people of Bountiful support us wholeheartedly."

Not everyone, she thought as she recalled the motel owner from last night.

"And if we find irrevocable evidence to link the murder to one of your Subjugates?" she asked.

"You won't. Because I know they didn't do this."

"Then who did?"

"That, I'm afraid, is your job to work out."

"Has anyone ever made threats against you or the Complex?"

Attis shot Remmell a glance. "None we've taken seriously."

"Who?" Salvi asked.

Attis eyed her. "The next community over, Garner Town. It's a survivalist community. Another pullaway, only instead of believing in God they believe in guns."

"What happened?"

Attis shrugged. "They paid me a visit and said if any of my Serenes or Subjugates tried to enter their community they would be shot."

"Did you report this?"

"No."

"Why not?"

"Because right now our residents don't go anywhere near Garner Town. There's no chance that can happen."

"Someone made a threat of violence against your residents. You've had clear opposition to this facility. What if someone is trying to set up the Complex to get it shut down?"

Attis gave her a stony look. "Well isn't that why you're here? To find out who did this?"

"Yes, it is. But it would be easier if people mentioned important information like that at the start."

"The people of Garner Town like to talk a lot, but they rarely leave their community. They're not a threat. As for my residents, I've already told you. No one in my Complex did this. You're wasting your time and ours." He shot Remmell a glance, gave a nod of farewell to Salvi, then left.

She turned to Remmell, whose eyes were still on the door. "Are you really a religious man, Doctor?"

Remmell turned back to the mirrored glass. "Christ is our savior, Detective."

Salvi walked down the hollowed green-tinged corridor to the bathroom under Serene-41's escort. When they reached the door, he made her wait outside while he ensured it was empty. There were only male bathrooms at the Solme Complex, after all.

"You may go inside." Serene-41 bowed.

Salvi entered the room and saw no urinals, just three stalls lining the wall to the left, while wash stations lined the wall the right, and a large frosted window filled the wall ahead, allowing for natural light. She noticed how clean it was, noticed calming music filling the room, noticed the three stalls had no doors. She wondered whether this was a deterrent to stop the Subjugates from getting too familiar with themselves. She suddenly looked around for cameras, wondering whether there were any security measures. She spotted one in the corner and stared at it, wondered who might be watching on the other side. With no other option, she chose a stall and undertook her business swiftly, taking care to stay covered, then left the stall and moved to the automatic wash station.

She rinsed her hands, listening to the soothing music, trying to detect if it was having an effect on her, whether it would have a soothing effect on the Subjugates.

A noise disturbed her thoughts, however.

It was voices in the distance. Voices that seemed to sever the tranquility.

She realized they were coming from outside and moved to

the window. She couldn't see through the frosted glass, but along the top was a mesh airstrip. She listened again for the voices. They were shouts. Angry shouts.

The mesh airstrip in the window was too high up, so she climbed onto the wash station and peered out. There, in the near distance, was the farm. And there in front of a tractor was Levan Bander shouting into the face of a Subjugate who sat crouched on his knees, face scrunched in regret and hands clasped in prayer.

She watched as Bander yelled something that she didn't catch, then pulled out his baton and swung it heavily at the Subjugate. She flinched at the impact. Immediately the other Subjugates who had been watching turned away, closed their eyes and began praying.

Salvi's eyes widened and her breath caught, as Bander continued to hit the Subjugate, who in no way fought back. The Subjugate fell down to the ground, covering his head, desperately trying to protect his halo, as Bander swung the baton again and again. Eventually another guard, Jones, came jogging over and grabbed Bander's swinging arm. Bander, face red and furious, pushed the other guard away and raised his baton at the man. Jones cowered back, holding his arms in defense, and motioned back to the main building. Bander took a moment, catching his breath, then he lowered the baton and looked back at the bloody, still heap of the Subjugate on the ground. He moved over and wiped his baton on the Subjugate's uniform, then called to a group of three Subjugates standing close by, motioning them to collect the injured man. They rushed over to the Subjugate, eyes lowered to the ground, then lifted him and walked him back toward the main building again.

Bander hooked his baton onto his belt again, straightened his synthetic uniform, wiped his brow and continued on.

"Detective?" Serene-41 called from outside the door to the

bathroom. "Are you alright?"

Salvi looked back at the closed door. "Just a minute," she called, as she slid back down to the ground again, heart thumping against her ribcage. Calming her breath, she studied her reflection in the mirror, smoothed down her straight dark hair and ran her finger along the edge of her red lipstick. She made sure everything looked neat and tidy as normal. And it did.

Except for the crease in her brow that remained from the incident she'd just witnessed.

She moved toward the door, her eyes catching on the security camera in the corner of the room as she did.

Escorted by Serene-41, Salvi made her way back to the control room. As she stepped inside, she noticed that Margola was gone from the next room and Mitch sat alone at the table scrolling through something on his iPort.

After waiting several minutes, the door to the interview room opened and Bander walked in with Subjugate-52, Edward Moses. Salvi's eyes darted between the two men, equally curious. Moses was tall, about 6'3, and weighed at least 240 pounds. As she'd thought from seeing his subjugated photo the day before, he had less muscle definition than when he arrived at the Solme Complex, but clearly all the manual labor he did had managed to keep him relatively fit and strong.

Bander sat Moses down in the seat opposite Mitch, and she studied the caretaker carefully for any effects he might be showing after what she'd witnessed just minutes before. But she saw nothing. He stood back against the wall, quiet and calm, just as he did in the interviews yesterday. This was a man used to dishing out violence, all in a day's work. In fact, he looked like he could go a few more rounds yet. Bander too, was fit and strong.

She turned her eyes back to Mitch as he began to interview Edward Moses.

"Subjugate-52?" he said.

"Yes," Moses spoke as he gave a slight bow. His voice was deep, the accent refined.

Salvi's iPort alerted an incoming call, startling her. She saw it was Ford, and switched it to her lenses, turning away from Remmell's curious stares.

Ford appeared in her lenses, blonde hair tugged back into a rough bun, her blue eyes full of business.

"Brentt," she said. "I couldn't get through to Grenville. Where is he?"

"Interviewing a Subjugate. What's up?"

"A second vic just surfaced in Bountiful."

Salvi paused, her body tightened. "Where?"

"Riverton will send you through the address and I got Swaggert and Weston heading up on the SlingShot. Get out there before the local cops mess up your crime scene."

"On it," she said, then tapped her iPort, ending the call, and went for the door.

"What's going on?" Remmell asked.

"Interview's over." She walked out and headed to the other room, opening the door. Mitch, Bander and Moses turned to look at her.

"Detective," she said to Mitch. "We've got to go."

"You're not supposed to be in here!" Bander said, as Mitch stood.

Salvi gave Bander an indifferent look, then glanced at Moses, who sat still and calm, staring at her.

"Subjugate-52." She gave a nod. "We'll continue this later."

Bander abruptly turned to Moses, hand on the baton, giving him a hard look not to speak. Moses registered the look and lowered his eyes to the table.

Mitch stepped out of the room, ushering her with him and

closing the door. "What is it?"

"We got a second vic."

Mitch stared back at her a second. "Shit," he said, moving past her down the corridor. She turned and followed, as Serene-41 hurried to catch up.

9 : THE ANNIVERSARY

Salvi and Mitch ducked below the yellow police tape, cordoning off the crime scene where the second victim had been found. It was a small house a few blocks from the center of town, and a few blocks west of Sharon Gleamer's. Manicured gardens and fresh paint showed the owner cared for appearances. Or perhaps that she'd recently had Serenes around to do some work.

Sheriff Holt met them at the door.

"What've we got?" Mitch asked, placing his hands on his hips.

"Rebecca Carson. Twenty-nine years old. Lives alone," he told them. "Found by her friend, Loretta Sine, who came to collect her for some shopping. She was found in the sunroom out back. That looks to be where she was attacked."

Mitch gave a nod, grabbed a coverall off the officer standing by the door, slid it on, then made his way carefully into the house, snapping on some gloves. Salvi followed suit and they engaged the recording device on their badges. She took in the neat, comfortable home, her eyes catching on a picture of Mary and baby Jesus on the wall of the living room as she passed.

They stepped into the sunroom and fanned out around the sprawled body, covered in a sheet. Mitch reached out a gloved hand to lift the sheet and view the vic. Salvi moved to his side to join him.

The woman, of African-American descent, lay on her

stomach, with her head turned to the side. Her face was beaten, and she was naked from the waist down.

"Partially dressed. Looks like it was quick," Salvi said standing back up and looking around. "Not prolonged."

"Cause of death looks like a broken neck," Mitch said, studying the woman.

"Most likely, I'd say, the angle it's sitting," Holt agreed.

"How do we know this one's linked to the first vic?" Mitch asked.

Salvi watched as Holt, also gloved, bent down and pulled the side of the vic's body up to show them a pool of blood underneath and the word 'pure' carved into her belly.

"Yeah, OK," Mitch said, standing back up again as Holt lowered the body back to the floor.

"How did you know that was there?" Salvi asked. "You moved the body already?"

Holt nodded. "I needed to know if we had a serial on our hands."

"No, you needed to not touch the body until we got here," Salvi said.

He stared back at her. "Well if I hadn't, you'd still be elsewhere unaware we had a second vic."

"They still would've called us in," Mitch said firmly. "No one else touches her until our ME arrives."

Holt turned and walked away. Salvi moved over to the door of the sunroom and examined the lock. She felt Mitch come to stand beside her. "It's been tampered with," she said. "He broke in."

"Maybe he didn't know this one," Mitch said.

Salvi turned to look at the vic again. "He's left her like he did Sharon. On their stomachs, faces turned, arms up around their heads."

Mitch nodded. "Like they're holding their arms up in surrender."

"Or he doesn't want to look them in the eye," she said.

Mitch nodded again, then headed back into the house.

Swaggert arrived, camera dangling around his neck. "Another one, huh?" he said.

"Yeah," she replied, then moved past him. "Make sure you get the lock. Back door."

"Gee, thank you, Detective," he said sarcastically. "I wouldn't have thought to look there."

Salvi shot him a blank look, then walked into the house again. She found Mitch in the woman's bedroom, looking into the drawer of the bedside cabinet. He glanced back at her, then kept riffling. Salvi stood in the doorway studying the woman's room. It was clean and neat with a pale beige quilt cover and handmade furniture. Her eyes fell onto a wooden cross on her dressing table, opposite the bed. She moved over to it, picked it up and examined it. She looked up into the mirror and caught Mitch watching her curiously. He held up a pamphlet of some kind.

"Our vic attended Vowker's church," he said. "This is from the mass last Sunday."

Salvi put the cross down and turned to him as he placed the pamphlet on the bed and closed the drawer again.

"Why so different?" Salvi asked.

Mitch looked at her.

"This attack is very different from the one on Sharon Gleamer," she said.

Mitch shrugged. "They both had 'pure' cut into them. He left them face down."

"Yeah but Sharon was raped more than once. This woman looks like a hit and run attack." She folded her arms. "Sharon was blonde, white, eighteen years old. This one is almost thirty and dark-skinned. Our perp doesn't have a type. That worries me."

"Yeah, he does," Mitch said standing up from the bed and

making his way for the door. "He likes good, *pure*, church-going women."

They examined the scene, spoke to the friend Loretta Sine, watched as the evidence was bagged and Swaggert did his thing capturing 3D images of the scene. Salvi and Mitch looked around the back garden but found nothing unusual. The perp could've easily walked around the back of the house. The folks in Bountiful didn't care much for fences.

Again, Salvi felt a strange sense of agoraphobia from all the open space, the vic's backyard was so big. No wonder it was easy for someone to break into houses here. They had too much room to move, too many access points and not enough witnesses. She looked up into the sky wishing Bountiful had the same drone surveillance that the city had. The folks here had pulled away from technology, but right now it was the lack of technology that was allowing this killer to get away with his crimes.

"Oh, Detectives!" Swaggert called in a sing-song voice from the doorway, waving them forward.

Salvi and Mitch headed back inside to see Dr Weston leaning over the victim. She looked around at them.

"Look what I found," she said, holding an electromagnifier over the body.

There, in the middle of the vic's back, were faint traces of BioLume.

Salvi and Mitch exchanged a look.

"It's only faint," Weston said, "But I see slight drag marks. It looks as though he stomped on her with his boot, perhaps trying to stop her getting away. Her movement has caused his boot to drag a little along her skin and it's left a minute trace of BioLume."

"How long does BioLume last in the wild?" Salvi asked.

"Don't know. We'll have to check with the producers."

"Our killer keeps walking in it," Mitch said, eyeing the body then turning a dark stare to Salvi. He moved past her and headed inside once more.

Weston carefully watched him leave, then shot her a sympathetic look. "I'll send you the report as soon as I have it."

Salvi gave a nod of thanks, then followed Mitch through the door.

As she walked out the front door she saw Mitch standing by the Raider, looking down the street. She followed his eyes and saw a sleek white van from the Solme Complex parked down near the intersection. Levan Bander stood by the open door with three Serenes and one Subjugate. The Subjugate was Edward Moses. Bander and Moses both paused and stared down the street at her.

"Salvi!" Mitch called in a warning voice, motioning behind her.

She turned around to see Fontan Pragge standing behind her. *Close* behind her. She took a step backward.

"You," he said, lips moist with saliva.

Salvi stared at him, his weak blue eyes, his curved thick nose, his white woolly hair. "You," he said again, lifting his finger to point at her.

"Subjugate-12," she said evenly, remembering to refer to him by his official name.

"You, go. Don't stay. You go," he said, shaking his head, his voice partially slurred, as a line of drool began to seep out the side of his mouth.

"And why's that, Subjugate-12?"

He shook his head, then waved both hands like a baseball umpire declaring a runner safe. "No girls," he said. "Bad. No girls. No."

"SUBJUGATE-12!" Bander yelled from down the street.

"GET BACK HERE NOW!"

Salvi watched as Pragge visibly cowered at the sound of Bander's voice. His frightened, childlike eyes looked at her and he shook his head.

"Bad man. Get punished," Pragge muttered to himself. "Bad man. Get punished. No girls. No."

"But you're not a bad man any more, are you?" Salvi said.

"SUBJUGATE-12!" Bander yelled again, stalking toward them, tapping his baton loudly into his hand.

Pragge scurried around the Raider and toward the other side of the street to avoid the caretaker, who stopped and gave him a death stare as he passed. Pragge avoided eye contact, eyes lowered to the ground, as he moved back toward the van.

"Sorry about that," Bander called to her. "He gets attached to faces he recognizes. Can't seem to beat it out of him." He smiled, then turned and headed back for the van.

Salvi watched as Bander walked away, but her eyes soon moved past him to fall on Edward Moses again.

Subjugate-52 stood still and calm beside the van, eyes fixed upon her in return.

Salvi and Mitch arrived back at the hub late afternoon. Mitch disappeared to get coffee, while she moved to her desk to tidy up the interview notes that Riverton had transcribed for them, along with their commentary from the second crime scene.

Someone leaned their butt down on the side of her desk, and she glanced up to see Hernandez looking down at her, his arms folded across his chest.

"Where's Grenville?" he asked, darting his eyes over his shoulder.

"On a coffee run," she said.

"I heard you got another vic," he asked, his police eyes trying to read something on her face.

"Yeah," she said. "Looks like the same perp but it was a slightly different attack."

"How's he taking it?" Hernandez asked, glancing over his shoulder again.

Salvi eyed the door, wondering why Hernandez was acting strange. Then she realized he was worried that Mitch might walk in and catch him being nosy.

"He's fine," she said.

"Yeah? You sure about that?" he asked, like some concerned uncle or something.

"Yes," she repeated, staring at him. "Why?"

Hernandez shrugged. "Just curious. This case... I just thought he might be taking it hard, is all. Taking it *personally*."

"No more than any other case," Salvi said. Although she wasn't sure that was exactly true.

Hernandez nodded. "Just keep an eye on him," he said. "You think he's not handling it, you let someone know, alright?"

Salvi stared at him, offended that he thought she couldn't handle herself and would need to go running to someone else for help.

"Mitch is fine," she said firmly, "and if he wasn't, I'd handle it."

Hernandez stared at her for a moment, then shrugged again and waved his hands in the air indifferently. "Whatever you say."

She watched as he moved back over to his desk and sat down. Bronte glanced at both of them, but it looked like he was happy to stay out of it.

Mitch came back after a while, but his hands were empty.

"What happened to the coffee?" Salvi asked.

He sighed. "I changed my mind. I need a real drink instead."

"Really?" she asked.

"I told you, I only had a few drinks last night."

Beggs happened to be walking past at that moment and laughed at what he heard. "See! You are his mother!"

Salvi ignored him.

"I'm up for a drink," Beggs said to Mitch, glancing at his iPort. "Give us a few minutes."

Mitch gave him a nod then moved to sit at his desk. Salvi stared at him the whole time.

"What?" he asked. "Believe it or not, it helps me think. Loosens me up."

"So where did you go when you weren't getting my coffee?"

"I made a call," he said. "Locked in a new time to interview Edward Moses."

"Which is?"

"Day after tomorrow. Apparently the whole town is going to Sharon Gleamer's funeral tomorrow. Attis wants his Serenes and Subjugates to be there and of service to the Bountiful community."

"Yeah? Or is he just trying to put a little distance between us and his precious Subjugate-52?" Salvi said.

"Could be," he said, tapping at his console and eyeing his screen. "I checked who was in town yesterday around the time our second vic was murdered. Subjugates 46 and 52. Dolles and Moses."

Salvi stared at him.

"And we know they were both in town the day of Sharon's murder too," he said.

"You said you didn't really like Dolles for it."

He shrugged. "That was before I knew he was in town both days the murders took place."

"With Subjugate-52..." she said, thinking aloud. "Something about him sends a shiver down my spine."

"Moses? He's a big guy."

She nodded. "And his previous crimes are—"

"Much like our victims now," he finished her sentence.

Salvi considered his words. "Were they the only two in town both days?"

Mitch eyed his screen. "No. Looks like Subjugate-12 and Serene-41 are always there."

"Pragge," Salvi thought aloud. "The bad man..." She locked eyes with Mitch. "The brain-damaged ex-serial rapist."

Mitch nodded. "But he only raped before. He never murdered."

Salvi shrugged. "What if his treatment has made things worse? What if there's pent-up rage from his torture?"

Beggs came back over and slapped Mitch on the back. He stood. "You coming for a drink?" he asked her.

She stared at him. "Someone's gotta finalize the report on what we saw today."

Beggs smiled and slapped Mitch's shoulder again. "And that's exactly what the junior detective should do!" He looked over at Caine. "Ain't that right, Lewie?"

Caine didn't bother looking up from his display, he just raised his hand and flipped Beggs the bird.

"We'll see you down there when you kids are done!" Beggs gave a raucous laugh and pulled Mitch out the door. As soon as they left Caine eyed the doorway then looked across the room at her. "Assholes," he muttered. Then went back to work.

Salvi walked into the calming tones of her apartment, closing the door behind her. As the chime of the coded lock sounded, she pulled off her black boots and dumped her gun and her gear in her bedroom, then walked back out to the living room, straight over to the windows. She looked out over the city, at the twinkling lights and the black of night that surrounded them. And the police drones buzzing about. The Golden Gate was lit up but covered in a thick fog, giving it an eerie look. It reminded her hauntingly of the case. She had pieces of evidence but not yet the whole picture.

She pulled a chair over to the window and sat down, ate her pre-packaged meal while staring blankly out at the view. Her mind swam in a sea of a thousand thoughts. She pondered the second vic, Rebecca Carson, and how she was different to the first. The only connection being that she attended Vowker's church and had "pure" carved into her belly. And of course, the BioLume smear. She thought of Fontan Pragge approaching her outside Carson's house, telling her he was a "bad man" and would get punished. She thought of Attis Solme's passion for his facility, how he was adamant that his Serenes and Subjugates could not be responsible. She thought about Garner Town and asked Riverton to submit a background check on the place to their case file. She thought about what she'd witnessed in the Complex's bathroom, of Levan Bander meting out a brutal punishment to a Subjugate. She thought of Tobias crying over his Christian guilt. Thought of the preacher lecturing her and Mitch on forgiveness.

And sure enough, her thoughts turned to Faith.

She turned away from the window, put her dishes in the washer and moved to the bathroom. As she undressed, she stared at herself in the mirror, noticing the resemblance to Faith within her. The dark hair, dark eyes. Especially the eyes. She turned away from the mirror and moved to the shower, catching a glimpse of the scorpion on her hip. Black and menacing, it sat perched ready to strike. Ready to defend.

She looked away from it to the shower controls. She was tired and wanted to relax so she selected the spa mode. A section of the shower wall raised up and a platform emerged. Once it was fully extended, she lay down on it and set the shower on. Hundreds of streams of firm spray fell down upon her, massaging her entire body. She closed her eyes and focused on the sensation.

Anything to wash the day away. Anything to make her forget about Faith.

And it worked. She did stop thinking about Faith. But instead, as she lay naked being gently pummeled and massaged by her shower spray, her mind turned once more to Mitch.

And Hernandez's concern.

And Mitch's behavior of late.

And once more to the killer out there with two victims to his name.

She sighed, annoyed, and turned up the intensity of shower spray, wanting to forget them all.

Salvi awoke to the sound of her iPort ringing on her bedside table. She swatted the pink and purple jellyfish swimming around her and looked at the clock. It was 1.23am. She checked the caller's number. She didn't recognize it. She pressed "answer" and a hologram projected from the iPort.

"Hello?" she answered, squinting her eyes at the pierced guy with a blue mohawk.

"Yeah, is this Detective Brentt?" he asked, loud music pumping in the background.

"Yeah."

"I was told to contact you and tell you to come and collect your partner."

"My partner?"

"Yeah, Mitch Grenville. You know him?"

"Yeah. Where is he? Who are you?"

"He's down at McClusky's bar. I'm the barman. So if you don't come pick him up, I'll find some other cops who will. But they may not take him home, you know what I'm saying?"

"Shit." She rubbed her eyes. "What'd he do?"

"Just come and get him, alright?" With that the hologram vanished.

Salvi sighed heavily, threw her sheets back and got out of bed.

McClusky's bar was even more schizophrenic than she remembered it. She'd only been here a handful of times over the past three years. Half rock-and-roll dive bar, half electronica club flashing with bright neon LEDs, she walked through the door and took a moment to orient herself. The few patrons still there at this time of night looked over at her: a couple of old fat guys in factory coveralls sitting on bar stools, a small group of stoned college kids wearing dull monogrammed pantsuits and data-lenses, a young guy at a booth with three consoles around him, and a businessman in a suit, sitting with a young woman who wasn't wearing very much at all.

Salvi couldn't see Mitch, so she moved over to the bar and flagged the blue mohawked barman.

"It's me, Brentt, where's Mitch?"

The barman shot her an empathetic look. "He's back here." He waved his wristband over a section of the bar and it retracted, opening up a space. He motioned her through. She followed him out back to a cool room, where he swiped his wristband again and unlocked it. The door slid back and he motioned her in. She paused a moment, then cautiously moved to peer inside. There was Mitch, sitting on the floor, leaning back against a stack of beer kegs, his eyes closed, passed out.

"What the hell is he doing in here?" she asked, feeling the cold permeating out the door.

"It was for his own good," the barman said. "He was about to drink himself to death. I tried to cut him off, and he didn't take too kindly to it, so I got Wattunga to put him in here."

"Wattunga?"

"The doorman."

Salvi nodded and looked back in at Mitch. "Who told you to call me?"

"He was drinking with some guys earlier. When they left they said if he caused any trouble to give you a call."

"Did they," Salvi muttered, picturing a laughing Beggs in her mind. She sighed again and nodded. "I'm sorry if he was a problem."

"That's alright," the barman said. "As much as I like Mitch's patronage, I hope he sorts his shit out. The guy's getting messier by the day."

"He's a regular?"

The barman nodded. "Yeah, but these past couple of weeks he's been drinking more heavily than usual. Something's going on in his life."

"Yeah," Salvi said looking back at Mitch. "I guess it is."

"You want Wattunga to give you a hand?" the barman asked.

"No," she said. "I'll handle it."

"Alright." He nodded. "Close the door on your way out."

The barman left and Salvi stepped into the cool room. She walked up to Mitch and nudged his leg with her foot. He didn't move. She nudged him harder. He stirred.

She bent down in front of him. "Mitch. Mitch, wake up."

He didn't stir.

"Mitch!" she said loudly. "Wake up!"

This time he stirred, his eyes opening slightly, but then he closed them again. Salvi stared at him a moment, then unleashed a hard slap across his face.

That woke him up.

"Fuu…" Face scrunched, hand rubbing his cheek, he looked at her like she was crazy.

"Get up, Detective!" she said, standing. "We're going home."

Mitch looked around the cool room quizzically, perhaps a little confused about how he got there. Then he began rubbing his hands over his arms.

"Whysssitt so friggen cold?"

Salvi stood over him with her hands on her hips. "Get up before you get hypothermia."

Mitch moved to stand and she held her hand out to assist. She pulled him up and they stumbled a little. She suddenly realized just how unsteady he was on his feet, so she pulled his arm around her shoulder and supported him as they made their way to the front door.

They stumbled out into the car park, Salvi using all her strength to steer Mitch's taller, bigger frame toward her Zenith. As they neared, she raised her iPort and swiped it over the door handle, while trying to hold Mitch steady at the same time. He tried to stand on his own, but staggered, falling and flattening her against the side of the car.

"Jesus," she grunted, heaving him off. She swiped the handle again, it unlocked and the door opened of its own accord with the hiss of hydraulics.

Mitch peered in drunkenly. "It's tiny. How am I supposed to fit in there?" he slurred.

"By shutting that mouth of yours," she said, pushing his head down and ushering him inside like he was an arrested criminal. She locked him in, then moved around to the driver's side and got in.

She set the Zenith in motion, glancing at him and wondering if he was going to vomit. He looked OK, but she sent the windows down a little just in case. Besides, the fresh air was good; she could smell the booze leaking out his pores.

"Where do you live?" she asked, shivering a little at the cold air that swam inside the vehicle. He didn't respond, and she looked over to see his eyes closed again. She reached out and thumped his arm. "Mitch!"

He opened his eyes and looked at her.

"Where do you live?" she asked again.

He turned his eyes to the road ahead, looking around at their surroundings. She thumped his arm again. Harder.

"Damnit," he said, rubbing his arm. He looked back at her again. "So violent tonight." Then he gave a drunken grin. "I'll put Internal Affairs onto you."

Salvi slammed the brakes on and swerved the Zenith over to the side of the road. His eyes went wide and he threw his arm out against the car's dash for support. The Zenith came to a stop as another car swerved around it honking their horn and the driver yelling expletives.

"You can tell me where you live, or you can get out right now and sleep on the street, Mitch. I don't care. The choice is yours," she seethed, "but it is almost 2am, and I'm tired."

He looked back at her, even in his drunken state his eyes were curious. "The Folex Building downtown."

"Thank you," she said, then put her foot down and veered back into the traffic.

They pulled up directly out front of the Folex Building, named after some young whizz kid software billionaire. It had once been a co-op store that had been refurbished into what were known as "molecular apartments": tiny studio apartments designed for maximum density and minimum cost. She got Mitch out of the car and moved to the entrance.

"Access key?" she said, holding out her hand.

Mitch began fishing in his pocket for it. His jeans were snug and his drunken fingers not cooperating, nor were his wavering legs.

"Goddamn it, Mitch," she hissed, pushing him up against the wall and pressing her hand against his chest to keep him there. With her free hand she tugged his away from the pocket, and slid her smaller fingers in. While she fished her fingers around for the key, Mitch stared at her. His face just centimeters away, his dark green eyes watching her through the unkempt fringe falling in his eyes. Her fingers caught the edge of the key and she pulled it out. She pointed at him. "Stay!" she said, then moved over and swiped it over the entrance console. The doors slid back and she motioned him forward. He staggered toward her and she took his arm and steered him toward the elevators. She swiped his key over the console in the elevator and it automatically took them to the floor registered on the key.

She glanced at the time on her iPort and silently fumed. All the while he continued to stare at her.

"What?" she snapped.

His eyes shone with intrigue, albeit drunkenly. "Nothing … Detective *Salvi Brentt*," he said, accentuating her name as he spoke it. She stared back at him, wondering what he meant by it. It was the second time he'd done that. The elevator chimed and the doors opened on level nine. They stepped out, and as he staggered again she grabbed his arm and threw it over her shoulders once more.

"Apartment?" she asked.

"Nine fourteen," he slurred.

She found the apartment, unlocked the door and ushered him inside, flicking on the lights as she did. She heard a whirring sound and looked up to see a globe sheath pull back and a soft green BioLume glow spread across the room. She glanced around his apartment. It was molecular alright. The whole space was around the same size as Salvi's bedroom in her lush apartment. A small kitchenette sat along the left wall of the entrance, a small lounge area to the right, and the bathroom and bed lay along the wall opposite. Styled in gray hues, the apartment was dark, yet another light pulsed in from a round window punched through the opposite wall; the lights from a club in an alleyway behind his apartment.

She steered Mitch toward his bed as the pinks and blues and reds splashed across them both, cutting through the soft green BioLume glow.

She tried to ease Mitch's frame down on the bed, but he fell back heavily, pulling her down on top of him. She thrust her hand out against the bed and pushed herself off.

"Jesus, Mitch," she muttered.

He looked up at her and smiled with humor, as she lifted his feet onto the bed. She walked over, poured a glass of water and placed it on the small cubed table beside the bed.

"Drink this," she said.

"Yes, mom," he smiled.

"Fuck you," she said, and went to walk away but he grabbed her wrist and pulled her back.

"What?" she asked.

"I'm sorry," he slurred, blinking his eyes heavily. "Thank you."

She stared at him, at the way the lights through the window flashed upon his cheekbone and stubbled jaw.

"It was tonight," he slurred, still holding her wrist.

"What was tonight?" she asked

He slurred something and it took her a second to work out what he'd said.

"Anniversary?" she asked.

He nodded. "He killed her. Tonight."

"Who killed who tonight?"

"Alison," he said. "My girlfriend… Tonight was the night he killed her."

Salvi felt the tension in her arm ease off. She closed her eyes for a moment and sighed. She probably should've known this, but she'd never asked him about it. She sat down on the side of his bed. "Mitch, why didn't you tell me it was the anniversary of her death?"

He looked at her with intoxicated eyes. "You don't like to

talk about it."

She stared back at him. "Because this is what it obviously does to you. I know it's hard but... you need to accept that she's gone and move on."

He stared at her a moment. Then he nodded, pressing his lips together, as his eyes began to shine in the colored lights dancing across him. "You're right," he whispered.

Salvi suddenly felt bad. Who was she to tell him how to feel? Maybe she was a cold bitch after all. Any which way, now was not the time. She'd talk about it with him in the morning.

She went to get up but he tugged on the wrist he still held and pulled her back down.

"Life is precious, Salvi," he slurred, the grip on her wrist tight. "You need to live it while you can."

She stared back at him but said nothing. Wasn't sure what to.

"Who knows how long we have left?" he said. "Don't waste it."

She furrowed her brow. "I'm not wasting it."

He studied her another moment, then let go of her wrist. He raised his hand and cupped her cheek tightly, as though trying to get his point across. The touch of his skin on hers shocked her. "Don't waste it, Salvi," he slurred softly, brushing his thumb across her cheek. "Don't cut people off." His intoxicated eyes lowered to her mouth and she felt his thumb brush slowly over her lips, parting them.

She froze briefly in surprise at the gesture, then grabbed his wrist and pulled his hand away. "You're drunk, Mitch. Sleep it off." She placed his hand firmly across his chest, then stood and headed for the door. "I'll see you tomorrow."

10 : THE OUTPOURING

Salvi sat in the hub and glanced at her iPort. Mitch hadn't shown yet. She sighed and tapped her fingers against the desk in thought.

Kara from narcotics ducked her head around the doorway. Lean, with the bronzed skin of her Middle Eastern ancestors, her hair was coiffed up high and shaved at the sides which beautifully displayed her long intricate earrings – which no doubt hid the latest PD spyware.

"Hey Salvi," she said in greeting, the diamond piercing in her nose sparkling in the light. "I heard you got another body in Bountiful."

"Yeah," she replied.

"That's too bad. That's some horrible shit right there."

"Yeah, it is," Salvi replied. "What's the latest in narc town?"

"Word is there's some new super-nasty on the streets. Bad shit. But we'll stomp it out."

"Good luck," Salvi said. Kara gave a wave, then glanced at Caine and left. A few seconds later Caine casually stood and headed out the door. Salvi smiled to herself, wondering if something was going on between the two, although she'd heard he was seeing Bel from cyber. She shook her head. *Pretty boy's got his hands full.*

Not long after Caine left, Beggs walked in with a coffee in hand.

"Thank you," she said sarcastically, greeting him.

"For what?" he said walking over to her desk.

"For leaving my number with the barman last night."

"What barman?" he asked, sipping his coffee, eyes twinkling with humor.

"The one you left my details with," she said, lowering her voice.

"I didn't leave your card with any barman," he said, then looked over at Bronte as he approached, pulling on his jacket. "You leave Salv's number with the barman last night?"

Bronte shook his head. "Must've been Hernandez," he said.

"Hernandez?" she asked.

Bronte nodded. "I gotta go, got a lead to follow."

Beggs nodded, watched as he walked out the door, then turned back to Salvi.

"I'm going to kill Hernandez," Salvi said.

"Hey, look," Beggs said, "this Mitch thing. Cut him some slack, alright? You know what yesterday was, right?"

She nodded.

"We see some shit in this job and that's hard to deal with," Beggs said, "but it ain't anywhere near as hard as seeing it happen to someone close to you. Mitch is struggling a little, but I feel for the guy." He shrugged. "So long as he does his job, what does it matter if he's drinking a little? Whatever gets us through the day, right?" Beggs turned and walked off toward his desk.

As he did, a message sounded on her iPort. She rolled her wrist over to view the screen. It was from Mitch.

Running late. Meet you in Bountiful.

Salvi gave another sigh. She wondered whether he was really running late or whether he was avoiding her. Either way, she was actually grateful. She was glad not to have to sit in a confined car with her partner right now. She wondered if he remembered touching her face the previous night; touching her lips. She'd found it hard to get it out of her mind ever since. She couldn't remember the last time someone had touched her like that. And despite how drunk he was, she knew it wasn't a drunken gesture. It had been intentional. Honest. Whether Mitch was just drunk and wanted sex, or whether he meant something else by it, she didn't know. But it made her feel odd. And she didn't know if that odd feeling was good or bad. He was her partner. It shouldn't have felt good.

Again, she lamented the days of working with Stanlevski, an old married cop who'd kept things professional. It was always about the job with him. Nothing more, nothing less. Just the way she liked it.

She stood from her desk, checked the gun in her holster and moved for her black jacket. As she did Hernandez appeared and walked toward his desk.

"Hey," she said, stopping him. He looked back at her. "You left my name with the barman last night?"

"Yeah, so?" He shrugged.

"Why didn't you just take him home?" she asked.

He shrugged again. "Not my problem. Besides, you said you could handle things." He turned and walked off. She couldn't see the smug look on his face, but she knew it was there.

"Where's Grenville at?" she heard Ford call from the doorway to her office.

Salvi turned to see her standing there with her arms folded. Salvi gave her a relaxed wave, wondering how much she'd heard. "He's meeting me in Bountiful. I'm just on my way out now." And with that she quickly exited the station.

As Salvi drove to Bountiful, she wondered why Hernandez had bothered to go to the bar the previous evening. It was

pretty clear he wasn't a fan of Mitch, so why he would want
to go and drink with the man? Was Hernandez keeping an
eye on him? Was Ford? What did that mean? Did Ford think
she couldn't handle herself? Didn't trust her to watch Mitch?

With the Zenith's autodrive on, cruising the straight
stretch of road toward Bountiful, she sat back and let her
mind endlessly tick over the case. She thought of Mitch's odd
behavior, of Hernandez's mistrust, of what Beggs had said,
wondered about Ford and Attis' relationship, what influential
ties Attis had, the brain tweaks the Subjugates had undergone,
the bodies of Sharon Gleamer and Rebecca Carson, and the
BioLume found at both scenes.

And as she gazed out the window in thought and the
SlingShot raced past, she still had no answers.

She eventually pulled up in Bountiful a few blocks away from
the Children of Christ church. It looked as though the whole
of the town had turned up for Sharon Gleamer's funeral.
Sprinkled among them were the Serenes, like gaps of light
breaking up the black of the crowd, dressed in their beige
uniforms, their flattened silver halos pressed against their
skulls. As she got out of her car, she recognized Serene-41
smiling and ushering her toward the church.

She walked toward the entry doors, blending into the crowd
nicely with her black pants, boots, jacket and sunglasses. Her
white button-up shirt the only thing providing contrast at the
collar, aside from her trademark red lipstick, that is. Up by the
road, she saw Bander talking to Subjugate-12, Fontan Pragge,
directing him impatiently to do something. Not far from the
two of them was Subjugate-52, Edward Moses, who stood
scanning the crowd. He paused when his eyes fell on hers. As
she stared back, he gave her a slight bow. There was something
oddly intriguing about him. Fascinating. Even though he
was almost a Serene, he seemed somehow different. Where

the others blended blandly into the background, somehow Moses stood out. As much as she hated to admit it, as much as it made her skin crawl to think it, Moses was handsome. Striking. She wondered if that was how he'd drawn his victims in – like moths to the flame. He gave new meaning to the term "handsome devil".

Feeling a swirl of sickness in her belly at her thought, she turned her eyes away and tried to find Mitch. Unable to see him, she entered the swollen church.

Young altar boys stood by the door holding bowls of holy water, offering people sanctification before they entered. Salvi walked straight past them. She found a place along the back wall to stand and studied those present. The family of Sharon Gleamer were obvious. Sitting at the front, their blond hair and crying faces giving them away. Salvi spotted Tobias sitting with them, equally stricken. His roommate Kevin sat beside him, and a few pews back was Ellie Felling with her mother. Not far from them were the Gleamers' neighbors, the Fizzraeli family. She saw little Lucy with her red hair, face turned right around staring at Salvi with that accusing furrow in her brow. Then she noticed Attis Solme, dressed in a fine suit and bolo. He walked up to the Gleamers, passed on his condolences, then took a seat in the pew behind them.

Eventually her eyes fell on Mitch. He was standing against the wall on the opposite side of the church. He glanced her way, gave her a brief nod of acknowledgment before he turned his eyes away again. Given his state last night, he looked fine. She wondered if he'd taken a ReVitalize shot or two to pull himself together in time. Her eyes lingered on him as she recalled him accentuating her name; recalled his thumb parting her lips.

She moved her eyes over the gathered crowd again, until they landed on Graeme Vowker, who now stood at the lectern. The church quietened down, and the preacher began to talk of sending Sharon Gleamer safely into the hands of God in heaven.

Salvi managed to stomach about twenty minutes before she had to step outside. The talk was enough, but even the hymns were starting to grate on her. Outside, the fresh air, despite the chill, was a welcome relief. Although speakers had been set up for those who couldn't fit into the church – so Vowker's voice and the songs of prayer came with her. There was no escape.

She saw the Serenes huddled together out front, faces tilted down, eyes closed, hands clasped together in prayer. In the middle of the clump of Serenes stood the Subjugates in a similar pose.

All except two, that is.

Both Edward Moses and Lucius Dolles were distracted.

Moses had looked up from his prayers as she had exited the church, and Dolles was looking off to the side at a dog sniffing a tree and lifting its hind leg to pee.

Bander, who had been beside the group, stepped toward her.

"Detective," he said quietly, motioning her to follow him away from the Serenes. She did so. He looked back at his wards. "We don't disrupt them when they're at mass. It's important they listen and atone for their sins."

"I thought they weren't encouraged to think of their prior sins?"

"We're all sinners," he said with a smile. "And we have all sinned. What those sins are is irrelevant, so long as we repent."

"And what if you haven't sinned?" she asked. "Why must you then repent? Why punish yourself when no harm has been done."

"No one is free from sin," he said, raising his finger and tapping his temple. "It's human nature to think about sinning on a daily basis. That's what we're trying to teach the Subjugates. Every day they must cleanse their thoughts. They must offer themselves to God."

Salvi looked back at them, clustered together in a sea of beige. Moses and Dolles' faces were tilted down again, their eyes closed.

"I was thinking," she said, "about Fontan Pragge."

"Subjugate-12," he corrected her.

"Subjugate-12." She gave a nod in acknowledgment. "Why hasn't he been converted to a Serene as yet? His number is twelve. That means he's been a part of the Solme Complex for a long time."

"Subjugate-12 will never be a Serene."

"Why?"

Bander looked at her in study. "Because of his mental capacity. His brain no longer functions like a normal adult."

"So, he will never know right from wrong?" she asked, sharpening her eyes on his. Bander's eyes sharpened on hers in return and a smile slid across his face.

"No one from the Solme Complex did this," he said, motioning back to Sharon Gleamer's funeral.

"How can you be so sure?" she asked.

His smile grew wider, as he pulled out his baton and tapped it in his other hand. "Because I personally make sure of that."

The door to the church opened and they looked back to see Mitch standing there. His eyes fell on Bander, Salvi, and the baton. He moved toward them, and as he did, all the Serenes and Subjugates stared at them.

"Everything alright?" Mitch asked.

"Yes," she said, although Mitch wasn't looking at her.

"I was just explaining to Detective Brentt, how you're looking in the wrong place for your killer," Bander told Mitch, putting his baton away.

"Are we?" Mitch said. "Where should we look, then?"

Bander shrugged. "I don't know. That's not my job."

"No, it's not," Mitch said. "So, you stick to what you know," he motioned to the Serenes, "and leave us to what we know. Which is finding killers."

"You better hurry up and do your job, then," Bander said, "before another body washes up." With that Bander walked off toward the Serenes, who were still watching them. The caretaker pulled out his baton again and slapped it hard into his hand, sending their eyes to the ground again.

Salvi studied Mitch. "You're looking better than you did last night."

He tore his eyes away from Bander and the Serenes to look back at her. "What are you doing out here?"

She shrugged. "Couldn't stand listening to Vowker. Didn't realize his voice carried out here."

Mitch didn't say anything, just stared at her, analyzing her like he did. Any mention of Vowker igniting the curiosity in his eyes.

"So how much ReVitalize did it take to resurrect you today?" she asked, trying to shift his focus.

He didn't answer her, just turned around and walked back inside the church.

The wake was held in the Children of Christ's hall. The Serenes acted as waiters, fetching people drinks and handing out food. The Subjugates stood back behind the long tables, stirring pots of soup and buttering bread, keeping their eyes down. Salvi's attention kept falling on Subjugate-52, watching him, eager to interview him. He barely said a word, barely looked at anyone, only interacted with the other Serenes, stayed well back behind the tables.

Salvi stood alone by the door sipping a coffee that Serene-41 had furnished her with. Mitch was on the other side of the hall talking with Sheriff Holt. She was starting to think he was avoiding her. Tobias walked past and she gave him a friendly smile, but he turned his eyes away and continued on like he didn't know her. Or perhaps, like he didn't want her to know his dirty little secret. Ellie Felling, too, looked down into her lap when she'd made eye contact with the girl. Then there were the Fizzraelis. The mother still refused to make eye contact but her daughter, Sophia, more than made up for it. The little redheaded girl didn't take her glaring eyes off Salvi. She was starting to get the feeling the town wanted her to leave; not liking what she represented, uncomfortable with what her presence meant.

In that moment, Salvi had never felt more like an outsider. And here, in this crowd, that didn't bother her one bit. These people would never be her tribe.

"I'm so glad you could attend the mass," Vowker said, approaching. "Although I realize you're probably here in a professional capacity, but I hope you got something out of it?"

"No," she said bluntly, "I didn't."

Vowker took a moment, then smiled patiently. "Well, I guess in order to get something out of it, you would need to open yourself to it in the first place."

"I open myself to the truth. To reality. You're the ones hiding from the world and pretending it doesn't exist."

"We know it exists. We just don't allow the devil to infect our souls. We are strong of mind. We are not weak. We will not be slaves to sin."

Salvi stared at him. "Thank you for volunteering to give us your DNA sample." She hadn't tried to lower her voice. "We hope to have the results soon and clear you from our suspects list." Vowker's face paled and he looked around uneasily before returning his eyes to her.

"I feel for you, Detective," he said quietly, narrowing his eyes in study. "I've never met anyone quite like you before."

"What?" she asked sarcastically, "anyone so closed off to

your bullshit mind control?"

"Anyone so closed off, period," he said quickly, before his eyes softened with sadness, with pity. "So hostile. So bitter. So vengeful. You are sad, and lonely, and dead inside, Detective. You've let hate eat away at your soul… I know you think it's too late to heal yourself, but it's never too late. You just need to open up and let people in. Let God–"

"And how do you recommend I open up?" she said a little loudly, a little tersely. "Like Sharon Gleamer and Rebecca Carson did?"

He stepped backward, aghast, like she was some horrible beast he couldn't comprehend. Then he turned and walked away shaking his head in hopelessness and maybe disgust.

Salvi clenched her teeth and noticed she'd drawn attention. Mitch and Holt were staring at her, as were Bander and Attis Solme, and the Subjugates and Serenes, the Fizzraelis, the Fellings, Tobias. She met their stares and confronted each one, until they looked away. Then she turned and left the hall, dumping her coffee cup on the nearest table as she did.

Salvi didn't bother waiting for Mitch. They'd taken separate vehicles anyway, so she got into her Zenith and headed back to the hub. She didn't know why, but she just had to get out of Bountiful and away from the preacher's words, telling her she was dead inside.

She sat at her desk and went over the forensic reports of the two vics, staring at their photographs, willing herself to hit on something to catch the killer. What Bander had said to Mitch outside the church played on her mind. It was their job to catch this guy, and so far they hadn't. Now two women were dead. If they didn't do something fast, he would probably strike again.

The forensic report from Weston had confirmed the perp's bodily fluids were found at the second scene as well, but no clothing fibers or hair, pubic or otherwise, were found at either. No hair...

Her mind ran over the two Subjugates in town the day of both murders: Moses and Dolles. She wondered again why the victims were left face down. Did the killer feel guilt? Could he not look them in the eyes? Or did he think they were beneath him? That they were just pieces of meat and nothing more? Or could it maybe be a little of both?

Her iPort signaled an incoming call. It was Mitch. She didn't want to speak to him right now. She ignored it.

Riverton suddenly appeared on her console display.

"Detective Brentt," it said. "Footage recorded from Detective Grenville's holo-badge at the funeral has now been uploaded to the case file, and all known residents now logged in our facial recognition software have been identified. Yesterday's interviews have also been transcribed and the timeline for Rebecca Carson's case has been established and linked where appropriate. I have also captured the similarities between this case and Sharon Gleamer's in a linked document."

"Thank you, Riverton," she said.

"I have one other thing to report, Detective."

"Yes?"

"Senior Detective Hernandez accessed both case files this morning and viewed their contents."

Salvi paused. "He did?"

"Yes." Riverton displayed the access log.

"He just viewed it?" Salvi asked.

"Yes. As per SFPD protocol, editing is locked to all but the assigned officers."

"Anyone else been checking up on us?"

"Only Detective Lieutenant Ford."

"Right..." she said. "Thank you, Riverton. End request."

Salvi sat at her desk, mind racing. Why the hell was Hernandez checking their case files? Ford's name on the log didn't surprise her, she often did so to keep herself abreast of the current caseloads. But Hernandez?

When he walked in ten minutes later, she fixed her eyes on him. He noticed her intense stare and approached.

"What's up?" he asked.

"You tell me?" she said.

"Where's your partner?" he asked, motioning to Mitch's empty desk.

"What's it to you?" she said.

He studied her a moment, then shrugged. "You're his partner. You should know where he is."

"I'm not his keeper."

"You should be," Hernandez said, then leaned forward and lowered his voice. "Look, Salvi, you got a serial killer out there, and your partner's unstable. That's a big fucking problem right there. Do you understand what I'm saying here?"

A deep furrow crossed Salvi's brow. "Mitch is fine. We're gonna catch him."

"You got two vics now. So where is your partner? Drinking?"

"I know where Mitch is, Hernandez," she lied. "We're handling this."

"Are you?"

"What's it to you anyway? And why have you been checking our case files? You trying to take Ford's job?"

"Someone's gotta keep an eye on things."

"I said Mitch is fine. Stay out of my case."

"No, Salv," he said carefully, as though explaining something to a child, his eyes boring into hers. "Your partner's unstable, and you have a serial killer on the loose."

"We're doing our best, alright?"

"No, Salv," he repeated, leaning closer. "You're not listening. Your partner's unstable, and you got a serial killer out there. That's an explosive mix. Odd they're happening at the same time, don't you think?"

Salvi finally got his meaning and jerked her head back as her mouth fell open. "Are… are you kidding me?" she said. "Are you saying what I think you're saying?"

He stared back at her. "I'm just saying keep your eye on him, Salv. He's got a past. You're his partner. You're the only one who can vouch for him."

Salvi shook her head in disbelief. "I can't believe you just said that to me. What the fuck, Hernandez?"

"Look, do yourself a favor and go see Stan, alright?"

"What? Why?"

"Because he's got some information on your partner that you should know."

Salvi stared at him. "And he told you this information?"

Hernandez nodded.

"So why don't you tell it to me, then?"

Hernandez shook his head. "'Cause you won't listen to me. But you always listened to Stan. So, go see him. Go listen to what he has to say… *Mia*."

With that, Hernandez left, and Salvi sat in shock watching him go.

Salvi exhaled heavily. She didn't know what she was doing here. She contemplated turning around, but then changed her mind. She raised her hand and pressed the buzzer on the door.

She heard the sound of a dog barking from within. She frowned, wondering when Stan had gotten himself a dog. A few seconds passed before Conchetta Stanlevski's voice sounded over a speaker by the door.

"Oh! Would you look at that, it's Salvi Brentt!"

The door unlocked and opened, and Conchetta's plump frame and rosy cheeks beamed a big smile at her.

"Salvi!" she said. "How you doing? What brings you here?"

Salvi smiled as she saw the source of the barking. A virtual dog bounced around Conchetta's feet, projected from a small round disc on wheels. It looked like the Golden Retriever model. "I, er… I was in the neighborhood. Thought I'd say hi to Stan, while I was around. He about?"

"Sure," she said, before Stan appeared beside her.

"Well, look what the cat dragged in," he said, the old man's voice sounding craggier than Beggs'.

Conchetta hit him. "Stanley! Where's your manners!"

Stan looked at his wife as he pointed at Salvi. "I got a witness, right there, to your domestic violence," he told Conchetta.

Conchetta chuckled a wheezing laugh and hit him again. She looked back at Salvi. "He's lucky I don't kill him, the years he's put me through."

Salvi smiled, and Stan ushered her inside their cozy apartment. Conchetta disappeared into another room and the virtual dog bounced alongside Stan as he led her to a small balcony on the opposite side of the apartment. Salvi stepped onto the balcony and saw a thick wall of apartments ahead and an alleyway with rubbish bins below. Stan closed the door behind him, tapped a small console on the wall that sent the balcony cover down, blocking off the view as a light came on overhead.

"Where shall we go," he muttered to himself, looking at the console. He made a selection, and the balcony covering suddenly turned into a gorgeous view of palm trees and crystal blue beach. The light overhead turned warm like the sun and she heard seagulls in the distance.

"Hawaii?" Salvi smiled.

"What, you want Paris?" he grumbled. "You've always been a city girl, Salv. Well screw you, this is my retirement." He motioned for her to sit down.

"Hawaii's good," she chuckled, taking the proffered seat as the virtual dog raised its front legs up onto Stan, who stood by the door.

"Down!" Stan said. "Sit!" The virtual dog sat, tongue hanging out the side of its mouth as it panted, staring at Stan.

"I never took you for a pet owner," Salvi said, as Stan leaned back against the wall.

He waved her off. "Conchetta kept nagging me." He shrugged. "At least this thing doesn't shit or need walks. Although apparently there's a setting for that, for realism, but I asked them to shut that off at the store."

Salvi smiled. "Does it have a name?"

"Pluto," he said, and the dog barked happily.

Salvi smiled and nodded, eyeing the dog.

"So, what brings you to these parts, Detective?" he asked, eyes fixed curiously on hers.

Salvi shrugged. "I was just in the area."

Stan's eyes studied her, squinting like he did when he was trying to work something out on a case, accentuating the crow's feet. "You're a bad liar, Mia. Always have been."

Salvi smiled again and nodded, her eyes resting on a pot of pink roses against the far wall. She looked back at Stan. "Hernandez told me to come."

Stan nodded. "And?"

"He said you have information for me."

"On?"

Salvi studied him. She felt like she was on the opposite end of a suspect interview. Stanlevski had always been good at making suspects talk.

"My new partner," she eventually said, feeling a sense of guilt like she was betraying Mitch by being there. "Apparently there's something I should know about him."

Stan nodded, glanced around casually at the tropical beach before him. He looked back at her. "You sure you want to know?"

She shrugged. "I don't know. Do I?"

"How're you finding him?"

"Fine."

"He legit?"

"Yeah. I think so."

"So why are you here, then?"

"Stan, if you're playing games, I really don't have time."

"I know you don't. Two women dead now in that religious community, huh?"

"Hernandez?"

Stan smiled. "Hernandez likes to stay on top of things. It's his way of asserting his dominance. He asserts his dominance by knowing everything and having an answer for everything. So, he finds out everything. He's good police."

Salvi studied him. Stan looked a lot more relaxed than when they'd worked together. Retirement was agreeing with him. She smiled, happy for him.

"So, what does Hernandez know that he wants me to ask you?" she asked.

Stan studied her a moment, then moved over to take the seat beside her. He exhaled loudly as he sat, then looked at her. "An old friend of mine is stationed in the Chicago hub that Grenville came from. Turns out it wasn't a willing transfer when they sent him here. This was his last chance to keep his badge."

"Yeah, I heard the rumors. So?"

"After they found his girlfriend dead, he became the prime suspect, Mia. And he was the only suspect for a long time."

Salvi paused, staring at Stan. Her breathing became shallow. "What?"

She'd known about Mitch's girlfriend, had known about the transfer being forced, but she hadn't known that he'd been the prime suspect in her death.

"But… they had to drop it," Stan continued, "'cause they didn't have enough evidence to go on. They watched him like a hawk, though. And eventually they had to get him out of town, because he wouldn't let his girlfriend's murder go. Every waking hour he could, when he wasn't working the case he was assigned to, he was searching for her killer trying to clear his name. He was obsessed, overworked, drinking hard and they said… they said he started shooting up."

Salvi felt a small relief wash over her. "Yeah," she said. "He was ReVitalizing to combat the effects of his drinking."

Stan shot her a weird look, studied her for a moment. "Either way, he was on edge. He got a lead on a guy, some guy the girlfriend had worked with. Turns out she'd had an affair with him behind Mitch's back. Mitch wound up beating the guy pretty bad, put him in hospital. But the guy was innocent. Mitch was lucky he didn't press charges. The guy must've felt guilty for the affair." He paused a moment. "According to Hernandez, Mitch is still on edge. He's still drinking?"

"Yeah, but… it's only been recently that he started up. The first few months he was fine. But… it was the anniversary of her death yesterday."

Stan nodded, studying her some more. "You think he's innocent?"

Salvi looked away, out at the beach. "I don't know. I don't know enough about him."

"Is he good police?"

She looked back at him, thought for a moment, then nodded. "Yeah. I think so."

"Not as good as me, though, right?"

Salvi burst into a laugh. Stan smiled back, before his face fell serious again.

"What'd I teach you, Mia?" he said softly.

Salvi looked back at him.

"What's your number one weapon in the field? Screw all

the technology. What's your number one weapon?"

"My gut," she answered.

Stan nodded. "Your gut. It's more important, more powerful than any man-made weapon. More important than your gun, your iPort, your fists, anything. Science has proven that now. Our brains are linked with our guts, but our guts don't get clogged with emotion. It's our base survival mechanism. You listen to it. You absorb *everything*. Let it work in conjunction with your senses. Listen to the sounds, take in the smells, record everything with these," he pointed to his eyes. "And you listen to what your gut tells you. Your brain will process everything and give you the answers you need. But your gut'll give you the early warning you might need to survive. You hear me?"

Salvi nodded. She missed working with the old bastard. To her, he was like family. The only family she had. She suddenly felt a lump in her throat and the sting of tears in her eyes at the realization.

Stan was all the family she had.

He reached out, placed his hand on hers and gave it a quick squeeze. "You're good police, Mia." He let go of her hand and stared out into the ocean. "His girlfriend was raped and murdered. That's gotta cut anyone up pretty bad," Stan said. "If he's clean, then he's clean. But if he's not..." Stan looked at her, "you gotta watch your back."

Salvi nodded, looking down at her hands. "Why didn't you tell me this earlier?"

He shrugged. "'Cause you don't like being told what to do."

She looked up at him.

"And..." he shrugged again, "you're good police, Salv. Hernandez is being over-protective, but he don't know you like I do. I know you can stand on your own two feet." He gazed out upon the beach before them. "These murders started after Mitch moved out here, but that could just be a bad coincidence." He turned back, locking eyes with hers. "If he's clean, he's clean. And if he's not… then you take care of it. You do what you have to, Mia. Either way, you catch this killer. You know you can."

Salvi saw the twinkle in his eye as he looked at her. It was pride. She smiled back at him, and quickly, briefly, squeezed his hand too.

Stan stood and waved her off. "Now get out of here. I got shit to do."

Salvi laughed and watched him disappear back inside his apartment, while Pluto the virtual dog followed.

11 : CONNECTIVITY

Salvi tried to go back to the hub after her visit to Stan, but she just couldn't face it. She didn't want to see Mitch or Hernandez. Her apartment wasn't an option either – being left alone with her thoughts as she stared out her window at the city lights and police drones. No, she needed to take her mind off things for a while and give her subconscious time to sort through things. She needed to submerge herself in the city and become invisible.

She jumped one of the new Cylin trains, an inner city add-on to the existing BART system, and made her way into the city's heart. As she stood, feeling a smooth vibration travel through her legs with the movement of the Cylin, she studied the people in her carriage, sizing them up like she did. Like they were a suspect. Like she needed to remember their faces, how they were dressed.

They varied in age, sex and race, she noticed, but they all had one thing in common. Every single one of them was connected to technology in some way. As she glanced around she realized she was the only one disconnected. Three of them sat wearing Voakleys – VR integrated sunglasses. Two wore boxy headphones, one bopping his head to music, the other tuned in to the screens on the front wall of the carriage. She counted nine on various other devices – some tapping their fingers quickly playing a game of some sort, others typing messages or undertaking some other administrative task. And the carriage was silent.

Stone cold silent.

With each stop the Cylin made, some people exited and new ones entered. All were connected. Even those that appeared to be traveling together barely said more than a few words to each other unless it had to do with whatever technology they were interacting with at the time. Watching a young couple sitting side by side, she saw the teenage boy hold up his smart device to his girlfriend. On the screen was a love heart. The girlfriend held her device up to his and he knocked them together and the heart transferred to the girl's screen. The girl smiled at the screen, then tapped her device against her boyfriend's and sent the heart back to him. They cast each other a brief smile, then once again became absorbed in their individual devices.

Once upon a time, Salvi realized, those lovebirds would've kissed and hugged each other. Now they tapped screens.

It made her think of Bountiful, how they disregarded technology. Did they have a point? Was their community more physically connected as a result? Were the people in the city, with their access to technology, physically disconnected? Or was it merely a trade-off at the end of the day? Whether religion or technology, whichever way you looked at it, whichever enslaved you, was it really a case of freedom vs control? Were we all slaves to something?

Staring at the young couple, she couldn't help but think of Sharon and Tobias. How he'd told Salvi they'd tried other things to avoid temptation. She wondered whether Sharon and Tobias had managed to get their hands on some 'sinful' technology, whether they had once sent each other love hearts like the couple before her. Before it spilled over into real life. She recalled Ellie's claim of seeing them heading toward the Bountiful SlingShot station and wondered whether they had mostly just sat in the café and held hands as Tobias had claimed, or whether their visits to the city with Kevin had enabled them to indulge their love in other ways. Whether the technology and freedoms of the city had seduced them and tainted their innocent minds.

The Cylin reached the city center and Salvi exited. She made her way through the tubular stark white corridors and up the smooth escalators to ground level, watching all the people coming and going like ants in an underground colony. It reminded her of the Solme Complex but on a much larger scale.

As she stepped outside someone tugged on her coat. She pulled it away from their grasp and looked to where a young man sat on the ground. He was skinny and pale and desperate, holding a dirty cap out toward her. She saw a broken device on the floor before him. This wasn't a druggie needing money for a fix. This was a techie, an addict who couldn't survive without their tech and needed cash or supplies to hook them up again. Salvi turned away and kept walking.

Fresh rain had left the streets glistening and reflecting the bouncing, pulsing and flashing lights of the thriving metropolis around her. As she walked along she absorbed the overbearing impact of the lights, the sounds, the crowds, the smells. The distraction she'd sought, fulfilled. The anonymity she pursued, embraced.

The communities on the outside saw the cities and the technology they were drowning in as decaying cesspits. Many claimed technology would be our downfall, would result in the ruination of mankind, especially after the Crash. When it happened and people had died, some of the population had drawn their line in the sand, and that was when these communities on the outskirts grew in popularity as people vowed to live tech-free.

Their arguments had merit, but thinking about it now, in Salvi's eyes, they had simply traded one obsession for another. They left tech behind, but they'd traded it for gods or guns. Sometimes both.

Yet, despite the Crash, many remained in the cities. Many decided they could live without the neural tech, but they couldn't live without all the other mod cons of everyday life. The thought of adapting to the way their ancestors lived, or 'regressing' as some called it, was far too scary a thought. The truth was, many just saw it as a lot of unnecessary work for little reward. Why clean your house when a robo-cleaner can do it for you? Besides, now the neural tech had been retracted from the market, people felt safe again. The chances anyone could hack their brain had been erased.

Unless, of course, people like Attis Solme were successful in bringing it back again. From what Salvi could tell, the neural tech Attis used at the Solme Complex was only a small element of what had been on the market prior to The Crash, but still… Salvi loved technology, yet even she drew the line at neural tech. She would never leave a door open for someone to fuck with and control her mind.

She'd been down that road before, and would not let it happen again.

To help take her mind off things, she thought about seeing something at the AR movie house, but standing in the queue for a ticket, she changed her mind. And so on she walked, until just outside the heart of the city, she came upon the area known as the Mission, now called "Transmission" by the locals. It was the tech center of the city and it was packed with shoppers, street sellers, and of course, the tech-heads with their caps out. She looked up into the sky and saw a drone hovering overhead. There were always at least four drones dedicated to watching the Mission. She passed the windows of a variety of "specialists", from VR, AR, other high-tech gadgets, and robot specialists offering everything from robo-help to robo-security to robo-whores.

She hadn't walked around this part of town for a while and noticed several new stores alight with their bright LEDs and holo-sales personnel, encouraging her to step inside. She glanced further down the street and saw something that made her pause.

It was a bright green BioLume cross.

She moved toward it, crossing the street amid passing autocabs and tuk-tuks. She came to a stop in front of the building. From afar she'd questioned what she'd seen as the building had flashing lights and holograms projecting out front. But she hadn't been wrong. It was an actual church. A high-tech church.

She pulled the broad, heavy doors open and stepped inside. The layout of a traditional church was before her; rows of pews and an elevated altar at the front, but the aesthetics were very different. She felt as though she'd just stepped inside a nightclub or performance arena. Dim light filled the high-ceilinged building. Where stained glass windows should've sat along the side walls, now were video screens of interactive saints. Rows of green BioLume globes sat along the front where candles would've once been placed. And the music playing was not a traditional hymn, but some kind of modern interpretation undertaken by an electronica band.

A hologram came to life beside her, offering her holy water. She ignored it and stepped further inside. She noticed a few people scattered among the pews, heads down and praying.

Light blue neon footsteps lit up in the floor before her, and she watched as they slowly made their way toward the altar. She suspected she was supposed to follow them, but she slipped into one of the back pews instead and took a seat.

A spotlight suddenly came on, flooding the altar, and a figure emerged from the side. It took Salvi a few moments to realize that it wasn't a man but a robot. As soon as it hit the spotlight she saw the shine of its plastic veneer, shaded in a similar tone to human skin. The robot raised its arms to the sky, lifting with it the heavy robes it wore.

"Praise the Lord Jesus!" it called out.

One of the people in the pews ahead called back. "Praise the Lord!" Another startled as though he'd been asleep.

Salvi listened as the robo-preacher spoke of how Jesus loved them, of how he was there for each of them, of how Jesus would always be with them. A screen came to life behind the preacher as it talked. Salvi watched as advertisements began to roll for religious group meetings and the latest apps to connect with Jesus. She saw an interactive Bible app and a confessional app. *Instantaneous absolution!* Then she saw an ad for an app called *Sacrifice*™. It challenged users to make sacrifices then record and measure how they did, rewarding them with free Christian literature and music for those who sacrificed the most.

Then came the advertisements for "connected" games. She saw VR glasses that allowed you to walk with Jesus and partake in the Last Supper. Another was called *Good Life*™ where players would follow and assist Saints as they performed good deeds. Then she saw one advertised called *Sin Hunters*™, where players were encouraged to seek out sinners and punish them – giving them thirty-nine lashes or nailing them to a cross.

Salvi's mouth fell open at the last one. The graphics were … *very* graphic. Before she could gather her thoughts, a miniature drone flew down and hovered in front of her, shaped like a bird with flapping wings. A compartment opened, and an arm extended holding a box.

"Give back to the Lord," it half chirped, half spoke. "All donations accepted."

Salvi swatted it away and stood, took one last look at the robo-preacher and interactive saints, then left.

As she stepped outside, she saw three techies now sitting on the doorstep. They raised their hands to a chorus of "Please!" "Help out those less fortunate!" "Just a little!"

Salvi moved past their reaching hands and stepped onto the sidewalk. As she strode away she heard another voice say: "Hey, why don't you come inside? They'll give you free tech. Apps, games, whatever you like. All you need to do is just listen for a bit."

The voice sounded familiar and she glanced over her shoulder to see a young man ushering the three techies swiftly inside the church. It was Kevin Craydon, Tobias Brook's roommate.

Before Salvi's brain could compute that, her iPort registered an incoming call. She looked at her wrist and saw it was Mitch. She switched it to message. She looked back at the church and contemplated going back in, when the sound of raucous laughter rang out behind her. She looked around to see a group of teens walking along playing a game of virtual tennis, the bright yellow ball shooting back and forth between two players, swatting it with their haptic-gloved hands. Her eyes swiftly drifted past them, as she noticed a sign for the SlingShot station. She moved toward it and studied the screen outside showing which stops the station serviced. Bountiful was on the list, as was Garner Town and several others north to Seattle and south to LA.

She turned back to view the church, staring at the BioLume cross protruding from its roof. She thought of the BioLume lights inside, then thought of the BioLume smudges found at the crime scenes. She suddenly wanted to go back inside and take another look but couldn't risk being seen by Kevin. She hissed quietly, then activated her iPort and lenses.

"Hello, Detective Brentt," Riverton answered, in its golden, bald, androgynous form.

"Riverton, I need a drone to survey the inside of a building."

"Yes, Detective. Please give me your location."

Salvi authorized Riverton to access her geolocater.

"It's the Church of Connectivity," Salvi said, reading the

sign over the doorway.

"Parameters?"

"I need all traces of BioLume. Particularly on the floor. Anywhere it can be stepped in."

"Drone 10 on approach."

Salvi looked up to see one of the overhead drones swoop down. She quickly moved for the door of the church and opened it enough to allow the drone to enter. Several minutes went by before Riverton appeared in her lenses again.

"Appraisal done," it said.

Salvi pulled the door open again and the drone flew out. She quickly walked away as data began scrolling up her lenses. BioLume was registered among the row of lights near the altar and in several other spaces within the church, but none was detected on the floor or anywhere it could be stepped in.

"Shit," she muttered.

"Is that all, Detective Brentt?" Riverton asked.

"Yes. Item closed. File archived."

"Yes, Detective."

Riverton disappeared, as did the scrolling information. Salvi turned her lenses off and looked around again. She moved her eyes from the church to the SlingShot station to the road ahead where the area known colloquially as the "Sation", short for "Sensation", was located. It suddenly dawned upon her that she was literally standing at the intersection of the Mission and the Sation. And right there on the border between the two was the SlingShot station and the Church of Connectivity.

She reconnected her lenses again.

"Riverton?"

"Yes, Detective Brentt."

"Can you tell me who owns or runs the Church of Connectivity, at the location the drone just scanned?"

"One moment," Riverton said, pausing as it assessed her request.

Salvi tapped her iPort, clearing the view in her lenses. Standing on the sidewalk outside the SlingShot station, she scanned everyone who walked past her. Eventually Riverton came back onto her lenses.

"The Church is owned by a company called Neuricle Corporation."

"Who are they?"

"According to my records... Neuricle Corporation is owned and chaired by Mr Attis Solme."

"Solme?" Salvi said, pausing.

"Yes. It is the same corporation behind the Solme Complex."

Salvi felt her heart race a little with the information. "See what else you can find out about them, Riverton. Have it in my case file by morning."

"Yes, Detective."

She ended the call and stared at the church again.

Why was Attis Solme running a high-tech church in the city? The Solme Complex was high-tech, yes, but Attis voluntarily lived in Bountiful. He was a strong supporter of the Children of Christ, a church, and community, that vowed to live tech-free. If the Children of Christ considered tech sinful, then what would they think of this Church of Connectivity?

She wondered whether Preacher Vowker knew what Solme was up to here in the city. And if he didn't know, what would Vowker do if he found out that Solme was dancing with the devil behind his back?

Although, the truth was, at the Solme Complex, Attis was already dancing with the devil. Lots of devils, in fact. Devils dressed in beige uniforms with silver halos pressed against their skulls.

She thought of Kevin Craydon again. Did he really come

into the city to attend lectures? Or was he secretly working for Solme? Again, she wondered what Preacher Vowker would think of this; the young Kevin entering this pit of sin on the regular and indulging in all this technology. Even if it *was* just to bring people to God. Was this where Kevin had brought Tobias and Sharon? Could that have somehow led to Sharon's death? What about Rebecca Carson? Did she fit into this? Did this even have anything to do with the Bountiful murders?

She exhaled heavily, feeling less sure what to do now than ever. The plan to give her mind a break from thinking about the case was so far not working. Rain began to sprinkle down again, and she looked around for somewhere to seek shelter. Drawn by the blinking neon LED lights of the Sensation, she moved toward it, wanting to drown herself within.

As she walked, she passed a Silo Disco, a club where people stood on their own with earphones and danced the night away in their own little partitions – a way to go out dancing but not having to deal with other people. There was a high-tech gym where people stood in machines that made their muscles work for them – a way of getting buff without the sweat. Whorehouses openly displayed their wares through their long glass windows. Whatever you wanted they had it: women, men, robots, VR, AR. Several people milled about out front, enjoying whatever they could see for free – as their options stood on an elevated platform waiting to be chosen for a sale. Salvi paused in front of a male whore. Shirtless and handsome enough, he approached the glass and bent down to her face level. He smiled and raised his finger, beckoning her inside with a smile. Tempted, she considered it briefly. That would certainly take her mind off things, even if it was only for a few minutes. But images of Sharon Gleamer's and Rebecca Carson's bodies were fixed in her mind. She turned and walked away.

Her eyes fell on an establishment called the Dream Bar. Located beneath an erotic art gallery, the soft blue cloud holo-sign, smacked with red lips, caught her attention and drew her inside. She took an elevator with mirrored walls and blue neon lights down to the basement. When the doors opened she was greeted with more soft blue neon lights, and a wide space with a mirror ball dance floor on one side and a long bar down the other. In between the dance floor and the bar sat sunken circular tables, each half-buried in the floor like hot tubs and also glowing a neon blue. She found a table right in the middle and ordered the most potent drink she could find on her table's inbuilt menu, then sat back, trying to let the loud music, a mesh of electronica and metal, and the dim lights envelop her.

Her drink came quickly courtesy of a scantily clad waitress in a chainmail dress with a sleeve of shining silver tattoos. Salvi gave a nod of thanks, took the drink and had a long gulp, feeling the liquid warm her from the inside. For a moment she understood Mitch's drinking. He was using it to numb his pain. To numb his emotions, his thoughts. And now here she was trying to do the same.

Just like she'd done many times before in her past.

Running. Hiding. Burying herself.

Pushing herself to the limits. Wanting to punish herself.

Maybe she understood Mitch better than she thought she did. Maybe she was just as screwed up as he was. Maybe she was just better at hiding it.

Or denying it.

Maybe she'd just had more time to perfect the camouflage.

But she didn't want to think about Mitch right now. Or what Stan had told her. Or the way Mitch had touched her lips. And she certainly didn't want to think about what Hernandez had suggested.

She glanced about at the bar's clientele. All the women

were in short, tight dresses or skirts. She looked down at the black suit and white button-up shirt she wore and decided to take off her jacket. She rolled the sleeves of her shirt to her elbows, exposing her iPort, and opened the first few buttons to mid-chest.

She finished her drink and ordered another. She eyed a couple at the sunken table next to hers. The woman wore the thinnest material of a dress, which sat delicately on her large, fake breasts. The man sat with his shirt open all the way down, sitting back with his arms up on the raised floor around them as though he really were sitting in a hot tub. He saw Salvi watching them and smiled, as the woman placed what looked to Salvi to be a narcotic on her tongue, then snuggled into his side, kissing his neck and sliding her hand between his legs.

Salvi looked away as a shirtless waiter arrived with her second drink. The kid looked about eighteen years old going by his face, but his body was clearly enhanced as though he'd been using the machines at the gym down the road. She felt a little guilty for admiring the kid's chest and arms, as she took the drink and gulped immediately. The memories were swarming over her now. Of her youth. Of her rebellion. Of her determination to do everything she'd ever been told not to. It was coming back to her, and as she pictured Vowker's face in her mind, she felt the urge to rebel again. To push back. To fight against them.

"Well, I didn't expect to see you here," she heard a familiar voice say. She looked up, annoyed, wanting to be alone. It was Levan Bander. He was dressed in civilian clothes, smelling of aftershave.

Salvi glanced around the bar, then looked back at him. "I didn't expect to see you here either."

"May I?" he asked, motioning to the other side of sunken table.

She paused a moment, then nodded, and he stepped down into the sunken circle and took a seat.

"You're a long way from Bountiful," she said.

He nodded. "I like to get as far away as I can on a night off and the SlingShot helps things," he said, sipping the drink he carried in his hands. "When you live onsite for days at a time like I do, it sometimes feels like I'm one of the Serenes too. I like to remind myself that I'm not. That I'm normal, and I can do normal things."

Salvi sipped her drink, eyeing him. "And would Attis Solme approve of you coming to a place like this?" she asked. "It's not very Godly."

"No, it's not." He smiled. "But I won't tell if you don't."

She stared at him but didn't respond.

"Besides," Bander said as he leaned on the table between them, placing his glass down and folding his arms, "after the funeral today, I wanted to live a little, you know?"

Again, she said nothing but continued to analyze him.

"Look, I get a little wound up sometimes," he said. "When you spend your days with criminals, it's bound to affect you. Harden you. But it's part of the job. When I'm at the Solme Complex, I'm the 'caretaker' and I fulfil that role. But when I'm off duty, I'm Levan Bander. Just a normal guy. That's why I try to get away from Bountiful when I can. Stay the night elsewhere." He chuckled. "I don't want to end up a weirdo like Remmell. He never seems to leave. Besides, I can't exactly invite a date back to my lodgings at the Solme Complex, now can I? They'd run a mile."

Again, Salvi didn't respond. She just stared at him trying to figure him out.

"You come here often?" he asked.

"No," she said.

"So why tonight?"

She shrugged. "Felt like it, I guess."

He nodded, sipped his drink.

"Do you come here often?" she asked.

"I've been here once or twice," he said looking around. "I like to mix things up though."

She nodded.

"Listen," he said, "I wanted to apologize for earlier today. When I got the baton out I was just trying to demonstrate my authority over the Serenes. It wasn't meant to be threatening you."

"I didn't take it as that."

"I think your partner did."

She shrugged. "He'll get over it."

He nodded. "So. Two women now. Are you any closer to finding their killer?"

"You think I could tell you if I was?"

He smiled. "I guess not. I hope you sort it out soon, though. It's getting Attis and Remmell all edgy."

"In what way?"

He shrugged. "I don't know. They're worried you think it's one of the Subjugates. They're on edge. You're threatening all they hold dear."

"I'm not threatening anything. Yet." She sipped her drink as he stared at her.

He smiled again. "You're a hard woman to read, Detective."

"So I'm told," she said, then decided to shift his focus. "Do you have any theories about the killer?"

He shrugged and glanced around the bar, his eyes lingering on the couple making out at the sunken table beside them. The woman was now straddling the man, tongues firmly down each other's throats. Bander moved his eyes back to hers.

"You talk to the boyfriend?" he asked.

"Whose boyfriend?"

"Sharon Gleamer's. Tobias Brook. You speak to him?"

Salvi nodded, sipping her drink again.

"Those kids," he said, then paused and smiled, "they're not as holy as they make out."

"What makes you say that?"

He shrugged, wrestling with something he wanted to say.

"I'm all ears," Salvi said, encouragingly.

"Kids these days," he shrugged again, "they're smart. Smarter than we ever were. They find loopholes in everything. Don't get me wrong, they believe in God and being good, but... they've found a way to indulge, but to also *technically* be good."

"What are you talking about?"

Bander studied her. "You heard of U-Stasis?"

Salvi thought for a moment. "Heard of it but don't know much about it. It's a connected AR roleplaying world, right?"

Bander nodded. "Utopia-Stasis is the full name. It's all about creating your own perfect world and making it the norm, you know? Somewhere you can escape to. Some kids access pre-existing worlds and take on grand quests of adventure and puzzle solving, all pretty innocent, but some kids go on there to experiment in stuff they're not allowed to in real life."

"So how do you know about it?"

"I'd heard one of our Subjugates talking about it in his therapy. It's where he used to groom his victims. Then I found out from my brother that my niece had been playing on it. He said she just did dragon quests, but I warned him about what I'd heard. About these virtual drug labs where they can get off their minds without actually physically taking drugs, and then there's these sex rooms where you can do all sorts of things. You need passwords and stuff to access the hardcore areas, but they're easy enough to hack into if you really want. Like I say, kids these days are smart. They got a good hold on technology that we don't have. Well," he shrugged, "I'm alright, 'cause I've worked in security most of my life, so I had to deal with a lot of that stuff. Anyway, I offered to go on there and check it out, make sure my niece wasn't doing something she shouldn't. So, I did."

"And you saw Tobias Brook in there?"

He nodded. "And Sharon Gleamer."

"Don't people use avatars and fake names on those things?"

"Yeah."

"So how do you know it was them?"

"Some people use these rooms to find real dates. After I went on and couldn't find any obvious trace of my niece, I got curious, wanted to see who from Bountiful was on there." He smiled. "Tobias and Sharon were so naïve, they didn't pick randomly assigned avatars, they had ones created from their own likeness and they went by their initials."

"But how could you be so sure it was actually them?"

He smiled again. "I may have done a little hacking to find out their details to be sure."

"Are you admitting to illegal activities, Mr Bander?"

He shrugged. "I was already in that part of the program checking if my niece had any other accounts set up."

"What did you witness them doing? Tobias and Sharon."

"I saw them walking out of one of these rooms holding hands."

"The drug rooms or the sex rooms?"

"Sex. I don't know if they just did a voyeur tour or whether their avatars got involved in stuff there, it was an AR room after all, but they were definitely in there. That's when I realized, these kids, they're liars."

"Why are they liars?"

"Because they claim to be Children of Christ and pure and free from sin, but then they dabble in that stuff on the side."

"Pure?" Salvi questioned his use of words.

"Yeah," he said, staring at her. "They claim to be holier than thou, and think if they don't actually physically touch, then they're not doing anything wrong. So, they go into these rooms and let their avatars do what they can't. Then they pray afterwards and think that makes everything alright. Like it was just impure thoughts or something."

"Isn't that a little hypocritical?" she asked. "You make sure the Serenes and Subjugates toe the line, preaching about God and praying, and good clean lives and clean minds, then you come to a bar like this?"

He smiled again. "And find you here."

She stared back at him. "I'm not preaching about the good Lord and clean living, though, am I?"

Bander shrugged. "All I'm saying, is that Tobias was clearly having impure thoughts about his girlfriend. And for all I know engaging in these thoughts too. Whether she gave him a hand job with a haptic glove or in real life, it's the same thing, isn't it?"

"Tobias having impure thoughts just makes him like any other guy his age," she said. "That doesn't make him a killer. And it doesn't explain the second vic."

"Maybe he got a taste for it? And Sharon was gone, so?"

"Why are you so keen to pin this on Tobias?"

"I'm not," he said. "You asked me for my thoughts and that kid, *the dead girl's boyfriend*, is clearly a liar. I'm just saying you should never judge a book by its cover. You look at the Serenes, see how good they are now, and then you see their past crimes and judge them. Then you look at someone like Tobias Brook, assume he's a good kid because he goes to church, and then you look at what he was doing in his spare time…"

"I judge everyone the same," Salvi said.

"Yeah?"

"Yeah." She smiled. "Everyone's a suspect until they're proven innocent."

"Even me?" he asked, smiling back.

She stared at him, at the white collared polo shirt he wore, tight over his fit physique.

"Yeah," she said, "even you."

Bander nodded, knocking back what was left in his glass. "Does this mean I can't buy you a drink?"

Salvi stared at her empty glass, then looked back at him waiting patiently for her to answer. Her eyes moved to the couple in the sunken table next to theirs, still heavily making out, and maybe even actually having sex if she'd cared to take a closer look. She moved her eyes back to Bander, who was watching them too. He shifted his eyes back to hers.

"I won't tell if you don't," he said with a smile.

She looked at her empty glass again, then at his; saw his hand wrapped around it, the knuckles all rough and rocky like he'd busted them more than once. She pictured him through the bathroom window again, beating the Subjugate with his baton.

"No," she said. "I'm good."

"What, you don't trust me?" he said, amused. "You wanna cuff me or something, for peace of mind? I'm down with that."

"Detective Brentt," she heard Mitch's voice and looked up to see him standing by their table.

"Mitch?" she asked, straightening a little.

He gave her a slightly glaring look, then turned it to Bander. He looked back at Salvi again. "A word? In private."

"She's already having a word with someone," Bander said to Mitch.

Her partner gave Bander a cold, stony look.

Salvi stood, grabbing her jacket. "Thank you, but I'll decide who I have a word with." She looked at Mitch. "Both of you." Then she walked up the steps and straight past him.

As she hit the cold night air outside, she pulled on her jacket, and began heading back for the Cylin. Hurried footsteps sounded, and someone grabbed her arm and turned her around.

"What the hell are you doing?" Mitch asked a little exasperated.

"What the hell are *you* doing?" She pulled her arm out of his grasp.

"What were you doing with Levan Bander? Are you seeing him?" He screwed his face up.

"Seeing him?" She screwed her face up back.

"Well, I don't know, Salvi. I saw you talking outside the church, then find you here together."

"How *did* you find me here?"

"I traced you via the geoloc map in Ford's office."

"You what?!" she asked incredulously.

"What did you expect me to do?" he asked raising his voice. "You disappeared from the wake, wouldn't return my calls. We've got a serial killer on the loose. What did you expect me to do?"

"I can handle myself, Mitch," she said, turning and walking away. Within moments a hand clamped over her mouth and one around her arms and waist, swiftly dragging her into a dark alleyway and slamming her against the wall.

"Can you, Salvi?!" Mitch said angrily.

"Yes!" she hissed, thrusting her gun into his groin. He jerked back and let her go. "You *asshole*!"

"Why didn't you return my calls?" he panted.

"I didn't want to," she said bluntly. "I had enough of you for one day."

Mitch stared at her, catching his breath. "We're partners, Salvi."

"Yeah, we are. Do you remember me taking you home from the bar at 2am?" she asked.

Mitch looked away. "I'm sorry, alright," he said. "It was a hard night... but it's behind me now."

Salvi reholstered her gun. She glanced back to the street, caught her own breath. "Look, I know it was the anniversary, Mitch, but…" She shook her head.

"Yeah, I know." Mitch nodded. "So, what were you doing with Bander?"

"He walked in. I was already there. It wasn't planned," she said. "Besides, it was actually quite useful to talk to him out of uniform."

"Why's that?" he asked, putting his hands on his hips.

"He told me about U-Stasis. Heard of it?"

Mitch shook his head.

"It's an augmented-reality online community," Salvi told him. "Tobias and Sharon were on there. Apparently some seedy stuff can happen in there. I think this is what they were maybe doing when Ellie saw them heading to the SlingShot station."

"Seedy like what?"

Salvi moved away from the wall and rolled her shoulders. "Do we have to go into it now? It's late and I'm tired. Thanks to you."

"Well, I found out some things today too while you were AWOL," Mitch said. "The second vic was the daughter of a close friend of Attis Solme's."

"Rebecca Carson?"

Mitch nodded.

Salvi nodded back. "I found a church here in the city that Solme owns. I saw Kevin Craydon, Tobias' roommate, going in there. The church has BioLume. And it's high-tech. Nothing like the one in Bountiful."

"Solme and BioLume, huh? Let's compare notes."

Salvi looked at her iPort. "Let's do it in the morning when we're fresh."

"You want to get back to drinking?" He motioned back to the club.

"No. Do you?" she challenged.

"No," he said, a little awkwardly. "Last night... won't happen again."

Salvi stared at him, wondering what the comment meant. Did he mean that he wouldn't drink that much again, or was he referring to the moment between them, touching her like he did?

Now Salvi felt awkward.

"Tomorrow," she said. She stepped onto the sidewalk, then stopped and looked back at him. "And don't you *ever* grab me like that again."

"I was trying to prove a point."

"And my gun in your crotch proved mine," she said. "Don't grab me like that again, and don't trace my iPort. I wasn't in trouble. I can handle myself." She turned and began walking again.

"I know you can... *Salvation*," he said.

She halted at his words. Despite the freeze that iced over her, she turned slowly to face him. "What?"

"Salvation Brenttanovich," Mitch said. "That's your real name, isn't it?"

"Wh–" she stuttered. "You've been looking into me?"

Mitch shrugged. "You're a closed book, Salvi. I wanted to know who I was working with, why you were getting so worked up over the preacher like that."

"So you looked into my records?" She screwed her face up at him.

"Why'd you change your legal name?"

"That's none of your *goddamn* business!" she said. She swung back around, ready to storm off toward the Cylin, but spotted an autocab on approach. She rushed out, stepping into its path, forcing it to screech its brakes and come to a stop. The door raised up with a hydraulic hiss, Salvi threw herself inside, then gave a firm voice command for it to drive.

• • •

Salvi's body shook as both anger and shock shot through her. As soon as she was out of sight of Mitch, she ordered the autocab to pull over into a side street. She panted, catching her breath, her hands clutching her knees, the fingers digging in. What the hell had gotten into him, to look up her records? To trace her to the bar? She thought of Hernandez's warning, of her talk with Stan.

She suddenly looked at her iPort. Mitch had traced her to the bar using it. She tapped the screen to access the connectivity portal and shut it down, taking herself offline. She glanced around at the streets surrounding her, wondering what she should do. Why had Mitch been looking into her? Why would he pry into her life like that? Because he was curious about her reaction to Vowker? That couldn't just be it.

As her mind turned over, an idea formed. She ordered the autocab to drive past the Dream Bar again. As it did, she slunk down in the seat, out of sight of the windows, and fixed her eyes to the console monitors displaying the external autocab camera vision. She saw Mitch tapping at his iPort console and the silver glow of his lenses fade out as he climbed into the Raider.

"I want you to follow that car," she ordered the autocab. "License plate SFPD717."

"Do you have authorization for me to do this?" the autocab AI asked.

Salvi tapped her chest and flashed her badge.

"Instructions accepted," the AI replied.

Mitch had been looking into her, now it was time to look into him.

Salvi made the cab follow at a distance, almost losing the Raider once or twice. But she knew it couldn't get too close or Mitch would be onto her. Fear suddenly filled her stomach when she realized he was heading for Bountiful.

The fear turned to staunch curiosity when he pulled up at Bountiful's SlingShot station. She had the autocab cut its lights and pull over a couple of blocks back in the shadows of a large oak tree. Engaging her lenses, she switched to the binocular function and zoomed in on her partner. She watched as Mitch got out of the Raider and sat on the hood as though waiting for something, or someone.

Within minutes the SlingShot arrived. Mitch watched the doors carefully and a single woman in a bright yellow dress stepped off the train. As she walked down the platform to the car park, Mitch said something to her. She moved over to him cautiously and they began talking. After a moment, he slid off the Raider's hood. He hiked his thumb back to the Raider and the woman nodded, then looked around as though making sure no one was watching her. Mitch moved over and popped the doors of the Raider, and they climbed in. Salvi zoomed her vision in closer and saw the woman hold her hand out to him. Mitch looked down into his lap, then passed something to her. Money. The woman counted it, then gave a nod.

A prostitute?

In Bountiful?

Really?

And Mitch with cash? He said he didn't carry any.

He glanced around at his surroundings, but didn't see Salvi or the autocab as he set the Raider in motion and took off.

Salvi sat back in her seat, wondering what to do.

A flash of light revealed a second vehicle as it turned out from a side street up ahead. It was Sheriff Holt. She slunk down further in her seat, but he didn't see her or the autocab in the shade of the oak. Instead, his vehicle was driving away from her, disappearing in the same direction as the Raider.

"If you wish to proceed no further, payment is required,"

the autocab's AI said, breaking the silence.

She looked back at the autocab's console and sighed.

"Take me back to the city."

12: SUBJUGATE-52

Salvi stood out the front of the hub and watched as the sleek black shell of Mitch's Raider headed toward her. She'd just been reading the information Riverton had loaded on their case file, on Solme's Neuricle Corporation. Turns out, Neuricle Corporation had been heavily involved in the neural implant industry prior to the Crash taking place. No wonder he was so invested in getting it back in favor. He would've left a lot money on the table when the Crash occurred.

The Raider came to a stop; she got in and he handed her a coffee.

"Thank you," she said, keeping her eyes front; trying not to think about seeing him with the prostitute, trying not to think of him tracing her iPort or checking her records. Or dragging her into the alley. Whether trying to prove a point or not. Maybe Hernandez was right. Maybe Mitch was unhinged. But then she thought of Beggs' words, of cutting Mitch some slack. The anniversary of his girlfriend's murder had just passed. And now with these murders? That would be enough to set anyone on edge. Who knew what he had seen when he'd found his girlfriend's body. Who knew how the revelation of her cheating had affected him. Maybe these murders were dragging up too many painful memories for him. Salvi knew cops tended to be control freaks. It was their job to find holes in everyone's story and always watch their back – to not trust anyone. Maybe when he traced her iPort he was just being over-protective of his partner. After all, if you weren't loyal to your partner, then what kind of cop were you?

Unless, of course, that partner was actually a criminal.

A criminal who thought nothing of paying a prostitute for her services in a police vehicle, when technically he should've been busting her for street hustling.

But was Salvi any different? She didn't bust the woman in the club for popping the narcotics. She'd been off duty. Mitch had been off duty.

She thought of Stan then, and the key piece of advice he always drilled into her – to use her gut. So, what was her gut telling her about Mitch?

The truth was, right now she didn't know.

Mitch eyed her a moment, then focused his eyes ahead as the Raider headed out of town. "I'm sorry about last night," he said. "Grabbing you like that. I just... you gotta be careful, Salvi. That's all I'm saying."

She looked back at him, a flick of anger on her tongue. "I have to be careful every day of this job, Mitch. That will never change regardless of which perp we're chasing. The same goes for you too, you know."

"Our killer isn't into guys, Salvi."

"He could still kill you if he wants to."

Mitch nodded. "He could, I guess."

Salvi decided to change the topic and began giving him a rundown of what Bander had told her about U-Stasis the previous evening.

"I think we should go in and take a look around," she said, "see who's lurking in there?"

Mitch nodded, his mind ticking over, as an alert sounded on the Raider's console. Salvi tapped the screen, accessing the message.

"DNA from Sharon Gleamer is in," she said.

"Hit me."

Salvi scrolled through the results. "Tobias Brook is negative."

"No surprise there."

"James Stackwell, the neighbor, is negative."

Mitch nodded, then noticed her silence. He looked at her. "And the preacher?"

She stared at the results on the screen a moment, then swallowed and closed the file. "Negative."

Mitch eyed her carefully. "You sound disappointed."

"I am."

"Why? You really wanted it to be him so bad?"

"No, Mitch. Because if it's not any of them, we still got a killer out there."

Mitch clenched his jaw briefly. "What about the DNA of the Serenes and Subjugates? I think we've got enough to check Moses, Dolles and Pragge. They were all in town both days of the murders. Have Riverton check the files Dr Remmell gave us. DNA samples would've been collected upon their arrest."

Salvi tapped her iPort and engaged her lenses. Her eyes frosted over and within moments the AI appeared.

"Detective Brentt," it answered. "How may I help you?"

"Riverton, I need you to run a comparison of the DNA results from the attack on Sharon Gleamer with the criminal files of the Subjugates," she said. "First name is Edward Moses. Arrest made in New York state."

Mitch glanced over at Salvi while she waited for the response.

"Access is denied," Riverton announced.

"What? Dr Remmell gave us access."

"To their criminal files yes, but not to their DNA. There is a DNA suppression order on all residents of the Solme Complex."

"A suppression order?" Salvi said. "You're kidding me. How do we override it?"

"You will need authorization from the Solme Complex. All records now belong to them."

Salvi clenched her fist. "Are you sure there's no other way we can access this information? You're an AI, Riverton."

"I am an AI bound by law, Detective. Without the correct authority I am unable to access this."

"End request." Salvi ended the call.

"What?" Mitch said.

"The Subjugates and Serenes are protected by a DNA suppression order. I'm calling Ford now. See what she can do." Before Mitch could say anything, the call connected and Ford appeared in her lenses.

"Brentt," Ford answered, her eyes narrowed curiously. "What's up?"

"You see the DNA results?"

"Yeah."

"Our main suspects have been ruled out. We need to check the DNA against the Serenes and Subjugates who were in Bountiful the days of the murders, but Riverton can't access them for us."

"I'm not surprised," Ford told her. "It's part of the deal when they enter the Solme Complex. Their criminal record is erased and they cannot be tried for any other priors. They are considered new people and given clean slates when they come out the other end. I was surprised when they gave you a copy of their criminal records, to be honest."

"We've got a killer on the loose, who we think will strike again, and a high probability it was one of them. We need that suppression order overturned."

Ford was quiet a moment. "My hands are tied on the suppression order, there's nothing I can do."

"But–"

"Hear me out, Brentt!" she cut her off. "We can't access the DNA currently on file from their priors, but given the circumstances, we *can* get a warrant for new samples."

"A new warrant takes time."

"It's the best I can do."

Salvi swallowed her anger. "Alright. Any speed you can give it would be appreciated. Thank you." With that, she ended the call.

"Suppression order? New warrants?" Mitch asked.

"We can't access the DNA on file for their priors, but Ford's going to arrange a warrant to obtain new samples for this new crime."

Mitch shook his head. "Meanwhile someone else dies."

Salvi shot him a glance. "Let's hope not."

Silence sat in the Raider for a moment, until Mitch broke it.

"You know," he said, "Attis Solme knew the second victim quite well." They exchanged a glance. "Solme goes to mass at the Children of Christ. So did Sharon Gleamer, so did Rebecca Carson."

Salvi stared out at the road ahead. "Why would Attis risk his Complex? All that he built? All his hard work? He'd know suspicion would fall on the Subjugates."

"Maybe he couldn't help it? Maybe that's why he's so understanding of the monsters he houses. Because he's one himself. Or maybe he just didn't think he'd be caught."

Salvi sipped her coffee, mind turning over. "There was opposition to the Solme Complex being built and not just by some of the residents in town. Attis told me he'd received threats from a nearby survivalist community."

"Yeah, I saw Riverton's notes on Garner Town. But to kill innocent women just for the sake of getting the Complex shut down?" Mitch said. "That's a long shot. Even for those crazy gun-loving survivalists."

"Maybe," she said, "but it's also a motive. But I think if anyone wanted the Complex shut down, it would be someone closer to the situation. Someone in the town itself. Last night in the city, the church I saw, the high-tech one, it was called the Church of Connectivity. It's geared to target all the tech-heads. Attis owns the church, and Kevin Craydon, Tobias' roommate, is working for him."

"So?"

"It has BioLume lighting everywhere. It's across from the SlingShot station."

Mitch shrugged. "He said he was studying to become a teacher so he could spread the word of God. Maybe he's practicing on the tech-heads."

Salvi nodded. "I saw him encouraging some techies inside."

"So? What are you thinking?"

"The Church of Connectivity goes against everything that Bountiful encourages. It considers all that tech sinful, that's why they pulled away from it. And there is Kevin partaking in it, in the city. Dancing with the devil at Attis' request." Mitch glanced at her as she formed her thoughts. "Kevin is Tobias' roommate. He encouraged Tobias and Sharon to go into the city, to help him with the sinners. He would've spent plenty of time with Sharon. Maybe he's the one who tempted Tobias and Sharon into U-Stasis. The Church of Connectivity was offering all these games and apps for Christianity. Maybe he was the doorway that led Sharon online. Maybe it was online that Sharon met her killer. Or maybe Kevin was her killer. Maybe that's the possible love triangle we should be looking at. Not Sharon, Tobias and Ellie."

"Maybe." He nodded. "Or maybe Sharon's killer was mowing her lawn and saw her undress through that open bedroom window of hers."

Salvi stared back at him.

"Besides, it doesn't explain the second vic." Mitch tapped his fingers on the steering wheel. "Only two Subjugates align with the murders of both vics. Lucius Dolles and Edward Moses," he said, staring back at her.

"If we're comfortable ruling out Fontan Pragge and Serene-41. Pragge had similar offences to Moses. He never killed but he raped."

"But with his current mental capability, could he have undertaken these attacks? Both Dolles and Moses were in town around the time both the vics were killed, the crimes fit their previous MO, mostly, and they are both physically and mentally capable."

"Attis would argue that physically and mentally they aren't capable." Salvi looked out at the road ahead again. She pictured the group of Serenes and Subjugates standing clustered out the front of the Sharon's funeral; saw two of them with broken concentration; their heads not lowered, mouths not praying. It was Lucius Dolles and Edward Moses. Dolles watching the dog pissing on the tree. Moses watching her.

"Dolles never killed anyone before," she said. "He had class issues and could, I suppose, have something against these pure women now, but after the treatment he's received I don't see him suddenly turning to murder and carving into those dead bodies."

"Depends how much they were tortured at the Complex. Who knows what that treatment does to their brains, Salvi. Besides, Moses never carved words into his victims either."

"No, but he raped them, then he murdered them. And each crime was different. He cut one's throat. He didn't mind the sight of blood. Neither does our killer."

"Yeah." Mitch nodded. "But that would mean the years of treatment he's had, the brain tweaks, haven't worked."

"Or they've made him worse," she said quietly. "Or he's too smart for his own good and he's playing the system to survive... or seek his revenge upon those who torture him." Mitch stared at her. "Let me go in today," she said.

"What?" he asked.

"Let me interview him."

"Subjugate-52?"

Salvi looked at him. "Yes," she said plainly. "Let's see if I can get a rise out of him. Let's see if I can draw a code blue on that halo of his."

Mitch stared back at her. "That's exactly why they won't let you interview him. You might cause a setback."

"If they've done their job," she said, "then he won't react to me. If they've failed, and he does, then Subjugate-52 will become our prime suspect."

And hopefully, she thought, that will erase Mitch from the list.

"But how did he get away from his escort?" Mitch asked. "The Subjugates always have a Serene escort that stays close."

She shrugged. "Maybe the escort worked outside the house, while Moses went inside. The second vic was a hit and run, remember. The killer worked fast."

"Even if he did it in record time, the Serene wouldn't have left his side."

"Maybe he threatened the Serene? Subjugate-52 is still a little intimidating, don't you think?"

"Maybe," Mitch said.

"Or maybe he threatened the Serene with Bander."

"What do you mean?"

"Last time we were at the Complex, I saw the caretaker in action. In the grounds. He lost his cool and he was beating on a Subjugate pretty bad."

"When did you see this?"

"I went to the bathroom. I heard yelling, climbed up on the bench and looked through the mesh airstrip. I saw the whole thing."

"And you're just telling me this now?"

Salvi shrugged. "I'm sorry. I got out of the bathroom and you were about to interview Moses, then we got the call about the second vic."

Mitch exhaled heavily, eyes narrowed in thought. "I don't care much for Bander, but I got to sympathize with his job. I imagine he'd have to beat on a Subjugate every now and then to keep them in line."

"There's beating them, and then there's *beating* them. He wasn't holding back."

Mitch darted her a glance. "You think it was an accident him running into you at the bar?"

She shrugged. "I don't know," she said, then looked back at the road. "The bar was right by the SlingShot station. It's possible." She looked back at him. "You're thinking he could've done this? He's as adamant as Solme is at protecting the Complex."

Mitch shrugged back and exhaled heavily. "Until we get the new DNA warrants, we can't rule anyone out."

"No," she said. "We can't."

"This is against our policy," Attis Solme said. "I cannot allow it."

"Why can't I?" Salvi asked, as she and Mitch sat in his office. "It's just talking."

Doctor Remmell stood beside them, a slight furrow across his brow. He'd joined the meeting at Attis' behest. "We don't put our Subjugates in situations that may trigger unwanted emotions," he answered for the mayor. "Having you sit there and interrogate him may do that."

"You let the Subjugates into town to interact with women all the time," Salvi argued.

"Yes, with the guards and their Serene escorts," Remmell pointed out.

"There'll be a guard in the room," Salvi said. "And if you like, have the Serene escort there too."

"No," Remmell said, looking at Attis for backup. "Not Subjugate-52."

"Why not?" she pushed.

"He's been doing very well. You will not jeopardize our work on him."

Salvi turned to the mayor. "What are you trying to hide?" she asked firmly.

"Hide?" he asked her with raised eyebrows.

"Why are you so afraid that I will set Edward Moses off? Is he *that* borderline? One conversation with me could set him off?"

"It won't," Remmell said confidently. "I told you when you first came here, that there is no Subjugate we are more proud of."

"Then prove it," Salvi challenged. "Let me talk to him." She turned back to Attis Solme. "I promise to be nice."

Attis stared at her, mind ticking over.

Mitch sat forward. "Both Subjugate-52 and Subjugate-46 were in town on both days our victims were attacked."

"As were many other people in town," Attis told him.

"You want to find the person who killed your friend's daughter?" Mitch asked him.

Attis stared at him. "Of course I do," he said. "But you *won't* find him here."

"Then let me speak to Subjugate-52," Salvi said. "Let me erase all doubt and prove that the Solme Complex is doing good things. That your treatment works."

Attis looked back at her. "And if I don't?"

She shrugged. "Then you're obstructing a murder investigation."

"I'm not obstructing anything." Attis stared at her with cold eyes, the normally pleasant smile falling from his face. "I've told you, Detective Grenville can interview him."

"Mayor Solme–" Salvi began, but he cut her off.

"I wouldn't say any more if I were you, Detective. You're already *this* far away from me making a complaint to the

Chief of Police. I'm more connected than you think I am."

"And what would you make a complaint about?" Salvi said. "Me doing my job, trying to catch a killer."

"My Subjugates are not killers! Not any more."

"Then prove it."

"This is borderline harassment and I won't stand for it," Attis said. "Especially coming from officers of your stature."

"Excuse me?" Salvi said.

Attis looked at Mitch. "Surely you of all people would understand what it's like to be accused of something you did not do, Detective."

Mitch's eyes narrowed as he looked back at him.

"Yes, that's right. I'm capable of undertaking investigations too," Attis said, then looked at Salvi. "And you, Detective. You're a particularly interesting one."

"As are you," Mitch countered. "Would you like to tell us about your church in the city?"

Attis paused, staring at him. Dr Remmell glanced between both men, seemingly unaware of what Mitch was referring to. So Remmell didn't know...

"The Church of Connectivity," Salvi said. "It's incredibly high-tech, with a robo-preacher and all. Doesn't that go against your way of life here in Bountiful? To embrace all that technology?"

"Look around you, Detective. I embrace technology here at the Complex," he said in a low, almost threatening voice. "I make no secret of that."

"Yes," Salvi said, "and now you're embracing it in the city and drawing in all the tech-heads. Why is that?"

"I'm a religious man, spreading the word of God. You know that."

"Yes, apparently so. But you're also a businessman. I know you're keen to get neural implants back on the market. You've been testing things out here with the Subjugates' halos. But they're criminals. No one cares about them. Your work is still very much underground. You want to widen the scope, don't you? And if you can clear the tech-heads off the street, give them what they want – technology – then convince them to trial the neural implants that your company Neuricle Corporation is working on... Just imagine how many faces you can turn to God if you can control their minds."

"Is it such a bad thing if I clean up the streets? Get people to believe in something other than themselves?"

"It depends how much mind control you plan to implement. A whole city full of Serenes scares me a little to be honest. Especially while you're sitting back and getting rich off all the implant sales and your slave labor."

Remmell continued to dart glances between the two. "We're getting off track."

"What I'm doing in the city is no business of yours, Detective," Attis said, ignoring him. "I am doing nothing illegal."

"Does Kevin Craydon know what you're really up to?" she asked. "He's working for you, right?"

Again, Attis stared at her for a moment. "Kevin is a devout follower of God. It is his wish to bring more people to our way of life. Again, he is doing nothing illegal."

"Not illegal, no. But how does Preacher Vowker feel about Kevin hanging out in the city among all that sin, dancing with the devil? Encouraging the tech-heads to embrace all those Christianity apps and games? I particularly like the one where you encourage players to punish sinners with lashes and nails through their body parts."

Attis offered no reply.

"Vowker doesn't know, does he?" Salvi said.

"Preacher Vowker knows that I do not shy away from technology. If I did, he wouldn't have all my Serenes helping his Children of Christ, would he?"

"For a fee, yes." She motioned to her iPort. "Our AI has also done some investigation, Mr Solme. I know that the residents of Bountiful donate a large portion of their income to the Children of Christ. In return they get the free labor of the Serenes and Subjugates. You make out like they're doing free community service, but you're skimming your cut off the top. Preacher Vowker gets the lion's share, though, and the free workers are a draw card, luring more and more Christians to move to Bountiful. More faithful residents, more money. You don't just get them to hand over their souls, their very freedoms, but their wallets too."

"That's something for you to speak to Preacher Vowker about."

"You both benefit, Mr Solme. He gets rich, and you get to use Bountiful as a testing ground for your neural implants. But you're a businessman and progress must be too slow for you. That's why you're branching out into the city, wanting to start testing on the desperate tech-heads. I don't think you like the preacher holding you back. Do you get a secret satisfaction from taking Kevin into the city and telling him to embrace the technology that Vowker tells him to avoid? Tell me, were Tobias Brook and Sharon Gleamer working for you too?"

"I don't see how this is relevant."

"Sharon Gleamer is dead. So is Rebecca Carson. We need to explore every avenue of possibility. If Sharon was playing around with technology on your behalf, that may have exposed her to a killer."

"I thought you suspected Subjugate-52?"

"As I said, we need to explore every avenue."

"The Church of Connectivity is purely an avenue to God. And Subjugate-52 is soon to be a Serene. Both avenues are closed."

"Not until we say so," Mitch spoke up. "You can let us go in and speak to Subjugate-52 today or we will come back with a warrant... and anything else we dig up."

Attis' mind toiled as he stared back at them. The man's face was tight. It was clear he was working hard to hold down his anger. "I'll be speaking with Detective Lieutenant Ford about this."

"As will we," Mitch said.

"You think she's going to be able to do anything about it?" Attis smiled.

"Yes. She has connections too, Mr Solme," Mitch said.

"Yes, and she also has a past, Detective. A past, that if it came to light, would see her lose her job. A past that only I am privy to. Her career depends on me keeping her confidence." He leaned across the table toward them. "So, you see, that avenue is closed also."

"Did you just openly admit to possibly blackmailing Detective Lieutenant Ford?" Mitch asked, tapping his badge. "That's not very Christian of you."

"We all work toward the greater good," he said, sitting back in his chair. "It is God's will."

"It's not God's will," Salvi said. "People who say that are looking for a reason to excuse something terrible. To shirk responsibility. We are all responsible for our own actions and the consequences born of them."

"Tell that to Detective Lieutenant Ford."

The silence sat as they stared at each other and Doctor Remmell continued to dart his eyes back and forth between them nervously.

"I think I've made my position clear," Attis said. "I am a Christian man, and I am also a businessman. A strong man. I do not bow or break at others' commands."

"Whatever you say," Mitch said. "Now back to Subjugate-52. You'll let Detective Brentt interview him, yes?"

Doctor Remmell moved uneasily at Attis' silence. "Mayor Solme," he spoke up. "I highly object to thi–"

"Look, I believe you!" Salvi said, leaning forward to Attis, trying to convey to him her passion. "We may not see eye to eye on things, but I honestly believe you might be fixing them here. But we need proof of that. Let me talk to Moses. Help me clear his name from our suspects list. Show me what a good job you've done."

"Mayor Solme," Remmell began. "I–"

Attis threw his hand up in the air to hush him. He stared at Salvi for a moment, his mind ticking over.

"Show me how strong your faith is," she said. "Show me how you've turned these monsters back into men."

The silence sat again for a moment, before Attis finally moved. "Doctor Remmell," he said, his hard eyes fixed on Salvi, "allow Detective Brentt an audience with Subjugate-52."

Salvi and Mitch walked down the tubular corridor awash in the soft green BioLume glow. Headed for the interview room, Doctor Remmell stalked ahead angrily, not trying to hide his displeasure at Attis' decision.

Mitch leaned over to her and whispered. "Do you actually believe what you said to Solme?"

"No. Not yet," she said, subtly unbuttoning the top of her white shirt. Just a little. Just enough to enable Subjugate-52 to see her décolletage. Mitch caught what she did, his eyes glancing between the top of her unbuttoned shirt and her face.

"Visual stimuli," she whispered. "Let's call it a live test."

She glanced back at Mitch, and they walked onward like nothing happened.

When they arrived at the interview room, Serene-41 opened the door for her, and she exchanged one last glance with Mitch before they separated.

She took a seat at the table and waited while Serene-41 stood in the corner silently.

She studied him, the subservient geisha-like man; pale-skinned, eyes lowered, softly spoken. The silver halo wrapped around the back of his skull.

"Do you go into town, Serene-41?"

Remaining still, only his eyes traveled to look at her. "Yes, Detective."

"Every single day?"

"Yes. Every day."

"We're not recording!" Remmell's angry voice sounded over the speakers.

Salvi looked around at the mirrored window. "So, record me." She turned back to Serene-41. "How come you get to go into town every day, Serene-41?"

He gave a pleasant smile. "I am graduated, Detective. I do good things and I'm their most trustworthy Serene. It is my job to guide the others. I am the Serene-Supreme."

"Serene-Supreme…"

A thumping sounded against the mirrored window. Salvi glanced at it, then back at Serene-41, who had lowered his eyes to the ground again.

"It's OK, you may speak," she told him. "I give you permission, Serene-41. You guide the others. Other Serenes or the Subjugates?"

"Both," he said pleasantly, raising his eyes again.

"And how do you guide them?"

"Detective Brentt!" Remmell hissed again.

The Serene paused, his eyes darting to the mirror, unsure as to what to do.

She nodded to him. "Please continue, Serene-41."

The Serene hesitated, unsure. Salvi gave him a warm smile.

"I show them what to do and where to go," he said. "I check up on them and make sure everything is as it should be." He lifted his beige tunic and showed her a security pass that sat attached to the top of his beige trousers. "I am entrusted with access to the Complex."

Salvi stared at the pass. "So, you could come and go as you please from the Complex?"

Serene-41 thought for a moment, looking as though he'd never considered the idea. "Yes, I suppose I could. But it is too far to walk into town."

"Has anyone ever asked to use your pass?"

"No. I would never give it out."

"You've never lost or misplaced the pass?"

"Never. It is with me at all times. I am the Serene-Supreme."

Salvi studied him. "When you're in town, do you guide Subjugates-52 and 46?"

"Yes. Sometimes."

"And how do you think they're doing, Serene-41?"

"They are making good progress. We are very proud of them."

"What do they do when you're with them?"

The door opened, and Bander entered with Moses. The caretaker paused upon seeing her.

"What are you doing in here?" he asked a little bluntly.

She smiled. "I'm here to speak with Subjugate-52."

Bander glanced over to the window, before moving the Subjugate into his seat. He turned back to the window. "This was approved?" he asked the mirror.

"We can't hear you!" Remmell's tetchy voice came over the speakers. "You need to fix the system!"

"Again?" Bander glared at the window, then exhaled heavily. He moved over to the table in front of Salvi and pressed the on/off button on the console. "Can you hear me now?"

"Still nothing," Remmell's voice responded. "It's not a system lockout. I checked. The fault must be in there."

Bander looked at Salvi, the relaxed face of the night before long gone, and the pissed-off guard firmly in its place.

"Excuse me," he said, motioning that he needed to get under the table. Salvi stood and moved out of the way, glancing at Moses as she did. The Subjugate sat there still and silent. And serene. His skin was pale, but she could just make out the outline of where he shaved, halfway down his thick neck. A neck that sat atop broad, strong shoulders. Although not as broad or strong as they had once been, but broad enough. She tried to picture him in his former life: as a lawyer in a suit, or the narcissistic gym fanatic in some sweats. Or the murderer raping and killing innocent women. She could see how he would've gotten close to his victims. The handsome Moses with some added, albeit fake, charm. Many women would fall prey to that, be fooled into a position they didn't realize they'd been put in until it was too late. Until the facade dropped and the killer stood before them.

The question was, is that what Moses was doing now? Presenting a facade? Pretending to be Serene while the devil still lay within waiting to come out?

She struggled to comprehend why a man with a good job, a nice body and a handsome face, who probably could've had any woman he wanted, would turn into the brutal raping killer that he had. According to his criminal file, his excuse was that he'd simply been bored. He was bored of getting everything he wanted all the time. He wanted to have to fight for it. To earn it. To win it. So, he made his victims fight him. Fight for their life, for their survival. And he would take it from them. He would fight them, and he would win, stating that he'd never felt so alive. And, of course, it had been the fault of his victims for their own death. Not his. The women, he'd said, had literally flirted with death. Moses, with his high IQ, enjoyed the hunt, he enjoyed outsmarting his victims. So, was that what he was doing now?

Bander came out from under the table and smacked the microphone button hard. "Now?" he asked.

"Perfect, Caretaker," Remmell answered calmly and lightly, as though reminding Bander to be the same.

"The devices seemed to get turned off quite a bit, don't they?" Salvi commented. "That must make it difficult to record what happens in here."

The caretaker glanced her way, but virtually ignored her, moving to stand by the door.

"You may begin," Remmell's voice sounded.

"Thank you." She flashed a big smile at the mirror, catching sight of her bright red lips, which she then turned to Moses.

"Subjugate-52, I'm Detective Brentt. I want to ask you some questions about what you do when you're in Bountiful."

"Yes, Detective," he said with that deep, refined voice.

"How long have you been traveling into Bountiful now?" she asked, keeping her face light and friendly.

"I'm not sure," he answered. "We do not believe in tracking time at the Complex. They are all God's days and we serve without question."

"Ten weeks," Bander answered for him. "He's been going in ten weeks."

Salvi nodded and looked back at Moses.

"And you attend church?" she asked.

"Yes," he said, giving a slight bow. "Every Sunday."

"And that's the only time you go to the Children of Christ?"

"To the church, yes. But we do attend the Children of Christ hall for other things."

"Such as?"

"We attend their Bible studies. We help the preacher when they have fairs, and we help their charity groups."

"Do you like going there? To the Children of Christ?"

"Yes. Very much."

"Who else goes to this Bible studies group? Is it just for Subjugates?"

"No, the townspeople go too. They share their stories with

256   THE SUBJUGATE

us, of how they found God."

"I see. Did you ever see Sharon Gleamer there?" Salvi asked. "She was young, pretty, blonde?"

Bander's eyes flicked to hers. A silent warning.

"Yes. I remember her," Moses answered.

Salvi studied the Subjugate a moment. He was the first one to recognize the vic by name. The others had to be shown a holo. "Did you talk to her?"

"Yes. She was a nice person."

"What about Rebecca Carson?"

Moses gave her a blank look.

"She went to the church," she said projecting a holo of Rebecca Carson from her iPort. "Have you see her around?"

"Yes," Moses replied, eyes fixed on the hologram. "I've seen her at church, and sometimes in the hall with the charity groups."

Salvi nodded, studied his face; his dark blue eyes, his square jaw, his full lips. "Did you know these two women were now dead?"

Bander cleared his throat and glanced at her; a warning to watch her step, as Moses marked a sign of the cross upon himself.

"I knew that Sharon had passed, yes," Moses answered frankly. "I attended her funeral. But I did not know about Miss Carson. I am sorry for your loss."

"I didn't know them," Salvi said. She pulled her arm back then placed her elbows up on the table and leaned forward, a move that pushed her cleavage together and offered Moses a view. "How did they seem to you?" she asked. "What kind of women were they?"

"I don't understand what you mean," Moses said, looking her in the eyes, seemingly oblivious to the top of her opened shirt.

"Did they seem like nice girls?" she asked, tilting her head to the side and biting her bottom lip.

The Subjugate's eyes looked down to her lip but returned just as quickly to her eyes. His face remained impartial. "Yes," he said. "They were Children of Christ."

"So, you never saw them with bad people?"

"No." Moses seemed to study her back. "Why do you ask this of me?"

"Well," Salvi said, "the way they died–"

A gentle musical chime suddenly sounded and a bright red light began flashing beneath the Subjugate's beige uniform shirt. Moses looked down at it.

Bander stepped forward.

"What is that?" Salvi asked, looking at the light pulsing and glowing beneath Moses' uniform.

"His personal alarm. It's time for his injection." Bander checked his watch.

"What injection?" she asked.

"The injection that helps keeps him serene," Bander said.

"We have two a day," Moses told her calmly. "They are crucial to our wellbeing. This must be attended to."

Bander motioned for him to get up. Moses did, standing taller and broader than the caretaker. Which was saying something, because Bander wasn't exactly small.

"Move!" Bander ordered and Subjugate-52 left the room with his Serene escort and Bander in tow.

Salvi sighed, annoyed her interview had been cut short. She wondered if Attis had planned it this way, knowing she wouldn't have long with Moses before he'd need to leave for his shot. She needed more time. She'd gotten nothing from the Subjugate during it. From what she could tell, he didn't seem to react to her at all. He glanced down at the biting of her lip, but it was a natural reaction. Had anyone else been sitting in Moses' place, they probably would've done the same thing.

She stood from the table and headed for the exit. Mitch met her at the door and was about to say something, when his iPort signaled an incoming call. He engaged his lenses and the silver shimmer swam across his eyes as he turned and started walking down the corridor, answering the call. Salvi went to follow, but a hand clasped tightly on her arm jerking her back. It was Remmell.

"I saw what you did!" he hissed, looking down at the open top of her shirt. "That's entrapment!"

"Yeah, it was," she told him. "And would you look at that, he passed." She jerked her arm out of his grasp.

"You ought to be ashamed of yourself," he said, looking her up and down with disgust.

Salvi gave him an unaffected stare in return, then moved off down the corridor.

Mitch ended the call and turned to her with a look of dread on his face.

"That was Ford. We got another vic."

Mitch pulled the Raider up in front of the third vic's house. Salvi got out and surveyed the surrounding streets. Nice, well-maintained houses and manicured gardens. She caught staring faces in windows, but they vanished upon being seen. No one was on the street. Fear had now gripped the community.

"It's close to the center of town," Mitch said. "Just like the others."

"Yeah," Salvi said, glancing about.

"Walking distance for the Subjugates and Serenes."

They exchanged a look as they approached the steps of the small duplex house, engaging the cameras on their badges. Salvi heard crying and turned to see a small boy in the arms of a pale-faced woman, who sat in the back of an officer's car, trying to console him. An officer stood close by and Salvi guessed this must've been the person to have found their third vic.

With names checked and coveralls and gloves on, Sheriff Holt met them at the doorway to the vic's abode.

"It's one of ours?" Mitch asked him.

Holt nodded, leading them through to the body. "She's got 'pure' cut across her, but it's been crossed out. This one was a sinner." They entered the vic's living room and saw the body lying on the floor covered in a sheet. "Carly Fresner, thirty-two. Bountiful's dirty little secret. Also Bountiful's worst kept secret." He made his way over to the body and lifted the sheet. "She's a known prostitute."

Salvi paused when she saw the torn bright yellow dress the woman wore.

It was the same woman she'd seen getting into Mitch's Raider the night before.

The back of her head was red with blood; part of her skull had caved in. She obviously died from severe head trauma. Salvi looked up at Mitch and saw him silently reeling, eyes wide. He looked like she felt. Like the blood had just run out of him.

"Something wrong?" Holt asked, studying Mitch carefully.

"No," Mitch said quickly. "No, I… show me the carving."

Like Rebecca Carson, this woman was lying face down, her dressed pulled up around her waist. Holt lifted her body up and back with gloved hands. They saw the front of her yellow dress had been sliced open all the way, and there carved into her belly was the word "pure". Although as Holt had said, a line had been carved across it as though canceling it out.

Salvi looked back at Mitch. He looked like he was struggling to breathe, like someone had punched him in the gut. He turned his back to them and began to look around the apartment as though searching for clues, but Salvi knew he wasn't really looking at anything.

Her eyes fell back down to the body as Holt lowered it to the ground again. She felt herself breaking out in a sweat as her heart kicked double time. She forced her mouth to move. "You moved the body again," she said to Holt. "To see the carving, you moved the body again."

He glared at her. "I wore gloves and the movement was minimal. I know what I'm doing. You may be running this investigation, but this is my town. These are my people. I got a right to know what's going on."

She remembered seeing Holt driving after Mitch the previous evening. Did Holt know?

"Who else has contaminated the site?" she said. "Who placed the sheet on her?"

"Just the neighbor. She found her," he said. "She was babysitting Fresner's son. Fresner didn't come to collect him when she was supposed to, so the neighbor brought the son back about an hour ago and found her."

Salvi glanced at Mitch again. His eyes were fixed on the floor, searching around aimlessly, his mind clearly racing. He suddenly engaged his lenses and the silver sheen washed over his eyes. "Riverton? How far away are forensics? Yeah … Alright." He ended the call and glanced at her. "Ford's got 'em on the SlingShot. They'll be here soon."

She nodded, then scanned the room. "It would be risky to attack her with the neighbors so close," she said, darting her eyes to Mitch, who now stood by the window looking out into the street, his back still turned.

"Unless he did that to her head first," Holt said. "There'd be no sounds of struggle then."

"The side window looks tampered with," Holt said, standing up again. "Looks like he got inside that way."

Salvi looked around for evidence of a struggle. The furniture didn't look disturbed, but she saw visible blood splatter and possibly skull fragments. He mostly likely subdued her quickly.

"No sign of the weapon that did that to her skull?" Salvi asked.

"Not that I can tell," Holt said. "Must've took it with him. I'm sure your forensics team will tell us what it was soon enough," he said, throwing Mitch another glance, then he gave a huff of a laugh, though it contained no humor. "Hell, they might as well just stay here in town, the way things are going."

"If everyone knew she was a prostitute, why was she allowed to live here?" Salvi asked.

Holt shrugged. "Because she went to church every Sunday. Vowker likes the sinners. He likes the challenge of converting them, I guess. He's the one that OKed her to move here."

Salvi stared at Holt, then turned her eyes to stare at Mitch's turned back.

"Anyway," Holt said. "I'll get back to canvassing the neighbors." He eyed Mitch again, then walked back out of the apartment. "Let you know what I find out."

Salvi watched him go. Alone with Mitch and the dead body, she stood frozen. She looked from Fresner's dead body to Mitch's turned back, heart still thumping against her chest. Should she mention what she saw last night? Did she admit she'd followed him? Should she get in first, before Holt did? But what if Holt hadn't seen anything?

Besides, so what if he slept with her? Why would she pay to have sex with her, then attack her? Unless he took his money back afterward?

Silence filled the room and still Mitch didn't move. Salvi looked back at Fresner's bashed-in skull.

"He's getting more violent and more frequent," she said, heart and hands rattling. "Sharon was strangled, Rebecca had her neck broken, and this one... her head smashed in. He's getting more aggressive. He's getting angrier... Or he's growing in confidence and enjoying it more... I don't know which one is worse."

Mitch eventually turned around to face her. His skin was pale, as he clenched and unclenched the gloved hands that rested by his sides. "She's against type," he said softy. "She's not pure."

"Neither was Sharon Gleamer," Salvi said, as a sudden thought struck her. "I bet if we look harder into Rebecca Carson, we might find that she wasn't so pure either."

Mitch locked eyes with her and nodded.

"I'll process the scene," she said carefully, wanting Mitch away from it. "You go make sure Holt's canvassing our witnesses correctly."

Mitch gave a silent nod, face still pale, then left.

13: U-STASIS

Salvi sat in the passenger seat of the Raider, eyes fixed on the road ahead, willing the car to get them to their city hub as soon as possible so she could get out. Her body still felt frozen. She kept seeing the prostitute's yellow dress, kept seeing the woman get inside Mitch's car.

Sitting right where she was now.

Salvi subtly glanced down at the leather seats, wondered if he'd had sex with her in this very car. Wondered if he'd killed her in this very car. Was there evidence? Blood?

She recalled taking Mitch home when he was drunk. Remembered that he had BioLume lighting. And the morning the second vic had been reported, when she'd woken him at the motel, he'd had that long scratch down his back.

Could she really be sitting next to the Bountiful Killer?

She pulled up her iPort, engaged her lenses and called Kim Weston, whom they'd left at the scene.

"Detective Brentt," she answered.

"Dr Weston, any traces of BioLume yet?"

"Not yet, but I'm looking. I'll let you know if something comes up."

"Thanks. Did you find out how long the BioLume lasts outside of the globes?"

"I'm still waiting on the Solme Complex to get back to me on that. I'll follow them up again."

"Thanks," Salvi said and hung up. She noticed Mitch was staring at her.

"I want to see if he left his footprints again." She recalled Mitch comparing his shoe to the prints in the Gleamer house. They were a similar size.

Mitch nodded and looked back at the road. His face was still a little pale, his jaw clenching and unclenching. His knuckles white as they gripped the steering wheel. He looked nervous. On edge.

But as Salvi thought about it, she realized this reaction from him was new...

He hadn't acted like this after any of the other vics. If he had killed all of them, why would his reaction to this one be so different?

And what possible connection could he have with them? He didn't go to church, wasn't religious in any way. As far as she could tell he had nothing against those who practiced religion, nor women who liked to have sex. Wasn't he always telling her to live a little? And if he was going to rape and murder women, wouldn't he just do it in the city? Why drive all the way out here?

Unless he caught the SlingShot.

But the SlingShot had cameras. Mitch wouldn't be that stupid.

She suddenly wondered if he had a personal vehicle. She'd only ever seen him in the Raider, but that didn't mean he didn't have another car to drive around in.

But still, why Bountiful? Here in Bountiful, Mitch would be a stranger in a small community with less anonymity. The city would be safer to stalk victims.

Or would it? Bountiful didn't have drones watching the streets. And Mitch was a cop. He would know how to get away with murder.

She glanced over at him again. His eyes were still staring at the road ahead, his knuckles still white as they gripped the steering wheel. He was freaking out but trying to hide it. That much was clear. If he'd actually killed Fresner, would he be acting like this? She'd seen the look on his face when he saw the body. This had come as a surprise to him. A shock.

Or was he just surprised by what he'd done? Some killers claimed to have blackouts, to not remember the things they'd done. Was this happening to Mitch now?

Maybe he'd had sex with her, then he'd gotten drunk and attacked her. Maybe his mind had blanked out what he'd done. But there would be defensive wounds. She glanced subtly at his neck, his hands. Nothing.

She looked back at the road ahead, Stan's words swirling about in her mind, telling her to trust her instinct.

And the truth was she was finding it hard to believe that Mitch had done this.

But was that just because he was her partner? Was it just because she didn't want to believe that she'd missed the signs? That these women's deaths had been her fault because she couldn't tell it was her own partner?

Or was it something else.

Could she not believe it was Mitch because she felt sympathy for him? For his girlfriend's murder? For him being so screwed up? Because Salvi identified and understood what it was like to be so screwed up and yet somehow functioning. Because the sympathy she felt was actually empathy.

Or did it run even deeper than that?

She pictured Mitch running his hand over her cheek again, his thumb parting her lips. Did she have feelings for Mitch that went past partners? Past friends even? Is that why she didn't want to believe it was him? Was she letting her hormones get in the way of her gut? Was she letting an attraction to Mitch cloud her judgment?

Had she been fooled, seduced, just like the victims of

Edward Moses had been?

She closed her eyes and turned her face to the passenger window.

No, it couldn't be Mitch. He'd just slept with the prostitute and now he was in a panic because his DNA might be found on the body. That's it. It had to be.

Didn't it?

Could she be so certain about a man she hardly knew?

She remembered their argument the night before, of him grabbing her and dragging her into the alley. He said he was just trying to make a point, but what would he have done if she hadn't pulled her gun on him?

Was he really just being a control freak, concerned for her safety? Was he really just trying to prove a point? Or was it something else? Was he trying to prove dominance over her? Had he been jealous at seeing her at the club with Levan Bander? Had he taken it out on the prostitute?

She recalled seeing the prostitute walk out of the SlingShot, saw Mitch waiting on the hood of his car for her.

The SlingShot … that silvery snake of sin, luring the devil to Bountiful.

"Stop!" Salvi said. "Turn around."

"What?" he said.

"We need to go to the SlingShot station."

"Why?"

"Riverton just confirmed Fresner was spotted on the Slingshot last night," she lied.

"When did Riverton tell you this?" he asked.

"Just now."

"I never heard a message come through."

"Well it did. So turn around and let's go to the SlingShot." She stared out at the road ahead. "Besides, I want to know what Tobias and Sharon were really doing down there."

• • •

They pulled up at the SlingShot station in virtually the same location Mitch had the previous evening. She saw him eye the security camera on the platform nervously as they approached it. From the positioning, it would've captured Fresner getting into the Raider. That would not bode well for Mitch.

A large digital clock told them the time until the next train into the city. In five minutes a southbound SlingShot would arrive.

Salvi walked along the platform until she reached the arcade game outlet. She stepped inside and began walking along the rows of retro games in the form of pinball machines and racing cars.

"Can I help you?" a thin man, maybe 5'10 and 80 pounds, with a crucifix pin on his lapel asked.

Salvi glanced around the store again. "Can I access any connected games or sites from here?"

"Oh, no." He shook his head. "We don't allow that in here. The station is still in the community limits of Bountiful, so no connectivity games are allowed. We just have good old-fashioned isolated, *clean*, games here."

Salvi heard the warning signal of the SlingShot on approach. "Thank you."

When she stepped back outside, Mitch's eyes were silver. He glanced at her, then quickly ended his call.

"Anything?" he asked.

Salvi shook her head. "No. There's no connectivity here. Sharon and Tobias must've accessed U-Stasis on the SlingShot or in the city."

They watched as the SlingShot pulled into the station. No one exited, but they stepped aboard and flashed their badges to the SlingShot's AI driver console, requesting access to the cabin security footage. They got their clearance to watch the footage, but the SlingShot AI would not halt the train while they did so. The SlingShot system prided itself on a fast and reliable service, so they would not delay things now. Salvi and Mitch were going to have to ride into the city and jump the next SlingShot back to Bountiful whether they liked it or not.

As the SlingShot pulled out from Bountiful station, they had Riverton lock into the footage and they watched on their lenses. They located Fresner and watched her journey. She stepped aboard at the city station and rode the twenty-minute journey alone reading an old paperback book.

"Riverton?" Salvi asked.

"Yes, Detective?" it answered.

"Find out where in the city she was working. It must've been at a proper establishment. She didn't look like a street walker."

"Yes, Detective. Would you like me to obtain access to the station footage also?"

Salvi saw Mitch tense up.

"Why don't you do that?" Salvi told Mitch. After all, she'd already seen it, and she didn't want to give her hand away just yet. "I'm going to take a look around the SlingShot.

Mitch gave a nod. However, the tension in his body didn't dissipate, and he kept his eyes fixed on her as she walked away.

Salvi passed through several seated cabins until she found the recreation cabins: a small bar cabin, a silent reading cabin, and a gamer cabin where Salvi spotted AR consoles – the kind required to enter something like U-Stasis. But they were out in the open among the other consoles. From what she'd heard about these sex rooms, private AR console enclosures would be required. She couldn't see Tobias and Sharon openly doing something like that here. Not when someone from town could witness them.

When Salvi found Mitch again, he looked agitated.

"See anything of interest?" she asked him, watching him carefully.

He shook his head.

"Riverton didn't pick up anyone using facial scans?" she asked.

Again he shook his head. "No. I had Riverton focus on locating Fresner's place of work and trying to identify a client list. I checked the footage. It was clear." He locked eyes a moment, then averted his gaze. "We need to see if anyone from Bountiful was on her client list."

Salvi nodded as the SlingShot began to pull into the city. She looked out the window, trying to wrap her head around the fact that Mitch had just blatantly lied to her. How long did he think he could hide the fact that he had been with Fresner the night before she died? It was only a matter of time before Riverton would scan the footage out of procedure anyway and make notations in their case file. She knew too well that circumstantial evidence did not mean guilt but lying about it only complicated matters. Mitch knew this too, so why was he doing it?

She watched the people moving about on the city platform, scurrying like ants, rushing to their next destination. The stores along the platform all seemed to be doing well from the commuter trade. She saw a Kittson's drugstore, a whole chain grocery store, a couple of cafés and bars, a gift store specializing in games ... and right there next to it, was a specialist store for tech experiences, called AdventureLand. It was basically a nice name for a tech-sex store. She noticed a sign in the window advertising private AR lounges.

"Mitch," she straightened. "We need to get off."

"What?" he asked, the edginess still clear on his face.

"Private lounge." She pointed. "I bet that's where Tobias and Sharon were going. Come on." She turned for the exit.

"What about the Raider?"

"We'll get it afterwards."

• • •

Salvi stepped off the SlingShot and made her way toward the store, zigging and zagging among the commuters as the smell of coffee and spiced croissants filled her senses, making her stomach rumble.

"Salvi," Mitch said, jogging to catch up, though his words were drowned out by a station announcement. "We don't have time for this now."

"We need to see what they were doing in there," she called over her shoulder.

"What Sharon and Tobias were doing in there is irrelevant if we can't tie it to the others."

"So, have Riverton do a search." She turned to him as the neon pink lights of AdventureLand bathed them both, blinking in time with her heartbeat. "See if the others had accounts on U-Stasis."

Salvi stepped inside the store and approached the counter, where a short, tubby guy wore a full VR headpiece and held his hand out in the air, swishing it this way and that, as though he were painting a masterpiece.

"I'm interested in your private AR lounge," she said interrupting him.

The guy flipped the lens part of his headpiece up and pointed to a second counter at the back of the building. Salvi gave him a nod as Mitch entered the store, silver sheen fading from his eyes as he ended the call with Riverton.

"It's working on the warrants we need to access the information," he told her.

"Good," she said and moved to the second counter at the back of the store where an older woman with several face piercings sat reading a 3D book. Salvi saw galloping unicorns and some warrior charging its sword. The woman behind the counter looked up as they approached and closed the book down, making the unicorns and warrior disappear.

"What can I do you for?" she asked with a voice that

suggested she vaped too much.

"What have you got?" Salvi said.

"Just about everything," she said, bringing up a clear screen that displayed the menu of services in bright orange text.

"Salvi," Mitch said coming to stand beside her and looking back at the door eager to leave.

"Can we get access to U-Stasis?" Salvi asked the woman. "The sex rooms."

"Sure," the woman said, and motioned to Mitch, "you want a twofer?"

Salvi held still a moment, then looked at her partner. Mitch was looking around the store, but his eyes came back to her, questioning.

"Yes," Salvi told the woman. "Access for both of us. Together." She wanted to take Mitch inside U-Stasis, and she wanted to watch him like a hawk.

"Sure thing," the woman tapped the screen. "You want to get in on the action or just voyeur mode?"

"Will voyeur mode allow us to see in all rooms?" Salvi asked.

"Some of 'em. But it depends on the other users. If they've marked their activity as no voyeur, then you can't see 'em. I'd suggest you take one of our action packages. We got four modes. *Straight* action, will be you and your man here, getting it on alone in a room of your choice. *High Voltage* action will be you and your man getting it on and people stopping by to watch. *XXX* action will be you and your man getting it on and other people joining in. And the fourth level is an all-access action pass, which means you can do what you want to anyone else with the same access."

"Anything we want?" Salvi asked.

The woman nodded. "Depends what floats your boat. The only thing that's illegal is doing children or animals. We don't have programs for that. Although if you really want that, if you look hard enough there's places out there that will cater for that. Under the counter, you know what I mean."

"I'm good," Salvi said holding up her hand to stop the woman, glad their coats covered their badges. She made a mental note to report that to the cyber unit later. "When you say anything goes... could you rape and murder someone in there?"

The woman looked at her, then at Mitch. "Murder, no. As for the rest, it's anything goes. When you set up your avatar you can set the rules. There's no 'don't rape me' option, but there is a 'I like it rough option.' Read into that what you will."

"So, you can beat someone around in there?" Mitch asked, stepping closer, suddenly more interested.

The woman nodded, looking between the two. "If that's what you want. You just get an all-access pass, set your parameters, which would be you," she looked at Salvi, "selecting 'I like it rough'," then she looked at Mitch, "and *you* selecting 'I like to dominate'." She shrugged. "Then you go for it."

Salvi and Mitch stared at her.

"Sorry," the woman said. "Unless you want it around the other way, where she beats the shit out of you and gives it to you rough. Then you'd make the reverse selections."

Salvi and Mitch stared at her again a moment, then glanced at each other.

"Is that what you want?" the woman asked.

"Voyeur will be f–" Mitch said.

"All-access," Salvi cut him off. "We want all-access. No restrictions." Salvi looked at Mitch. "We want to see everything that goes on in there."

He stared back at her. "Then voyeur should suffice."

"Such a good little boy, Mitch," Salvi said, throwing the words he'd once spoken to her back at him. "Take a risk once in a while."

His brow furrowed, then he looked back at the woman who was staring at them. "All-access, please."

They paid the account, and the woman led them through to a small room where two AR chairs sat side by side and began running them through the procedure. Curved in the shape of a crescent moon, soft joints in the spine of the chair enabled various movements – stretching out and retracting, and twisting and turning, etc. They were to each wear haptic suits made of a thin, delicate material, which covered their bodies from head to toe. Once dressed they lay back in the chair and plugged themselves, their suits, into the chair's console and placed their skull caps on and goggles down over their eyes.

Once they were both locked into their chairs and ready to go, the woman enabled their access and left them to it.

When Salvi's suit connected to U-Stasis, she found herself standing in a lavish hotel reception. White marble floors and gold fixtures abounded as she looked around; the vision was pristine, and it looked and felt very real. She glanced at Mitch's avatar standing beside her. He'd opted for a tall, blond guy with blue eyes and a muscular torso called "Billy", and it too looked very real. Salvi had opted for a curvaceous, busty, redhead wearing head-to-toe shiny black spandex, name of "Sindy".

"So, what do we do?" the blond Mitch asked.

"Next please!" a man behind the reception desk called, smiling at them.

Salvi walked up to him, noticing as she got closer that the man's African-American avatar wasn't realistic like theirs but drawn as though in cartoon form. He waved his hand in a rainbow arc across Salvi and her data appeared in the air beside her, which the man read. He then did the same to Mitch, and she saw his data scrolling up alongside his face.

"All-access passes," the man said. "Please use elevator four."

Salvi glanced at Mitch, then turned and stepped inside the elevator. It rose automatically and pinged when they arrived at their destination. They stepped out and saw another reception desk and another cartoon avatar – this time a blonde Caucasian woman. She wondered if these avatars were in cartoon format for a reason, to clearly distinguish the staff from the paying customers.

Salvi's data appeared in the air again and the woman behind the counter smiled. "Welcome. This is your first time?"

Salvi nodded.

"You're in for a wild ride." The woman winked. "Now let's just check that your suits are working." The woman reached out and grabbed at Salvi's breasts and crotch. Actions that she felt on her real person as the haptic suit contracted in those areas. Salvi managed to contain her surprise.

"You felt that, yes?" the woman asked.

"Yeah," Salvi said as the woman turned to Mitch's avatar and grabbed at his crotch.

"Yes?" she smiled.

"Yes," he said stepping backward from her.

"Looks like it's all working just fine to me," the woman said, as both Salvi and Mitch's data appeared in the air again. "Now, just head down that hallway and pick any room you like. If a door is locked that means you cannot enter and the activity has been classed private. If the door is unlocked, you may go in. There are no restrictions here unless you've specified that in your parameters, which all avatars must obey. But it looks to me that you're both up for anything." She gave a soft purring giggle. "Although, you've both chosen that you like to be dominant, so that should make for an interesting time. Have fun now!"

Salvi and Mitch cast each other a glance then moved down the hallway. The came across the first doorway – an old-fashioned kind with a doorknob. Mitch placed his hand on it and tried to turn, but it wouldn't budge.

"Locked," he said.

Salvi nodded and moved across the corridor to the second. This one was unlocked. She glanced at the blond Mitch then opened it.

The room inside was empty except for a floor filled with velvet cushions, satin sheets, hookah pipes, and four or five people mid-orgy. Salvi felt Mitch's avatar come to stand by hers as he looked inside at the moaning and grinding bodies. She looked back at him, then closed the door and moved onto the next one. He followed silently. The next door opened onto a room that appeared to be a dungeon. Inside were three people: two male avatars tied to posts while a female avatar whipped them hard. Salvi thought about the haptic suit when the female avatar had groped her. If she felt that, then what were these men feeling now? She glanced around the room and saw all kinds of implements. Some of which could certainly cause death in the wrong, over-excited hands.

The woman with the whip looked over at them, then raised her hand and enlarged their data, reading it. "You want in?" she held the whip out to Salvi.

She shook her head. "I'm just watching for now." The woman moved the whip to Mitch.

"Me too," he said, as Salvi felt something firm press into her lower back. She glanced over her shoulder to see a male avatar there. She felt her breast squeeze as the avatar's hand found its way to her front. Salvi pulled the arm off and turned around to see the man's avatar was naked.

"You've still got your clothes on," he said. "Want me to help you take them off?"

"No," Salvi said.

He read her data. "I see you like to be dominant. Want to go inside?" he motioned into the room. "You can hurt me."

"Not right now," she said.

The man shrugged and looked at Mitch's avatar. "What about you, handsome?" he groped for Mitch's crotch.

Mitch knocked his hand away. "Read the data," he said, and the man began scrolling the text beside Mitch's face.

"Oh. Heterosexual," the man said. "Do you know how many men come in here with that parameter, and within five minutes they scrub that section clean."

"I'm not one of them," Mitch said, then gave the guy a smile and moved past him.

Salvi followed, deciding to pull back a little now and let Mitch lead the way so she could watch him.

The next room they came upon looked like a classroom. Four people sat at desks watching while an older male avatar had a young male avatar bent over a desk at the front. Mitch closed the door and moved onto the next. Another orgy, this time with voyeurs on the outskirts, in a setting that appeared to be a hospital's emergency room: doctors, nurses and patients all getting in on the action.

They moved onto the next room. As they opened the door they paused upon finding a church setting. They glanced at each other, then stepped inside. It was empty of people, but they saw a confessional box at the side with its door closed.

"You've been bad, haven't you?" a male voice sounded. They looked around for the owner and found no one. "Get on your knees and pray!" it said. Salvi felt pressure at her shoulder, and suddenly she and Mitch were moving to the front and being forced down onto their knees.

"Dominant demons, hmm?" the voice said. "You must pay for your sins!"

Mitch looked at Salvi. "Is that supposed to be the voice of God?"

"I don't know. You think maybe Sharon and Tobias discovered this place?"

"Or maybe Kevin?"

Just then the confessional booth opened, and a young priest and nun exited. They saw Salvi and Mitch kneeling at the altar and moved toward them.

"Who wants to go first at confessing their sins," said the priest, who displayed his data to them. He was using the un-original name "Lover".

"They're dominants," said the nun, reading their data. She moved closer and dropped to her knees in front of Mitch; her data appeared, and Salvi read her parameters. This woman, if it was a woman behind the avatar, was going by the name "Panther" and apparently liked it rough. "I've had impure thoughts," she said to Mitch, sliding her hands up his thighs. "Would you like to punish me?" She leaned forward, pressing her face into his neck.

"No," Mitch said, taking her shoulders and pushing her back. "Thank you."

The nun looked back at him with sad eyes. "But you like to dominate?"

"Yes, I do," he said. "And I'm telling you no."

"Oh," she said, moving back from him.

"Can we watch you two then?" the young priest avatar asked. "We won't touch. We promise. Although you should probably specify that in your parameters next time. This is all-access after all. We just assume everyone is in for anything here."

The nun nodded. "Maybe they're just playing hard to get?" She slid a hand up both Salvi and Mitch's thighs this time. They both looked down at her hands. "Maybe they need a little enticing to warm up and come out of their shells."

"No," Salvi said, catching both her hands. "I'm also dominant and I'm telling you he's mine."

Both Mitch and the nun looked at her. The nun retracted her hands and smiled.

"Do you come here often?" the blond Mitch asked the nun.

She nodded.

"You ever see a couple of kids in here?" Salvi asked. "She was blonde, he was brunette? They went by initials. SG and TB?"

The nun shook her head. "No. Now, tell me what you would like me to do, dominant."

"Please do!" the priest nodded eagerly, getting familiar with himself.

"Enjoy yourselves," Salvi said. "We were just leaving." Salvi stood and headed for the door, but Mitch hesitated. She looked back, wondering why he hadn't followed. He stood there with his back turned and seemed to make an adjustment to the front of his avatar's pants. He turned back around and moved toward her, probably thankful his avatar couldn't show his real, most likely abashed, face.

She studied his avatar as it approached her, focusing hard on its face and not letting her eyes drop any lower. Which was a ridiculous thought given it was an avatar. Then again, the avatars did respond to the haptic suits.

"Got a thing for nuns, huh?" she asked as he reached her. "Do you like pure women, Mitch?"

He paused and stared back at her a moment. "No," he said. "I like the ones who aren't afraid to let themselves go." He moved past her. "I'm leaving. We've wasted enough time here already." And with that he walked out the door.

They finished up, silently, left the store and caught the SlingShot back to Bountiful, deciding to split up and check out the different carriages separately. An awkwardness now sat between them, and Salvi wasn't sure how to handle it. Wasn't sure whether going into U-Stasis with Mitch had done any good or solved anything in relation to the case.

She kept seeing Mitch drive off with Carly Fresner in her yellow dress. Kept seeing the body beneath that sheet.

But Salvi suddenly realized something. Something that she'd overlooked upon first seeing Fresner's body, due to the shock of it all. Fresner didn't look like she'd been dead long. Salvi had seen Mitch with her the previous night. And that was hours ago.

She found a spot in the main corridor and turned to look out the SlingShot's windows, as she engaged her lenses and put in a call to Weston.

"Brentt, what's up?"

"Can you confirm the time of death on Fresner yet?"

"Yeah," she said. "She was in partial rigor mortis when I examined her at the scene, so she hadn't been dead that long. At a guess I'd say she died sometime between 7 and 9am."

Salvi felt relief wash through her. Mitch had been in the Raider with her at that time. She swiftly felt a rush of guilt for having suspected him.

"OK. Thanks." She ended the call and turned to see Mitch approaching her. "That was Weston. She puts Fresner's TOD between 7 and 9am this morning."

Mitch nodded. He didn't appear to share her feeling of relief as he looked out the window at the SlingShot pulling into Bountiful. The truth was, if he'd slept with Fresner, his DNA could still be on her and that would still be a hard situation for Mitch to get out of. Especially with the security cam footage at the station.

He suddenly stiffened, and Salvi followed his line of sight to a group of Serenes and Subjugates working in the station grounds. Some were sweeping pathways, some collecting rubbish, some weeding. Mitch looked back at her. "The Subjugates start work in town at 8am."

They stared at each other as the SlingShot's AI announced their arrival into Bountiful. They made their way to the exit and walked down the platform to where the Raider awaited them. As they did they saw Dr Remmell approaching.

With Serene-41.

The Serene wore a hat over his skull hiding his halo.

"Doctor Remmell," Salvi said, then turned her eyes to his companion. "Serene-41." The Serene gave a bow and Remmell scowled. He was clearly still angry at her for trying to entrap Subjugate-52. "You're heading into the city?"

"We're on private business," he said, moving around her, but Mitch stepped in his path, blocking him.

"What business do you have in the city?" Mitch asked.

Doctor Remmell turned his scowl to Mitch. "I have a meeting. Is that alright with you?"

"And you're taking Serene-41?" Salvi asked.

"I would've thought that was obvious, Detective," Remmell said.

"If Serene-41 is going with you, who is watching your Subjugates?"

"We have many Serenes who fulfil this obligation."

"I thought they were all bound to Bountiful?" Mitch asked.

"They are. However, we must report on our progress to the various authorities and those we report to like to see things with their own eyes. So occasionally I have a Serene escort me to these meetings. It's good for their development to see the wider world. It is our aim to send them out there eventually anyway."

"You assured us they never left Bountiful," Salvi said.

"No, we assured you the Subjugates never left Bountiful," Remmell replied. "Now if you'll excuse me, we're going to miss our SlingShot."

"Why the hat?" Mitch asked, motioning to Serene-41.

"Why do you think?" Remmell said. He stepped around Mitch and impatiently waved the Serene forward.

"We'll need the names of who you're meeting with," Mitch called after him.

"Talk to Solme," he muttered, then continued onward up

to the platform. They watched them enter and take a seat. All the while Serene-41 kept his eyes to the ground and hands clasped in prayer.

Salvi turned back to watch the group of Serenes and Subjugates working close by. She spotted Moses and Dolles among them. Moses watched the SlingShot as it moved away from the station, then glanced back at them and gave a bow.

"Come on, let's go," Mitch said, then continued on to the Raider.

"Before we leave Bountiful, I think we should speak to Kevin Craydon," Salvi said to Mitch. "I want to ask what he's doing with Attis Solme, and what he did with Sharon."

Mitch gave a nod and turned the Raider around.

When they knocked on the door, Tobias answered.

"Hello?" he said, tentatively. "What's wrong?"

"We'd like to speak with Kevin, please," Salvi said.

"Kevin? Why?" Tobias' face paled.

"Yes?" they heard Kevin's voice behind Tobias.

"May we come in?" Salvi asked him.

"Of course," Kevin said. "Tobias, let them in."

They entered the living room and Kevin ushered them to sit. Salvi did, but Mitch remained standing.

"What's this about?" Kevin asked.

"We'd like to know what your involvement is with the Church of Connectivity," Salvi asked.

Kevin and Tobias paused a moment at the bluntness of her question, then exchanged a glance before Kevin answered.

"We are spreading the word of God."

"Isn't technology against your code here in Bountiful?"

"Yes. In Bountiful. But if we are to combat sin, we must enter the lair of the devil and save whomever we can."

"So, you use sin, technology, to draw them in?"

"Yes and no," Kevin said. "We use technology, but it is not sinful technology. The Church of Connectivity deploys Christian technology. Clean technology."

"So, you've never been inside U-Stasis?"

Both Kevin and Tobias stilled.

"I–" Tobias began to blurt an excuse, but Kevin held up his hand, cutting him off.

"We are missionaries, Detectives," Kevin told them. "Just as our ancestors once traveled to ancient lands to spread the word of God, we in this modern era do the same. However, our journey is to go online. That is where we find the sinners, save them, and bring them to God."

"Was it necessary for you to travel to the sex rooms in U-Stasis?" Mitch asked, calling his bluff; the warrant hadn't cleared yet to access any account information.

Kevin looked at him, then averted his eyes, marking a sign of the cross upon himself. "I was tricked. By the devil himself. I met someone at the Church of Connectivity and spoke to them about God and they told me there was a church I might like to see in U-Stasis. I did not realize what it was until I opened the door and entered. As soon as I found out what filth it was I left immediately."

"You didn't think anything was strange when you had to set your parameters before entering?" Mitch asked.

"Yes. But I was naïve to technology back then. And, I admit, I was curious. I wanted to see the church. And when I did," he swallowed and marked another sign of the cross upon himself. "When I did, I realized how *vile* and *sickening* and *far reaching* the devil's sin was in the city and online. And I vowed to do everything I could to fight it."

"With Attis Solme's support?" Salvi asked.

"Yes." Kevin gave a nod. "It is our vow to destroy sin and bring people back to God."

"Destroy sin…" Salvi mused aloud.

Mitch looked at Tobias. "So why did you and Sharon go into U-Stasis?"

Tobias paled again.

Kevin looked at him. "I told you *never* to go in there!"

"W-we wanted to be m-missionaries too," Tobias stuttered to Kevin. "I know whatever you saw affected you. We wanted to see what it was. We had to see the devil with our own eyes in order to defeat him."

"But you were seduced by the sin," Mitch said.

Tobias looked at Kevin, his eyes wide with fear.

"W-we didn't mean to…" he voice faded. "We were weak."

Kevin stared at Tobias a moment, before reaching out and squeezing his shoulder. "I feared the devil and his sin had worked his hooks into you both." Kevin shook his head. "I was wrong to send you into the city so soon, brother. I should've known you did not have my strength."

"Tell me, Kevin," Salvi said, "how do you feel knowing a Child of Christ has indulged in the online sin you fight to destroy?"

He looked at her. "I am upset the devil has won this battle. But it is only a small battle. We will win the war." He looked at Tobias. "And Tobias will pray and repent for what he has done. I will make sure of that. I will guide him, back onto the path of the Lord."

"You won't punish him?" Salvi asked.

"No." He shook his head. "It is not for me to punish. That is for the Lord to do. God is our witness."

Tobias bowed his head and marked a sign of the cross.

"So, you didn't find out that Sharon had succumbed to sin and then punish her?"

Kevin stared at her as the realization of her words fells upon him. "No. I did not."

"You sent Sharon and Tobias in, to help bring people back. Then you feared they were instead drawn into sin. That didn't anger you at all?"

Kevin looked at Tobias, who hung his head and began to cry. "I won't lie, I am very disappointed to hear this." He looked back at Salvi. "But I have only just heard this. I did not kill Sharon. I am a missionary of God. It is my mission to save people. Not hurt them." He stood from his seat and moved for the door opening it. "If you wish to speak with me further, it shall be with Mayor Solme's lawyer present."

"He prepared you, didn't he?" Salvi asked. "He told you we might come."

Kevin didn't answer but held his body strong in resolve.

"You're very close with Mr Solme, aren't you?" Mitch said.

Kevin stared at them both with firm eyes. "I am a religious man, but I am no fool, Detectives. Mayor Solme is a smart man and he mentors me. He believes I have what it takes to follow in his footsteps. And that I shall. Now, you have outstayed your welcome. Please leave."

Salvi and Mitch exchanged a look, then moved to the door.

"Tell me something," Salvi said, stopping in front of him, "seeing how you're so smart. Is the Solme Complex really fixing those Subjugates?"

"No," he said. "Religion is. It is saving mankind, one sinner at a time. Good day."

The drive back to the hub was long and undertaken in a heavy silence, their minds racing over the morning's events. As the Raider finally pulled up, Mitch kept the motor running.

"I gotta do something," he said, darting his eyes briefly to hers. "I'll meet you here later."

Salvi looked at him. "What do you have to do?"

Mitch glances at her again. "I just got to check something out. Go start on Carson. See what you can find, see whether she was pure as she made out. I'll be back soon."

"Did Riverton say how long it would take to get the

warrants to access the U-Stasis accounts?"

"A day or so."

Salvi nodded and got out of the car. Then she watched him drive away, wondering whether letting him out of her sight had been the right thing to do.

14: SMOKE AND FIRE

Salvi checked her iPort. Several hours had now passed and Mitch still hadn't returned. She'd read over the data on their second vic, Rebecca Carson, and still wasn't any the wiser. Carson had attended church groups, worked at the local hairdresser and played in a unisex softball team. Nothing stood out as unusual. But then again, on face value, nothing had stood out as unusual about Sharon Gleamer either.

Salvi considered the church groups Carson took part in, knew that Subjugates and Serenes would've been present. Then she made a call to Carson's friend, Loretta Sine, the one who had found her, and they had a chat. She'd read Holt's notes but wanted to go over things one more time. Salvi found out the names of those in Carson's softball team. The only name she recognized was Ben Holt, the Bountiful sheriff.

Salvi pictured Holt in her mind; saw him at every crime scene, the way he handled the bodies, remembered his car driving past right after Mitch had left with Fresner. Curious, Salvi did a search on him, wanting to rule him out more than anything. He was single, thirty-nine years old and had lived in Bountiful for several years. She remembered their first meeting. Holt wasn't backward about his dislike for the Complex's residents. Did the sheriff dislike them *that* much? Would he go to these extreme lengths to set them up for a fall? The sheriff would, she had to admit, have a good understanding of how to get away with murder. She checked Riverton's records to see whether Holt's house was on the grid or whether he maybe used BioLume. It was on the electrical grid.

Her iPort signaled an incoming call, disrupting her thoughts. She didn't recognize the number but engaged her lenses.

"Hello?" she answered tentatively, eyeing the middle-aged guy with a three-day growth who stared back at her.

"Is this Salvi Brentt?"

"Who is this?"

"My name's Gus. I work for Solid State, the company that handles security for Sky Tower 4." He tapped a button and his credentials appeared on screen. "Your apartment alarm registered on our system a short while ago. We'd like to confirm if that was you or whether you'd like us to check in with the auto-concierge and ascertain if there's a problem?"

Salvi paused a moment. "How long did the alarm register for?"

"Only a few seconds, but it's standard procedure for us to put a call into you. According to our records you haven't had any problems with it in the past."

"No," Salvi said. "Please check for unauthorized visitors and scan the apartment's security. Let me know if there are any abnormalities. Call me back."

"Will do."

She ended the call and jumped in fright as she suddenly noticed Mitch standing beside her desk.

"Jesus!" she said. "Don't creep up on people."

"Something wrong?" he motioned to the iPort, his eyes narrowed.

"No." She shook her head.

"You find anything?" he said, taking a seat at his desk.

"Not really." She eyed him curiously. "You?"

He didn't seem to hear her, eyes fixed on his console screen.

"Mitch? You said you went to check on something?" she asked.

He looked back at her. "Riverton found no links to the prostitute in the city, so I put in a few calls, spoke with the neighbor and eventually found an associate of hers. I spoke to them about getting the names of her clients."

"And?" She stared at him.

"They're pulling together a list and sending it over to me."

She nodded, mind ticking over. "Why the hell would Preacher Vowker allow a prostitute to live in the community?"

"I wondered the same thing, gave the preacher a call."

"You did?"

"Yeah. I thought it best not to have you take part, given your interaction at the wake."

Salvi ignored the comment. "What did Vowker say?"

"He said he was helping Fresner change her life. Said she wanted to get her boy out of the city, so he gave her somewhere to stay, on the proviso she turned her life around, turned her face to God."

"But she hadn't."

"Not yet, but she was working on it. She had a debt to pay with a pimp before she could pull out entirely."

"A debt to the pimp and a debt to Vowker. Ain't that dancing between two devils?"

Mitch shrugged. "She was getting her boy out of the city and away from that life. It was always going to cost her, no matter where she lived."

Salvi nodded. "It cost her, alright. But the question is, did her killer follow her to Bountiful from the city, or did her killer live in Bountiful all along?"

"You found no city links with Carson?"

Salvi shook her head. "Nothing obvious."

"Hey, Grenville." Beggs came up and slapped his shoulder. "You up for a drink with me tonight?"

Mitch shook his head, eyes fixed back on the screen.

"No?" Bronte smiled from across the bullpen. "You feeling alright?"

"We got a third vic," Salvi told them.

"We heard," Beggs said, dropping his smile, then looked at Mitch, "that's why we thought you might like a drink."

Mitch glanced at Beggs and shook his head again, then looked back to his screen. Beggs gave a shrug then walked off.

Mitch suddenly stood. "I need a coffee. You want one?"

Salvi studied him. His face was less pale, but he still seemed edgy. His dark green eyes stared into hers.

"No," she said. "I'm good."

He nodded and headed for the door.

"Mitch?" she called.

He stopped and looked around at her.

"You alright?" she asked.

He nodded, averting his eyes, then left.

Salvi sighed heavily and looked back at her screen. A photo of Rebecca Carson in her softball uniform stared back at her.

Her iPort signaled another call. She answered it.

"Miss Brentt? It's Gus from Solid State again. Auto-concierge scan looks fine. There's nothing suspicious on the security feed. Several other apartments have registered their alarms too. Must've just been a glitch."

"Thank you." She hung up the call and sighed.

A shadow crossed her face as Hernandez sat down on the desk beside her. She looked up at him.

"A third vic, huh?" he asked.

She didn't answer.

"Mitch looks a little jumpy," he said. "You talk to Stan?"

Again, she didn't answer, just stared at him. Well, now it was more of a glare.

Hernandez put his hands in the air in surrender. "I know, I know. You can take care of yourself." He lowered his hands again and sighed. "I'm just trying to look out for you, Salv. They were Stan's parting words to me when he retired. 'Keep an eye on Mia'."

"Stan wouldn't say that," she countered. "He trained me. He knows I can handle myself."

Hernandez raised his hands again, then leaned off her desk and walked away.

Mitch never returned with the coffee. She waited and waited but he didn't show. Her stomach was in knots. Where had he gone? Was he just somewhere trying to get his head around what happened and the mess he was in? Or was it something else?

Why hadn't he come to her for help? Had she been such a closed book that he didn't think he could?

Why was he hiding his contact with Fresner? He had no reason to. He was in the Raider with Salvi that morning. She was his alibi. Wasn't she?

Or could Mitch have caught the SlingShot to Bountiful, killed Fresner, and then come back to the city to pick her up at the precinct? The SlingShot was a twenty-minute ride either way. He could've gone out there, killed Fresner around 7am, then been back in time to pick Salvi up at 8.30am.

He could have…

But did he? She couldn't ask Riverton to check the security footage for that morning, she would need to do it herself. Even then, there would be a log of her activity and Riverton may question why. Although the AI worked to serve its detectives, it also served Internal Affairs, clamping down on corruption. Every day, the AI would run through the case files, looking for any clues missed or anything unusual. This was a time bomb ticking.

Salvi recalled the AI telling her that Hernandez had been reviewing their files. She quickly accessed the log and checked. He'd been in again. So had Ford.

"Shit," she muttered. She had Hernandez and Ford checking up on her, Holt possibly doing his own surveillance in Bountiful, and an AI that was designed to be thorough and check facts and faces. It was only a matter of time before Mitch was called out. Salvi just had to hope that she had not been spotted by Holt the night she followed Mitch. If he had, and Mitch turned out to be a killer, she would be found to be sitting on evidence. Her career could be at stake.

So why the hell was she stalling?

Because she wasn't ready to finger Mitch as the Bountiful Killer. All she had was circumstantial evidence. Right now, she had no motive. And *that* was the real killer when it came to tanking a case.

The faces of all the suspects flashed through her mind. There were so many possibilities. Was it one of the Subjugates or Serenes? She pictured Edward Moses staring at her, thought of his heinous previous crimes, his intellect. Could he have outsmarted the Solme Complex's treatments? She saw Lucius Dolles watching the dog pissing on the tree, thought of his hatred for women he thought acted like they were better than him. She saw Fontan Pragge approach her, telling her he was a bad man, thought of how he would never graduate to a Serene due to his mental capacity – something brought upon him by the Complex's torture. She saw Serene-41 talking proudly of his Complex access pass and his status as Serene-Supreme, of how he had the trust of Attis and Remmell and could move freely about the Complex and the town. And she pictured him getting onto the SlingShot with Remmell.

And then there was Doctor Remmell himself, the way he grabbed her arm, yanking her back and eyeing her with disgust, telling her she ought to be ashamed of herself. She recalled him saying that he'd spent too much time with the Subjugates, indicating that he had forgotten how to talk to normal people. But was it just the speech aspect? How much more like the Subjugates had he become?

She saw Levan Bander beat that inmate, thought about his double life as religious caretaker by day and "normal man" by night.

She saw Sheriff Holt drive past after Mitch and Fresner, roaming the streets at night. Thought of when they first met and how from the start he tried to subtly finger someone at the Solme Complex.

She recalled Attis defending his facility, practically threatening her if she tried to find one of his residents guilty. All his talk of God and forgiveness, and yet he authorized the violent and sadistic torture the inmates were put through. Just how far would Solme go to protect his empire? The man led a duplicitous life with the Children of Christ and the Church of Connectivity, sending young missionaries out into sin to do his bidding. Was he saving souls or corrupting them? He was brainwashing the Subjugates, and from what Salvi could tell, he was doing the same to Kevin Craydon, his little protégé.

Then she thought of the neighboring survivalist colony, Garner Town. Had they just made empty threats, or had they followed through? She'd read the data Riverton had supplied on them. The community was small, only one hundred and fifty-six residents. There were no prior arrests or criminal records among them. Nothing serious anyway. According to Holt's notes, he'd paid them a visit and interviewed a bunch along with one of his officers. They'd provided sufficient alibis each substantiated by several witnesses, and because it was a pullaway, there was little Riverton could do to seek further information.

Despite being cleared of the DNA, she still pictured the preacher talking to her of forgiveness, of his guidance to those who strayed from the way of chastity. Did he know

Sharon had broken her vows? Did he know something about Rebecca Carson who also attended his church? Had she confessed her sins to him? Was Carly Fresner taking too long to extract herself from her sinful life? Was it causing problems for him in his clean and holy town, letting her live there? And did he know what Attis was up to in the city? Did the preacher know that he was luring his star Children of Christ into a world of sin, all the while he was trying to pull others back from it? What would he do to protect the sanctity of his community?

Despite the cleared DNA, she saw Sharon Gleamer's neighbor spying on her through his window. A non-believer living in Bountiful only for the free ride, with no intention to follow God. Then she saw Tobias' innocent face cry tears of sorrow at what he'd done...

Salvi sighed and closed her eyes, tried to clear her mind. "Go back to the basics," she told herself. "Go back to the first crime scene."

She thought again of the BioLume footprint at the first scene. Of the BioLume smear on Rebecca Carson's back. And her mind came back to the Solme Complex. She heard Attis Solme talk about the factory, saw one of the workers with BioLume spills on their coveralls. Remembered the BioLume lights in Mitch's apartment and the hardware store in which Tobias worked, selling the globes. Saw the BioLume cross adorning the Children of Christ church and the Church of Connectivity.

And still she had no answers. She was going in circles.

Her head was drowning in thoughts. She needed some air. She needed a break to let her mind breathe.

And strangely enough, for the first time in a long time, she didn't want to be alone.

She thought of Beggs mentioning drinks, then decided to try to find him.

She went to McClusky's, the same bar around the corner from the hub that she'd picked Mitch up from the other night. But she couldn't find any of the guys there, nor anyone from narcotics or cyber.

She did, however, pause upon seeing Ben Holt eating dinner in one of the booths.

She pictured Rebecca Carson in her softball uniform again, saw Ben eating his fries and sucking the salt off his fingers. She went to the bar, ordered a bottle of vodka and made her way to his booth.

"Do you mind if I join you?" she asked.

Sheriff Holt looked up, surprised. He finished licking his fingers then shook his head and motioned for her to sit.

"Sorry to interrupt your dinner," she said with a smile.

"That's alright," he said.

"You here on business?"

He looked down at his plate. "I had an errand to run here in the city. Decided to stop for dinner."

She studied him a moment. "It's funny, our hub is just around the corner."

"Oh yeah?" he said, but any surprise he may have felt was lacking from his face. He glanced at her again, then dipped some of his fries in the sauce smeared across his plate. "So, what brings you here, then?"

"Pleasure," she said, pouring the vodka into a glass. She offered to pour him a drink but he waved a "no".

"You got a whole bottle there," he said. "Planning on a big night?"

"Who knows?" she said. "We'll see." She sipped her drink, felt it heat her body all the way down from her throat to her belly.

He eyed her for a moment. "Well, just make sure you don't go drinking and driving or I'm going to have to arrest you."

Salvi laughed and threw back the rest of the drink, then

poured another. "Would you like that?" she said. "To see me in cuffs?"

Holt paused, looking at her, but then continued eating without responding to the comment. "What are you celebrating?" He motioned to her bottle of vodka. "You caught the killer?" He looked at her eagerly for her response.

"No. But we're getting closer," she lied.

He studied her again, nodding to himself. She wondered if he could see through it. Cops were good at sniffing out lies.

"So tell me, Ben," she said. "What are your thoughts on our killer? Who do you think it is?"

He studied her again, as though checking whether her question was serious or not.

She shrugged. "You know the town and the people. What's your take on things?"

Holt shrugged back, finished the last of his fries, and washed them down with a mouthful of soda. "Well, he's a sick son of a bitch, that's for sure. Doing that in our town, of all places."

Salvi eyed him. "You think he lives local?"

Holt seemed to consider this as he sipped his drink. "Local enough."

"Local enough? You sound like you already have a theory?"

Holt shrugged and pushed his plate to the side, then folded his arms on the table. "I got the same suspicions as you."

"Which are?"

"Well, you've been out to the Solme Complex a few times, right? Gotta be a reason for that."

"We're simply following up witness leads."

"And what better lead is there than a bunch of rapists, murderers and serial killers living on our doorstep."

Salvi knocked back her second drink. "You're really not a fan of the Complex, are you?"

"Why would I be?" he said, taking another sip of his soda.

"Bountiful is my territory. It's my job to enforce the law and keep people safe. How the hell can I do that, with those animals living there?"

"Have you ever had any trouble from them?" she asked.

"Well, no," he said, "but it was bound to happen. Sooner or later one of them was going to crack, and now they have. I tried to warn them, but they wouldn't listen to me."

"Who wouldn't listen?"

"The damn council! But Attis Solme had the money and the influence, so the regular folk of Bountiful were ignored."

"You voted against the Complex?"

"Yes, I did." He took another drink. "What am I, stupid? Bountiful has always been nice and quiet. I've lived there for years. Now look at this!" He leaned forward over the table and stabbed his index finger as though banging a gavel. "This would *never* have happened if they hadn't allowed those monsters into town! It was one thing having the Complex close by, but to let them out among us?"

Salvi poured another drink. "A lot of people like the Serenes, though. They say they're doing a lot of good for the town."

"I don't care." He shook his head. "As far as I'm concerned a leopard don't change his spots. I've worked this job long enough to know that. I wasn't always the sheriff of a sleepy religious town, you know. I did my city time. Sacramento." He finished the rest of his soda. "Those Subjugates and Serenes hang around the church where two of those women went. And the third? Well, she was a purveyor of sin. I guess that was bound to happen. With everyone else being cautious and staying indoors, she was the only fresh meat left on the market."

Salvi sat back in her chair, the bite of his words stinging her a little.

"You think that's fair?" she asked.

"What?"

"Talking about her like that? She was a single mother doing what she could to feed, clothe and house her son."

Holt looked at her with a plain face. "There are plenty of jobs that she could've done. She chose to earn it on her back."

"Well, men are prepared to pay a lot more for sex than they are for someone bagging groceries or cleaning their house. Can you blame her?"

"Yeah," he said standing, and pulling out his wallet, "I can." He shook his head. "I told the preacher about this, you know. Bountiful has been going downhill for a while now. At the start it was just us religious folk, but bit by bit the normals have been moving in and setting up house. Why? Because it's cheap and we have all that free labor with the Serenes. But that's just the problem, you see. People want the cheap houses and the free labor, but they don't want to live by our rules. They don't believe in God. They say they do, but they don't. They're outright liars and they should *not* be allowed in town. But Vowker thinks he can save them, thinks he can turn them. Attis too. I say they can't. Why? Because a leopard *doesn't* change his spots."

She downed her third drink while he threw his money down on the table. He studied her a moment and held out his hands.

"Wanna give me your keys?"

She looked at his opened hand. "Why?"

"I've just watched you down several drinks. You are not allowed to drive."

"Thanks, but I'll hold onto my own keys," she said. "And, ah, here in the big bad city, in our cars, we have this thing called autodrive."

"Autodrive is still illegal if you're intoxicated, Detective. You need to be of sound mind to set the controls correctly. I'm sure you know this."

"We also have autocabs, the Cylin trains, tuk-tuks–"

He pointed a finger at her. "I catch you driving, Detective, I will arrest you."

She smiled back at him. "You're outside your jurisdiction, Sheriff. I'm sure you know this. Why are you here again?"

His brow furrowed as he stared at her, then he shook his head and walked away.

Salvi watched him leave, mind ticking over, then poured herself another drink.

Her iPort signaled an incoming call. It was Mitch. She contemplated not answering it but figured she ought to. After all, if he really wanted to, he would just trace her iPort again and find her anyway. Besides, wasn't it better to meet in a crowded place?

She engaged her lenses. "I'm still waiting for my coffee."

"Where are you?" he asked. He looked to be standing in the hub.

"McClusky's bar."

"We've got our third vic and you're drinking?" he asked.

"You of all people are saying this to me?"

"Salvi, we need to talk. I'll meet you there."

Waiting for Mitch, Salvi had now downed five shots. She didn't know why she was doing this. Knew it was a stupid thing to do. Drinking wasn't her. *This*, being a mess, wasn't her. Not any more. Not for a long time. But she just had too much swimming around in her brain. She was tired and needed a buffer from thinking about the case. And truth be told she wanted to numb the thoughts that put Mitch on her list of potential suspects. That's what bothered her the most. He was her partner; she was supposed to be able to trust him with her life. But who was he really? Could he have done those things to the vics? Could he have done it to his own girlfriend? Surely not. She'd worked with him for almost four months. He was the guy that brought her coffee every morning.

But how many people had she heard that from before. *He was always such a nice, polite, young man...*

Mitch was the guy who'd traced her iPort to find out where she was.

She felt a sense of betrayal, that her partner could've been the one doing this all along. That she hadn't picked up on it. She'd always prided herself in judging someone's character. But was she really feeling betrayal, that he could be the one? Or was it a wounded sense of pride, that she'd been wrong about him? That she'd failed in her duty to recognize him? That in her quest for privacy, she'd failed to find out who her partner really was.

That she'd been weak. That something else deep down inside had caused a lapse in judgment. Something that she didn't even want to look at. She recalled him, once again, cupping her cheek and running his thumb over her lips, parting them.

He suddenly slid into the other side of the booth, breaking her thoughts. She poured her sixth shot.

"What's got into you?" he asked, studying her as she downed it. He grabbed the bottle and her glass when she was done and poured one for himself.

"Nothing," she said, feeling the alcohol warm her all over, easing the tightness in her muscles.

"You don't drink, Salvi," he said, studying her with his dark green eyes. "You're drunk."

"No, I'm not."

"Yes, you are," he said, then gave a half smile. "You look relaxed for once. Last night it was the club, tonight it's here."

She didn't answer, just felt the glow of the alcohol as it sheltered her, began to cocoon her.

He downed his shot and studied her again. "Relaxed but

troubled. And drunk. What's up?"

She gave a laugh. "What's up? We have a serial killer out there, Mitch." She stared at him, analyzing him as best she could. "A sick, twisted, fuck."

"Yes, he is."

They stared at each other across the table.

"You said you wanted to talk?" she asked, glancing around the bar. Through the front window she saw Holt's police car drive by. Wondered what he'd been doing outside all this time. Had he seen Mitch arrive?

First Bander in the city, now Holt. And then there was Remmell earlier that day...

"You first," he said.

"You called me."

"You're the one acting out of character."

"Acting out of character?" She laughed, almost bitterly. "You know nothing about me, Mitch."

"No, I don't," he said, pouring another drink and downing it. "So, tell me. Why'd you change your name?"

"Why did you look me up?" she blurted. "Why did you search me? That's called stalking, you know?"

"I told you. You play your cards close to your chest. I was curious. The preacher got to you. I wanted to know why." He shrugged. "I'm a detective. Call it a bad habit."

"You invaded my privacy."

He shrugged again. "Maybe I did. So why did you change your name from Salvation Brenttanovich? Why did that preacher get to you? Why has this case gotten to you?"

"This case has gotten to you too, Mitch. Don't make this all about me."

"People tend to legally change their name because they're hiding from something or someone, or they're ashamed of something. So which is it, Salvi?"

"What business is it of yours?"

"You're my partner, Salvi. And this," he motioned to the bottle, "isn't you. This case, the preacher, it's got under your skin and turned you upside down. Whatever it is, just let it out so you can move on."

She stared at him through the blanket of vodka coddling her; felt her cheeks flush warm and pink. She wanted to yell at him, tell him he was the reason she was drinking. But she didn't. She pictured Hernandez's face, then Stan's. Stan's face looked at her calmly, his eyes pleading for her to be a police officer, to find the evidence she needed to catch this killer. To follow her gut.

"Alright," she said. "I'll tell you why, if you tell me about the prostitute you were with last night."

Mitch paused, and his face fell. "What prostitute?"

"Our third vic," she said leaning forward on the table. "You were with her last night and she was found dead this morning."

Mitch said nothing at first, just stared at her. "Riverton scanned the station footage?"

"No," Salvi said. "You traced me to the bar, so I followed you afterward. I saw you, Mitch. I saw her get inside your car and I saw you hand over money."

He lowered his head, running his hand through his hair as he exhaled long and slow. He looked back at her. "It's not what it looked like, Salvi."

She burst out laughing. She didn't know why. Blame the vodka. She shook her head. "Mitch, you knew as soon as you saw the vic and you said nothing. What do you think is going to happen when Riverton decides to review the station footage, when Weston finds your DNA all over her?"

"My what?!" he said incredulously.

"You're screwed, Mitch." Salvi sat back in her seat, all humor gone from her voice.

She swallowed hard. "Was it you?"

"Was what me?" he asked, long fringe resting on his furrowed brow.

Salvi reached for the bottle, but he whisked it away, still staring at her.

"Was *what* me?" he asked again, eyes fixed sharply on hers.

"Did you kill her?" Salvi asked, trying to keep her voice steady. Not sounding as firm as she'd like. "Are you the sick fuck I'm after?"

"Are you kidding me?" he asked. "You're really asking me that?"

"It's my job to ask you that, Mitch."

"You think I did this? You think I killed her? Killed the others?" Mitch shook his head, then looked back at her and clenched his stubbled jaw. "And I suppose you think I killed my girlfriend too." He shook his head again. "And here I was thinking you were different from the rest."

Salvi stared at him through the circle of light that lit the table's booth.

Mitch clenched his jaw again. "You think I did, Salvi? Do you? Tell me. Look me in the eye and tell me you think I did it." He leaned forward over the table, putting his face in the light.

"I don't know," she said. "I don't know that much about you."

He leaned further forward. "You think. I killed. My girlfriend?" he asked again, accentuating each word.

Salvi lunged, grabbed the bottle and took a drink straight out of the neck.

"You don't know everything about me, Salvi, but you know enough," he said firmly. "So, you look me in the goddamn eye and tell me you think I did it."

Salvi glanced around the bar, mustering up the courage, then finally looked back at him. His dark green eyes stared back at hers, demanding an answer.

"Hernandez, right?" he asked. "You've been talking to Hernandez." He sat back in his seat, his face falling into partial shadow again. "Yeah, that's it. He cornered me the other night. Told me he didn't trust me. Said he was watching me." Mitch sat forward again. "You think I didn't have everyone back in Chicago ask me the same question, Salvi? It's what we do. The first person cops look at in a homicide is the partner. And trust me, they looked hard. And I was cleared. It wasn't me! I…" his voice broke a little. He took a moment to regain his voice. "I loved her, Salvi. We were having problems, sure, but I… loved her."

"I heard she had an affair behind your back. That didn't make you angry?"

Mitch looked at her, paused, then dropped his head a little. "At first. But then I realized that I'd driven her to it." He shrugged. "I was never around. When I was, I was always crashed out and sleeping, or my mind was caught up in a case."

"What about the prostitute?" she asked, her heart thumping despite the alcohol in her veins.

"What about her?" he asked.

She stared back at him, her eyes asking the question.

"I didn't sleep with her, Salvi," he said, eyes piercing back.

"You paid her money–"

"For information! Who knows the people in town better than the local prostitute? The one sinner in an otherwise holy town. We're looking for someone who has a thing for sinners, right? The killer is a sinner themselves. When I left the bar the other night I just drove to Bountiful, I don't know why. To think, maybe. To go over the cases. I pulled up at the SlingShot and she came out and we got talking. I told her I was a cop and I was investigating the murders, told her she was brave to be walking around at night by herself. She said it was horrible what had happened. I asked if she knew anything that could help. She hesitated, then told me maybe she could help. I found out she was a prostitute. Who better to tell me who in the town is maybe not as squeaky clean as they make out? Prostitutes don't come free no matter what the service, Salvi. I paid her for information, we went for a ride, out of sight, and we talked. That's all!"

"So why didn't you mention it then?"

Mitch sighed and ran his hand over his face. "It was late and the next day we got to interviewing Edward Moses."

"No, Mitch. When we found the body, why didn't you tell me then?"

He sat back in his seat. "Because I knew what it would look like," he said quietly. "I knew Hernandez was watching me, and this... If he found out... I know Ford's watching me too. I saw the access logs on our case files, Salvi."

"You know it would've come out eventually. Riverton will rescan the footage at some point, pick you up and flag it as a gross error. A hole in our data, which you failed to mention."

"I know!" he said. "And I freaked out!" He leaned forward again. "Don't you get it, Salvi? Our killer has been going for good girls turned bad. Suddenly he switches to a bad girl. You know what that means, right?"

"It's about punishment. He's punishing sinners."

"No. I mean, yes, but why out of everyone in town would he hit her? Why *her*?" He stared across the table with gravity. "Because he's watching us, Salvi. He knows we're on the case. It's a warning. It's a warning that he knows what we're doing. He's trying to get us to back off. Making me look like a possible suspect is a good way to do it."

"But why target you?"

"Because I'm investigating the case." He shrugged. "If he makes me look guilty, it slows things down and hampers the investigation." He leaned forward again. "This guy is punishing sinners, but he's having fun while he does it. He likes playing with people, controlling people. He likes being dominant."

Salvi felt more drunk now. This was not what she wanted; to have to think about the case, about the suspects. She moved for the bottle again, but he pulled it back out of reach. She stared at him.

"Salvi," he said. "You believe me, right?"

She studied his eyes as they stared back hopefully into hers.

"Ben Holt never wanted the Solme Complex near Bountiful," she said, changing the subject. "He voted against it. He was on Rebecca Carson's softball team."

Mitch stared at her, brow furrowed. "You think it could be Holt?"

"He drove past me after you left with the prostitute. I think he might've been following you." Salvi glanced around the bar. "He was here tonight in the bar... but maybe... Maybe he saw you like I did. With the prostitute. Maybe he's watching you, running his own investigation." Salvi shook her head, and her whole body swayed with the movement. "I just don't know any more," she said putting her elbows on the table and lowering her head into her hand. She closed her eyes and fought hard to clear everything out of her mind.

"Come on," he said. "I'll take you home."

Salvi looked up at him. "I'm fine."

"No, you're not."

"Mitch–"

"Detective," he said firmly, pulling rank. "I'm taking you home."

People at the next booth looked over at them. Not wanting to create a scene, Salvi stood, snatching the bottle of vodka and stumbling slightly out of the booth. Mitch took hold of her upper arm and steered her toward the door.

15 : SALVATION

"I'll take an autocab," Salvi said as they stepped out into the cold night air.

"You're drunk and we've got a goddamn killer on the loose who might be watching us," Mitch said. "No. I'll take you."

She pulled her arm out of his grasp. "Drunk? You mean like you were the other night when I had to take you home."

"Yeah," he said, looking back at her with a plain face. "So, I owe you one. Get in."

The Raider was parked close by. She watched him walk over to it and pop the doors. He looked back at her. A moment passed.

"I didn't kill my girlfriend, Salvi. I didn't kill any of them."

"Yeah, that's what they all say," she slurred slightly.

"Get in," he said, sliding behind the driver's wheel.

She looked around again, sighed, then stumbled over to the passenger door. Had she been sober she probably wouldn't have taken his ride, but drunk Salvi was a self-loathing risk-taker. And that's exactly why she didn't drink any more.

As soon as she was strapped in, he set the Raider in motion. They sat in silence and she looked out the window, letting the cool night air blow in her face. After a while, she realized he was heading in the right direction for Sky Tower 4.

"How do you know where I live?" she asked him. "I never told you."

He looked over at her. "When I couldn't find you the other night, I got your home address and tried you there."

"Riverton gave my address? You've been to my apartment?" She screwed her face up in anger.

"Yeah, I have," he said nonchalantly, glancing at her. "Sky Tower 4. *Nice*. You're just full of secrets aren't you, Salvi? I mean, *Salvation*."

"Fuck you!" she said.

"No, fuck you, Salvi! You said you'd tell me if I told you about the prostitute. I told you, now you tell me."

"You haven't finished telling me about the prostitute. What information did she give you?"

He exhaled heavily. "She'd been approached by some of the locals. She said she had all the names of her clients in a book, along with dates and times, that was kept somewhere safe, with a friend, for insurance. She said she'd get a list to me, but she never got the chance because someone killed her."

"But she must've told you some of the names when you talked?"

"Let's talk about *your* name first," he said, pulling over to the curb out the front of her apartment.

"No, let's talk about clearing *yours* first," she shot back.

"So, you don't think I did it?"

"I didn't say that."

He exhaled heavily again and turned the Raider off. "I showed her holos for positive identification, focusing on faces from the Solme Complex and the town. She ID'd Dr Remmell, James Stackwell and Sheriff Holt. The book will tell us how often and when they last visited her."

Salvi stared at him, thinking over the names. "OK, Remmell and Stackwell I can see. But Holt?"

Mitch nodded. "She said he just sought her out for the occasional blowjob. They never actually had full-blown sex. For some reason he refused to do that with her."

"Anything kinky with the others?"

"With Stackwell she said they just had straight sex, with Remmell he liked to be dominated," Mitch shrugged. "I guess he does enough dominating in his real life and likes to turn the tables on his time off."

"Remmell, Stackwell and Holt," Salvi repeated, thinking aloud with her drunken mind. "No one from the church?"

Mitch stared at her. "No. And I asked her about the preacher too. It would seem he really is a good boy after all."

"Or he just doesn't like paying for it, so he takes it instead."

"Salvi," Mitch stared at her. "His DNA was cleared from Sharon Gleamer's murder. What is it with you and the church?"

She looked at him. "Don't start." She unbuckled and opened the door of the Raider. By the time she got out and walked around the car, Mitch was waiting for her by the door.

"I got it from here," she said.

"No, I'm going up with you."

"Detective Grenville," she said formally. "Do you remember my gun in your crotch the other night? I'm quite capable."

Mitch put his hands in his pockets and stared back at her. "It's my duty as your partner to ensure your apartment is safe."

Salvi looked at him. "Oh, please. Give me a break. This is a Sky Tower. We got security, trust me."

"Yeah. I overheard the tail end of your conversation with your security company earlier."

Salvi put her hands on her hips and stared back.

"Goddamn it, Salvi," he said. "Would you let me in? We haven't finished talking here."

She stared at him a moment, wobbling a little. Uncomfortable about inviting someone into her secret world. She'd never done that before. But he knew where she lived now. Her secret was out. What did it matter if he saw the inside too? Besides, she knew he wasn't going to give up. She glanced around then looked back at him. She didn't see a killer before her. She just saw Mitch.

She sighed and swiped her key card. The grand glass doors slid back allowing them entrance into Sky Tower 4's reception. The auto-concierge came to life, greeting them. Mitch watched it curiously, but she ignored it as they walked to the elevators. No one else was around, their shoes clipping the polished tiled floors the only sound.

They rode the elevator in silence. She kept her eyes on the seamless control panel, while he kept his eyes on the floor numbers, clearly curious as to how high they were going to go. The elevator came to a stop at the seventy-seventh floor. Mitch looked at her.

"Penthouse, huh?"

"Not quite," she said, stepping out of the opened doors. She shared this floor with one other apartment. She moved over to her front door and swiped her pass again. The door unlocked, and they went inside.

Mitch stopped just inside the door and scanned the surrounds. He gave a whistle.

"Who'd you rob to get a place like this?" he asked. "That why you changed your name? You in Interpol or something?"

She flashed him a humorless look, walked over to the kitchen bench and placed the bottle of vodka from McClusky's down on it. She fished for glasses, poured the vodka and handed him one. He took it, eyeing her curiously, then raised his glass to hers.

"To me not being the killer."

"I haven't decided that yet," she said, refusing to raise her glass.

A smile curled Mitch's mouth. "Even drunk, Salvi, you're too smart to invite a killer up to your apartment."

"I didn't invite you. You insisted," she said, moving over to her couch and sitting down. Mitch followed, sitting in the chair opposite.

She watched as he sat forward, holding the glass in both hands, staring at it as his mind ticked over.

"You're not drinking," she commented. "There's definitely something wrong with you."

He looked up at her, face serious. "I've been through a rough patch, Salvi. I admit it. The other night, when you came and got me… it was like a wake. It was the anniversary of her death." He sighed and rolled the glass and its contents around. "Four years she's been gone… and for four years, I haven't moved on. I've been stuck on this awful carousel, carrying guilt for not being there, hatred for her killer … and frustration that I may never find who did it." He knocked back the drink, then leant forward and put the glass on the coffee table between them. "I should've been home," he said, his throat sounding tight with emotion, his jaw clenching. "I was working on a case, was close to nailing the perp. I'd been working back a lot. She'd had enough, and it was causing tension in our relationship. I'd promised her that I'd be home on time that night. But we got a break and I…"

Mitch's mouth twitched with emotion. "I was home three hours late that night… When I got there, she'd been dead for two." Mitch looked up at her, his eyes shining. "If I'd been home when I said I would, I would've been there to protect her. But I wasn't." His brow furrowed and he pressed his lips together, fighting the emotion. "I've had to live with that, Salvi," he said quietly. "The past four years. That I was a selfish asshole who not only drove her into another man's arms, but also let her die… It's been tough. And it's been no secret that I've struggled. That's why they shipped me out here."

He nodded to himself. "I made a mess of things," he said reaching for the bottle and pouring another drink. "But you were right," he told her. "I feel too much. I felt too much, and it was killing me. So, the other night, on the anniversary…

that was me saying goodbye. That was me accepting that she's dead, that she's not coming back... That I may never find her killer... But that I gotta let it go before it kills me too. It was one last purge."

Salvi felt a heavy sensation in her chest, like her ribcage had been stuffed with wet towels. She swallowed, noticing her throat was tight.

"Mitch," she started, but he held his hand up to stop her.

"I'm not looking back any more," he said. "I'm moving forward. I'm not going to drink so much. I'm going to be focused..." He locked eyes with her. "And we're going to catch this killer, Salv. And I'm gonna clear my name from this."

"Mitch, when I said..." Salvi closed her eyes and ran her hand over her face, feeling like a lump of lead sat in her belly. A lump of guilt. "Don't listen to me. It's OK to feel something. She was your girlfriend."

"It's done," he said firmly. "It's over. I'm finally putting her to rest... I gotta focus on the present. I gotta focus on this killer, and make sure he doesn't hurt anyone else. I need to make sure no one I care about ever gets hurt again."

Salvi stared at him. "Is there someone you care about?"

Mitch glanced at her, an uncomfortable look washing over his face. He downed his drink, put the glass back on the table. "I'm just trying to explain, Salvi. To apologize. You're my partner, right? When I tried to call you the other night and you didn't answer, I panicked. That's why I traced your iPort to the club." He sighed, ran his hand through his hair. "I overreacted. I'm sorry, alright. I'm not a stalker. I'm just a cop who doesn't trust a lot of people. I just wanted you to know; I wanted to explain things." He stood from the couch and smiled sadly. "I do wear my heart on my sleeve. I feel things too much. I care too much. Maybe a little too much for this job... I crossed the line and I'm sorry."

He began to head for the door. Salvi felt a flood of regret

wash over her. For doubting him. For contemplating that he could be the killer. For her ice-cold heart. She stood from the couch and followed him.

"Mitch. Stop."

He looked around at her.

"You don't have to apologize," she said. "I should. There's nothing wrong with feeling something. She was your girlfriend. Who the hell am I to tell you not to feel something?"

He stared back at her, a sadness to his face. A loneliness she suddenly understood. An emptiness.

She felt the lump in her throat swell. "I… I know what it's like to feel something," she said quietly, her eyes beginning to sting. "To feel something so much it tears you up inside… I know how much it hurts. I know how hard that is to move on from."

He turned his body to face her and she squeezed her eyes shut, rubbed her hand over her forehead.

"I used to feel something, Mitch. I used to feel a lot. But it hurt so much I had to shut it away." She opened her eyes again and a tear escaped down her cheek. She quickly brushed it away. "I envy you," she said. "I envy your passion. Your emotion. That you can let it run so freely… I can't do that."

"Why not?" he asked.

"I just can't." She shook her head, and pressed her lips together as another tear ran down her cheek. She brushed that one away too.

"Why not, Salvi?" he asked again.

"Because it will kill me," she whispered.

"Why?" he asked, brow furrowed. "Why will it kill you to feel something?"

She shook her head again and turned away from him, damning herself for having all that vodka and losing her control. For weakening her foundations and allowing her façade to crack. She raised her hands to her face and wiped her cheeks.

"Salvi," Mitch said, closer this time. "What happened to you?"

"No," she said, still shaking her head and sniffing. "I can't."

A moment of silence passed before he spoke.

"What happened?" he asked softly. "To Salvation. What happened to her?"

At the sound of him saying her real name, the floodgates opened. She hunched her shoulders, covered her mouth, and began sobbing as tears streamed down her face.

She felt Mitch's hands touch her shoulders, holding them firmly. "It's alright, Salvi. Let it out. Whatever it is, just let it out."

"I can't. I can't," she managed.

"You can."

"No, it will kill me," she said, as another wave of gut-wrenching sobs escaped her lips.

"Salvi," he said, trying to pull her closer. She tried to fight against the movement, but she couldn't do both – fight the emotion *and* him. He turned her around and pulled her into a hug. "Hey. Hey, it's alright, Salvi. It's alright," he said softly.

She resisted his embrace, the intimacy, but he didn't relent. Finally, she dropped her fight and just let him hold her; felt the warmth of his body, the touch of her forehead against his chin and neck; felt the structure of his arms holding her. Mitch was just as fucked up as she was, so who would he be to judge her for it? Maybe she could really let go?

God, how she wanted to let it go...

She didn't know how long they stood there, but it was long enough. Eventually he gently led her back to the couch and they sat down. She thought about reaching for bottle of vodka again but decided against it. That was what had gotten her into this weeping mess.

She wiped her face again, saw the mascara on her fingers. She calmed herself down, while Mitch sat patiently, close beside her in support. She glanced at him, saw he was waiting to hear more.

She turned away and looked out her floor to ceiling windows at the city lights in the distance, felt the darkness beyond the glass like a cloak of anonymity.

"My parents were religious," she said softly, feeling as though she were in a confessional booth. Feeling as though she owed him an explanation after what he'd told her about his girlfriend. She knew she didn't have to, but she actually felt she wanted to. Felt like she'd carried it long enough. She just wanted it out now. To use Mitch's words, she wanted to purge.

It felt strange talking about it. Rough. Like a set of old rusted kitchen pipes that were finally running again. Brought back to life.

"We were raised religious. Me and my sister. Our parents were very strict. They…" she swallowed, wiped her face again, sniffed away her tears, "…they were evangelists. They were famous among their kind; had their own show on cable TV. Pillars of their community, they were. Good citizens. And me and my sister were their good little girls. Such brilliant examples of what young ladies should be." She glanced around her apartment. "Then we grew up. And like any other girls, we started noticing boys. But we were good girls. My parents knew they could trust us… Faith. That was my sister's name. Faith and Salvation," she gave a tired laugh, "you can't get any more religious than that, huh? Faith was older by two years. She was pretty. Athletic. We had the same dark hair, same dark eyes. But she was stunning." Salvi gave a sad smile.

"She met Brad not long after her fifteenth birthday. They both did track and field together, but he was older and from a different school. His family weren't religious, but they grew close. They both made the state championships. Faith was happy, always walking around with this smile on her face. She fell in love," Salvi said, as a tear escaped and slid down her cheek. She wiped it away. "She knew our parents wouldn't approve, but she loved him. She kept him a secret from them, but she would tell me all about him. She started to loosen up a little. He showed her there was a world outside of the one our parents had raised us in. Then one night they went to a party, had a few drinks, and one thing led to another. They slept together. There was nothing untoward about it. It was innocent. They were both consenting... But this guy from Brad's track and field team, Steven, he saw them go into the bedroom, and he thought it would be a laugh to record them through the bedroom window." Salvi felt her face fall. "He thought it was hilarious. He showed everyone, posted the video online with some obscene title like Evangelist's Devil Daughter... It went viral." She heard Mitch exhale sympathy beside her.

"Within hours it was everywhere," Salvi continued, eyes glazed as she stared at nothing in particular. "It was everywhere and my sister was tainted a slut, while Brad was painted the stud." She looked down at her hands. "My parents found out... You can imagine the gossip it provided for our town. The holier-than-thou evangelists and their whore of a daughter!" She shook her head. "My parents had Brad charged with statutory rape. He was older than her. She was legally underage. My sister pleaded with them to drop the charges, but they wouldn't. She tried to tell them that she loved him, that it was her decision, that if she had the chance she would do it again." Salvi paused, as her eyes glazed over again with the memories. "They had this huge argument. My mother slapped her. Told Faith she was so disappointed in her. Said 'may God forgive you'..."

"They kept us both home from school after that. Our parents taught us, made us pray for hours every day. They wanted me to learn from my sister's mistakes. Wanted to make sure I didn't repeat them." Her eyes came back to focus on her apartment. "Brad was convicted and sent to prison... He'd had consensual sex with his girlfriend, and because of one stupid jerk, both their lives were ruined. Faith was beyond devastated. The thought that Brad had been sent to jail, the thought that her naked body was flying around the internet for other people's amusement... it killed her." Salvi stared at the empty couch opposite, as a single tear rolled down her cheek. "She couldn't stand it," she said, her voice barely a whisper. "And then I found her, hanging from the ceiling fan."

"Fuck..." Mitch said softly. "Salvi, I'm sorry."

"My parents were beside themselves. I remember them crying and praying, trying to get her body down. I had tried to but I... I couldn't... I had to wait for my parents to get home. I just had to sit there staring at Faith hanging from the ceiling... Things got worse after that. My parents were constantly praying and wondering why their little girl turned out so damaged, saying the devil had taken her from them. Said that God was testing them. Then all eyes turned to me."

"I was the hope left in their lives. Faith had fallen to the darkness, but I was their *Salvation*. My father told me that, you know? He said he just knew when I was born that I would be their salvation... I hated them... I couldn't forgive them for what they did to Faith, or Brad. As soon as I was strong enough to stand on my own two feet, I rebelled. In every way I knew how. I openly slept around. Men, women, I didn't care. I drank too much. I tried all kinds of drugs. Anything to avenge Faith. Anything to make them realize that *she* was the good one. That they were wrong about her. They tried so hard to bring me back into the fold, so determined not to lose another one. They locked me in the house, had their fellow parishioners come and kneel in my room praying, like some kind of exorcism or something. But I fought, and I *fought*." She wiped her face. "I ran away at sixteen, and I never spoke to them again."

"And you still haven't?" he asked gently.

Salvi shook her head, as a curtain of tears streamed down her face. "When I was twenty-one a lawyer tracked me down with a letter in his hand. They'd died in a car accident. It rolled down a ravine…" She paused a moment as the sobbing took hold of her. "I never forgave them," she whispered. "Hadn't spoken to them in years, and here was this guy handing me my inheritance, all the money they'd made from their TV show, from donations. At first I just let it sit there. I didn't want to touch it. Then I was going to donate it all, find some charity. But then I saw it as my way out. I was living in a shitty apartment, working in a shitty bar. This was my way out. I went back to school, graduated, and became a cop."

She wiped her face but it was useless. There were too many tears. "I never forgave them, and they'd left me everything they had. All their money, their house, life insurances, and this letter, telling me that they forgave me for everything. For disowning them. For turning my back on God. They said they loved me. That they always loved me and Faith. They begged my forgiveness, said they'd meet me in heaven… and I… I think I died myself that day." She nodded vaguely to herself. "The guilt… it killed me. Killed my heart… I swear it stopped beating… and… I don't think I've ever let it beat again since." She leaned forward, placing her face in her hands, as the emotion overwhelmed her. Mitch leaned closer and put his arm around her shoulders.

"I'm so sorry, Salvi," he whispered, pulling her gently against his side.

She pulled back and looked at him with her wet face. "So, you see, I'm even more fucked up than you are, Mitch. So don't listen to me when I tell you to stop feeling things.

I'm just jealous because I haven't let myself feel anything in years." She looked away again.

"It's not too late," he said, sliding his hand over her cheek, turning her face back to his. "You gotta forgive yourself, Salvi. Just like I had to. We gotta move on. We can't change the past."

"You didn't kill your girlfriend, Mitch. My parents? I often wondered whether their car going down that ravine was an accident. It was a fine day. The roads were dry. They were driving a straight patch of road at the time."

"Salvi–"

"Sometimes I wonder whether they just gave up and drove right off the edge…"

"Salvi, you can't think like that."

"…Whether I drove them over the edge." She looked away, but he turned her face back again.

"Salvi," he said firmly, locking eyes with hers. "You can't think that."

"You can't think that maybe if you gotten home earlier that you could've saved her."

"But I know I could have," he told her. "If I'd been home when I'd promised, she would still be alive."

"Or you could be dead too."

He looked at her, not sure what to say.

"What if he had a gun, Mitch? What if he shot you, then still did that to her?"

"What if your parents had a genuine accident? What if your father or mother or whoever was driving had a heart attack at the wheel?"

Salvi stared back at him through blurred eyes.

"That's what I've *finally* learned, Salvi. The 'What if's' will kill you. Her killer is still out there, but I have to let it go. And so do you. They're gone, and there's nothing we can do to bring them back. All we can do is forgive ourselves our mistakes and move on before we waste any more of our lives."

His hand remained cupping her face. She studied the dark fringe resting against his forehead, his eyes as they stared into hers, felt the soft caress as he wiped her tear-stained cheek. She couldn't remember the last time someone had touched like this; with care, with feeling. She couldn't remember if *anyone* had ever touched her like this... She dropped her eyes to his mouth.

The silence sat for a moment.

"I should go," he said quietly, standing.

"Why?" she asked, looking up at him.

He looked at her. "It's late and you're drunk. You should go to sleep." He turned for the door.

"Just like that?" she asked.

"Just like what?" he asked.

She stared at him. "All this time you push to find out who I am. You finally get it out of me, the family shame, the reason why I changed my name, the reason for the nice apartment." She waved her hands around. "And the second you get it out of me, the second you turn me into this pool of crying weakness, you make me open this door, then you just leave?"

"It's not weak to show emotion, Salvi," he told her. "It takes strength." He turned and headed for the door.

"And still you leave," she said, unable to hide the bitterness. She stood from the couch. "It's *weak* to leave."

He stopped and turned around, studied her. "No," he said, shaking his head. "It takes *strength* to leave."

She picked up the glass from the table and threw it at him. He dodged it and it fell onto the carpet.

"What the hell, Salvi!"

"You *asshole!*" she said walking up to him. "Go on then. Go!"

He stared back, brow furrowed. "What the hell is wrong with you?"

"What's wrong with me? What's wrong with *you*? You pushed me and pushed me. Kept telling me I need to live a little, I need to let go. That I need to *feel* something." She pushed him backward. "Then finally I feel something and you run away."

"And *you* kept telling me to stop feeling so much. So *that's* what I'm doing!"

"Get out," she said pushing him again.

"What do you want from me?"

"What do *you* want from me?" she shot back. He didn't answer her, just stared. "Get out!" She pushed him again, but this time he didn't budge, and her body slammed into his. He grabbed her wrists to stop her hands from pushing him back again.

"What do you want from me, Salvi?" he repeated, breathing heavily, trying to lock his eyes on hers.

"Get out," she said, averting them, trying to get her wrists back.

"What do you want?" he demanded, squeezing her wrists. "If you want something, say it, Salvi!"

She refused to answer him, focused her drunken mind on freeing her wrists.

"You want *me* to feel something?" he asked her. "Is that it? Huh? You want to go there? You *really* want to go there?"

"Go where?" She looked up at him confused.

"You know where, Salvi. And you know that's why I'm leaving. But if you want to stop me from leaving, if you want me to stay, just say the word, and I will."

She stared back at him, breathing heavily, but no words would formulate in her mouth. She could smell the faint scent of his aftershave, tried not to soak up his piercing gaze or the feel of her body pressed against his, as memories of her wilder days invaded her. Memories of times when she let herself go. When she had no fear.

She felt the fight within her disappear, lowered her arms.

"You want me to feel something?" he said again. "Well, I will if you will." His focus dropped to her lips, before returning to her eyes. "Tell me what you want, Salvi. If you want me to stay, say it."

Salvi worked to catch her breath. He let go of her wrists but remained standing close to her. She felt his breath on her face.

"W-we're partners," she said, glancing around, her head still spinning a little from the alcohol. "This… isn't a good idea."

"No. It's not," he said, but didn't move. "And you're drunk," he added.

She nodded, looked back at him. "So why are you still here?"

"You're the one who stopped me from leaving." He held his arms out. He stared at her for another moment, then nodded to himself as though understanding something. "Goodnight, Salvi." He went to turn around but she stopped him. He glanced down at her fist scrunching the front of his shirt.

She looked at him, awash in vodka, drained of tears.

The urge to feel the warmth of his body pressed against hers again, wanting to taste his kiss, was overwhelming.

But he was her partner. This was a bad idea. This was a *very* bad idea.

But for the first time, in a long time, she wanted somebody. Needed somebody. Wanted *him*.

"You want me to feel something?" she said quietly, staring into his eyes.

"Yeah. I do," he said back.

She scrunched his shirt tighter and pulled him closer. "Then God help us both," she whispered and pressed her mouth against his.

He exhaled heavily, closing his eyes briefly and savoring the kiss. He opened his eyes again, studying her carefully as he slid his hand over her cheek and kissed her again.

She felt the vodka swimming through her bloodstream, let it drown the common-sense part of her brain, sending it into hibernation. She pooled her energy into her senses, focused on the way his mouth kissed hers, warm and firm and wanting. The way his chest felt pressed against hers as she rolled off his coat. The way his hands slid around her back, pulling her closer to him. The way hers slid around his neck, the fingers raking through his hair.

She didn't want to think about the fact that he was her partner. As she moved him toward her bedroom, all she wanted to do was feel.

16 : TORMENT

Salvi slowly rose to consciousness on a sea of sporadic dreams. Images flashed like shards of daylight piercing through branches that blew in the breeze. Memories of vodka, of tears, of Mitch. She saw Mitch's fingers trace over the scorpion tattoo on her hip, saw his mouth press against the Faith tattoo over her heart. She heard him panting in her ear, felt a wave of ecstasy rolling through her body.

Then she noticed the dryness in her mouth, the ache in her head, and realized she was awake.

She opened her eyes, felt her naked skin against the sheets and knew she hadn't been dreaming. Lying on her stomach, she slowly rolled onto her side and looked over her shoulder. And there he was. Mitch Grenville. Her partner. Sleeping beside her.

He was lying on his back, his face turned away, the sheet draped lazily and low around his hips, providing enough evidence that he was naked too. She watched his chest, saw it rising and falling evenly. He was still in a deep sleep.

She slid out of the bed as carefully as she could, not wanting to wake him. She needed to sort out the pain in her head so she could get her thoughts together, to process what had happened between them. What they'd done.

She moved into the bathroom and closed the door quietly. Resting her forehead against it, she sighed and squeezed her eyes shut tightly. She'd slept with Mitch. She'd had sex with her partner. One of the biggest unwritten rules of being police – and she'd broken it.

The worst part was, if her hazy memory served her correctly, she'd enjoyed every second of it. And so had he.

She slid underneath the spray of her shower, trying to wake up, trying to shake off the hangover, trying to figure out what to do. The images from last night continued to flash through her mind: his naked body pressed against hers, the warmth in his eyes, the way she'd hungrily kissed him. She tried hard to shake them from her mind, but they wouldn't leave. Or maybe she wouldn't let them leave. Maybe she didn't want to let them go.

"Hey," Mitch's voice sounded from behind, giving her a fright. She turned around and saw him standing naked at the door of her shower, stepping inside.

"What are you doing?" she asked, her head still hazy, automatically covering herself.

He looked down at the arm across her breasts, the hand covering further below.

A smile curled his lips. "I hate to break it to you, Salvi, but I saw it all last night. Up close... Up *real* close. And my memory is probably better than yours is today."

She shot him an insulted look, and he reached out and gently pulled at her arms. She lowered them. His eyes washed over her body before he scooped some water and ran it over his face. As he did, she eyed his naked form back, swallowed hard, hesitated, then stepped out of the shower.

"You doing a runner on me?" he asked.

"No, I'm just done," she lied, grabbing a towel and leaving the room.

Mitch came out a few minutes later, his hair wet, lean but toned chest glistening with water droplets and a white towel wrapped around his waist.

Salvi was dressed, her lenses were in, and she was sitting on the edge of her bed, pulling her black boots on. Despite her rusty head from the vodka, she found it hard to look away from him.

"This how it's going to be?" he asked her.

"How is what going to be?" she asked, playing dumb, strapping her iPort on.

Mitch stared at her. "Us. Last night. You don't want to talk about it?"

She stood up but averted her eyes, moving to the mirror to put her red lipstick on. "I'm getting ready for work, Mitch."

He nodded, still eyeing her. "So, you're just gonna pretend last night didn't happen?"

"Mitch. We're late."

"You asked me to stay, Salvi," he said calmly. "You *wanted* me to stay."

"Mitch, you're making a big deal out of this," she said, heading for the bedroom door, but he caught her arm. She looked back into the green eyes that were fixed upon hers.

"You asked me to stay, Salvi," he said again. "You invited me into your bed, now you're going to freeze me out like I did something wrong?"

"Mitch," she closed her eyes and ran her hand over her forehead, "I haven't even had coffee yet. Do we have to do this now?"

"Yeah, we do," he said. "We're partners, Salvi."

"I gotta go," she said, pulling her arm from his grasp and heading out into her kitchen.

He followed her. "Your car is still at the bar. Wait a minute and I'll give you a ride."

"No," she said, grabbing one of the two key cards by the door and slipping it into her pocket. She poured a glass of water. "I'll meet you there. We should arrive separately anyway."

Mitch watched her silently while she swallowed some painkillers.

"I got a ReVitalize shot in my car," he offered.

"I'm fine," she said, grabbing her coat and heading for the door.

Mitch moved to block her exit.

"Salvi–"

"Mitch, we're late for work. We got a serial killer to catch."

"I know we do," he said.

"So, let me go do my job," she said.

"*Our* job." He stared at her.

"Mitch, I can't deal with this now. Seriously." She pulled the front door open. "I'll meet you at the station. You can let yourself out."

Salvi sat at her desk, staring at her console display. The painkillers were working, but she was still so thirsty. The thought of that ReVitalize shot was tempting, except for the fact that she was avoiding Mitch right now. She stared at the picture of Rebecca Carson, dressed in her softball uniform, smiling back at her. Salvi was trying hard to focus on the case and trying hard not to make eye contact with Hernandez or Beggs or Caine or Bronte. Especially Hernandez, scared he might read the truth on her face.

More than that, she was trying not to think about what a bitch she'd been to Mitch that morning. He was right. She'd asked him to stay, had wanted him to stay, and she'd enjoyed it. It had taken every ounce of her willpower to drag herself out of the shower that morning, away from him, to not have sex with him again right there and then. Now she was making him pay for the confusion she felt, the tattered remnants of her past billowing inside her. The loneliness. The connection she'd felt with him. Their shared guilt, their shared need to forgive themselves. He understood her pain. And she understood his. They were both fucked up yet functioning. Both needed someone. But they were partners. God, what a mess.

Mitch finally arrived and walked up to her with a coffee in hand, just like he did every other morning.

"Glad you could join us!" Hernandez called out from his desk. "Big night, huh?"

Mitch ignored him, handed Salvi the coffee. She took it, offering a quiet "Thank you," then he moved to sit at his desk like he did any other day. He was acting normal, giving nothing away about their previous night, about their fight this morning. She was grateful for that. Although she found it a little uncomfortable trying to work while he sat opposite in her line of vision. The smell of the soap from her shower wafted over to her.

A message came through from Riverton. She opened it and saw that it was a profile on the vics' online activity from the cyber department.

"You seen the cyber report?" Mitch asked, not taking his eyes off the screen.

"Just reading it now."

"Vic one and two had high level accounts with U-Stasis," he said. "That meant they were regulars."

"Rebecca Carson too?" Salvi paused a moment, dropping her eyes to the section of the report outlining that.

"Looks like she used a blind dating room." Mitch turned his face to look at her. "Carly Fresner's not on there, though. So, our perp may not have met them in U-Stasis." He tapped his fingers on the desk, thinking, then stood up. "I'm going to pay cyber a visit, see what other names they can dig up."

With that he took his coffee and left. And all the while, Salvi noticed, Hernandez watched him like a hawk.

Salvi racked her brain trying to find a connection between all three women. From what she could tell, Sharon Gleamer and Rebecca Carson had two links: they both attended the same church, and they both had accounts on U-Stasis. But Carly

Fresner, the prostitute, according to the cyber report, didn't have a U-Stasis account. But why would she? She was in the business of providing actual *physical* contact.

So why would the perp suddenly switch type? Was he trying to throw them? Was it even the first two victims' killer? Could it have been a copycat? Or was Holt right, had Fresner just been the easiest target as everyone else was staying off the streets at night? But then again, how would Holt know that? Because he'd been out on the street doing patrols that night. He'd know better than anyone else.

And he had been a previous client of hers. Was he erasing evidence?

Still, each attack *had* been slightly different. Sharon's had been a more drawn-out affair, then she'd been strangled. Rebecca Carson's had been a hit and run. She'd been raped and her neck broken, all in a flash attack. Carly Fresner had her skull smashed in. The only single link between all three cases had been the word "pure" carved into their bodies. And maybe the smears of BioLume.

Salvi quickly checked her messages to see if anything was in yet from Kim Weston, but there wasn't.

The thought of those BioLume footprints stuck in her mind. She finished her coffee, then she pulled up the files for the Subjugates again. Something about the BioLume niggled at her. She began flipping through the files, focusing on the three Subjugates that most intrigued her: Lucius Dolles, Fontan Pragge and Edward Moses. Then of course, there was Serene-41. But she didn't have access to his file. She'd never finished her discussion with him the other day, about his visits to town, and his escort of Moses. Serene-41 was half the size of Moses. So how was placid little Serene-41 supposed to keep the Subjugate in check?

One by one she pulled up their prior records again. Fontan Pragge, was of course, a serial rapist who didn't have a type.

His previous MO fit the bill, mostly, but with that brain damage did he have the capacity, or perhaps even the desire, to commit these murders – *and* be smart enough to cover his tracks afterwards? Lucius Dolles, the college rapist, could. But he never killed his victims. And even then, his physical violence was kept to a minimum. He didn't beat them, he just held them down and raped them. Edward Moses did both. He raped them, then killed them. And he'd been a lawyer. He was smart enough to cover his tracks and think of all the angles. She'd read the details of each of the attacks committed by Moses, and they had involved a mixture of circumstances. He didn't seem to have a type either or a preferred method of killing. For the seven counts of murder he'd been found guilty of, three had been strangulations, two had died from head injuries from a beating, one had a broken neck, and one had had her throat slit. Moses liked to change things up depending on his mood.

She sighed and closed the files. She couldn't deny that of all the Subjugates, Moses most fit the bill. He had similar priors, he had been allowed in the town and undertook work in the BioLume factory. But something still niggled at Salvi. How did he get away from his Serene escort? The guards were supposed to keep an eye on them too. With their brain tweaking and chemical injections, how could a Subjugate work up enough fury to have done what he did to the three vics? How could the treatment work on all the others, but not on him?

She needed the new warrants for their DNA, *now*. She stood and moved to Ford's office, but saw it was empty. Her iPort signaled an incoming call. It was her security company. She'd programmed in the number after they'd called her last time.

"Detective Brentt," she answered.

"Ms Brentt, Solid State Security here. Your alarm has

sounded again, albeit only briefly before it was shut off. We just wanted to check whether that was you?"

"When did it sound?" she asked.

"Just now."

Salvi looked across the bullpen at Mitch's empty desk. Maybe he didn't close the door properly this morning. She checked her iPort. He'd been gone a while. "It's OK," she said. "I'll go check it out."

"Would you like someone to meet you there?"

"No, it's fine," she said, moving back to her desk, opening the drawer and holstering her gun. "I got it."

She ended the call, logged out of her console, and headed out the door.

Salvi swiped her pass over the console and heard the door to her apartment unlock, which meant that it was previously locked. Perhaps it was just time for a service on her alarm sensors? Still, as the door opened, she kept her hand on her gun just in case. The door slid back and she surveyed her apartment. Everything looked just as she'd left it.

She stepped inside and closed the door behind her, listening as it made the musical chime. She sighed and moved over to the kitchen, poured herself a glass of filtered water and swallowed some more painkillers. The water was just what she needed, although part of her still pined for a shot of Mitch's ReVitalize.

As she stood there downing the water, she thought she heard something. A voice, a moan, coming from her bedroom. She put the glass down quietly, pulled her gun out and moved silently toward her bedroom. As she approached, she heard the sound again. There were two voices. Moans, panting.

She stepped through into her bedroom, gun firmly in front, swinging back and forth. The bedroom was empty, just like she'd left it that morning; the bed all messy, last night's clothes on the floor. She moved up to her bathroom and swiftly turned inside, gun swinging back and forth across the empty room.

Then she heard it again and looked back into her bedroom.

The TV was on.

Her brow furrowed. Did Mitch turn it on after she left and forget to turn it off?

She moved over to the console on her headboard and went to turn it off but paused at what she saw. At first she'd thought it was just some movie playing, but now as she looked at it properly, she realized what it was.

It was her.

The movie was her.

Her and Mitch. From last night.

She stepped toward the screen slowly, as a shaking began to overtake her body. She watched, frozen, unable to get her brain to understand what was happening. She watched herself straddling Mitch, riding him, as he squeezed her breasts in his hands. She glanced back at the empty bed, then looked back at the screen to see Mitch reverse their positions, lying on top of her, her legs curling around him. She saw him grab her hand and thread his fingers through hers, pressing it back into the sheets, as he kissed her. Saw him thrusting into her, saw herself moan and pant, as she thrust her tongue into his mouth.

Her whole body was rattling now, the gun visibly shaking in her hand. She turned around, a full 360 degrees, not knowing what to do. She looked back at the screen, saw herself come, saw Mitch follow. Her eyes shot back to the bed, then looked back at the screen again and realized the angle it had been filmed from. Her eyes moved to the air vent on the wall above the TV. She swiftly moved over and climbed onto the cabinet that sat below the TV, boosting her height. She clawed at the air vent, smacking it with her gun to get it loose; she pulled it off and there it was. A small camera and microphone. A red light indicated the camera was on. Whoever did this was watching her. Recording her.

It made her recall Swaggert flashing the red light in her face at the first crime scene. She snatched the camera, ripping it out of its hold, and threw it to the floor. She jumped back down from the cabinet and picked it up again, raced into her bathroom and smashed it against the tiled floor of the shower, again and again. She turned the taps on and flooded the remains with hot water. Catching her breath, she leaned back against the wall, eyes wide, body still shaking.

Who the hell would do this?

Who had access to do this?

She instantly thought of Mitch but struggled to contemplate it. If he was the killer, wouldn't he have just killed her last night? He was going to leave and she made him stay. He hadn't forced her. He hadn't done anything to her that she hadn't wanted done.

A tear rolled down her cheek as she stepped out into her bedroom again. Her eyes fell back to the screen; the footage still played. It was on repeat. She saw herself walking into her bedroom with Mitch removing their clothes.

She briefly lost her legs and fell to the floor, gasping for breath. She pictured Faith in her mind. This was what it must've been like for her. To have had someone invade her privacy like that. To record a personal moment meant only for the two people involved.

No one else knew about Faith. Only Mitch.

But she'd only told him that night? Or had he somehow found out? When he'd been looking into her?

She stood again, moved over to her bed and slumped down on the side of it. Still catching her breath, she looked around the room trying to make sense of things. Her eyes caught on something red, sticking out from underneath her white sheets. She stood and pulled the covers back a little. She gasped and ripped the top sheet right off her bed and onto the floor. There, written in red across her bed was the word "pure".

Her iPort began ringing then, scaring her. She looked at the caller. It was Mitch. The blood drained from her. She tore at the iPort's clasp, ripped it off and threw it on the bed, just staring at it. Then she lunged forward and thrust it beneath her pillow and clawed at her eyes and ears, pulling her lenses and ear piece out too, and tore the badge off her shirt.

Could he have done this?

No, it couldn't be Mitch. If he had wanted to torture her with memories of Faith, he wouldn't have had time to set this up. The cameras. He hadn't left her side once she'd told him.

Her brain started working overtime and a thought struck her like an axe to the spine. She suddenly raced out into her living room and began pulling at all the air vents. She groaned a cry as she found another camera in the living room, facing her couch. She moved onto the next and the next, working her way through the whole apartment. In the end she found three cameras: one in her bedroom, one in her bathroom and one in her living room. How long had someone been watching her?

She thought back to the first alarm call she'd had from the security company.

She suddenly recalled Mitch's concern about someone watching them. That someone had followed him to the prostitute that night. That someone was sending him a message. Just like she had now been sent a message. Someone was taunting them. Someone was having fun taunting them.

But was it someone else? Or had Mitch just planted a seed in her mind?

Her skin crawled at the thought of staying in her apartment any longer. She had to get out of there.

And she had to stay away from Mitch until she figured out who it was.

Salvi didn't know what else to do, but she got into her Zenith and headed for Bountiful. Before leaving, she'd checked in with the auto-concierge and asked to review the security footage. No one was seen entering her apartment. Only her and Mitch. But someone had written "pure" across her bed …

He was the only one that could've done it. So why couldn't she believe it was him?

She needed to find the killer fast, and Bountiful was the best place to look. At least that was what her gut was telling her. She wanted desperately to prove that it wasn't Mitch. That it couldn't possibly be Mitch. That she wasn't a fool who had just slept with the Bountiful Killer.

She drove around the streets, past the houses of his victims and into the center of town. She found herself out front of the Children of Christ complex, staring up at the large green cross atop the church. She thought of the BioLume pulsing within its confines. She got out of her car and moved toward it. This time her magnet wasn't trying to repel her, but instead drawing her toward it. Pulling her with determination to find the killer.

The church was empty, and she stepped inside the quiet. Nothing but her and the BioLume lights along the altar. She walked toward the altar, hands in the pockets of her jacket, eyes fixed to the large Jesus Christ nailed to his cross against the wall beyond. Everything, including herself, awash with the green glow.

She didn't know what to say, what to think. She still harbored so much anger for the religion, for the way it held human freedoms prisoner. She thought of her parents, of their extremism. She thought of Faith and of the footage that had driven her sister to suicide.

Then she thought of the footage she had just seen in her apartment. Saw herself letting go. Saw herself finding solace in another.

And she thought of someone taking that moment and soiling it. Taking her freedom. Taking her right to live her life as she wanted in private and using it for their enjoyment.

Someone trying to control her with fear.

Someone who was angry she wasn't pure.

"The lost souls always find their way back." A voice startled her from behind.

She spun around to see Preacher Vowker standing there, a soft smile upon his face. She stared at him, defiant, her eyes shining with angry tears.

"You looked troubled," he said gently.

She couldn't speak, her whole body was clenched, trying to hold the anger inside, to keep it at bay. This man, who raised so many unpleasant memories within her.

"What troubles you, Detective?" he said. "Let me help you."

Salvi looked back around at the Jesus on the crucifix, then she looked back at Vowker. "I don't want your help," she managed. "I'm going to do this alone."

She walked past him and headed back out onto the street.

Salvi walked along the road toward the third vic, Carly Fresner's house. She stood outside and stared at it, her body frozen, her thoughts racing. In her mind she saw Sheriff Holt raise the sheet, saw the yellow dress, saw Mitch's pale face, saw his back as he turned to the window. She recalled the scratch she'd seen on his bare back through the motel room doorway. The morning they'd found the second vic.

She walked to Rebecca Carson's house and did the same thing. She studied the house, tried to look at it from the perp's point of view. Thought of him sneaking around the back of her house. Pictured him breaking her neck.

Then she walked to Sharon Gleamer's house and stood at the base of her porch stairs. Thought of the young girl lying naked on the kitchen floor. Thought of her parents walking in and finding her. She sensed eyes on her and turned around to the Fizzraeli house across the road. There, behind the screen door, stood little redheaded Sophia, staring at her. Salvi began to approach, but as she neared Sophia stepped backward and shook her head.

"Stay away, sinner! You're going to hell!" she said, closing the front door and locking it.

Salvi stood in the middle of the street, staring at the closed door. She sighed heavily and turned around to study the Gleamers' house again. She felt the open space around her. The flat land, the low houses. The daylight, the trees, the birds singing. The simple way of life. They had removed daily temptations, and yet the sin had still found its way here.

And it had killed Sharon Gleamer, and Rebecca Carson, and Carly Fresner. And Salvi was next. "Pure" had been marked across her bed, a virtual target placed upon her. The question was, would it be her fate to join the other women? Or would she make it her fate to catch this killer and avenge their deaths? In a way these women were like her sister, Faith. Their lives stolen for some asshole's titillation. Faith's death had pushed Salvi into law enforcement. And now she was going to use that to find justice for these dead women.

She moved up onto the sidewalk again, analyzing the house carefully. All three victims' houses were close enough together to walk between. All of them were close to the town center.

She looked over at Jason Stackwell's house and began to move toward it but paused when she reached the gap between their houses. She looked down the side of Sharon's and saw a clear view from the street into her bedroom.

A shuffling noise sounded behind her and she turned around to see Subjugate-12, Fontan Pragge, approaching. His eyes were fixed on her, one fist clenched in the other.

"Bad man," he said, thumping his fist into his open hand. "Bad man." He motioned up to Sharon Gleamer's house, to her bedroom window.

"Yes, Subjugate-12," Salvi said, analyzing him carefully. "A bad man was here."

He nodded. "Bad man look," he said, pointing to Sharon Gleamer's house. "No. No. Bad." He shook his head, waved his hands like a baseball umpire. "That's bad. That's a bad man. Bad man."

Salvi looked at Sharon's bedroom window, then back to the Subjugate.

"You watched her?" she asked. "You were a bad man?"

Subjugate-12 shook his head. "No, no, no, no. Bad man watched her. Bad man watched her. No, no, no. He's a bad man." The Subjugate stepped right up to her and she stiffened.

"Who's a bad man?" she asked, stepping back.

"No, no, no." Subjugate-12 shook his head. "No, no, no, no. Bad man hurt me. Bad man hurt. No, no, no, no."

"Who will hurt you?" she said, stepping toward him now.

Subjugate-12 shook his head, kept smacking his fist into his hand.

"Who will hurt you, Subjugate-12?" she asked firmly.

"No, no, no," he said, still shaking his head.

"It's all right, you can tell me," she said, her voice softening. "I know you want to."

"Bad man watch," he said, eyes wide. "I saw. Bad man watch."

"Who?" she said, more demanding. "Who, Subjugate-12? Who's the bad man?"

"There a problem here?" a voice said.

Salvi turned and saw Sheriff Holt, leaning out the window

of his car as it pulled up alongside them.

Salvi stared at him. "No. There's not." She turned back to Fontan Pragge. "Tell me, Subjugate-12."

A loud whistle caught their attention. She saw Edward Moses approaching them, and Bander further on pulling his fingers out of his mouth.

"Subjugate-12," Moses said. "It's time to go."

Salvi looked back at Fontan Pragge. His eyes were still wide and he kept moving from one foot to the other, fidgeting, glancing from her to Holt, to Moses, and back.

"Subjugate-12," she said, firmly. "Tell me what you know."

Moses moved closer, and Pragge seemed to cower, darting his eyes between Holt, still leaning out his car window, and Moses on approach.

"SUBJUGATE-12!" Bander yelled from down the road by the van. "GET HERE, NOW!"

Moses unfurled his strong arm, holding it out to Pragge. "Come, Subjugate-12. It is time to go."

Subjugate-12 hunched his shoulders, cowering like a child in trouble, and began to walk toward Moses, still slapping his fist into his open palm and muttering, "Bad man, bad man."

Sheriff Holt drove off down the street then. As Pragge reached Moses, the other Subjugate ushered him forward, then looked back at Salvi. Moses gave her a smile and a slight bow, then turned back toward their van. And as he did, Salvi saw a glint flash along his halo. It was fast, it was brief, but it made her pause.

She couldn't tell if it had simply been the sun's rays reflecting off it, or whether she had just seen a code blue...

Salvi walked quickly back to her Zenith and set it in motion toward the Solme Complex. She needed to speak with Fontan Pragge again, alone. She was sure he was going to tell her something, but the arrival of Holt in his car, and Moses and

Bander calling for him, had spooked the Subjugate.

She wasn't sure how much she could trust the words of a brain-damaged man, and a hideous former criminal at that, but maybe that was just the thing. Maybe everyone doubted him. Maybe if Pragge had seen something he shouldn't have and the perp had caught him, maybe they'd assumed no one would listen. Well, Salvi would. It was worth a shot.

As she drove along she ran over the scene again and again. Pragge had been fine until Holt and Moses showed up. He cowered when Bander yelled at him, but that was understandable. Bander was the caretaker and it was his job to mete out punishments. No doubt Pragge had been on the end of his baton before. But Subjugate-12 had no need to be afraid of Holt or Moses.

And the one thing she couldn't erase from her mind was the glint from Subjugate-52's halo. Had it just been a flash of refracted sunlight? Or had she witnessed something else entirely? Something that could put the future of Attis' program at serious risk.

If the likes of Edward Moses was coding blue and allowed into town …

As she neared the facility, the console in her car beeped. It was a message from Kim Weston. Too distracted to put the Zenith into autodrive, Salvi swerved over to the side of the road and stopped. She opened the message. It was the forensics report on the third vic. Fresner had died from head injuries, and had indeed been raped. So far there were no hits on the DNA, but it matched the other victims. Time of death had been early morning, the revised times being between 8am and 10am. But Salvi's eyes paused when saw the word BioLume. Weston confirmed that minute traces of BioLume had been found on the vic's dress and on the carpet inside her apartment. Fresner's house, she noted, did not have BioLume lighting.

Weston also stated that she'd heard back from Attis Solme, who confirmed that the BioLume bacteria could only survive twenty-four hours outside of its special gel-filled globes. Given that the BioLume had been found on or near all three vics, it was safe to assume that the perp was stepping in BioLume regularly.

Every day, in fact.

Salvi's eyes left the console screen and looked up through her windshield. There in the near distance was the Solme Complex. The silver silos shining in the afternoon sun. She pictured the main BioLume plant, pictured the vats and their contents in all shades of green. She pictured the Serenes and Subjugates working in there. Pictured the BioLume spills on their coveralls. Pictured the spills, no doubt, that wound up on the floor. On the soles of their shoes.

This, she thought, was strong proof that the Bountiful Killer was a resident of the Solme Complex. Someone who worked directly with the BioLume. Someone who trod in it every single day. Someone who brought that BioLume into town with them.

She pulled her Zenith back onto the road and continued on. She drove up to the gates and as she pulled up, the guard on duty walked out to her.

"I wasn't expecting you today," he said, scrolling through data on his silver helmet visor. "You're not on my list."

"No, I'm not," she said. "Something's come up and I need to speak with one of the Subjugates."

"You know you can't visit without prior authorization from the mayor."

"Well, can you call his office? I'm sure he'll let me in."

"He's not here," the guard told her. "He's been gone all day."

"He has?" she said. "Do you know where?"

"No. You'll have to come back," he said stepping away.

"Wait!" she called. "What about the caretaker? He here? Can I speak with him?"

The guard studied her a moment, as though contemplating whether to give in to her request. He eventually relented. "I'll give him a call." He walked back to his booth to make contact. All the while Salvi sat, hands clenched around the steering wheel of her Zenith, watching the drone hovering in the air above the Complex's main building – watching her back.

The guard returned. "Alright, he said you can come through. Just let me scan you."

Salvi nodded and waited while the guard scanned her car, then waved her forward to meet the drone and follow it to the appropriate parking spot. She did so, turned the car off and moved to open the door, but was startled to see Serene-41 standing outside her window.

"Detective," he bowed in greeting, opening the door for her.

"Serene-41," she said back, getting out of the vehicle. "Take me to the caretaker, please."

"Of course." The Serene turned around and set off toward the main building.

"Serene-41," she said, moving after him. "When you went into town these past few days with Subjugate-52, did you ever lose sight of him?"

Serene-41 looked around at her, then seemed to think. "It's quite possible."

"Quite possible?"

"Yes." He gave a slight bow. "But the Subjugates must always travel in a pair, with a Serene or a guard. If I was not with Subjugate-52 then someone else was."

"And what about the Serenes?" she asked. "I saw you the other day, putting flowers on the Gleamers' doormat. You were alone."

"Yes. I am allowed to travel alone. I am Serene-Supreme.

I am trusted."

She studied him carefully as she followed him inside the main building.

"Please wait here in reception," he said. She nodded and watched him leave, then began to pace the curved-walled room with beige hues and BioLume lights. An empty, silent, shell. Much like the Serenes that dwelled here, in this vacuum of killers.

She soon heard footsteps and turned expecting to see Bander, but instead Dr Remmell stood there.

"We weren't expecting you," he said.

"No." She smiled, not wanting to raise any alarm. "I just had some questions I would like to ask of Subjugate-12."

"Have you the authorization from Mayor Solme?" he asked.

"No."

"Have you the authorization from me?"

She stared at him. "Not yet."

"Why do you wish to speak with him?" he asked, his untrusting beady eyes glaring out of his dark-rimmed rectangular-framed glasses.

Salvi considered carefully what to say, knowing that Remmell had been one of those identified by the prostitute. She decided on bluntness. She decided on the truth. She wanted to see his reaction. "I think he knows who the killer is."

Remmell scoffed a small laugh. "Subjugate-12? And why do you think that?"

"I think people underestimate him," she said. "His brain is fried so people pay him no mind. But he still has eyes and ears. And if the Solme Complex has done its job," she said with a smile, "if *you* have done your job right, then he will know what is good and what is bad. He will know what is right from what is wrong. And if he's seen something bad, something wrong, I think he can tell me."

"I assure you we have done our job and Subjugate-12 knows right from wrong. But he is also very fragile. He cannot handle stress."

"Well, what he's seen may have caused him undue stress," she said. "Has he been acting unusual this past week since Sharon Gleamer died?"

Remmell stared at her.

"He has," she answered her own question. "So, let me speak with him."

"No," he said firmly.

"Why not?"

"Because if he's under stress, you will not put him under any more."

"You're happy to let this killer do it again?" she asked.

Remmell stared at her. "I will speak with him."

"I need to be present."

"No, you don't."

"Yes, I do."

"Why?" he asked, stepping toward her. "So you can undo your blouse, confuse and entrap him, like you tried to do with Subjugate-52?"

She stared at him.

"I won't have that," he said. "Subjugate-12 is my patient."

"Dr Remmell, you're impeding a murder investigation right now."

"I will speak with the Subjugate!" he said bitterly. "If there's anything to report, I will let you know. Good day!" With that, Remmell stormed out of the room, almost knocking into Levan Bander on his way out.

"What was that about?" Bander asked, stepping into the room with Serene-41.

"I need to speak to Subjugate-12 and he won't let me see him."

"Why?"

Salvi exhaled. "I think he knows something."

Bander stared at her, then looked back at the Serene and motioned for him to leave. The Serene obeyed. Bander looked back to her. "You don't think it's him? Pragge?"

"No." She shook her head. "But he knows something. He's seen something."

Bander pouted his lips and nodded. "Well, when the mayor isn't here, Remmell is in charge of resident welfare. Not much I can do."

"But you're the caretaker."

He nodded. "Yeah, I oversee the security of the Complex, but personal welfare of residents comes down to Remmell." Bander stepped forward. "What'd he say to you today in town? Subjugate-12?"

Salvi looked back at him. "Nothing. He just gave me the impression he knew something."

Bander gave her an awkward look. "You know he's retarded, right?"

"Yeah," Salvi nodded, "but he still has the ability to witness a murder, or witness something that he shouldn't have."

"I guess," he said, scratching his head. He looked back at her and shrugged. "Well, until Remmell gives you the OK, there's nothing you can do. You'll have to come back."

She sighed, looked around the reception area. Thought back to the incident on the street; Holt sitting in his car, Edward Moses approaching him. She turned back around to Bander. "What about Subjugate-52?" she asked. "Can you take me to see him?"

Bander stared at her. "You trying to get me fired?"

"No," she said. "Look, Remmell wouldn't let me see Subjugate-12 because he thinks I'll cause him undue stress. He said nothing about me seeing Subjugate-52."

"So what do you think 52 can tell you that's so urgent it can't wait until tomorrow?"

"Let me ask him the right questions and we'll find out," she said confidently.

Bander studied her, eyes narrowing. "You think 52's the killer?"

"I don't know," she said, rubbing her forehead. "And I won't until I talk with him." She fought to hide the frustration in her voice. "I just need to speak with him one more time. *Please.*"

Bander considered her a moment, then glanced around at the doorway that Remmell had disappeared through. He looked back at Salvi, then checked his watch.

"I can give you ten minutes," he said quietly.

"Great!" she said. "Let's do it."

17: SILO SIX

Bander walked Salvi through the tunneled corridors toward the glass bridge that led to the BioLume factory. Serene-41 tried to follow, but Bander waved him away again.

"Go wait in reception," he told the Serene.

They crossed over as the sun was beginning to set. Salvi stared off into the farms, saw Serenes among rows of vegetables, and further beyond in the vineyard. They looked like they were packing up for the day. She recalled Bander's comments about how business was booming here at the Complex. Attis Solme was getting rich off all the free labor. He was exploiting them, but at the same time it couldn't be denied that he had taken them out of the prison system and had them doing something positive with their lives, repaying their debt to society. Regardless of whether Attis Solme was getting rich off his slave labor, or luring the tech-heads in the city, working to get neural implants back on the market, there's no way he would jeopardize the good thing he had going. There's no way he would be the killer.

She looked back at Bander and saw him swipe his security pass and submit to the retinal scan. He wrenched back the lock with a loud clank and wheeled the white metal door open. She followed him inside and saw the factory below was empty except for the four vats of BioLume glowing up at her in their various shades and reeking of that wet mossy smell. Bander moved alongside and looked over the railing.

"Subjugate-52!" he called out. There was no answer. "He

must be working in the silos," he said. "This way."

They walked down a set of stairs to the factory floor. Salvi studied each of the large vats as they moved past. Then her eyes fell to the concrete floor, saw numerous smears of green here and there.

"How often to do you get spills on the floor in here?" she asked.

Bander glanced at her over his shoulder. "Regularly," he said, "but it's never much. A drip here and there. There's no health hazard in that. Why the interest?"

"Just curious," she said, glancing down to his feet. They looked a similar size to Mitch's. A similar size to the perp's.

She looked up at Bander's broad shoulders and back as she followed him. She thought about his comments on U-Stasis, how he'd used it to follow his niece and found Sharon Gleamer on there. His name wasn't mentioned among the prostitute's clients, though. But then again, would the killer pay for sex when he so clearly enjoyed taking it by force?

It made her of think of Mitch then, and of last night. Mitch had access to her apartment that morning, but he'd also had access to *her* the night before. And she'd been drinking. Killing her would've been easy. But he hadn't. They'd had consensual sex, then they'd both fallen asleep.

Because Mitch wasn't the killer.

She thought of the prostitute again, and of Dr Remmell being one of her clients.

"Does Dr Remmell ever come in here?" she asked Bander.

"Yeah," he said. "He comes to study his patients, see how they're coping in a working environment. Takes notes."

Salvi nodded to herself, as Bander opened the door. The cold air hit her as they stepped outside the factory and headed for the six large teardrop-shaped silos, each connected by a silver pipe that ran back to the building housing the vats. They walked along, passing each silo until they reached the one last in line.

"He's in here," Bander said.

"How can you tell?" she asked, looking up at the silver walls.

"Air hatch up top," he said, checking his watch again.

She looked up and saw a portion of the wall near the top of the teardrop was open like a window. Bander took hold of an iron ladder welded onto the side of the silo. He looked back at Salvi, giving her the once over. "You alright to climb?"

"Of course," she said.

He nodded. "Alright." Bander began climbing the ladder and she followed, turning her mind back to Subjugate-52. Had Edward Moses been the one to attack these women? His priors were the most compatible with the current crimes. But could he have done this while under watch? And how did this explain Salvi's apartment? Moses would not be able to leave Bountiful. There's no way he could've gone into the city to her apartment.

Unless he'd seen Serenes traveling with Dr Remmell and decided that he could too.

What if he had managed to slip past his watchers and take the SlingShot? But how would he pay for it? Steal? And how would Moses break into her apartment? Moses had been a narcissistic lawyer with a fetish for gyms. He was smart, but not necessarily technically minded. But his MO fit these murders... Could he have worked with someone else? Could Moses have committed the crimes with someone else's assistance? While someone else watched, maybe?

She thought of Dr Remmell then, of seeing him taking the SlingShot into the city. He was familiar with technology, with cameras and microphones... But so too was Bander. And Remmell always needed Bander to fix them for him.

Or was *he* just playing dumb?

The first chance at getting off the ladder was a metal grid

walkway about three stories up. Bander stepped off and held his hand out to help her off. She eyed it, then took it. They moved around the walkway a few feet, where Bander wrenched opened a hatch. He looked back at her again. "Watch your step."

Bander disappeared inside, and Salvi took a quick look around before following. The sun was close to setting, the sky falling dark, and she could no longer see the farm and vineyard grounds. She spotted her Zenith, still parked out front of the Complex, though, then ducked her head and stepped inside the hatch.

She immediately heard the thrum of a generator and saw the bright glow of the green BioLume below, and was hit again with that wet, mossy odor.

Salvi stepped to the railing and looked down to the bottom of the silo to see Edward Moses working at a control panel on the wall. She watched as he tapped away at the screen, accessing a software program.

Maybe Moses was more technically minded than she thought...

Had they taught him new skills here? She recalled Bander fixing the comms in the interview room. Had Bander taught him?

"Subjugate-52!" Bander called out.

Moses looked up at them. At her.

"Yes, Caretaker?" his deep, refined voice said.

"Come up here," Bander ordered. "The detective wants to speak to you."

"I'll just finish programming the stir speed–"

"No. Now," Bander ordered.

Salvi watched as Moses hesitated, then stepped back from the console, wiped his hands with a rag. "Yes, Caretaker."

She turned her eyes to the large vat below, watching the large metal two-pronged stirrer spinning around, this way and that, keeping the BioLume in a state of constant movement, while more of the green sludge slowly dripped down from a large silver pipe that fed through the wall of the far side.

Moses moved toward a ladder which lead up from the ground to the walkway upon which they stood. He wiped his hands again, pausing a moment to watch the speed of the stirrer.

"Now!" Bander barked, smacking his baton on the metal railing, startling Salvi and Moses both.

"Yes, Caretaker," Moses said, beginning the climb.

Salvi heard a tapping sound. She looked back to see Bander pacing behind her along the curve of the walkway, tapping the baton in his hand. She looked back to Moses. Saw he'd cleared the first floor, continuing his ascent.

She heard a familiar musical chime sound and saw Moses pause and look down at the red light pulsing through the beige cloth of his uniform.

"He's due for his injection," Bander told her. "MOVE IT!" he yelled at the Subjugate. Bander began to pace again, tapping his baton. "You don't have long, Detective."

"It won't take long," she told him. She turned her eyes to Moses again, climbing the ladder. What was she going to say to him? What was she going to ask him that would let her know that he had killed those women? Her mind switched to earlier that day on the street; of Holt pulling up to ask if she was OK, while she was talking with Pragge. She saw Moses approach, telling Subjugate-12 to come. She saw Pragge cower. Pictured him saying "bad man, bad man." Saw him smacking his fist into his open palm.

Then she heard that tapping sound again.

The sound of Bander tapping the baton into his open palm.

A freeze seemed to roll through her body. She looked over her shoulder at his hands, saw the movements were not dissimilar to those Pragge had made to her. Bander paused and looked back at her.

"What?"

She looked down to his feet. Wondered what size he was. Wondered if it had been his boot that had left BioLume prints in Sharon Gleamer's basement, on Rebecca Carson's back, on Carly Fresner's carpet.

"Did you ever come across Rebecca Carson in U-Stasis?" she asked.

"What?" He furrowed his brow.

"The second victim," she said turning around. "She had a U-Stasis account. Did you ever come across her in there?"

"No. Why?"

She shrugged. "You said you ran into Sharon Gleamer there."

Bander's stare froze on her face. "So?"

"Did you know Carly Fresner?"

Bander didn't answer.

"She was a prostitute," Salvi continued. "You ever call on her for services?"

Bander stepped forward casually and Salvi subtly pressed her forearm against her gun for reassurance. Silence sat between them; the only sound interrupting it was the footsteps of Edward Moses getting closer.

Bander brushed past her, looked over the railing.

"Go back down," he told Subjugate-52.

Moses looked up at him. "I'm sorry?"

"Go. Back. Down," he said.

"What are you doing?" Salvi asked Bander. "I want to talk to him."

"Well, you lost your chance," Bander said. "It's too late."

"Too late for what?"

Bander stared at her. "I don't like your tone, Detective. I'm trying to do you a favor, risking my job, and all you're doing is demanding stuff."

She gave him a challenging look. "Perhaps I should be asking you these questions instead of Subjugate-52?"

"Questions about what?" He tapped his baton into his open palm.

She glanced back down at Moses, who had begun to descend again. "Subjugate-52!" she called.

Moses paused and looked up at her, his silver halo shining under the silo's artificial lights, the red of his personal alarm splashing in his face.

"Did Subjugate-12 ever tell you who the bad man was?" she asked.

Moses stared back at her, and the instant his eyes shifted to rest on Bander, she knew.

She turned back to the caretaker, one hand ready to go for her gun, one ready for her iPort.

Her iPort!

It was still on her bed where she'd thrown it after Mitch's call.

"What the hell are you playing at?" Bander asked her.

She stared at Bander and nodded to herself. "You used to work at a security company. You're comfortable with technology, going into places like U-Stasis, hacking into the secure areas. You know how to bypass alarms, break into people's houses, don't you? People's apartments."

"Excuse me?"

"Were you pissed that the geeky Tobias managed to score a babe like Sharon Gleamer and you couldn't?" she asked him.

Bander stared at her.

"You saw Sharon in U-Stasis, her and Tobias doing unholy things and you figured she was up for some, didn't you?" Salvi said. "But she wasn't. Not with you. Not even in virtual reality, let alone *reality*."

"I'd be careful with your accusations if I were you, Detective."

"You mentioned a dating section of U-Stasis. Is that where you met Rebecca Carson? But she turned you down too, didn't she?" Salvi pushed. "What about the prostitute? Her I don't get."

"The dead whore?" he asked, his face suddenly flat, his eyes cold.

"Her name was Carly Fresner."

"What would I know about whores?" he said. "Maybe that's a question you could help with."

"I'm sorry?" she said, then suddenly realized what he meant. The footage. She nodded to herself and smiled. "You couldn't hack into the precinct hub, not with our AI on watch, so you hacked into my apartment and set up the cameras. You wanted to know how we were doing on the case. That's why you were in the city that night. Did you follow me to the bar? Or did you hack my cards and see me buying drinks? Either way, you hit on me and I turned you down, left with Mitch. You followed us that night. Saw me following him. Knew I would doubt him if you killed the prostitute I'd seen him with. Attis told you about Mitch's past, didn't he? And you expected me to turn him in, didn't you?"

Bander said nothing, just stared at her.

She nodded to herself again. "But I didn't. And then last night you watched me have sex with Mitch. You've taken it personally, haven't you? Another woman rejecting you for someone else." She had to keep talking, had to keep pushing buttons to see if he would lower his guard and give her the evidence she needed to make an arrest. "I see why you like to get away from the Complex on your days off. Because here in Bountiful, you just can't shake the stink of this place from you, can you? The criminals you spend your day with. The means you use, daily, to keep them in line. It makes people, *women*, uncomfortable. They don't want anything to do with you."

Bander still didn't speak, but she saw his chest rising and falling with more vigor, a sparkle to those cold eyes. A hunter watching his prey, wanting to strike.

"You're a violent man, Caretaker," she said. "A frustrated, violent man, who is used to applying force to get what he wants. Submission. Obeisance."

"Trying to pin these murders on me?" He smiled, running the baton up and down the callused palm of his hand. "Really? You're that desperate?"

Salvi smiled back. "You've spent too long with these criminals, haven't you, Bander? Listening to their gory stories, meting out the torture and violence to desensitize them to the excitement of their crimes. But in the process, you have become desensitized to the violence and the torture, haven't you? With every beating you gave, with every form of torture you inflicted upon them. It became second nature to you. The violence no longer bothered you. It seemed normal. And you became comfortable watching the images of sexual violence shown during the Subjugates' PPG therapy. Comfortable, then eventually turned on by it. Until one day you realize that it takes more than normal to get you off now. You need to up the ante to feel something. And the frustration. Oh, the frustration that these seemingly good little girls in town won't sleep with you. Won't go near you. They'll sleep with everyone else but not *you*. Well, you showed them, didn't you? You proved your dominance. You made them submit, you made them obey you."

"I'd watch your mouth if I were you," he said quietly, tapping the baton in his hand again.

"Or what?" she challenged. "You'll make me the fourth victim? That's your plan, right? That's why you broke into my apartment and wrote 'pure' on my bed. Well, I'm not like those other women, Bander. I'm a cop... And you're under arrest."

"Yeah?" he said nonchalantly. "And where's your proof? All I hear is a lot of hot air from a slut detective who's admitted to sleeping with her partner when she should've been reporting him and investigating this case."

"What shoe size are you?" she asked, unable to hide the menace in her voice.

Bander stared at her, eyes colder than ice, jaw rigid with hate.

She smiled. "I wonder how many shoes you own that have BioLume caught in the tread? I wonder if your DNA will match the semen we found in Sharon's basement?"

Bander gave a quiet laugh, nodding to himself. He scratched his head, muttering. "Ah, you're just like the rest of 'em." He looked back at her. "A fucking little whore."

He lunged.

Salvi dodged his swinging arm, hearing the baton slam down hard on the side of the railing. She pulled her gun and swung it up, but the baton came smashing back down hard against her forearm. She yelled in pain and dropped the gun. Bander kicked it away, then grabbed her and threw her back against the railing. She thrust her arms out in defense, trying to fight him back as pain sliced down her arm telling her it was potentially broken. He pressed his weight and the baton against her neck, bending her right back over the railing.

"You fucking *bitch*!" he hissed, veins popping angrily in his neck. "You think you're so smart, huh? You think you're better than me? I deal with Subjugates every single day. Hardened, murdering fucking criminals, and *they* don't beat me! But you think you can, huh?" He eased off the baton a moment, only to land a hard punch in her face. As her head was flung back she caught a dazed glimpse of Edward Moses, frozen on the ladder where'd she stopped him before. He stared up at them, one leg hooked through the ladder, red light flashing at his chest, eyes uncomprehending about what was happening.

Bander pulled her off the railing. "You think I give a shit about you?" he said. "You think I would actually lower myself to fuck a whore like you? Huh? I saw you last night, you pathetic bitch. A stupid little girl crying over her dead whore sister!"

Salvi kneed him hard in the groin and he buckled, then she thrust the palm of her good hand into his throat, pushing him back. He coughed and splattered, then swung the baton again and it caught her good arm, near the shoulder. She groaned in pain as the baton came flying again. She got both hands around his wrist, trying to hold the baton back, but he was strong, and one arm of hers was fractured and weak, despite the adrenaline coursing through it.

He roared, ramming her back into the railing again.

"You think I would fuck you? Huh?" he said. "No." He smiled through gritted teeth, then dragged her over to the gap in the railing were the ladder was. She fought him, lashing out, trying to hit his nose, his eyes, then finally dug her nails into his neck and scraped her hand down his skin. He yelled in pain and she smiled at him.

"Thanks for the evidence," she said.

Bander's eyes went wide, then he suddenly let her go and stepped back. She latched onto the edge of the railing to stop herself from falling backward through the gap, panting, darting a glance at Moses, still paused on the ladder below, looking up at them.

Bander raised his hand to his neck and saw the blood on his fingers. He stared at her, mind ticking over, then he suddenly straightened again.

She darted her eyes to her gun. It was on the floor over by the wall. Too far. He would get to her before she could grab it.

"There was nothing I could do," Bander said to her, his face suddenly soft and boyish.

She stared at him.

"I did everything I could," he said.

"What are you talking about?"

He stepped toward her. "I told her no, sent her away, but she didn't listen," he said, shaking his head. His face fell serious. "She found Edward Moses in Silo 6, accidentally locked herself inside with him." He stepped forward again, his eyes suddenly dark and soulless again. "She pushed him too hard. Just kept pushing him. And he lost control." He said, voice devoid of emotion.

"Bander, it's over," she warned.

"There was nothing I could do," he said, stopping within reach of her, "to stop him from killing you."

And with a hard shove, he caused Salvi to lose her grip and she went flying backward off the walkway.

One moment Salvi was rushing through the air, the next she felt a jarring pain in her ankle; her body abruptly stopped, slammed into the railing and bounced off, then she felt a soft wet feeling on her fingers. She heard a whoosh, felt air rush past her face, and saw a large metal stirrer had just skimmed past her.

It took her a moment to realize what had happened. She looked down to see herself hanging over the large vat of BioLume; her face barely a meter above the surface, her hands immersed in the bright green bacteria. A drop of blood fell from her nose and disappeared within the green glow. She heard a strained groan. Dazed, she looked upward and saw Edward Moses leaning back from the ladder by his knees, her legs caught in his strong, straining, grasp.

"It's alright, Detective," he said, breathing calmly. "I've got you."

Salvi heard a low guttural laugh and glanced up further to the top floor. Bander stood looking down over the railing.

He smiled darkly. "She's all yours, Edward Moses. Don't do anything I wouldn't do."

Then he disappeared from sight, taking his laughter with him, and they heard the hatch of the silo close.

Edward Moses groaned and heaved, pulling Salvi up onto the first-floor walkway. She caught her breath, her BioLumed fingers clinging to the metal grating of the floor, glad to be on flat ground.

"Are you alright, Detective?" Moses asked, kneeling on the dim walkway in front of her, the red light of his silent alarm flashing in his face.

She grasped at her ankle. "It's not sitting right."

"I am sorry. The force of my catching you may have slightly dislocated it," he said. "May I look, Detective?"

Salvi eyed him, swallowed, then nodded. Moses took her ankle and rolled it around gently, making her gasp. Then with a quick, forceful movement, she heard a click and felt her ankle sitting right again. Salvi reached for it, eyes wide, exhaling through the shock of it.

"H-how did you know how to do that?" she asked.

Moses seemed to think for a moment, a slight look of confusion in his eyes. "I don't really know."

Salvi stared at him. Even with his Serene-like qualities now, she still saw the imposing criminal he once was. The lawyer, the gym fiend. Maybe that was why he knew how to fix her ankle. Maybe he'd injured himself a time or two before in his gym days. Grateful as she was that he had put her ankle back in place, she wondered if this was how he'd found his victims; coming to the rescue of a woman in the gym with an injury. Perhaps helping her home…

"You were fighting with the caretaker," he said. "He hit you. Why?"

"We need to get out of here, Subjugate-52," she said firmly.

"Of course. Can you walk?"

She nodded. She had no choice. Her face throbbed, her shoulder hurt, and she was pretty sure her right forearm was fractured, but she would walk, goddammit. Moses helped her to stand.

"We will have to climb up to get out," he said.

She limped over to the ladder, her ankle feeling incredibly tender, and looked up the two floors they would need to climb.

"Can you can do this?" Moses asked her. "Perhaps I could go for help alone."

"No," she said. "You stay with me, Subjugate-52. You're my witness."

"Your witness?" he asked, confused.

She nodded. "You saw the caretaker attack me. You're my evidence. He's a bad man, Subjugate. We need to stop him."

Climbing onto the ladder, she began to make her way up slowly to the top floor, both arms and her ankle making her movement slow and awkward. But she'd be damned if she was going to let Bander get away. When she made it to the top level, her eyes instantly searched for her gun, but it was gone.

Bander had taken it.

"Shit!" she hissed. Would she find his next victim killed by a bullet from her own gun?

She crawled onto the floor and scrambled over to the hatch. Moses was soon by her side and she motioned for him to open it. He pulled down on the handle, but it wouldn't budge.

"That is odd," he said calmly, taking hold of the hatch arm again and tugging hard.

"No, it's not," Salvi said, stepping back. "He's locked us in."

"The caretaker?" he asked.

She nodded.

"Why would he do that?" Moses asked, looking back at the

door. "He knows I do not have a pass to get out."

Salvi studied him; tall and broad, nearly twice her size. "Because he wants you to kill me."

Moses looked back at her, a deeper furrow now in his brow as he marked the cross upon himself. "I don't understand."

She looked down at the flashing red light beneath his uniform. "You ever gone without an injection before, Subjugate-52?"

He looked down at his alarm light. "No. I haven't. I must attend to it urgently."

Salvi nodded again. "How long until someone knows you're missing?"

"I'm due for my medication. If I don't collect it, they will come looking for me. It is crucial to our wellbeing."

"And if the caretaker lies and tells whoever gives you your medication that he'll take care of it?"

Moses stared at her blankly. "I don't understand."

Salvi's mind raced. Her car was still parked onsite. Someone would notice that it was still there. Someone would have to come looking for her.

But would Bander just leave it there, or would he move it? Hide it? He could always erase the drone footage afterward.

"Do you share a room with anyone, Subjugate-52?" she asked.

"We sleep in wards, but we each have small personal enclaves. We sleep alone in these sealed enclaves."

Salvi nodded again. "So, if the caretaker lies, says you've had your medication and that you're in bed asleep, is there anyone else who might check on you in the night and note you're missing?"

"No. There is not."

Salvi sighed and looked around the silo. "Is there any other way out of here?" She glanced up high. "What about the ventilation window?"

Moses stepped forward, clasping the rail and leaning forward to look up at. She eyed the halo around his skull carefully. "It's been closed."

Suddenly the artificial lighting in the silo went out. Salvi and Moses stood there in darkness, broken only by the green glow emanating from the large BioLume vat below.

And Subjugate-52's flashing red personal alarm.

"Why have the lights gone out?" he asked. "Have they forgotten we're in here?"

Salvi heard the generator still purring, could see the stirrers still stirring.

She turned back to Moses. "How long until someone will notice you're missing?"

Subjugate-52 stared back at her, his face tinged with green and splashes of red. "If I do not show for breakfast, my personal escort, Serene-41 will notice I am missing."

"What time is breakfast?" she asked.

"We dine at 7.00am."

She tried to remember what the time was when she'd arrived at the Complex. "Fourteen hours," she said. She looked back at the flashing light beneath his uniform. She had to remain calm, and she had to keep Edward Moses calm. She closed her eyes a moment, trawling her brain for whatever Attis Solme or Dr Remmell had told her about the program. She had to adhere to their strict protocol. She had to keep his mind focused on the present, on serenity. She had to keep his past erased. She must never call him Edward Moses.

Like Bander had just done...

She cringed, thinking of what Moses must've heard in her conversation with Bander. Slut. Whore. Sex. Violence.

"Subjugate-52," she said firmly, "we need to get out of here before then. Is there another way out?"

"No," he said, looking back down at the vat of BioLume. "The silo's exit chute only opens from the outside."

"Well, how does the BioLume get in here?"

Moses pointed across to the opposite wall. "When a vat has been mixed it is sent through the transfer pipe. As each silo's vat fills, we direct the flow into the next silo until all six silos are at capacity. The six silos are always at capacity."

Salvi looked up to the closed air hatch again. That wasn't an option, even if they could get it open. It was too high up and from memory there was nothing on the outside to cling onto. She looked back at the transfer pipe.

"Can we move through the pipe? Will that lead us back to the factory?"

"It does, but the pipe is not much larger than myself. We would need to crawl through BioLume for at least a hundred meters in cramped conditions."

"A hundred meters?"

"Yes," he said calmly. "But it would be dangerous to expose ourselves to the BioLume. Its effects on the human body are not yet fully known."

Salvi subtly wiped her green hands on her jacket. "How full is the pipe at any one time? Could we keep our head above the sludge line? Keep our faces out of it?"

Moses studied her, his face still a mixture of the BioLume glow and splashing red from his personal alarm. "The pipe would be at capacity, which is approximately half full. Then we would need to account for our weight displacement. It is too dangerous, Detective. We should wait until someone notices that I'm missing."

"Meanwhile the caretaker is out there and another woman gets murdered," she said, then looked back at Moses, who was marking a sign of the cross upon himself. "Or maybe two of us do."

"I don't understand," he asked, brow furrowed again.

She cursed herself for using a banned trigger word. *Murdered*.

"The caretaker is supposed to help us," Moses said, his face taking on the appearance of an innocent boy's. "He will come back and help us."

"The caretaker is a bad man, Subjugate-52. You know this."

He shook his head. "You must not talk like that. The caretaker helps us. He ensures we do the right thing."

"He's a coward," she said. "He's using you, Subjugate-52. He wants to blame you for all his victims."

Another trigger word. *Victims*.

"I-I don't understand," Moses said again. "I am a Subjugate. I am soon to be a Serene."

"But you're not a Serene yet, are you? He's going to make it look like you failed, like you killed these women."

"No." Moses marked another sign of the cross. "I am soon to be Serene," he said quietly, a slight furrow in his brow as he looked back to the vat below. "We must not hurt others or we will be punished. The caretaker will punish us. God will punish us."

Salvi squeezed her eyes shut and realized she'd just reminded Moses of his past. Oh, to hell with the trigger words. She needed to get through to Moses the seriousness of the situation.

"The caretaker *is* punishing you, Subjugate! He's going to tell lies about you. Very bad lies. He's going to tell the mayor you did very bad things."

He turned his face back to hers, his brow furrowed still, and for the first time, she thought she saw emotion flash in his eyes. Confusion, maybe hurt, perhaps betrayal. He was upset at not fully comprehending what was happening. Upset that someone might think he'd done something bad. Upset because parts of his brain had been numbed and he couldn't quite respond to the situation correctly. Is this what stress did to them? Is this why Remmell wouldn't let her speak with Subjugate-12? Could their brains, their programming so-to-speak overload, glitch, because they couldn't express things like normal people could? Is this why the Complex worked hard to keep them in a constant state of serenity?

"I am good," he said, brow still furrowed. "I am Serene."

And then she saw it.

A spark of ice blue flash along his halo.

It was only brief. Very brief. But it had been there – like a flicker of lightning in the distance. She was sure of it.

Moses' halo had sparked, however briefly, a code blue.

She tried to hold her surprise. How was it possible? Moses had had the augmentation, the numbing tweaks. Perhaps he hadn't had enough…

Or perhaps he was just smart enough to choose good behavior over more torture, more tweaks. Whether his brain was simply overloading, or whether he was losing his own control, Salvi needed to act. Fast. And carefully.

"We need to get out of here, Subjugate-52," she said calmly. "If you get me out of here safely, you will become a Serene, I promise. I won't let anyone take that from you."

He stared at her a moment longer, then looked back at the opposite wall below, to the transfer pipe connecting the silos to the factory.

"Alright," he said. "Come with me."

Salvi looked over the silver transfer pipe to where Moses studied its console. She eyed his halo, searching for any signs the code blue would return, but the device remained silver.

And she wondered then whether Bander had planned this all along. Had he known Subjugate-52 was a risk? Had he planned to set the Subjugate up to take the fall for his murders if the police got close? But how was Bander planning to overcome the DNA? Had Bander screwed up? Had he not known he'd left his DNA behind?"

It's at fifty-four percent capacity," Moses said. "That is

standard. We should be able to keep our faces above the BioLume, but we will need to be very careful."

"We don't have a choice, Subjugate," she told him. "I need to get out of here. I need to stop the bad man from hurting other people."

Moses eyed her, then gave a slight bow. "Then I shall assist, Detective." He ducked below the transfer pipe and reappeared on her side. He stepped up onto an elevated platform which enabled him to access the top of the pipe. He began rotating a metal arm attached to the entry hatch. She watched his face tighten, red alarm still flashing, as the muscles in his arm flexed and he gave a hard yank and pulled it open. His face was then immediately spotlighted by an intense circle of the green BioLume glow. He leaned into the hole and looked down each side, then leaned back again.

"It will be tight," he said, then looked at her. "For me at least."

She joined him on the platform and peered inside. It *would* be tight. While the wide streets of Bountiful had made her feel agoraphobic, this made her instantly feel claustrophobic. Second thoughts rushed through her. Did she really want to be trapped in a snug pipe of BioLume with Edward Moses? She leaned back and looked at him again. The Subjugate was staring down at the flashing red light emanating from his chest.

"This is very distracting," he said, a crease of concern beginning to show across his forehead.

"There's no other way you turn it off?" she asked. It was annoying her and it wasn't even right in her face like it was his.

"No," he said.

"Are you sure?"

Moses pulled the neck of his beige tunic down and Salvi stepped back in response at what she saw. Surgically implanted, the square flashing light sat beneath his skin, giving it a see-through appearance.

"It is embedded in our flesh," he told her. She eyed the surrounding skin, saw faint lines like white veins where tattoos had been erased.

"They implant it beneath your skin?" she asked.

Moses nodded. "It becomes part of us. We must always obey the light. It is the light of God." He glanced at her, a faint trace of worry in his eyes. "I must have my medication," he whispered. "Or I will be punished."

"Is it attached to anything?"

"I don't understand," he said.

"Is it connected to nerves or heart muscle or anything?"

"No. It simply sits beneath our skin and reads our biological systems."

"So, you could cut it out?" she suggested.

"We must *never* remove it," he said firmly, eyes staring at hers in earnest.

She studied him. Maybe the tweaks, the brainwashing, the torture had worked.

She nodded and looked back to the pipe's opening. "Well, the quicker we get back to the main building, the quicker you can have your shot and shut that thing off."

"Yes," he said.

She glanced into the pipe again then looked back at his big frame beside her. She pictured his hands around her ankles as she dangled above the vat. She stood back.

"You first, Subjugate-52."

He gave a slight bow then climbed up into the pipe and awkwardly wriggled down so that his feet were behind him, green BioLume splashing around as he did. He looked back at her. "If you get into trouble, Detective, please let me know."

Salvi nodded at him. "Thank you, Subjugate-52. And if you get in trouble, please let me know the same."

With that, he dipped his head into the pipe and began crawling through the BioLume sludge. She watched his feet shimmy past the opening, his heels kicking the roof of the pipe as he disappeared. When she saw sufficient distance between them, she pulled off her jacket, climbed up and stepped inside the pipe as well, then shimmied her body down to lie on her stomach.

She wasn't sure what to expect, but the BioLume in the pipe was room temperature and of a consistency somewhere between thickened cream and not-quite-set jelly. Lowering her head inside, she saw the tunnel of neon lime green luminosity before her, punctuated with the intermittent red flashes from Subjugate-52's alarm as he crawled away on his stomach. The wet moss odor was particularly overpowering, making her gag and cough a little, but she was just going to have to deal with it.

Using her good arm but injured shoulder, she pulled herself along, unable to take much weight on the throbbing forearm Bander had hit with the baton. She had just enough room to move, certainly more than Moses, but had to keep her head tilted up to avoid the splashback from both hers and Moses' movement. The runny gel occasionally kissed her earlobes and chin, but as long as she managed to keep her nose, mouth, and inner ears dry, she felt she would be OK. She would deal with the fallout of the contact on her skin later; sure she could take one of those special cleansing showers that Attis had told her about. Right now, her focus was getting out of this pipe without ingesting any of the gel.

She continued onward, soon catching up with Moses whose movements were restrained due to his size, like trying to squeeze a foot into a tight shoe. There was an eerie silence in the pipe, broken only by their breaths of effort. Moses' feet were just ahead, and they were large. She eased off to allow a little distance between them, wanting to be well out of strike range. Accidental or otherwise.

It seemed as though they had been crawling for some time before Moses stopped suddenly and raised a hand to the roof of the pipe.

"What is it?" she called out, coming to a stop also.

"The hatch for Silo 5," he called back.

Salvi stared at him. "We crawled all that way and we're only at Silo 5?"

"Yes, Detective," he replied, continuing onward, red alarm bouncing off the tube around them.

18: BROKEN

Salvi paused to rest. Her arm, shoulder and ankle were hurting, her face throbbing and swollen from Bander's punch, and maybe from smacking into the ladder when Moses had caught her fall. Either way, she couldn't wait to get out of this pipe.

Crawling along at a slow pace, focusing on Moses' shoes before her, they'd passed another three shut hatches.

Only two silos to go.

She willed herself onward. *We'll be out soon, we'll be out. Just keep going...*

She pictured Faith in her mind, pictured the three dead women whose lives had been stolen from them. She mustered her strength and began pulling herself forward again.

She had to get to Bander and stop him before he killed anyone else.

Salvi looked up ahead at Moses.

"What's wrong?"

He grunted, trying hard to open the hatch that led into the main BioLume factory, red light still flashing in his face.

"It's stuck, Detective," he said.

"It's locked, or it just won't budge?"

"I'm not quite sure," he said, tugging at the handle again, sending small waves of BioLume her way. She turned her face and tilted her neck, trying to keep away from the bright green sludge.

She glanced behind her. The thought of reversing back six silos was one she didn't want to entertain. She looked back at Moses. The space was too confined, making it difficult for him to get good leverage to twist the handle.

God, she didn't want to die inside this pipe.

She closed her eyes and thought of Mitch. How long had it been since he'd seen her? Would he be looking for her? Or given the way she'd shut him out this morning, would he be giving her space? If there was ever a time for him to be the control freak over-protective cop, now was it. Then she realized she'd thrown her iPort onto her bed. There was no way for Mitch to trace her. She fought the helpless feeling inside. She had wanted to do this alone, but the truth was, she should've done this with her partner.

But it was too late for regrets. She had wanted to do this alone, and now she was going to have to see it through.

She opened her eyes again and looked at Moses, still trying to open it.

"You're strong, Subjugate-52," she encouraged him. "You can do this."

He tugged and tugged but it wouldn't move.

"Try your feet!" Salvi told him. "Try stomping on the handle."

Moses looked at her, then glanced around the pipe. He saw a ridge running along the roof, clasped his hands on it, and squeezed around onto his back. He looked at Salvi.

"Please watch your face, Detective."

Salvi watched as he pulled both feet up as best he could, then stomped back hard on the arm of the hatch. A larger wave of BioLume came for her, but she turned her face in time, felt it caress her ear lobe and jawline; some splashed higher up on her cheekbone. She looked back but the handle hadn't moved.

"Try again, Subjugate!" she said firmly. "We need to get

out of here!"

Moses stomped and stomped again, but it wouldn't budge. She knew he could do a lot better, but right now he was too serene to tap into his full force.

She had to push him to find it. She had to break his serenity. She needed him to code blue.

"Try harder!" she barked.

He stomped again and again. Still nothing.

"Subjugate-52, we have to get out of here! Our lives depend on it. You need to open that hatch or you will never become a Serene. Do you understand me?"

He looked at her with a furrowed brow, splashes of red tainting his face.

"Do you want to fail, Subjugate?" she asked. "If you don't get us out of here, you will fail!"

His halo flickered. Briefly.

It terrified her how easy it was to do. She didn't know what was causing it. Anger, frustration, hate? All she knew was that there was a chink in Solme's chain.

But she had to keep going. Right now she needed it to fail.

"The caretaker is going to tell lies about you to Mayor Solme. Do you want that? He's going to try and take away your Serenity. We must stop him! Use your strength! All of it! Stomp hard, Subjugate! Stomp now!"

Moses gave a pained whine, whether through annoyance or anger, she wasn't sure. But it was working.

"I know Serenes are not allowed to get angry, but I need you to, Subjugate. Just this once you're allowed to. I give you permission. Help me and I will make sure you become the Serene you want to be. Now stomp the handle! Stomp it! *Get angry*!" she shouted.

Moses groaned, his face contorted. He inhaled a deep breath and stomped down on the handle. It moved slightly.

"HARDER, SUBJUGATE!" she yelled.

She could tell that Moses was feeling the pressure and was not sure how to handle it. He'd been trained through torture not to take to violence and aggression any more. He'd had the tweaks, and he was torn. His brain, his emotions, unsure of how to process what was happening. But at the end of the day he was still human. If she pushed hard enough, forced him to react, would he break his Serene shell?

"Come on, Subjugate! Come on!"

She could see his muscles tightening, trying to pool whatever he was feeling into his inner strength. Cramped in the tight space, red light flashing in his face and her yelling at him, Edward Moses was starting to overload. He was starting to lose his serenity. But right now, that is exactly what Salvi needed him to do. It was her only way out.

"HARDER, Subjugate-52!" she pushed, knowing it was a fine line. "Do *not* fail me! I need you to kick hard for our freedom. Kick hard so we can find the man who is telling lies about you. Kick hard to prove what a *good* Serene you really are!"

His halo flickered again. She saw Moses suck in a breath as his muscled arms pulled himself up ready to unleash a frenzy of kicking.

"KICK, SUBJUGATE! KICK!"

Waves of BioLume rushed past her, splashing her exposed skin, but she squeezed her eyes and mouth shut, strained hard to keep her ears and nose out of the BioLume waves.

"Again!" she barked. "AGAIN!"

Moses grunted again and again with effort, stomping wildly, his halo flickering ice blue, until eventually they heard the metal groan.

She watched as Moses paused and stared at the handle of the hatch, panting. He moved himself back into position, using his arms to pull the handle of the hatch around. It popped open and fresh air rushed in to greet them.

Salvi's body slumped in relief.

"Oh, thank god," she breathed.

Salvi looked up at Moses' extended hand.

"May I help you?" he said.

She nodded, and with his help, pulled herself through the hatch of the transfer pipe.

As she stood up, the BioLume sagged her clothes downwards with gravity, molding the clothes to her body like a second skin.

"The electricity is out in here too," Subjugate-52 noted, looking around the factory. His clothes molded to him like a second skin. His ghostly green neon form made him look like some kind of radioactive creature. His halo, although covered in the BioLume, had thankfully turned back to silver.

It's a warning sign, she reminded herself. The code blue was a warning to take action before bad things happened. She had time, but not much.

"It's the caretaker," she told him. "He doesn't want us to leave." She stepped out of the hatch onto the ground floor, and Moses turned to help her. "Thank you," she said, calmly.

The Subjugate gave a slight bow, red light still flashing in his face, then he moved over to the stairs. He ascended to the observation walkway and toward the hatch that opened onto the glass bridge. Salvi followed, still limping slightly from her tender ankle. She watched as Moses tried to open the door, arms bulging with strain. He grunted and she saw his halo flickering blue, but the door didn't budge.

Salvi stepped toward him. "Subjugate," she said calmly, "I don't think you're strong enough to open this one."

Moses released the handle and stepped back from the door, eyeing it. "No. I don't suppose I am."

"Come on," Salvi said, then made her way to the stairs and began to descend again. As she reached the concrete flooring of the ground, she looked around the walls of the factory. Moses moved past her toward another door. But it too was locked.

"The windows!" Salvi said, pointing back up to the observation walkway.

They climbed the stairs again and with each step Salvi gritted her teeth. She could feel her ankle and face swelling further by the minute, as she cradled her fractured forearm.

Moses moved over to one of the windows and examined it.

"They don't open," he said.

Salvi looked up and saw a large air vent twirling overhead. Far too high to reach for either of them. She looked back at the windows, like large cruise ship portals dotted along the walls of this level.

"Can we break them?" Salvi asked. "Kick them out, maybe?"

Moses looked from her to the window. For a moment he looked serene, despite that red light flashing in his eyes. Then he stepped back, tensed his body and kicked at the glass.

There was a loud bang, but nothing happened. He tried again.

"Wait!" Salvi moved closer to the window and ran her fingers over it. Her shoulders slumped as she realized it was made of a hardy industrial-strength plastic. There was no way they were going to be able to break through it. It shouldn't have surprised her. The Solme Complex was effectively a prison after all. It was just a well-camouflaged one.

"We need to find another way," she said.

"But how?" Moses asked. "There's no other way out. The caretaker oversees security, and if what you say is true…"

"He doesn't want to let us out." Salvi looked around again, still cradling her forearm. "If we can't get out," she said, "we need to get someone in. We need to draw attention."

"How?" Moses asked.

She looked back at him, glowing bright green from his head to his feet, bright red light splashing his face.

She smiled. "With BioLume."

Salvi didn't know how long it had been, but they'd been dancing around in front of the windows, waving their arms toward the residents' accommodation, for what seemed like an age. Focusing on the few windows that were still lit up, finally they had caught someone's attention. They'd seen the tiny figure scuttle away, then moments later come back to the window with a second figure, before both then disappearing again.

Now, she focused on the guard running toward the building, heart thumping in her chest, and smiled.

"It's not him!" she said. "It's not the caretaker."

"It's guard Jones," Moses said. "Serene-41 is with him."

They both moved down the stairs again, toward the exit, ready for their freedom.

"Put your hands in the air!" Guard Jones yelled from the other side of the door. "Come out with your hands up!"

Salvi and Moses glanced at each other.

"I'm opening the door!" Jones yelled again. "You stand back, then come out with your hands up! Do you understand?"

"Why is he yelling? Are we in trouble?" Moses asked, brow furrowed, red light still flashing in his face.

"It's OK!" Salvi called back to the guard. "We just got trapped in here. We're coming out. We're unarmed."

The door opened and Serene-41 stood there shining a bright torch on them. He gasped at the state of their BioLumed bodies, then again at Moses' flashing chest, and stepped backward.

"On your knees!" Jones yelled at Moses, aiming his taser at him. "On your knees, *now*, Subjugate!"

Salvi stepped out first with her hands up, glancing back at

Moses. "Do as he says, Subjugate-52."

She limped out into his torchlight and the moment the guard saw she was injured, saw her swollen face, he pulled her out the way and aimed his weapon back at Moses.

"GET ON YOUR KNEES NOW, SUBJUGATE! GET DOWN NOW!"

"I have done nothing wrong," he said, hands in the air.

Jones fired a quick blast of his taser at Moses. Salvi gasped as the pulse hit and his body locked up.

"No!" Salvi yelled at the guard, knocking his arm down. "He didn't do anything!"

Moses fell to the ground groaning as Jones turned the weapon to her. "GET ON THE GROUND! KEEP YOUR HANDS HIGH! YOU ARE TRESPASSING! GET DOWN NOW!"

"We're not the enemy!" she shouted at him. "I'm a cop. You need to let us go!" She moved to light up her badge but it too was back at her apartment.

"GET DOWN NOW!" he screamed, moving up to her and pointing the weapon in her face.

"Look, look you've got it wrong!" she told him calmly.

"Tell that to the caretaker! He's on his way."

"No!" Salvi said, eyes wide. She glanced at Moses as he pulled himself up from the floor. His halo was no longer sparking blue, it was now pulsing, long and slow. The guard turned back to Moses and saw it too.

"Shit," he muttered, "code blue," and blasted him again with the taser. The Subjugate roared in pain, while Serene-41 cried out in anguish. Salvi rammed herself into the guard, but he quickly struck back with an elbow knocking her back.

But that was all the time Moses needed to get to his feet again.

And this time his halo had turned completely ice blue.

The Subjugate growled as he lunged at the guard, knocking him to the ground, hands around his throat.

Serene-41 cried out again, hands to mouth, eyes wide.

"MOSES, NO!" Salvi yelled, and the sound of his name made him look up. "Don't hurt him, Subjugate-52!" she said, trying to convey calm. "That's not you any more. That's *not* what you do! You're a Serene. Become the Serene!" she commanded.

Moses looked down at the guard and eased off. Guard Jones saw the opportunity and elbowed him in the face, then shocked him again.

"No!" Salvi screamed. "Stop! He's my witness!"

But it was useless. Jones was already calling into his comms.

"Caretaker! It's Subjugate-52! He's coding blue! I got him! He's down!"

And Salvi knew then that she had no other choice. She had to call for backup before the caretaker got his hands on them again.

She looked toward the main building, then ran for her life.

19 : CRUCIFIXION

Salvi ran for the main building, ignoring the pain in her ankle and racking her brain for where the nearest phone might be.

Solme's office!

She saw a side entrance located beneath the glass bridge from the BioLume factory and raced toward it. She pulled at the doors, but they were locked.

"Shit!" she hissed. She heard footsteps and spun around to see Serene-41 on approach.

"Where are you going?" he asked. "You must not walk around unescorted!"

"Please!" she begged. "I need to get to a phone immediately!"

Serene-41 studied her a moment. "I-I don't know what's happening!"

"Serene-41!" she said calmly but firmly. "I'm a detective. You can trust me. Now, please, I need a phone. Urgently."

"Of course," he gave a bow. "This way."

He swiped his pass and began to walk hurriedly down the long-curved corridor to reception, but Salvi stopped him.

"In here!" she called, pointing at the door into Solme's office. "In here! A phone!"

"But reception is down here," the Serene pointed.

"No, goddammit!" she yelled. "I need a phone now!"

The Serene cowered at her voice, but did as he was told and swiped his pass. "This is the mayor's office," he said. "You're not supposed to be in here."

As soon as the door unlocked, Salvi barged her way inside

and moved straight to the phone on Solme's desk. She picked it up and glanced back at the door, but Serene-41 was gone. Salvi turned back to the handset and punched in 9-1-

"Put it down," she heard Bander's voice. A chill ran down her spine.

She looked up at the main doorway that led in from reception and saw him standing there with a gun pointed at her. *Her* gun. She looked back at the phone as Bander stepped inside the office and locked the door behind him. She threw a glance to the side door through which she'd entered.

"Don't be stupid," he said, waving the gun. "You know I will."

"You're going to anyway, right?" she said. "So what does it matter?"

"Oh, but we're going to have some fun first." He smiled. "Put the phone down," he said. "*Now*." He stepped carefully toward her. She looked at the gun and decided not to risk it. Every moment she could stay alive, even if it was fighting him, was worth it. Bander couldn't possibly kill every witness in here. She placed the handset down.

The second it was down, Bander pulled out his baton with his left hand and smashed the phone several times until it broke apart. Salvi cowered away from the flying pieces.

"Caretaker," they heard Dr Remmell's voice sound from the second doorway. They both turned to look at him. "What are you doing?" he asked carefully.

"Controlling the situation," Bander said quickly. "Subjugate-52's been on the rampage."

"No!" she blurted desperately. "Bander tried to kill me!"

"SHUT UP!" Bander yelled. "You're trespassing!" he looked at Remmell. "She set 52 off."

"No!" Salvi shook her head, eyes pleading with Remmell's.

"Alright." Remmell stepped into the room carefully, hands out placatingly, glancing between the two of them. "Put the gun down, Mr Bander. She's unarmed. She's no threat."

"Don't tell me how to do my job." Bander stared at him, panting. "I'm the caretaker and I'm controlling the situation."

"Detective Grenville called earlier," Remmell said carefully. Salvi's eyes widened at Mitch's name. "He wants to speak with you," Remmell said to Bander, then glanced at Salvi again. "He thought Detective Brentt was missing."

"Bander locked me up with 52!" she blurted.

"SHUT UP!" Bander screamed, then looked back at Remmell. "This bitch snuck in and set off 52. Jones found 'em in the BioLume factory. He's got 52 there now. Go check, if you don't believe me!"

"I did, Mr Bander," Remmell said serenely. "After Grenville's call, I went to 52's enclave. His bed had been stuffed with pillows. You'd signed off his injection but Serene-41 said he hadn't seen 52 receive it."

"So?" Bander said. "41 wasn't around. I don't know how 52 got out but I'll check the security footage."

"Erase it, you mean," Salvi snarled.

Bander turned his murderous eyes toward her.

"It's over, Mr Bander," Remmell said. "I don't know what evidence Grenville has, but it's over."

"What's over?" Bander screwed his face up.

"This. All of it. Put the gun down."

Bander turned the gun on Remmell. "52 did this. He killed those girls! You know he's been coding blue. That's why you didn't want her to speak with him."

"Mr Bander," Remmell said carefully. "I know this wasn't Subjugate-52. This is my fault, you know. I saw the warning signs. I knew you were escalating but I did nothing to stop you."

"Escalating?" Bander said, swinging the gun between the two of them. "At your request, Remmell! Go harder, you say! More pain! You're the one who ordered me to hurt them. You get off on it, don't you, doctor?"

"No, Mr Bander, I don't. But I see now that you do. Put the

gun down. Let's talk this over."

Bander's chest rose and fell heavily, his body still coursing with adrenaline. "I don't what you're talking about, Remmell; you've lost your mind. You're the one who's spent too much time with these people. Maybe Grenville should be talking to you."

"What did you do with Detective Brentt's car?" Remmell asked.

Bander paused.

"It was out front before, now it's gone. But she's still here."

"Serene-41 must've–"

"Bander," Remmell said, shaking his head as he inched forward, "it's over. Put the gun down. Let's talk. I just want to talk. You know you have nothing to fear from me. I'm not strong enough to hurt you or overpower you. You know this. I just want to talk."

Bander's shoulders slumped a little and his arms softened. Remmell stepped closer. "This is my fault," he said softly. "Let me make it up to you. Let me help you."

Remmell reached out slowly toward the gun.

"Don't trust him, Remmell," Salvi warned.

"Ssshhhh," Remmell said softly, reaching out and placing his hand over the gun in Bander's hands. "It's alright. Mr Bander knows I'm going to help him. Don't you?"

Bander looked at him and relinquished the gun. "You mean you're going to subjugate me."

In one swift motion, Bander pulled out a blade from the back of his trousers and slashed it across Remmell's throat.

Salvi gasped in shock as Remmell threw his hands up to his neck. His eyes flashed wide as blood spurted over the doctor's hands. Gargling and choking, with blood running down his arms like water, he sank to his knees.

"No, no, no! Bad man, bad man!" Pragge's voice sounded as he ran into the room, heading for the caretaker.

Bander dropped the knife and swiftly dodged his advance, belting him hard across the head with the baton he still carried in his left hand. Pragge groaned in pain, raising his hands to his halo, and fell to the floor in a heap.

Salvi saw Remmell fall flat to the ground, then looked back as Bander leaned over Pragge and belted him some more, as the Subjugate cried softly in pain.

Horrified, Salvi saw her chance and ran at Bander. He saw her coming around the desk and grabbed the gun that had spilled from Remmell's hands. He raised it at her, but she grabbed his wrist, twisted it and disarmed him. The gun fell back to the floor, but his baton soon swung and caught her in the back. She yelled in agony and he swung again, catching her across the back of her legs. She stumbled to the floor in pain, and he grabbed her by the hair, yanked her head back and thrust the baton across her throat, then heaved her up to her feet. Salvi struggled hard against him, her feet kicking Remmell's lifeless body as they moved past, but Bander dragged her over to Solme's desk and slammed her face down on it.

He leaned over her, pulled the baton away from her throat and pressed it across the back of her neck, as he venomously breathed, "I should never have left a Serene to do a man's job!"

Salvi struggled with all her might to push herself off the desk, but Bander was just too heavy. Her eyes caught on the stone statuette of Mary on the corner of Solme's desk. She grabbed it and swung it back into Bander's face. She felt the deep thud of the connection and Bander moaned, stepping backwards from her. She turned around, saw blood running down the side of his face, and tried to run for the door. He shook his head as though trying to clear the pain and grabbed Salvi. She swung her elbow back at him, but he pulled her back then launched a fist into her face. It connected with her cheekbone with a force that spun her sideways. Bander slammed her back onto the desk, panting heavily as his blood dripped onto her face.

She heard fast heavy footsteps then. Something collided with Bander and knocked him right off her. She stumbled away from the desk and saw it was Moses. He'd rammed Bander right into the wall and now they were wrestling. Bander found his baton, however, and began beating him back. Salvi searched frantically for her gun, but before she knew it Bander had snatched it and fired into Moses.

"No!" Salvi yelled, as Moses stumbled back, holding his gut. The blood pooled quickly, and he collapsed back onto the floor, tripping over Pragge's unconscious frame.

Salvi looked around for another weapon; couldn't see where the Mary statue had fallen, but her eyes caught on Solme's cross on the wall. She snatched it and smashed it against the desk, breaking the wood, and ripped the silver Christ off it. Then she ran at Bander's back as he stood over Moses, and stabbed it in. Hard.

He yelled in pain and threw an arm back, connecting her in the side of the head. She stumbled, smacking into the wall and fell to the floor. She saw Bander's feet beneath the desk as he moved over to the second door and locked it, then strode back toward her.

"Goddamn Moses," he said, through gritted teeth, panting. "He lost control tonight! Just couldn't stop him!" He charged at her and she raised her hands in defense. One blow to her broken forearm made her scream in pain. He grabbed a handful of hair and pulled her upwards. She punched him in the gut with her good arm and he buckled a little, gave a winded sound, but he yanked her back over to the desk and threw her atop it.

• • •

Salvi landed on her back with a *whump* and kicked at Bander as hard as she could, one foot landing in his face, but he soon caught her legs and pressed them down. As he did, she saw the silver Christ flash from behind him. It was still sticking out of his back. He must not feel it any more with the adrenaline flowing through him.

He lunged forward, hands reaching for her throat. She tried to block them but he hit her swollen forearm and pain shot through her. If she'd questioned whether it was broken before, she no longer did. His large hands clasped her throat and he squeezed hard.

"SALVI!" someone called from outside the door, banging on it.

Bander's eyes went wide and he looked up to the door.

"SALVI!"

It was Mitch. It was goddamned Mitch!

Her own eyes widened and she tried to call back, but Bander's hand tightened and squeezed the air out of her throat.

"Guess we gotta skip the main course and go straight to dessert, then," Bander said, looking down at her and tightening his face as he leaned all his weight on her throat. "No witnesses…"

She heard loud furious thumping against the door as Mitch tried to ram his way into the room. Salvi tried with all her might to pull Bander's hands away, but it was no good, his grip too tight, the weight too heavy, her broken arm too weak.

And as her vision became spotty, she knew that she would soon be dead.

But then she heard more voices. Saw light pour in from the corridor. Heard gunfire. Saw Bander's shoulder open up and splash blood over her. He let go of her throat and stepped backward. She gasped for breath and cast a glance to the doorway. Mitch stood there with his gun raised.

Bander growled and lunged for Salvi again, but she raised her legs and kicked hard. They hit their target and Bander stumbled back into the wall. As he hit it, he gasped and looked down at the middle of his chest. There, poking through, was the silver crucified Jesus.

As his chest pooled with blood, Bander coughed, before his face fell flat and his body slid down to the ground.

Mitch rushed in, gun still aimed at Bander, but the caretaker didn't move. The man was dead.

Salvi continued to gasp for breath, coughing and choking, sliding on the desk in the BioLume that still covered her. Within an instant Mitch was hovering over her, wrapping his arms around her, pulling her up to sit. "It's OK, Salvi," he told her. "It's OK. It's over."

She clasped him weakly, desperately, trying to regain her breath. He continued to hold her, rocking her, as he stared at Bander's dead body and looked around at the limp bodies of the Subjugates and Dr Remmell on the floor. He glanced back at the guard from the gate, who stood in the doorway with Serene-41. The guard scanned the room bewildered, before he quickly moved inside and checked Remmell's pulse. Then he moved to Moses, kneeling and pressing his hands against the Subjugate's bleeding body.

"Get a guard and go wait for the ambulance!" the guard ordered Serene-41, who still hovered by the door. The Serene gave a bow and scuttled away. The guard glanced over at Remmell's dead body, at Subjugate-12, unconscious from a bleeding wound to his head, before turning back to Subjugate-52, who breathed heavy gasps of pain.

"Hold on now," the guard told the Subjugate. "Help is on the way."

20 : ATONEMENT

Salvi awoke slowly and found she was in a hospital bed and it looked to be morning. Her body ached the more it awoke, and she suddenly realized just how much Levan Bander had thrown her around; how much the adrenaline had fought off the pain at the time. Her right arm was in plaster from her fingertips to her elbow, her throat was sore and dry and scratchy, the side of her face felt like a balloon, and her whole back was stiff and tight.

A soft tap on the door caught her attention and she saw Hernandez and Bronte standing there.

"Hey," she said.

"How you doing?" Hernandez said, walking in. In typical cop style they stood either side of the bed.

"I'm good," she said without really thinking. The look on Hernandez and Bronte's face didn't seem to agree.

"You look like you got worked over pretty good, Salv," Hernandez said. "Lucky that fucker is dead or I'd be paying him a visit right about now."

"Oh yeah," Bronte agreed in his baritone voice.

Salvi tried to smile, but her mouth hurt too much. "It's OK, I already took care of him."

"Yeah, we heard," Bronte's said with amusement. "A crucifix, Salvi?"

"Well, I just kinda finished him off," she said. "If Mitch hadn't shot him…"

"Yeah," Hernandez said, pursing his lips. "Mitch." Salvi

looked at Bronte. "Can you give us a minute?"

"Sure thing," he said. "I saw a coffee machine down the corridor." Then he flashed a smile. "Right near the nurse's station."

Salvi tried to smile again, as Bronte walked out the door. She looked back at Hernandez.

"I know what you're going to say," he said.

"You were wrong about him," she said.

"Maybe."

"Maybe?"

"Hey, look, if he toes the line, he ain't got a problem from me."

Salvi sighed. "You were wrong," she said again.

Hernandez stared back at her, then gave a nod. "I was wrong." She smiled.

"You just get back on your feet, alright?" Hernandez said. "Anything we can do, just say the word."

"Tell Stan I'm fine." She gave him a confident look.

Hernandez gave her a wink and a cheeky smile, then left the room, just as a nurse came in with a bunch of flowers.

"Flowers?" Salvi asked.

"Aren't they lovely," the nurse said, handing them to her.

Salvi moved her body delicately to check who they were from. She found the card and turned it toward her. They were from Preacher Vowker and the Children of Christ. The message read:

For it is by grace you have been saved, through faith, and this not from yourselves, it is the gift of God. – Ephesians 2:8

Salvi stared at the message, then shook her head.

"No," she said to the card, to the image of Vowker in her mind. "God didn't save me. I did. Mitch did. The Subjugates did."

"I'm sorry, honey?" the nurse said.

Salvi handed the flowers back to her. "I think these will look a lot nicer in the nurses' station."

"Oh, really? You're sure?"

Salvi nodded.

"Why, thank you," the nurse said with a smile. "That's so lovely of you."

She took the flowers and left the room, and Salvi closed her eyes again. Content.

The crucified Jesus may have been Bander's death nail, but Salvi had been the one to drive it home.

Salvi watched as the doctor tapped the small glass pane in his hands.

"We'll need to keep monitoring you," he said, "to make sure the exposure you had to the BioLume does not have any long-term effects. But you should be fine given you had the special cleansing shower when you first came in. I think regular checkups every month to start with should suffice, unless you experience any unusual symptoms before then."

"So, I can leave?" she asked.

"Yes," he said, signing off his pane. "If you prefer to recover at home, I'm happy to approve that. But you must rest, Detective. I'll not approve your return to work for at least a couple of weeks. Even then, with that fractured arm, you'll be stuck on a desk for a while."

"That's fine," she said. "Home is good."

The doctor gave a nod. "I'll go see to it."

She watched him walk out of her room, thinking of her apartment as he did. Her cloud, her cushioning from reality. But then she suddenly remembered the last time she'd been there, with her bed defiled and the footage running on her TV. A shiver went down her spine at the thought of Bander roaming freely in her apartment, but it soon dissipated with thoughts of Bander's body slumped dead against the wall of Solme's office.

Another knock on her door caught her attention. She looked over and saw Mitch standing there.

"You up for a visitor?" he said.

"Sure." She nodded.

He moved into the room and came to a stop near the foot of her bed. She'd been in hospital for almost two days now and this was the first time she'd seen him since they'd brought her in. She remembered being on a stretcher, remembered him holding her hand, but they'd given her painkillers and when she'd awoken in hospital he was gone. But she'd seen Ford, who'd told her that Mitch had been busy wrapping up the case for them.

"How you doing?" he asked, stuffing his hands in the pockets of his coat. He looked tired. Worn. Like he hadn't slept in days.

"I'll live." She smiled. "The doctor's about to release me home."

"Yeah?" Mitch asked, surprised.

She nodded again and the silence sat for a moment.

"How did you find me?" she asked. "How did you know I was there?"

"When I left you, I went to visit cyber. I asked them to look further into the U-Stasis account activity of our vics. I left them to it and came back to the bullpen but you were gone. I tried to find you but couldn't and you weren't answering your iPort." He paused a moment. "So, I waited. I tried calling you again and again. When you didn't answer, I'm sorry – but I traced your iPort again. It registered that you were in your apartment. Only, you didn't move for some time. I thought maybe you were sleeping, but I checked with Ford and you hadn't called in sick. So I went to your apartment." He pulled his hand out of his pocket and showed her one of the key passes for her apartment. "I don't know why, but I'd grabbed this when I left your apartment that morning."

She nodded.

"I knocked, you didn't answer," he said. "So I went in … and saw what was there. At first I thought …" He scratched his head. "I didn't know what to think. I thought maybe you'd filmed us … but then I saw 'pure' written across your bed, and your iPort and lenses left behind, your holo-badge." He looked her in the eye. "And I freaked the fuck out. I had your apartment security scan their footage, saw you walking out alone. So I knew you were alive, but I didn't know how long for. I saw the report Weston had filed, saw that you'd viewed it. It was risky, but I asked Riverton to give me the geoloc where you'd accessed it. It told me you'd accessed it from your personal comms unit in your Zenith. It pinpointed the access location as Bountiful, so I headed straight out there. But I drove around and couldn't find you. I even went out to the Solme Complex but your car wasn't there either."

"Bander moved it." She nodded to herself.

"Yeah," he said. "So I drove back into Bountiful, didn't know what to do. I knew if I called you in as a missing person, if you wound up dead … I was going to be the prime suspect. But I had no choice. Just as I was about to call you in to Ford, Riverton contacted me with the new report from Cyber. It showed Bander as being online in U-Stasis at the same time as both Sharon and Rebecca. Their activity status indicated there was interaction between them. We needed a further warrant to find out what that interaction was, but I thought it was enough to question him. I called the Solme Complex to find out if he was there. I got put through to Dr Remmell. He told me you'd been there earlier that day but that your car was now gone. But he thought Bander was still about, so I headed out there. Only, the guard on the gate wouldn't let me in. When he tried to get Remmell, he didn't answer. I think he was off undertaking his own investigations at the time."

"Yeah." Salvi nodded to herself again. "So how did you get into the Complex?"

"As the guard was trying to send me away, Bander called over his comms saying there was a code blue and that Subjugate-52 was on a rampage. He ordered the compound locked down and that no one was to leave. I thought if there was a chance you were inside?"

"So what did you do?"

He gave a slightly bashful smile. "I rammed the Raider through the front gates."

"You did?" Her eyes popped.

He nodded. "I got inside but didn't get far before the drone guard fried the electrics."

"So, what happened?"

"The guard pulled his gun on me and made me get out of the vehicle. I did, but then we heard a gunshot coming from inside the main building."

Salvi nodded again. "That's when Bander shot Moses."

Mitch nodded back. "I ran for the main door, the guard tried to stop me but I just yelled at him to call 911. The guy just kinda said 'shit' and ran for his booth to make the call. He realized that I wasn't the threat."

"So how'd you get inside?"

"The doors were locked, but I saw Serene-41 cowering inside. It took a little begging, but I convinced him to open the door. Once inside I just grabbed him and asked where you were. He pointed to Solme's office but told me to use the other door down the corridor. Only I got there and it was locked. I had no idea if you were inside or still alive, so I just started ramming the door. But it wasn't budging. Serene-41 came running up and swiped his damn pass. The door opened, I saw Bander choking you, and... I fired."

Salvi smiled, and the silence took hold again as they both recalled the moment.

"What's it like out there?" she asked him. "What's been going on?"

Mitch exhaled heavily. "Everything. I've been finalizing reports with Riverton, taking witness statements, processing the scene, cleaning up your apartment..."

"Yeah," she said, dropping her eyes to the bed. "Did anyone else see...?" her voice trailed off.

"It's OK, Salvi," he said. "I got rid of the footage. And the cameras."

She looked up at him; his green eyes staring back at hers, the dark fringe resting on his forehead, his stubbled jaw.

"You did?" she asked.

He nodded. "Riverton uncovered the hack Bander had done to your security to give him access to Sky Tower 4's systems. I figured that was enough to prove you were a target of his. I got rid of the sheets. Bought you some new ones."

"Thank you," she said softly.

He nodded gently back. "It's no one's business but ours."

She swallowed, her throat still hurting. She reached out and picked up the glass of water sitting by her bed, took a sip and placed it back.

"Bander's room at the Complex was clean," Mitch continued, "but he had an apartment in the city and it was stocked with a whole array of footage hacked from people's private security cameras, from his old job. It looks like he started out as a voyeur and it slowly built from there." Mitch shrugged. "I guess his free license to be a violent sadistic asshole at the Solme Complex went to his head. He got sick of watching and started doing."

Salvi nodded to herself. "How's Subjugate-52?"

"He caught a bullet in the stomach," he said. "He'll be in hospital for a while, but he'll be alright."

"Did he get his medication?"

Mitch nodded. "First thing they did, even before the ambulance came."

"And Subjugate-12?"

"He got a fractured skull, but they say he'll be alright in time. Attis Solme is arranging a whole bunch of counseling for them with a new psychologist he's bringing in."

"It's been two days and he's already moved on?"

Mitch nodded. "The media is all over him. He's trying to manage the collateral damage."

"And the fallout in the town?"

"Mixed," he said. "Solme released a statement to the press, painting the Subjugates as heroes. But people are uneasy. Like it or not, the killer came from the Solme Complex. Sheriff Holt is calling for an inquiry into the facility."

"They never showed any aggression toward me. If anything, the fact that they've had the violence bleached out of them was the problem. Serene-41 was useless. He was too centerline to know how to react appropriately. Pragge was an easy target to knock down, and Moses was only effective in knocking Bander off me because he hadn't had his meds. Because he still had the ability to feel something enough, to do something, albeit only slightly."

"That's a good thing, Salvi," he said. "Don't forget their pasts. These were horrible, horrible men before. Just like Bander was. They need to remain tightly controlled or they will offend again."

"I know," she said. "And Moses coded blue. And they knew he was still coding blue. That's why they were hesitant to let me speak with him... Still he didn't hurt me. And he genuinely seemed to think what Bander was doing was wrong. That's why he tried to stop him. They were monsters once, but I think Solme might've actually been turning them back into men again. His methods are questionable, but if it hadn't been for them, I'd probably be dead right now. Or at least, in a lot worse condition."

Mitch clenched his jaw as though she'd brought back a memory he cared not to think of. She wondered what it must've felt like for him to come through that door and see Bander choking her on Solme's desk.

"Thank you," she said. "For coming when you did."

He nodded, clenched his jaw again. "I'm just glad I got there in time... This time."

She nodded, gave him a sad smile.

He cleared his throat. "Don't ever leave your iPort behind again, Detective."

"I know," she said, "but I saw my apartment and I freaked out."

"And you thought it was me," he said, eyes fixed on hers.

"No," she said, then paused. "I was confused... because my gut told me that you could never do something like that."

He pursed his lips, looking down at the floor.

"You had every right to be screwed up after your girlfriend's murder," Salvi said, then gave a smile. "I was a heartless bitch. I admit it."

He looked up at her, and a smile curled the corner of his mouth. "Well," he said, "that's in the past now. For both of us. We need to move forward."

"Yes, we do," she said.

Another moment of silence passed between them before the doctor walked back in.

"Here's your clearance, Detective," he said, holding out the pane and motioning for where she should sign. She did. "You're free to leave whenever you like."

"Thank you," she said, and watched him leave again. She looked back at Mitch.

"You need a ride?" he asked.

"Yeah. I do."

• • •

Salvi smiled when she saw Mitch moving toward her Zenith.

"Where's the Raider?"

"Still recovering from her run-in with the drone," he said, throwing her a glance. "She's in the shop having her electronics overhauled. Ford is pissed."

"I see," she said, then smiled. "This is what happens when you take it off autodrive."

Mitch smiled back at her. "I guess so."

"Does Ford know about you talking with Fresner?" she asked as they reached the car.

Mitch nodded. "Riverton found it and flagged it with her. I told them we thought it was a setup and didn't want to say anything until we knew who was setting me up."

"Yeah? They bought it?"

"Yeah," he nodded, "although I may have mentioned to Ford about Solme blackmailing her."

Salvi stared at him, mouth agape. "You have bigger balls than I thought you did."

"What, you were that drunk you can't remember?" Mitch grinned.

Salvi blushed a little. "I can remember fine, thank you." They both climbed inside the Zenith. "So, did you find out what he was blackmailing her over?" She changed the topic of conversation.

Mitch nodded. "Ford crashed her car drunk twenty years ago. Solme got into the driver's seat for her and took the hit. He hasn't let her forget it."

"Huh," Salvi said.

They rode to her apartment in silence. As they stepped out of the elevator on her floor, Salvi felt a little trepidation. Mitch seemed to sense it, reached into his pocket and pulled out her swipe.

"You should probably have this back now," he said.

She took it and used it to let them inside.

As the door swung open she saw the air vents were back in place, the smashed cameras removed. And as she stepped into her bedroom, saw the bed was made with clean sheets and the TV off.

"What did you do with the footage?" Salvi asked him.

He reached into his pocket, pulled out a disc and handed it to her. "Thought you'd want to be the one to destroy it," he said. "For peace of mind."

Salvi took it and turned it over in her hands. "You haven't made a copy?"

He looked at her, another smile curling his lips. "Nah. I never was one for watching TV."

She smiled back.

"I've double-checked everything, Salvi. Your security's tight. I had the company change your codes and swipes." He glanced back at her, then held his hand up in apology. "I didn't mean to overstep. You can change them again so I don't know them."

She nodded. "It's alright. Thank you." She glanced around her bedroom. "You've been busy the past couple of days."

"Yeah," he said, then glanced around and exhaled heavily. "Well, I guess I should leave you to rest. If you need anything, just call me."

Salvi stared back at him, not sure what to say.

"I'm glad you're alright, Salvi," he smiled gently. "You don't know how much."

"Yeah, I do," she said, returning his smile. "You wear your heart on your sleeve, remember?"

"Ah, yes." His smile broadened as he nodded. "I need to work on that." He started walking toward the door.

"Mitch," she called out, stopping him. He turned around. She placed the disc down on her bedside table, then turned back to him. "I spoke to Ford earlier, when she came by the hospital." She looked at him, trying to find the words she wanted to say. "I told her…" she cleared her sore throat. "I told her that I can't be your partner any more."

His face fell, as did his eyes to the floor. He nodded, ran his hand down over his mouth, then looked back at her. "What did you tell her?"

She stared at him. "I told her I can't partner with someone like you…"

Mitch moved uneasily, turned his body like he was going to walk away.

"Someone I have feelings for," she finished.

He paused and looked back at her, not sure he'd heard right.

She shrugged softly. "You wanted me to feel something, Mitch. Well I do… For you."

He turned his body back to face hers.

"So, what does this mean?" he asked.

She shrugged. "It means Ford thinks I have a crush on you, so she's splitting us up. I'm going to be with Beggs, and you get Caine." She smiled. "I think you get the better end of the deal, by the way."

"Ford doesn't know we slept together?"

"No," she said. "It's nobody's business but ours."

He nodded. "So, what does this mean?" he asked again. "For you and me?"

"It means… We're going to stop punishing ourselves for our past mistakes. We're going to forgive ourselves. Move forward."

"Together? Or alone?"

Salvi took a moment, and a subtle breath in. "I think I'm done with being alone."

He nodded, the intense look upon his face slowly melting. "Yeah. Me too."

She smiled softly. "Let me get back on my feet, make sure this BioLume hasn't turned me radioactive, and… we'll see where this goes."

He nodded again and smiled back. "Whenever you're ready, you know where to find me."

With that, Mitch left, and Salvi turned to her apartment windows.

She moved over to them and looked out upon the city. She saw the Golden Gate hiding in the mist, saw the drones buzzing about amid the gray skies. Her eyes drifted to focus on the buildings, and she wondered what was going on behind all the closed doors out there. Wondering who, right now, was crossing that line between man and monster. Wondering which criminal she would be chasing next.

She thought it strange that, after all that happened, she was ready to get back out there and get into it again. Get working on a new case.

She thought of Vowker again, how he'd told her she was dead inside. She wasn't. She was just dead to Christianity.

And it suddenly dawned upon her then, the path her life had taken.

She'd been born into religion. The structure, the discipline, the control. She'd fought hard against it, but the truth was, it had been so ingrained into her system. The structure, the discipline, the control, was firmly in her veins. She didn't know any other way to live her life.

She thought she'd left religion behind but she hadn't. She'd simply left Christianity behind, and she'd replaced it with a new religion.

Law enforcement.

ACKNOWLEDGMENTS

Although writing a novel is at first a solitary effort, it takes a village to bring it to publication. Thank you to the following for making this book's publication possible:

To my beta readers, Tia, Todd and Joan – you always read the less perfect versions of my books and help make them better. Thanks for continuing to come back for more.

To my agent, Alex Adsett – thank you for your persistence and patience.

To Marc and the team at Angry Robot – thank you for taking a chance on me. Here's to a long and fruitful relationship.

To my editors, Paul Simpson and Claire Rushbrook – thank you for helping to make this book stronger and sleeker.

To Lee Gibbons – thanks for the great cover.

To my family and friends – you're accustomed to it now, but thanks for your patience and understanding of my time constraints, and for your continuing support of my work. It means a lot.

Lastly, but never least – thank you to my wonderful readers who follow me from book to book and continue to ask for more. You are the very reason I do this!

IT'S IN THE BLOOD...

"EMERY IS A CHARACTER I LOVED FROM THE START...
SUCH A GREAT ADVENTURE." — FRAN WILDE

LAUREN C. TEFFEAU

CONNECT ▪ ENCRYPT ▪ CONSPIRE

IMPLANTED

ANGRY ➡ ROBOT

"IMPLANTED takes readers to the bleeding edge of a
hopeful future and dives headlong into the risks required
to make that future real. Such a great adventure!"
*FRAN WILDE, Andre Norton Award-winning author
of the Bone Universe series*

"Lauren C Teffeau brings us a fully-realized world
filled with conflict, drama, and insight."
*WALTER JON WILLIAMS, multiple-award-winning
author of HARDWIRED and the Praxis series*